A
CERTAIN
APPEAL

A
CERTAIN
APPEAL

VANESSA KING

G. P. PUTNAM'S SONS
NEW YORK

PUTNAM
— EST. 1838 —

G. P. PUTNAM'S SONS
Publishers Since 1838
An imprint of Penguin Random House LLC
penguinrandomhouse.com

LIBRARY OF CONGRESS CATALOGING-IN-PUBLICATION DATA

Names: King, Vanessa (Vanessa L.), author.
Title: A certain appeal / Vanessa King.
Description: New York: G. P. Putnam's Sons, [2021] |
Summary: "A sparkling
contemporary retelling of Pride and Prejudice set in the tantalizing
world of New York City burlesque, perfect for fans of The Kiss Quotient
and The Roommate"—Provided by publisher.
Identifiers: LCCN 2021033386 (print) | LCCN 2021033387 (ebook) |
ISBN 9780593330715 (trade paperback) | ISBN 9780593330722 (ebook)
Subjects: LCGFT: Romance fiction. | Novels.
Classification: LCC PS3611.I58666 C47 2021 (print) |
LCC PS3611.I58666 (ebook) | DDC 813/.6—dc23
LC record available at https://lccn.loc.gov/2021033386
LC ebook record available at https://lccn.loc.gov/2021033387

Printed in the United States of America
1st Printing

Interior art: Art deco pattern © Picksell/Shutterstock

BOOK DESIGN BY KRISTIN DEL ROSARIO

To my daughter, True.

You are the work of my life.

Now hand this book back to me.

You're *seven*; you're not reading past this page until 2030.

A
CERTAIN
APPEAL

CHAPTER

1

"It is a *redacted* universally acknowledged, that a *throbbing redacted* in possession of a *thick redacted* must be in want of a *redacted*." Andrea bites out each "redacted" with a distaste that grows more resigned with every repetition, the final utterance leaving her on little more than a throaty British sigh. A Mad Libs sheet hangs limply between the tips of her thumb and forefinger, the page held away from her, as though to keep the vulgarity she so thoughtfully "redacted" from staining her white blouse.

She lowers her reading glasses to hang from the gold chain at her neck, eyes shifting to study each of us in turn. The Twins carry on with their stretches on the far side of the dressing room, Ginn slouching and bored in a front split, Tonic doing her best to look shocked as she holds cobra pose. Ming sits at a makeup station, feigning innocence, a row of false eyelashes dangling from her fingers like a cigarette.

"Dare I ask how this ended up on table two?" Andrea's narrowed eyes land on me, and her lips flatten to a matte red line. With her severe black bob and alabaster skin, she looks like a cartoon villain even when she's smiling; her current expression has me wondering which of us she plans to turn into a coat.

I shift side to side, the weave of my fishnets pressing into the ball of one foot, then the other. Ming did the Mad Libs last weekend, when I brought in the pad to play with between shows. She filled in every noun with the word "penis," inspiring a debate about whether the repetition was funny or if she'd drained the novelty from the word. I argued she should have diversified, but now I'm not sure; Andrea's lilting West Midlands accent gave the piece an almost musical quality, even with the substitution.

Still, I keep quiet, trying to feel her out. As the general manager of a venue with a burlesque show, Andrea deals with this degree of raunch on a near-nightly basis. Hell, she's just as nasty as Ming.

She releases the page, letting it drift to the surface of the low file cabinet beside her. "I don't care what you get into while you're down here, but don't bring the juvenile humor upstairs. It's beneath you."

Ming's brows shoot up, and I choke back a laugh at the suggestion she's above anything, let alone a dirty Mad Lib.

"Why are you grilling *us* about this?" Ginn props her chin in her hands, elbows on the ground between her legs. "It could have been the guys in the band, or Jane—"

"The boys have more creative words for 'penis,'" Andrea counters. I arch a brow at Ming, who rolls her eyes. "And Jane is a gentleman."

"Plus, he dots his i's with little circles," I add brightly, hoping to defuse the tension. "He does it on our rent checks. It's charming."

Before Andrea's eyes can properly beseech the ceiling for

deliverance, a gasp sounds from the supply closet across from us. The door swings open to reveal Jane, who's the picture of refinement in his vest and trousers, the pale gray wool a striking contrast with his dark skin. The little closet is where he warms up his voice; I didn't expect him to hear me.

Jane sags against the door frame, hand smoothing the Bic-close shave of his head as he sighs with dreamy affectation. "Kitten Caboodle, do you really think so?"

"You know I love your i's, darling." I blow him a kiss. He mimes catching it, clutching it to his heart, then tugs the door shut with a dramatic swoon.

His performance breaks us. The Twins collapse forward in their respective bends, giggling madly. Ming releases her wicked, machine-gun cackle that reduces me to snorts of laughter. Even Jane's muffled chuckle comes from the closet.

"I'm sorry, Andrea." I dab below my eyes to check that my makeup hasn't run. "It was my fault. I used the pad as a writing surface when I did tonight's reservation notes and a page must have fallen out."

Andrea's hands go to her broad hips. "Well, be careful. Our guests are here for a specific brand of titillation, not potty language." She peers at the offending page. "For heaven's sake, Ming, get a damn thesaurus."

We dissolve into laughter again, Ming's roar setting the beads of her shimmy belt rattling against the metal folding chair.

Andrea finally smirks. "Whatever am I going to do with you all?" She points at me. "You're supposed to be the reliable one."

"Hey, I just pick up panties," I say, palms up in innocence.

She rolls her eyes. At a burlesque show, the responsibilities of the stage kitten can generally be reduced to *pick up what the others take off*.

In my two years here, my role has evolved to take on duties Andrea prefers not to do herself, talent wrangling included. But there's only so much I can do about Ming's base level of smut.

Andrea nods at the notes I hold. "There haven't been any reservation changes, so what you have is current. Girls, have a great show." Her smile drops. "This one counts."

I open my mouth to ask what she means by that, but she shakes her head, patting me on the shoulder.

"Pop a pastie, luvs!" she calls, turning down the hallway.

"Pop a pastie," we chorus, the others already back to their stretches and makeup.

I watch Andrea make her way down the hall, her usually purposeful stride more of a trudge. A sliver of anxiety weaves into my preshow jitters, but I have to shelve my concern. We have half an hour left, and there are a few things to cover before we're stage-ready. "Ladies, family meeting."

Ginn and Tonic look up expectantly. The aerialists are "Twins" in stage name only, as evidenced by their vastly different coloring, and have been been performing together since high school. They are also a rare exception to the show's focus on classic burlesque, performing their peels suspended above the stage.

Ginn pulls her red hair into a messy bun. "Fire away, Kitten."

"Should we get Jane?" Tonic asks.

"Nah. We talked songs on the ride in. Ladies," I direct to the Twins, "you're trying the new aerial number with the silks, right?"

"Silks!" they chime.

"N'kay. I'll have them ready." I jot a note beside the set list. At the top of the page, the club's name, Meryton, is spelled out in fine, looping lettering, with "the *Meryest* Burlesque Revue in NYC" printed below.

"It's Ming, Twins, Jane, then Twins, Ming, Jane, for the eight o'clock," I say, citing the performance order. "We have three confirmed bachelorette parties for that show. Ming, the one at table five chose the 'naughty' theme—I'm sure they'd appreciate a little extra attention. They'll be the ones with the dick straws and the bride in the phallus-tipped tiara. And that was two separate synonyms for 'penis'; I hope you're taking notes."

"I like what I like," Ming sniffs, and dabs at a blob of pearlescent body paint in her belly button.

"And you do like penis," says Ginn.

"*Anyway,*" I interrupt, "that's all I have. Anyone need anything?"

Ming cranes her neck, rubbing the dislodged body paint over the swells of breast cresting the cups of her bra. "Did Andrea bring our bubbles?"

I glance at the file cabinet, where Andrea deposits the preshow prosecco and stems, but the only thing breaking up the gray metal surface is Ming's Mad Lib. That anxiety from earlier tightens around my middle. Andrea might have been distracted by the Mad Libs, but it would take more than that to sideline her from bringing down a bottle. "I'll go."

On my way out, I check in with Jane. "I'm going upstairs. You need anything?"

He straightens his tie with a broad smile. "*No, I don't, but thanks for checking first,*" he croons, each word a note on the scale.

Turning, I point to my back, where my corset stays hang in need of tying. "If you'd be so kind?"

"Do you have the ladies where you'd like?" he sings, higher this time.

I peek at how I've situated my boobs. With an overbust corset, you have to be careful. Too low, they're smooshed; too high, they look like a butt trying to smother you. "Should be good. Pull?"

Jane yanks, I grunt, and he ties a quick bow in the back, double-knotting it. I take a few breaths to make sure I get sufficient oxygen, and thank him.

I linger in the doorway. "How much did you catch with Andrea before? She seemed . . ."

"More tightly wound than usual?" Jane offers. At my nod, he crosses his arms, resting a shoulder against the door frame. "I wonder what that was about. She wasn't even this ruffled the night the chef quit."

I chew the inside of my lip. Scheduling changed last month, with acts and shifts no longer booked more than two weeks in advance. The announcement resulted in a minor exodus from the front of the house, costing us two servers and the chef with less than an hour before service. Andrea didn't bat an eye, promoting the sous on the spot and delegating food-running duties to Jane and me between our stage appearances.

While the evening's extra tips were appreciated, the new scheduling threw Jane into a panic. I have a day job, but the steady pay from Meryton keeps him afloat most months. Without it, he'd only be left with side gigs and his voice lesson students. They're not enough to cover his half of the rent, no matter how charming his i's are.

Jane's thoughts must end up in the same place, because his brown eyes go distant, familiar lines of worry creasing his forehead.

Crap. I shouldn't have said anything. "I'm sure it's nothing." I force a confused frown. "You're singing Prince and . . ."

"'Little Red Corvette' and 'Light My Fire.'" He smiles, which eases some of the tightness in my middle. "We talked about it earlier, space case."

I feign a pout at the cheeky insult, then continue to the hallway, trying to ignore the twisting in my gut. I pause at the full-length mirror on the door of the walk-in freezer—the ladies are *definitely* where they need to be, and Jane's help with the corset has given my athletic frame the defined waist I'm otherwise lacking. The front of my dark, wavy hair is pinned into a series of rosettes, and I fluff the bit I left loose in back for a little more oomph.

Tonight's lip color, a high-gloss stain named Rouge Deluge, brings out the hint of blush that warms my otherwise fair complexion. Brows have been shaped, false lashes adhered—*ah!* The snipped waistband of my fishnets peeks above the waist of my black undies. I re-situate it, running my fingers around the top of my satin bikini to make sure the band hasn't bunched up anywhere else.

That sorted, I scoot to the adjoining room, where the five members of the show's band play poker with our emcee, Johnny Ryall. The guys are in matching dark suits, and Johnny is in one of his remarkably hideous tuxedos. Tonight's crime against taste is a mint-green number with black piping at the cuffs and lapels, paired with a black ruffled shirt. I don't know where he finds the things.

Walking by, I get a few mumbled "Kitten"s in greeting. I take no offense to the brusque salutation; their poker games are intense. If this hand doesn't finish before showtime, they'll keep their cards in their pockets while they're performing and wrap it up at intermission.

As I push back the heavy curtain separating the talent space from the downstairs landing, I have to sidestep two women in black minidresses waiting for the restrooms. They do a double take, making zero effort to conceal their examination as I cross to the stairs.

"Is that a *corset?*" one asks, directing the question more to her friend than me.

"I don't know how anyone wears those," the other woman replies.

"Oh, they just take some getting used to." I start up the stairs. "Enjoy the show!"

Halfway up, I stop to give the butterflies a chance to settle. It's been at least three hundred shows for me: one each Friday, two on Saturday nights, and a few special events through each year. The first glance at the crowd makes me catch my breath even when I'm not constricted by a corset.

I interact with the crowd more than the other performers, playing the part of "Kitten Caboodle" as I hawk souvenirs during set breaks. The persona is as much an act as anything Jane and the girls do onstage, and when I'm on the floor, I'm *on*. It's exhausting and freeing at the same time, where I'm on the spot but have all the answers . . . if for no other reason than I'm only asked the same handful of questions. If I had a Meryton bingo card, the corset comment downstairs would be on it, along with *How do they do that?* after a performer does a tassel twirl, and some tired iteration of *Will you be getting naked, too?*

I climb the rest of the stairs and place my hand on the green, egg-shaped light fixture at the end of the railing. We all do it at the start of any performance, the ritual predating me. I don't know if it's meant for luck or simply habit, but the muted warmth under my palm settles the loitering jitters, leaving me with only midgrade anxiety about Andrea's earlier behavior as I take in the scene.

The guests for the first show are filing in, settling at their tables more quickly than the ten o'clock crowd does. This show's audience is generally tamer, too; eight's early for a New York Saturday, and this is usually folks' first stop of the night. It also explains the concentration of bachelorette parties. Andrea always schedules them early. Hen parties devolve notoriously fast; the least we can do is provide a base layer of solids before they start drinking in earnest.

Waiters bustle among the tables on the elevated platforms at the back of the room, igniting tea lights and pouring champagne into the flutes of a soon-to-be-seated party. A narrow aisle separates the tables from the rest of the dining room, where two- and four-tops fill the remainder of the space, nudging the small stage. It's a tight fit, but that's part of the fun. Performers have to get from the stairs to the stage via whatever path they can forge; anyone in their way risks becoming part of the production.

The lights of the dining area are down low, softening the edges of guests and muting the wear and tear of the club itself. But I know where to look. The bubbled spot in the damask wallpaper to the left of the stage; the mismatched sconces along the far wall; the worn velvet upholstery on the banquette seating in back. Usually, the lived-in touches add to Meryton's charm, but paired with Andrea's odd behavior downstairs, they fuel a concern that's simmered on the back burner since I started working here.

There is no *way* this place makes money.

The jazz shows get a decent showing, and the English tea service offered weekdays does all right, but the weekend burlesque revue keeps Meryton afloat. This is Tribeca; any business that isn't flourishing is liable to be turned into a Pilates studio or a baby boutique. With the club owner's out-of-nowhere change to the scheduling, I can't help but think he might be angling that way.

My stomach pitches at the thought, but I summon a smile and head for the hostess station, twinkling my fingers at guests as I pass. A gal with a hot-pink, saucer-sized "maid of honor" pin beckons to me with her phone, and I join the group for a photo, recruiting a waiter, Esteban, to snap the pic.

I press on, but my steps falter when I spot Andrea looking over some papers at the far end of the bar. Usually, she'd be mingling with guests or helping the hostess, armed with a dirty martini and her crimson smile. The martini's there, off to the side of the paperwork, but the closest thing to a smile is the crescent of lipstick at the glass's rim.

My chest goes tight again. She could be looking at anything: order forms for the kitchen, bar stock, toilet paper inventory. But the tension rolling off of her says otherwise.

I sidle over with a conciliatory grimace. "Sorry again about the Mad Libs."

She waves off the apology, barely looking up from the paper. "I shouldn't have been so snippy about it." Her voice is flat, doing nothing for the sensation in my chest.

I press my hands into prayer, playing up some kicked-puppy eyes. "Do we get bubbles or are we on the naughty list?"

Her dull expression sharpens. "The prosecco! I'm sorry, pet." She takes off her glasses, squeezing the bridge of her nose. "Michael! Be a luv and get Kitten a bottle for downstairs?" The bartender holds up his index finger to let me know it will be a moment and gets back to a guest.

I nod to the stack of paper. "Everything okay?"

She swishes her martini glass on the bar top, setting the contents swirling. "It's Manhattan real estate, darling. Nothing's ever *okay*." She exaggerates the last word with a hard American accent.

Unease crawls up my spine. "Is this . . ." I don't want to voice the nameless worry and try to keep my tone light. "Related to the new scheduling?"

Her silence speaks for her. My stomach drops.

"Andrea—"

"Don't fret." The two words are an order. "It's not what you think."

I cross my arms, unwilling to play along. "What *do* I think, then?"

"Kitten!" Michael calls from the opposite end of the bar. "Want your bubbles?" Andrea snags her martini, spared further interrogation.

I push off the bar. "This conversation isn't over."

She clutches her free hand to her chest. "I'm shaking in my ankle boots, kitty cat."

I hold my hand up, fingers curled like claws, and she blows me a kiss before shooing me away, reading glasses already back in place.

Michael greets me with a bottle of prosecco and a smile. The bar's muted lighting gives his shaved head a soft glow. "You're looking gorgeous this evening. New glad rags?"

"Newish." I smooth my hands down the cool satin of my emerald corset. "But don't think I'm going to let you be evasive, too. What's going on?" I tip my head toward Andrea. She and Michael are close, and he's as generous with his gossip as he is with his pours.

"It's fine. Or, it should be." He sends a cautious glance toward our manager, and I lean against the bar, the corset boning pressing into my ribs. His voice is low, his mouth barely moving as he says, "She's trying to buy the building."

"*What?*" I angle closer. I'm going to have a bruise from the corset boning, but I don't care. "Can she swing that?"

Michael gives me an insistent look, and I try to rein in my enthusiasm, but my heart skips. "Her backer is an old-money guy from California," he says. "The only competition is some flaky nephew of the owner. Things look good."

I nod to myself, thinking of Jane. At the very least, scheduling should get back to normal. "Is there a timeline?"

"If all goes well, they'll be closing the end of next month. She also wants to renovate, but that timeline is a bit looser."

The word "renovate" has me tracing the outside of my left hand, feeling for the calluses along my pinky. Three years away from the drafting table has softened them, but traces of the tougher skin remain. I glance down, half expecting to see the smears of graphite that were as much a part of me then as corsets and false eyelashes are now.

My attention lands on the faint white scar on my palm, and I come back to myself with a start. "Thank you for the scoop." I hold out my hands and splay my fingers. "Sir?"

Michael fetches a quintet of champagne flutes. He wedges three into my right hand, two into my left, then nestles the bottle between that thumb and forefinger. "Got it?"

"You can take the climber outta Colorado but you can't take away her grip."

"Noted. Have a good show. And not a word to the others," he warns. "They'll swarm Andrea and she's already stressed enough. I can't guarantee she'll be in a charitable mood."

I sneak another look at Andrea, still at the end of the bar. She frowns at something on the page, then takes a long pull from her martini.

"You're the bartender," I reply, and raise the bottle of prosecco. "Charitable moods are your job, no?"

CHAPTER

2

"Ladies and gentlemen!" Johnny calls. The band begins a sax-heavy rendition of "Harlem Nocturne," sending my butterflies into flight. "Beautiful people of all identities, show some love for *Ming DyNasty.*"

The spotlight shifts to illuminate Ming, who's tracing lazy circles over the top of the green egg with a gloved finger. She's a vision in crimson, from her towering showgirl headdress to the boa on her shoulders and the gauzy robe over her gown. From my spot a few steps below, I inventory the pieces to look for when I'm picking up after her set—seven, depending on whether she takes the boa when she leaves the stage.

The light follows her sultry prowl toward the "naughty" bachelor-ettes, who squeal in anticipation. As I step up to the egg, Ming drapes her boa over the bride-to-be, flossing it across her chest vigorously enough to set the girl's penis-tipped tiara askew. The table erupts in peals of laughter, and the bride shimmies her shoulders, sending her ample cleavage bobbing. Ming releases the woman, who earns a few stray feathers in the process, and sashays toward the stage.

I cast a wary eye over the crowd. The show attracts a varied audience. For many, the high price tag makes the experience a novelty, a place for a special event, like bachelorette parties or birthdays. Others are assorted couples who are out for a night of rowdy, consensual objectification in a comfortable environment that serves a killer plate of mussels and frites. We also appeal to large groups of wealthy Russians, who, I suppose, merely enjoy seeing women disrobe without dying of exposure. Minor celebrities roll in with their entourages, hiding behind dark glasses that make their navigating the stairs to the bathrooms a study in unintentional comedy.

Burlesque is niche enough that these groups have had to seek us out, and most attendees know what to expect and how to conduct themselves.

Others . . . not so much.

Most offensive are the young Wall Street types. They do coke in the bathrooms and sneer at performers whose bodies don't fit their narrow standard of desirability; one look at Ming's dimpled backside and they're shaking their heads in disgust. They're infuriating. And bewildering. In New York, no one is ever more than two blocks from the abundant cleavage of a Victoria's Secret billboard. If they want a display of scantily clad, conventionally attractive female bodies to drool over, all they have to do is look up. But they come here, where the variety in the human form is celebrated, and they can't cope.

Women in the audience fall into this trap, too, but with a response so coded, I doubt they're even aware how patronizing it is. They watch Ming take the stage and whisper about "bravery," like Ming's performing *despite* her proportions. These women can't imagine someone with Ming's build feeling comfortable enough to bare it all in public.

If such a woman is anywhere, she's often with a bachelorette party. But as I survey the three groups, their attendees are watching Ming with the appropriate degree of reverence. They're spirited but not sauced, and the whole room has a good energy for eight o'clock. Not an empty seat in the house.

I relax against the wall. The paper's textured detailing tickles my bare shoulders, and the sensation sends my attention to the bubbled spot by the stage, though the flaw has lost the edge it had earlier. Now I see potential. Ditto the sconces in back, which—I wrinkle my nose—*c'mon, that's an easy fix.*

The acrylic light fittings are too modern for the room, anyway. And the wallpaper's just *fussy.* I noticed that the first time I came in to watch Jane sing. With the performers decked out in feathers and fringe, the clean lines of an art deco print would be better suited to us, maybe a solid block of matte color behind the stage to better define the area.

I close my eyes. The idea takes shape in my mind, a narrow arc extending from the sides of the stage to a few feet below the ceiling. My right hand finds its way to the calluses of my left again, fingers itching for a pencil . . .

A wolf whistle pierces the air and I flutter my eyes open with a start. I scan the room, hoping I wasn't caught daydreaming. Esteban watches me from where he stands by the risers, his overly manicured eyebrows high.

"*Coffee?*" he mouths.

I wave him off, mouthing back, "*I'm fine.*" He winks and walks on, revealing an empty seat at the table behind him.

Odd. We're supposed to be totally booked. I glance at the single individual seated at the two-top—

My glance stretches to a gawk as I take in his striking arrangement of appealing facial features: defined cheekbones; solid jaw; thick, dark eyebrows that peak a little in the center. Either Meryton's lighting is working overtime, or this is one good-looking diner. I can't determine which end of his thirties he's closer to, but I'd place him at the younger side—

He's looking at me.

My heart skitters. I smile, mortified I've been caught ogling, and pivot back to Ming. She's in the process of shedding her robe, the boa already draped across the front of the stage. A roll of her shoulder eases the robe down her bicep. She arches a coquettish brow, inspiring another whistle.

I give myself a count of ten as I study the crowd, gradually making my way back to He of the Appealing Jawline.

He's still watching me.

Pleasure ripples through me, sending a flush across my cheeks. I suppose I have a decision to make.

There's a general congeniality expected of my interactions here. I'm more than happy to provide it, but I don't actively court specific attention. The line between playful flirtation and legitimate interest can get thin in any situation, and when the one flirting is in her underthings, folks can get the wrong idea.

Early on I was a little more accommodating. I shared my Insta handle and accepted some phone numbers, but it always went south after a few DMs. Guys assumed I'd "perform" for them, or that I'd be game for nudity in other public situations. One fellow proposed we meet up at a bar, which, my date eagerly shared upon my arrival, was hosting a wet T-shirt contest. Fortunately, I'd brought Ming with me. She and I enjoyed a robust sampling of top-shelf cocktails on the guy's tab before sneaking out the back while the audience was being probed for volunteers.

Tonight, though, with these particularly appealing facial features taking me in so intently, I'm willing to stick a toe over the line.

I smile, letting the slow spread hint at more interest than I'd usually reveal. His eyes dart to Ming. I shift my focus her way as well, watching the performance but also giving my new friend the opportunity to look me over.

Ming's moved on to her sequined strapless gown. She teases the zipper down her side, holding the bust to her chest as the back of the dress peels away, revealing pearlescent flesh and the crimson rhinestones studding her bra band and shimmy belt. She dances her fingers over her ribs, trailing them sensuously along the indentations. With a shift of her hips, she drops the dress to expose her bead-draped backside.

I do a tease of my own, playing along my skin on the off chance there are eyes on me. Tipping my head to the side, I let my fingers light along my collarbone and slide up to my throat. I reverse the route and repeat the cycle, keeping the motions idle. It's a move straight out of Burlesque 101: employ your hands to direct the audience to imagine their hands in place of your own.

I catch him watching me again. His look is cautious but direct, and when our eyes meet, he doesn't avert his gaze. *Bold move, Mr. GoodFace.*

I jerk my chin toward the stage, giving him a hard time for missing the main event. He frowns, brows low, and I laugh. I can't help it; he looks baffled.

Again, I turn to Ming: she's in the process of removing her bra. She takes her time, and the band repeats a few measures of the song, heightening the tension until the reveal. Flicking open the final hook and eye, she tosses the rhinestoned double-D cups toward the band. The upright bassist plucks the glittering garment as it sails above his head, draping it over his shoulder and resuming playing in one graceful movement.

Applause fills the room, and Ming shimmies her shoulders, sending her nipple tassels spinning. As the audience celebrates her mammarian prowess, she lifts her arms overhead and flexes her left pectoral. Her implant-enhanced breast jumps, the tassel spinning independently of its mate. The room overflows with gasps and appreciative whistles.

Johnny announces, "Folks, give it up for Ming DyNasty!"

Ming bows, her feathered headdress sweeping the floor, and plucks the boa from the stage. She situates it with a practiced shrug, arms outstretched, the feathers draped over her like a Christmas garland. She grins, head high, inviting the audience to drink her in.

As masterful as her peels are, this final beat is my favorite part of any number Ming performs. Stripped down, she is a lavish creature, all luxurious curves and extravagant, delicious joy. Her smile is a summons to join her in celebrating the sensory delights of life, every inch of her body's softness a compelling case for indulgence.

With a demure step, she descends the stage. There's an audible scraping of seats as awed diners make way for her, a Moses in pasties parting the Red Sea. I let her pass, then cut through the path she blazed to the stage.

Johnny arrives behind me and begins some filler chatter while I loosen the long hanging silks for the Twins' aerial routine. As I work, I'm conscious that this is my staring partner's first unobstructed view and perform the task with more emphasis on form than expedience.

When I bend to retrieve Ming's gown, I shift my hips, exaggerating the arch of my back as I rise. Imagining his gaze gives me a little charge, playful but exciting, adding a new high to a regular night at the show.

Johnny's banter trails off, and I brace for my intro. The spotlight is warm on my back as he says, "This scantily clad spark plug behind me is our stage kitten, Kitten Caboodle!"

I saunter to Johnny with Ming's gown and robe draped over an arm. "Johnny Ryall, you usin' my name in vain?" I rest an elbow on his shoulder, adjusting my stance to a three-quarter turn to highlight both northerly and southerly assets.

"Just wanted to introduce you, kitty cat. Crowd, say hello to Kitten."

The audience plays along, responding with a hearty, "Hello, Kitten!"

I twinkle my fingers at them, though I can barely make out anyone over the spotlight.

"As stage kitten," Johnny continues, "she'll be tending to the stripper sheddings, but that's not the only time you'll be seeing her. At the break, Miss Caboodle will make her rounds with oodles of goodies for you to choose from—tassels, pasties, playing cards, good stuff for young and old. Take something home for the kiddies."

I nod along until Johnny dismisses me with a wink and then cross to the band. Ming's excellent aim was not reserved for her bra, as both her gloves and her heavy, beaded shimmy belt ended up on band members. The latter could have been a problem, though, and the drummer grumbles as he unwinds the belt from where it tangled around his neck.

On my way back through the audience, a guest pushes out his

chair, blocking my way, and I wait as he rummages beneath the table. I'm directly across from Mr. GoodFace, who's raised his hand like he's trying to flag down a waiter. A tall blond guy by the bar waves in response and moves toward him. I'm momentarily chagrined to see the men hug, but the quick exchange of back pats is more friendly than intimate.

The man in my way scoots in his chair, wielding his recovered napkin victoriously. Johnny announces the Twins, kicking off the girls' progress to the stage, and I finally get to the dressing room. Ming rests against a makeup station, dabbing between her breasts with a paper towel. A few feet away, Jane lounges in an office chair, turning side to side as he hums along to the music upstairs.

"Ming," I say, remembering the drummer's complaint. "Be careful. Dion would rather not be garroted by your shimmy belt."

"Eh?" she asks, patting delicately at an armpit.

"Don't chuck heavy stuff at the band," Jane clarifies, stopping the swivel of his chair to face Ming. "Their hands are busy."

Ming cups her mouth. "Shit! Is he okay?"

"He's fine. But you might want to apologize later." I go through the items. "Gown, two gloves, robe, murder belt, bra. Everything's accounted for."

"Thank you, Kitten!"

I carry my load to the clothing rack on the far side of the room, arranging the gown and robe on a hanger before draping the remaining items on another.

Jane joins me. "You good?" He hands me my champagne flute. "You seemed preoccupied earlier."

I take a sip of my drink. Guilt plucks at my insides, but I don't want to tell Jane about the potential sale on the chance it goes south.

He doesn't rebound well from disappointment—unfortunate, given the audition-heavy nature of his work.

"Just distracted," I say, which isn't a lie, and wiggle my eyebrows. "There's a dreamboat at table nine. We were making eyes for most of Ming's set."

"Oh?" Jane beckons toward the door with a cheeky smile. "I'd better have a look."

◆ · ◆

We arrive in time to catch the end of the Twins' routine. I try to point out the handsome one to Jane, but the latecomer's position blocks my view. It's just as well. The Twins haven't perfected their aerial set, and their costume pieces are scattered across, behind, and away from the stage.

I'm struggling to count their items from afar when Jane lets out an appreciative, "Oh, *my*." I smile, assuming he's caught a glimpse of my quarry, but it's the blond Jane's spotted. "Is *that* the one you were talking about?" he whispers.

"No, he's the friend. Super cute, though." Jane has always had a thing for the Scandinavian types, and the strapping blond is giving off a distinct Valhalla vibe.

"Hmm . . ."

I do a double take. I know that tone. That's Jane's "I probably shouldn't . . . *but*" tone. It's the sound of an indulgence being weighed, the one I get when I suggest we spring for takeout or buy the "nice" toilet paper. But Jane doesn't indulge where boys are concerned. It's self-preservation for him, too, but more a life choice than my Meryton-specific policy.

"I'll feel him out at the break, if you'd like," I offer.

Jane bats his lashes, feigning innocence. "Well, you'll already be out here . . ."

I give him a playful bump of my shoulder and we watch the girls wrap up. The descent's been choreographed to display their coordinating tattoos: a juniper bush along Ginn's right side, and a fever tree adorning Tonic's left. The ink work provides more coverage than the pasties and G-strings they've stripped down to, their lithe dancer's bodies a testament to the hours they spend on the silks.

If only they'd pay as much attention to their peels, I think, noting a bra between a pair of wineglasses on a two-top. The couple doesn't seem to mind the intrusion, however, and when I pick up the bra on my way off the stage, the husband is composing a photo of the arrangement. He beckons for me to get into the frame, and my fishnet-clad legs make a clever backdrop.

At the stairs, I pause to listen to the first few verses of Jane's performance of "Corvette." It's a guaranteed crowd pleaser, and while it doesn't do his talent justice, he's putting a little extra energy into it. I wonder if it's for Mr. Valhalla. A quick glance to his table shows me the blond in profile—he's smiling as he watches Jane, which is good, but his head is blocking my view of his friend again, which I don't appreciate.

I tote the Twins' items downstairs and slip on the garter belt with the little bag I use for change, then grab my tray of goodies. When I return to the main floor, I approach the naughty-themed bachelorette party. "Ladies, may I interest you in some pasties? Handmade by the incomparable Ming DyNasty." I hold up a sampling of pasties, the sequined and rhinestoned disks used to conceal nipples, and then the tasseled versions, which allow for more creative feats of boobery.

All eyes fall on the bride-to-be. She chews her glossy lower lip, barely restraining a grin. I wait them out. When the energy nudges close to a go, I brandish my roll of fashion tape, twirling it around my index finger. "If the only thing holding you back is a lack of adhesive, I can tape them up for an extra two dollars a pair."

The bride-to-be squeals, holding out her palm. "Gimme!"

I beam. "Any other takers?"

Inhibitions properly dashed by their leader, the remaining six women each shoot a hand into the air. I get a $5 commission per pair, so this is a good get, though if the other parties are equally enthusiastic, we might run out of pasties. I make a mental note to ask Ming about raiding her backup stash downstairs.

Bachelorette party number two isn't as passionate about the goods as the first, pooling their cash for a pair of rhinestone pasties for their bride. I pose for pictures and check off several more boxes on my bingo card, including *How do you even apply false eyelashes?* and colorful commentary about Ming's boob flexing.

Then I'm beside the pair of good-looking fellows. I'm a little apprehensive, given the ogling earlier, but I angle my tray to rest on the table. "Gentlemen! Can I interest you in any of my goods this evening?"

"What are you offering?" the blond asks with a flirtatious flair that tells me Jane is solidly in line with his preferences, and I, barring an experimental phase on his part, am not.

I cast them an apologetic glance. The sheer density of the dark-haired one's eyelashes almost makes me falter. "Honestly, not a lot that might appeal to you. Though I'd be remiss not to mention tassels can work for men, too."

The blond smiles. "Not tonight. It's good to know, though."

"I also have naughty playing cards." I produce a hand of cards from my tray, fanning them out with a flourish. "Fifty-four ladies—and gents—in varying stages of undress, including all of tonight's performers, you lucky so-and-sos."

Valhalla cocks his head. "Gents, you say?"

"*Boy*lesque is out there, too." I flash him the card featuring Gorgeous George, the bronze slab of a man on the Two of Diamonds. His assets are concealed by a hat, which I know firsthand is suspended solely by said assets.

"Is this when we're supposed to ask if you're on one?" asks the guy I've been eyeing. His voice is so low, it's practically a rumble, but the pleasing timbre is flattened with—*boredom?* The sound tugs at my flirty high.

"I've always felt that question was a *little* forward," I muse, "but, yeah. That's the usual angle."

He smirks, unimpressed.

Oh, this will *not* do. I inch the tiniest bit closer, idly fanning myself with the cards. "Right? It's like they expect me to bat my lashes and say"—I plant the most smoldering look I can on GoodFace, whose smirk gives way to a satisfying flutter of surprise—*"one way to find out."*

I release the last bit on a husky whisper, every bit the femme fatale, and wait. This starchy fellow is in need of rumpling, and if burlesque has taught me anything, it's that time and tension will undo the most rigid of squares.

It doesn't take long. As my sultry look lingers, his surprise ebbs to something warmer, the temperature rising as his gaze shifts to take in my parted lips. When his eyes return to mine, the heat is enough to make me feel a little rumpled myself.

I snap back to perky salesgirl. "But I'd never do that. It wouldn't be ladylike."

The blond claps his hands, leaning back in his seat with a laugh. "You are *outstanding*. We'll take two. He'll pay."

The designated buyer reaches for his wallet, eyes still glazed.

"And you're Kitten?" the friendly one inquires.

"For a few nights a week."

"Brilliant! I'm Charles, and the money clip across from me is Darcy."

"Pleasure to meet you both." I nod at Darcy. "Well, Money Clip, that'll be forty dollars."

He nods and thumbs through the bills in his wallet. I certainly do not notice the abundance of hundos, because that would be tacky, and take a quick inventory of his attire, like I might for one of the performers. No wedding band or man jewelry, thank God, and his navy suit has the cashmere sheen the Wall Streeters could only dream of.

"The cleanup thing you do," Charles continues. "That's where your name comes from?"

"Stage kitten? That's correct."

He rests his elbows on the table. "This just a stepping stone? Do you have to work your way up before getting onstage to drop the whole *kit 'n' caboodle*?"

I grin at the wordplay, and at the way Darcy pauses his cash inspection to scowl at his friend, as though the inquiry was in poor taste. "It's a blast up there, but I have zero head for choreography. And rhinestones are expensive. It would take a lot of time and money to be half as good as those gals." I shrug. "Besides, if I were onstage, I wouldn't get to make the rounds and meet lovely people like you. It would be tragic."

Charles grins at Darcy. "I love this one. I love her!"

Darcy hands me one of the hundreds, and I reach to make change.

"Keep it," he says, his voice low but light.

I stare at him, thrown by the generosity; this is the largest tip I've ever received. I recover with an affected gasp, then beam at Charles. "I love this one. I love him!"

Darcy almost, *almost* smiles. He's regained some of his starchiness since our little moment, but there's something curious in his look now, an intrigue that wasn't there before. I can work with that.

I make a minor production of stashing the bill in my garter, patting the little pouch where it's situated high on my thigh. "Thank you," I tell Darcy, and lift my tray from the table. "I promise to spend it irresponsibly, and think of you fondly as I do."

"Then I stand by my investment." Again, his voice betrays no emotion. But his focus hovers at my thigh long enough for it to feel like contact. Instinct has me shifting closer, my leg a breath from the table's edge. His fingers curl around his wallet, and he jerks his attention away from me.

Not sure what to do, I wink with a parting, "Gentlemen," and move toward the next couple. I get two steps before the tug of missed opportunity has me backtracking. I bump Darcy with my hip.

Charles tosses his head back in laughter, clapping again. Darcy looks at me with a wide-eyed expression I have no name for but "dour bafflement." For a staggering heartbeat, I watch him. He really is devastating, even when he's staring at me like I've insulted his mother.

His grip on the wallet goes white-knuckled.

I swallow hard and nod at the decks on the table. "Four of Clubs."

CHAPTER

3

I get to the dressing room in time to drop off my tray and head right back for the Twins' second act. It's a well-established routine, and I don't have to track any errant undergarments, which is good, because I'm still reeling from my interaction with Darcy. It wasn't simply the good face. And he didn't say anything particularly compelling. So why . . . ?

I flash back to the last few seconds beside their table: his attention on my thigh, the way he clung to his wallet like it was the only thing keeping him from reaching for me.

I wrinkle my nose. *Or he thought I was going to swipe it.*

Later, Jane joins me to watch Ming, and I distract myself by giving him the lowdown on Charles: "Charming, good sense of humor, and unless my senses are completely off, I'd put him down as a definite potential. I give you leave to like him."

Jane keeps his eyes on Ming, but he makes a thoughtful "hmm" sound.

"Jane." My voice is hard, making him look at me. "You know what you have to do."

"*No*," he says with a hint of annoyance. "Absolutely not. It's too forward."

"Jane, it's a new dawn. It's a new day. It's a new life." I break up the lyrics like I'm trying to make a point with each line. "You're feeling *good*."

He narrows his eyes. "You're a terrible influence, you know that?"

"Well, this terrible influence told ya boy's friend about the Four of Clubs."

Jane's glare goes wide-eyed, and I stand straighter, compensating for a sudden burst of self-consciousness. "Elizabeth Bennet, you don't do that." The use of my real name makes his statement of fact even more resonant. I shrug.

Jane watches me for another beat, and my stomach gives a guilty pitch. I don't want to badger him. If he's not feeling it—

"I'll do it."

"Really?"

Jane rolls his shoulders and smiles. "You're stepping it up. I can be brave, too."

The excitement ricochets in my chest. "I'll spread the word."

Jane waves me off, and I skip to the top stair. Johnny has already started toward the stage when I intercept and update him. Ming takes her bow and I cross the room the long way, past the far end of the stage, to address the band. Arthur nods as I approach, eyebrows high as he continues playing the piano.

"Jane has a wild hair," I tell him. "You and the guys up for Miss Simone?"

"Seriously?" His playing speeds up, the others catching on within a few notes. "Is he trying to get everyone in the place laid, or just himself?"

"Consider it a good deed for all," I offer, and scoot to the stage for Ming's costume.

In the dressing room, the Twins stand in front of a fan, still in their pasties and G-strings from their earlier number. Ming's dabbing more glitter onto her lipstick, clad in the bra and shimmy belt she'll wear when we take our final bows.

I place the pile of clothing on the filing cabinet. "Jane's singing 'Feeling Good'!"

A beat of silence follows my announcement, then the room erupts in movement. Robes are donned in a flurry of silk and marabou, and I lead the charge upstairs with the trio at my heels. We stop halfway up, letting Jane stand alone for his intro. When he glances our way, the four of us titter excitedly, and he beams.

He'd never admit it, but he loves singing this song. It's his one vanity, and if he's ever feeling down about a bad audition or a gig he missed out on, it's his go-to pick-me-up. Granted, he's never used the song to intentionally pick anyone *else* up before, but if Charles is even remotely curious about Jane, this song will seal the deal.

"Folks," says Johnny, "you're about to be treated to a very special performance. So get cozy with the nearest sexy body and give it up for Meryton's own sweet Sweet Jane!"

The spotlight illuminates Jane, who looks away, striking a pose of bewitching distraction. The audience responds with polite applause.

Ming squeezes my arm. "They have no *idea*," she whispers.

Jane cradles the microphone in one hand, the other resting on the green egg. The clapping tapers to quiet. After a beat of silence, he begins singing.

At first, it's just Jane's smoky voice as the spell is cast. The effect is gradual, building as he assures bird and sun and breeze that they know how he feels. By the time he croons the first *"And I'm feeling good"* of the song, I have chills. The band comes in, brass-heavy and seductive, and Jane saunters into the dining room. We girls match each leisurely step with one of our own, making our way to the main floor. We rest against the slim bars of the railing, slowly melting.

Ming holds a hand to her chest in an earnest swoon, and her head falls to my left shoulder. "The basement. Is. *Flooded.*"

I can't even laugh. Chin propped on the crossbar, I send a dazed look over the audience. No one is immune to Jane's siren song. Couples clutch hands and lean against one another, expressions pleasantly glazed. The two women who asked about my corset are straight-up making out with their dates, while the bachelorette party on the risers simply stares, inactive phone screens dimming one by one.

I get to Charles. His jaw hangs open, his frame slack, as though the back of his chair is the only thing keeping him upright. The man is gobsmacked and, I suspect, a few seconds shy of drooling.

I grin. Earplugs will *definitely* be in order this evening.

And Darcy—

Is looking at me.

In the sway of Jane's performance, the eye contact is electric. My lips part in a gasp, and his eyes drop to take in the movement, then lower, drifting along my form with an intention that feels like a promise. I grip the railing so hard my knuckles crack.

Jane sings the final *"And I'm feeling good!"* extending each word for maximum effect. As the words carry through the room, Darcy's chest rises in a long, slow breath, the kind of intake that precedes sudden movement, and I know, as sure as I know my own name, he's going to come to me.

This is happening . . .

Darcy's hand pushes against his table, his chair moving as he shifts to stand. I rise from the railing—

Johnny clears his throat into the mic, and I crash back to earth so suddenly I have to cling to the rail for balance. My eyes dart back to Darcy. His gaze is low, eyes blinking rapidly as if he, too, is coming back to himself. He's firmly in his seat, hand gripping the table.

Disappointment seizes my chest, and I sag against the railing.

It was the song. And it's over.

＞－ · －＞

With the rest of us waiting in the wings, Johnny closes the show with our roll call, summoning us from the stairwell one at a time once the thunderous applause for Jane dies down. I'm first, the band playing a light, brassy tune as I make my woozy way to the stage, quickly followed by Ginn, Tonic, and Ming. We crowd the tiny dais, where the six of us take our bows, and Ming initiates a conga line to guide us off.

I scan for Darcy as we pass through the audience, but the crush of the other performers blocks my view, and I'm steered down the stairs. At the landing, I recover my mental note about restocking the pastie tray for the second show. Ming pulls me into the coat check, the alcove unused in the warmer months, and we draw the heavy red drape shut to avoid any chatty guests.

I rest against the wall, still muddled by the influence of Jane's song and . . . God, what *was* that?

Whatever it was, a few more beats of that heat and my undies would have *ignited*.

I replay that deep breath from Darcy, his grip on the table. Hell, a few more seconds and—what *would* have happened? He was coiled like he was going to pounce.

My thighs clench. *I could go for a pouncing.*

"Heads up!" Ming stands on a chair, riffling through the stock she keeps in the corner. She tosses the little bags of pasties down to me. "So, what was the occasion for Nina? Jane feeling feisty?"

"Kind of." I lurch to catch a pair of tassels and peek through the gap in the curtain at the guests queuing for the bathroom. "He spotted a cutie earlier and wanted to make an impression."

"Oh?" Ming sounds unconvinced. When I look over, she has a hand on her hip, still standing on the chair in the corner. "That's not very Jane."

I shrug and return to the gap, hoping to spot a specific face. "I *may* have encouraged him."

Ming chuckles. "Good for you, giving him a nudge. Our boy doesn't recruit enough action here."

Damn. No Darcy. I let the curtain fall shut. "You know Jane."

She nods, eyes going distant. "It's been, what? Three years since all that went down?"

"Three in July." Like I could forget: the breakup was the catalyst for my move here. Jane was devastated when his fiancé left him, but in typical New York fashion, the practical took priority over the emotional. He needed to split his suddenly doubled rent with someone. I was reeling from my own crisis and jumped at the opportunity to move cross-country and start fresh.

I'd only met Jane twice before then, through my cousin in LA. But when I lugged my few boxes into the apartment, I was stunned at the change. He drifted around like a ghost for months, and it took him the better part of a year to get back to the brilliant creature he is. Even now, he's reluctant to plunge into the dating pool. He's dabbled in hookups and casual dates but hasn't gotten excited over anyone since his ex. Wielding Nina tonight is a huge step for him, even if Charles doesn't bite.

Ming frowns. "Come to think of it, you don't reel 'em in either."

That look from Darcy scorches through my memory, and I resist the urge to peek past the curtain again. "Maybe because *someone* makes me stock pasties when I could be otherwise occupied."

"*Oh?*" Ming's frown turns into a salacious grin. She holds a hand to her chest and steps down from the chair. "Far be it from *me* to interfere with a lady's pursuit of booty. Go get yours!"

I lift my chin, embarrassed to have admitted my intentions but determined to have them realized. I take one last peek at the landing—

Charles and Darcy are out there!

I hold a finger to my lips and wave Ming to the curtain. I point out Charles. "The blond," I whisper. "He's the one Jane sang for."

"Jane does love a Norseman," Ming whispers with approval. "But who is the sex god beside him?"

Indeed, this is the first time I'm seeing Darcy at his full height, and "sex god" about covers it. He's removed his suit jacket, and I admire the broad shoulders and trim waist. He also has the sleeves of his dress shirt rolled up to the middle of his forearms. I don't know what it is about that look, but oh, yes, *please*.

"*Mine*," I tell Ming.

Another filthy smile. "Reconnaissance?"

Absolutely. I twist the dimmer switch to turn down the already faint light in the alcove, and we strain to listen.

"I just don't get the allure," says Darcy. "Especially for you."

"Are you kidding? This is brilliant! And the singer—Jane? Sensational. That was . . ." Charles shakes his head. "I don't have the words. That was *sex*."

I pump my fist, and Ming whispers a singsong *"Jane's gonna see Thor's hammer!"*

Darcy doesn't say anything, and Charles sighs.

"Come on, Darcy," Charles replies, his tone rife with disbelief. "You can't pretend you didn't have a good time tonight."

"It's just so artificial," he adds stiffly. He crosses his arms over his chest, clearing his throat. "And too . . . *much*."

Ming nudges me, making an exaggerated humping motion toward the curtain. I hold in a laugh, though Darcy's word choice, "artificial," doesn't sit right.

Charles laughs. "You're such a prude, man."

"I prefer the intimate remain intimate."

Despite Darcy's flat tone, the comment has me cocking my head. *This* I like; real intimacy isn't for show. Granted, I've never considered what goes on here to be intimate. If I did, I wouldn't be able to do it.

Regardless, methinks the gentleman doth protest too much.

"It's all for fun. Come on." Charles smirks. "What about Kitten?"

Ah! Ming smacks my shoulder and I wiggle my eyebrows. *Yes, what about Kitten?*

I wait, eagerly anticipating the response. The door to one of the bathrooms opens. Charles nods to the woman who steps out, then catches the door, still waiting for Darcy's reply.

Anticipation winds through me. After this long a pause, I can only assume Darcy is searching for words adequate to convey his insatiable lust.

"She's thoroughly tolerable, but not enough to tempt *me*."

A record scratch tears through my brain. *Excuse* me? I replay the comment, but there's no room for interpretation. His emphasis was clear: good enough for *some*, but not *him*. The slight is a needle into my ballooned ego, bringing it sputtering from the ceiling to plop at my feet.

Ming's jaw drops and she mouths an elongated, "*Damn.*"

"*Thoroughly tolerable?*" I mouth back, incredulous. Ming snorts back a laugh, then covers her mouth with her hand. But when I peer out again, the landing is empty.

I shove back the curtain with a huff. "And I sold him a deck earlier. I have half a mind to take back the card I'm on."

Ming gasps. "Well, that settles it. If anyone can turn you down after the Four of Clubs, they're not worth pursuing, anyway."

The disappointment settles on my chest like a physical weight. I really thought there had been a connection. All his watching, and the moment during Jane's song; it felt like we were building to something.

Ming links arms with me, and I force a stiff upper lip as we march back to the dressing room with the pasties, my tattered ego limping along after us.

❦

We don't see the men again, and when Esteban brings down a stack of receipts with messages for Jane, none are from Charles. The notes range from appreciative to downright lewd, and while Ming leads the group in a series of dramatic readings ("*Sweet Jane, let me tame your little red love machine!*"), I search Jane for any signs of disappointment. To my pleasant surprise, I don't find any. Instead, there's a buzz about him the rest of the night, some confidence that elevates both his songs in the second show. It energizes him to the point where he arranges to sing for the band at their after-hours gig, though I beg off, my hand still itching to sketch out my design ideas for Meryton.

At home, I tuck tonight's kittening getup away among the corsets and girdles I wear at Meryton. I pause to pluck a new ensemble from the standards, avoiding the number on the price tag, which Tonic's employee discount only *just* managed to make doable. The fine-mesh bra would require pasties, and the coordinating garter belt draws the eye to my crotch, the arch created by the straps framing the area almost indecently. It'll be one hell of a look if I get the nerve to put it together.

With a sigh, I return the hanger to the closet and smooth my hand over the pale pink fabric. *Someday, lovelies . . . maybe something more pleasure than work.* I bite my lower lip; *that* would take more nerve than wearing it at the show.

Unbidden, Darcy's face pops up in my mind, accompanied by a brutal echo. *Not enough to tempt me.*

"Liar." I yank the closet door shut, the panel shuddering in protest. He *was* tempted, thank you so much. There was . . . *something.*

I thought there was something.

Even hours later, the slight stings more than I'm comfortable with. I decide to indulge in a little ego stroking. Jane has Nina, and I have a fallback of my own. I take a seat at my desk and open the shallow drawer in the center, pressing down on the bulging manila folder within so it doesn't catch on the lip of the writing surface. Inside the file are the prints from the card deck shoot.

It happened early in my time at the show. The photographer was in the dressing room chatting with Ming when he received a text from someone bailing on the next day's shoot. He griped about finding a last-minute replacement and Ming gestured my way, with the offhand comment, "Kitten's hot. She'll do it."

I was hopeless, my poses stiff and awkward, all weak imitations of what I'd seen other performers do while I'd been waiting my turn. With back muscles knotting and frustration edging me toward tears, I had to break to stretch—and the photographer snapped my photo. The shot caught me mid-arch, my arms raised and lips parted, my eyes soft.

The effect is intense. At first glance, I appear totally naked. I'm not; I'm in pasties and a G-string, and am seated on a pile of sky-blue boas with another draped over my shoulders. But the eye is drawn to very specific areas—two, to be exact—and if I may say so, they look outstanding.

Hella better than "thoroughly tolerable," thank *you* so much.

Ego slightly revived, I move to return the file to the drawer, but a second folder demands my attention. I look at my watch: *1:07 a.m.* I grimace, drumming my restless fingers on the edge of the drawer front. *It's late. No need to start on that now* . . .

My memory flickers to the ideas I had at the beginning of the first show: simpler wallpaper, the dark arc behind the stage—it's not like I have any plans for tomorrow, anyway.

I toss the folder onto the desk and flip it open before common sense interferes. Staring back at me are two years of notes, sketches, wallpaper samples, and newspaper and magazine clippings, organized by concept and location. Some are for the interiors of bars, and there are a few ideas for concert venues and restaurants, too. Last month's search for a space to host a merger party for my day job put me into overdrive; at this point, the place I ended up reserving could have a file of its own.

I select the pile bound in a folded sheet of the letterhead I used at the start of my evening: Meryton.

Jane was only working Jazz Nights when I moved here. I'd lurk at the bar, letting Michael's heavy pours take the edge off my hurts while Jane sang around his own. Such was the extent of my social life until Jane added the burlesque shows to his repertoire.

I knew nothing about burlesque outside its reputation as "fancy stripping." But the first time I saw Ming prowl across the room, I was hooked. The costumes, the playfulness, the control the performers had over every moment they were on: it spoke to me. They were 98 percent bare and nothing short of invincible. And I needed invincible.

I sat at the bar through both shows, rapt, and when we got home, I signed up for the New York School of Burlesque's intro class. And then I drew.

I sketched Ming slinking across the stage and Johnny sassing the crowd. I drew Jane in his three-piece suit and another performer, a fire-eater from Coney Island, rolling a flaming baton over her skin. I sketched for hours, but I didn't draw Meryton. Interior design was still too raw, but after months in creative limbo, it was invigorating to have an outlet again.

Now Andrea is buying the building. *And* renovating . . . A thrill dances up my spine at the prospect, more intense now that I'm in front of my work. Meryton has facilitated so much good in my life; the least I can do is contribute to this new chapter of its story.

With that appreciation, I sketch out my idea about the arc behind the stage. I lose track of the time, adding a rendering of the Twins on their silks. When I reach for my laptop, I cut myself off, knowing damn well I'm about to tumble down an internet rabbit hole of wallpaper searches.

I sag into the seat, surveying my work. It really is good. *I* really am good.

A heavy melancholy settles over me, bearing down with the familiar weight of regret and shame. But the late hour overtakes it. My aching eyelids demand to be relieved of the layers of shadow, liner, and residual eyelash glue, and I go to the bathroom to get ready for bed. By my return trudge to the bedroom, exhaustion has set in. Jammies are a bridge too far, and I collapse into bed after taking off my clothes, twining the cool sheets around my bare body. As I settle, blue and red lights flash around the edges of my blinds, and I grope for the sleep mask and earplugs on my nightstand.

One more time, the two words bounce in my brain: *"thoroughly tolerable."*

"Hmph." I situate my mask. I wedge in an earplug on one side, then the other, and tug the comforter up to my chin. "Tolerable my *butt.*"

CHAPTER

◆ 4 ◆

I'm drifting back to consciousness when a familiar jostling sets me rocking. I peel back the corner of my sleep mask and glare down at Jane, sprawled across the foot of the bed, wearing only his blue paisley pajama pants. He twinkles his fingers at me.

I sit up, mindful to keep the sheet high over my bare torso, then note the time on the clock: 10:17 a.m. *Not too bad.* I push the mask onto my forehead and pluck out my earplugs. "And when did you crawl in?"

"Around four." He props himself up on an elbow, head in one hand as he traces the vine pattern on my duvet cover with the other.

"Really?" Four's late for him. I reach to the nightstand and drop the earplugs into the jewelry tray, then arrange the comforter around my shoulders. "How'd the after-hours show go?"

The floorboards on his side of the apartment creak. He gives me a coy smile as I draw my lips into an "O," clutching imaginary pearls.

"You little minx!" I lean to peer through the open doorway. "Jane Okogu, is there a gentleman in your boudoir?"

Jane inspects his nails, but his smile stretches ear to ear.

"Why are you in here?" I prod him with my foot. "Go tend to your fellow."

"I don't want to be clingy," he replies, voice low. "Plus, I wanna show him off. I did *good*."

"Um, hello?" a voice calls. "Jane?"

"In here," Jane says, watching me.

Footsteps sound in the hall, and there's a rap at my open door. A blond head pokes in.

Charles?

At the sight of Jane, Charles smiles. "Hey—oh! Good morning—" He aims a finger gun my way, eyebrows down in recall. "Kitten?"

I school my shock into pleasant surprise, though it's touch-and-go when he steps in and the friendly face is accompanied by a shirtless form that speaks of an admirable devotion to a fitness regimen. Ming's "hammer" joke comes to mind, and I will myself to keep my eyes above the waist of his dark boxer briefs.

"Good morning to you, too." I smile back, internally cursing Jane, who is lounging on top of my robe. "And you're right, it's Kitten. Off-stage, I'm Bennet. Charles, right?"

"Good memory." He crosses the room, hand outstretched.

Clutching the comforter, I reach over Jane's legs to shake. His hand is soft, but calluses scrape against similar rises high in my own palm. I wonder how he got his. Judging from his chiseled form, whatever it is, he does it diligently.

"The two of you room together?" Charles places a hand on Jane's bare shoulder.

I shoot a quick glance at Jane, who relaxes into Charles's touch. *Interesting.* "Yeah. Family got us connected."

Charles nods, eyes sweeping the room, and I do a quick scan for anything unseemly. My design file is still on the desk and last night's dress hangs on my chair, but that's the worst of my offenses. Well, that and my nakedness, I guess.

He points to the cluster of lanterns tiered around the window and bed. Tulle and silk tendrils stream from them in light shades of blue and violet. "Jellyfish?"

"Meryton was in the Mermaid Parade this year," I explain. "It's an art parade in Coney Island, kind of kicks off the summer. Those were from our float. We were all jellyfish."

I get a phantom itch at the memory. Redecorating my room ended up being a productive way to spend the two days I needed to recover from the sunburn I earned frolicking on the boardwalk in only pasties and a frothy tulle skirt.

"Very nice. You have an interesting arrangement." Charles rubs Jane's shoulder, as though the intimate contact is something they've established over months, not hours. "Is there a common area?"

"My room's supposed to be the living room." Jane rests a hand over Charles's, twining their fingers. "This is a one-bedroom."

I keep my features neutral, but inside, I'm floored. Rare as they are, Jane's even-keeled when it comes to hookups: some friendly chitchat in the a.m. and then he sends the lucky fellow on his merry way. This hand-holding and petting is a first; that he's literally showing off last night's conquest borders on surreal.

Beneath the covers, I wedge my foot under him again, digging my toes into his side to get him moving. With such an exceptional situation, he'd best keep the momentum going.

Jane pops off the bed, sidling up to Charles in one smooth motion. "Sorry for disappearing. I didn't want to wake you. I was telling Bennet about brunch plans." He links arms with Charles in another move that has me restraining a baffled *Wha?* "I got her and me roped into eating with Andrea."

"Brunch with *Andrea?*" We've only ever had drinks with her outside of Meryton once. Jane and I left staggering. "I don't know if I have it in me."

Jane shrugs, using the motion to gain further contact with Charles's bare side. "She plied me with an additional booking next week." He squeezes Charles's arm, then starts for the door. "You were there. You can vouch."

"Andrea?" Charles replies, letting himself get escorted. "Yes, she can be very persuasive." He turns to wave, Jane already in the hall. "It was nice seeing you again, Bennet. You, ah . . ." He smiles. "You made quite an impression last night." The smile broadens into that charming grin of his. "Even *I* appreciated your Four of Clubs."

For Jane's sake, I don't share that I know perfectly well how shallow that supposed impression was. So I grin back, throwing my arms up in the same position as on the card—forgetting about my nudity.

In the split second it takes for the comforter to drop from my shoulders, I go from embarrassment to mortification. But the goose down piles into a barrier just above my boob region, and Charles is spared an eyeful.

He makes a show of covering his eyes, then continues to the hall, still chuckling.

◆ · ◆

I take my time getting ready, in case Charles and Jane need more than a few minutes to say or otherwise convey their goodbyes. The front door opens and closes late in my hair regimen, the scrape of the door over the thick mat competing with the hiss of my hairspray.

I poke my head into Jane's room, hoping for some sign of whatever he and Charles got into during those predawn hours. But the space is as perfectly put-together as ever, the charcoal bedding and goldenrod throw at the foot of his bed with corners so tight, Jane barely makes an indentation where he sits putting on his shoes.

"*So.*" I settle beside him, almost bouncing on the taut bedding as I arrange my skirt. "How did *that* happen?"

"He came back! Not long after you left, he and his friend came in for a drink." He purses his lips in delight. "He *looked* for me. Spotted me at family meal and asked if I was free to join them." His voice is dreamy, like he still can't believe it.

"His friend excused himself, and after we finished our drinks, Charles came to the after-hours gig. I sang, then he had a *car* bring us down to the Slope and we caught another drink and a bite at the Black Horse, then, ah—" He averts his eyes. "Then we came here."

Before I can voice my appreciation for my earplugs, he nudges me, grinning.

"By the way, his friend? Will, I think. Charles calls him by his last name, like how people do with you. Darcy? *Gorgeous.* I didn't notice at first, because of Charles, but *damn.*"

"Agreed on the gorgeous. Too bad he's a dillhole."

Jane smacks my shoulder. "He seemed nice!"

I share the overheard commentary. At this point, it's kind of funny:

"*thoroughly tolerable*"? Who talks like that? But Jane can tell it rubbed me the wrong way and sticks out his lower lip with an appropriate degree of sympathy.

"That is harsh," he says. "Charles mentioned that he takes a while to warm up. Darcy doesn't like crowds, and Charles sprung the show on him last-minute and got there late. Maybe he was in a bad mood?"

I shrug. Darcy said that "tolerable" line with confidence; he'd made up his mind. Still, I'm willing to entertain the possibility of redemption, if for no other reason than it would be a waste of such a gorgeous face for his personality to be so lacking. "You gonna see Charles again?"

Jane bites his lower lip.

"*Wow.* You are in some deep smit, friend."

"He's *really* nice. And really cute, but he's only around for a few weeks. They're in from the West Coast for some business stuff. I dunno; I checked out during that part. I was watching his lips move."

"They are very nice lips."

"They are *amazing* lips."

"*Oh?*"

"More like O-*face*."

"Oh. My. God," I marvel. "He has you making sex puns. This boy toy has potential."

"Do you think?" His voice is bright.

I smile and stand, reaching out to haul Jane from the bed. "You are hopeless."

◆ · ◆

When we arrive, the line at Stone Park Cafe has already curved around the patio seating, the potential diners shifting to accommodate the constant flow of scooters and strollers en route to the playground across the street. I spot Andrea waving at us from a four-top, her large sun hat drawing us in like a black hole. Jane and I "Pardon me" and "Excuse us" our way through the front door, and the beleaguered hostess shows us to our seats.

"Quickly!" Andrea snaps her fingers to get a waiter's attention. "Do either of you want biscuits and gravy? We have to get the order in immediately, they're almost out."

"Oh, very yes," I say, and Jane makes a request as well.

Andrea snags a server, places the order, then busies herself with pouring us mimosas from the pitcher she's already largely consumed.

"Jane," she says, her tone too light to be genuine. "How*ever* was your evening?"

"I had an excellent night, thank you very much." He takes a dainty sip of his mimosa. I respond with a Ming-inspired cackle, and he smacks at me with his free hand.

Andrea chuckles along, and her smoker's rattle borders on sinister. Jane glances my way, and I find my unease reflected in his expression.

She puts down her drink, her laughter ebbing. "Jane, my dear, your evening may prove to have been *excellent* for all of us." She taps the stem of her glass tunelessly, her painted face growing solemn. "You should know we are in a bit of a situation at Meryton. The landlord's considering selling the building—"

"What?" Jane gasps. I do my best to feign wide-eyed shock.

Andrea scowls. "Oh, for Christ's sake, Kitten, I know *you* know. Michael can't keep his mouth shut. *Anyway*," she continues, "as Kitten is well aware, *I* plan to buy in."

Jane crosses his arms, facing me. "Why didn't you tell me?"

"We had other priorities."

He tips his head, eyes going dreamy. "Yeah . . ."

Andrea clears her throat, and Jane and I straighten, properly chastened. "The owner had the building appraised and got some numbers on renovations. The back of the house is in desperate need of upgrades, and there's no question the dining room could use some love. He's reluctant to put in the money and is considering offloading the property."

I scowl, suspicion eroding the novelty of a free meal. Why is she telling *us* all of this?

"Our current options are to find an investor to back me, relocate the show, or simply be at the mercy of whoever ends up taking on the space."

"But you have a backer, right?" I say, hoping further evidence of Michael's loose lips doesn't get him in trouble.

"Oh, I have a moneyman." Andrea grins. "You chatted him up quite thoroughly, Kitten, but Jane won the day—or night, I suppose."

The implication creeps up on me, a slow march toward the obvious. "*Charles?*" I blurt. "Jane's *Charles* is the one backing you?"

Andrea takes a smug sip of her mimosa, which turns into a downing of her glass. She places the empty champagne flute on the table with a raised pinky. "He's the one."

Jane's jaw goes slack. "Charles wants to help you buy Meryton?"

I fall against my chair, shaking my head. That explains his comment about Andrea's being persuasive. "Why didn't you say anything about him coming in?"

She shrugs, refilling her glass. "It's just as well I didn't. I assumed the Charles Bingley in question was the *senior*, not the junior. Old money can be so eccentric," she muses. "Handing off fortunes to their offspring like they're doling out Monopoly money."

"Why are you telling us all this?" As I ask, a possible reason comes to mind. "Don't you say anything about using Jane as a damn honeypot. That's gross."

"But everybody wins." Andrea waves her champagne flute to take in the general area. "We keep the show going; Jane enjoys a sweet, handsome fellow with a fortune; and Charles gets a talented, delightful boyfriend and a fun investment in the Manhattan property game."

"I'm sorry," Jane interrupts, his palm raised like he's a student waiting to be called on. "You're talking like I'm not right here. Are you saying it's on *me* to keep Meryton intact?"

"No, Jane. I'm simply informing you of the situation."

"But no pressure." I prop my chin in my hand and finish my mimosa. *Lord.*

"Of course not," says Andrea. "The odds are simply more favorable if the young Bingley has a vested interest in the show's success."

Our food arrives. We're quiet as the plates of biscuits and gravy are distributed, and the waiter departs with Andrea's request for a refill on the mimosa vat. My irritation with Andrea isn't mixing well with the bubbles and orange, so I dig in before my hanger hits in earnest.

"There's a slim possibility the current owner will pass the property on to a nephew," Andrea says, picking up the thread of conversation as she slices into a biscuit. "Unlikely, though. He's already had a few failed ventures and wouldn't have the talent connections—"

I swallow. "Unless we're willing to stay on with him."

Andrea freezes, her fork just shy of her mouth. "Well, that's the rub, isn't it?" She places the fork back onto the plate. "If it goes that way, there's no guarantee the nephew would employ the same concept, but given the show is the club's biggest draw, the best move would be to change as little as possible."

"Where would you be, in this scenario?" Jane asks.

"That . . ." She pauses. "That remains to be seen. Charles's involvement is specific to Meryton; outfitting some other venue for our shows would be too much of a gamble for him. I certainly don't have the assets to start anything of my own, and finding another investor would take time." She sniffs. "You all would scatter to the four winds, getting scooped up by other producers and shows."

I roll my eyes at the unnecessary drama and make my next bite large enough to let me avoid having to placate her. It earns me a kick from Jane, but I chew on, defiant.

Jane sighs. "We wouldn't abandon you, Andrea."

Andrea's eyes soften, likely more at Jane's acknowledgment of her emotional fronting than his loyalty. "Let's just hope it doesn't come to that. Thank you, darling," she says to the waiter, who has returned with another ungodly amount of $2 bubbles and orange juice concentrate. He tops off each of our glasses, and Andrea raises hers in a toast. "To artful negotiations. And happy couplings."

◆— · —◆

"On a scale from one to *Silkwood*, how badly do you need to shower after that conversation?" I weave my arm through Jane's, and he gives mine a squeeze. We've opted to aid digestion with a stroll through the park instead of heading straight home.

He sighs. "Andrea gonna Andrea."

Andrea left as soon as her plate—and mimosa vat—was clear. At least she'd done us the courtesy of paying for the meal. I'm still livid over her suggestion about Jane, but Jane's been quiet. When I peek at his face, his expression is shuttered, brows low in thought.

"It doesn't have to change anything with you and Charles," I say.

He blinks. "Why would it? Andrea's just being *her*, and I don't mind that Charles didn't mention it. I don't know when it would have come up."

"I bet not." I elbow him. "*You got a love bite on your neck—*"

"That's two Cher references in less than thirty seconds, Bennet."

"That one was Olympia Dukakis."

"Still *Moonstruck*."

"Still stalling."

Jane releases my arm. I let him walk ahead a few paces. He turns, scrubbing his hand along his jaw. "I like him, Bennet. I want to get to know him better in the time he's here. We only talked a little bit about him; he was the one asking what brought me to New York and about my interests and . . ." He shakes his head, eyes distant, then bright. "I *really* like him."

While I love seeing Jane so buoyant, my thoughts touch down on the potential fallout of this hypothetical love affair. An image of Jane, depression-dulled and couch-bound, mainlining nature documentaries, flickers in my memory.

I force it aside. It's been three years. He'll always be a softie, but Jane's more resilient now. Plus, he's braced for a short-term thing here. "Then that's all that matters."

Jane nods, beaming. "I saw your folder out, by the way. Andrea did mention renovations." He links arms with me again, and we turn onto a path lined with benches. "You feeling inspired?" His angling hooks the excitement I've been holding in check all morning.

"I don't know," I admit. "I *am* sorry I didn't say anything about the sale last night. Part of it was how wrapped up I was with Ol' Tolerable, but . . ." I grit my teeth. "I didn't want to mention it, in case it fell through."

Jane tugs me to take a seat on a bench. A few yards away, a group of children play in a water feature, a man-made stream that will be turned off in the coming weeks. For now, the weather is still warm enough to keep it running.

A little girl in a pink sundress beelines for the water, launching herself into it. The resulting splash flecks our shins. She holds her arms up in triumph, though a few smaller kiddos wail at the unexpected deluge.

Jane chuckles at the spectacle, then tips his head my way. "I know you closed that chapter, Ben. I also know you love interior design. You're good."

"I am good," I concede, helpless in the face of the praise.

"And I *do* have a special relationship with the moneyman."

I let my head fall onto his shoulder. "Dearest, are you volunteering to honeypot yourself for little ol' me?"

"*Only you,*" he croons, and kisses my temple. "Now c'mon. All that Cher talk has me wanting to watch *Mermaids.*"

CHAPTER
✦ · 5 · ✦

The phone's shrill ring bounces off the glass walls of the reception area. I pick up the receiver without taking my eyes from the computer screen, smile already plastered to my face. "Work It, this is Liz speaking. How may I help you?"

Toby laughs loud enough that I have to pull the phone away from my ear. "Liz, you sound like my mom."

Toby is my day-job boss, the president of Work It, a (since last month's friendly acquisition of three competitors) *national* chain of communal workspace facilities. I'm his administrative assistant here at HQ: a glorified receptionist of the highest order and reliable semi-adult who can man the fancy Italian espresso machine in the break room.

"Your mom *hired* me." I pivot to face him at his own desk,

separated from the lobby by a partition twenty feet away. Headphones set his glasses askew, making him look about a decade younger than the thirty-three years already undermined by his baby face. *"Reception, admin . . ."*

"Occasional babysitting," he chimes, concluding the list of duties in the job posting I stumbled on two weeks after I got to New York. Assuming the last bit meant childcare, I applied. Toby's mom, who'd been functioning as admin since Work It got off the ground, had written the post. She meant *him*.

The traditional nine-to-five nature of my day job baffles the burlesquers, who seek work with flexible hours or have side hustles more in line with their creative efforts. Jane teaches voice and piano, Tonic does aerial lessons in addition to her job at the high-end lingerie boutique, and Ming is the go-to seamstress for the better part of the burlesque scene, creating and adjusting costumes and clothing for those of us who don't know our way around a sewing machine.

"How may I help you?" I ask.

"I was looking over the contract for the venue hosting Saturday's function." He squints at his computer screen. "Is that all we're paying, or is more due later?"

I sit taller. Toby told me to go all out when finding a venue for the merger party—"Spare no expense!"—but I kept my feet on the ground. One of my "babysitting" duties is reining in his occasionally impulsive spending habits; he got the espresso machine on an afternoon when I was at the dentist. Incidentally, his mom was filling in for me and called to tattle.

"I haggled," I admit. "Pemberley is new to the scene. We're one of their first contracts, so they were willing to deal."

"Great. And, your, um"—he clears his throat, voice high with forced nonchalance—"*friends* from your weekend thing. They'll be . . . appropriate?"

"You said you wanted it to be memorable," I say, feigning confusion.

Toby's eyes go round, shaving another handful of years from his features, forcing me to laugh. I recruited the Twins and Jane for entertainment. They'll do their respective things, though Ginn and Tonic will keep their act second-tier-city-friendly, and the venue has a piano, which is where Jane comes in.

"No nudity," I assure him, and he relaxes into an expression less likely to get him carded. "Just acrobatics and Gershwin."

"Perfect." Toby's attention shifts back to his computer screen. "It's an amazing space, Liz. You really have an eye."

He's right on both counts. Pemberley's exterior is lovely, a brick façade with a giant chrome sunburst over its broad double doors, but the interior is like nothing I've ever seen. An indoor lake takes up half of the venue's main floor, with seating on little islands connected via a walkway. Seeing Pemberley in person a few weeks ago, I about swooned. I handed over the deposit check without a second thought. While it meant I had to figure out how to incorporate the venue's stage into the flow of the room, there was no way we were going to have that party anywhere but that Hell's Kitchen gem.

I put my hands behind my head, rocking in my desk chair. "Anything else you'd like to compliment me on? I'm terribly important and busy."

Toby laughs. "You're a lifesaver, Liz."

"It's what I do."

Toby hangs up, cutting off his chuckle, and I open the email I received from Andrea earlier. Pemberley's owner had inquired after liability insurance for aerialists, and I asked Andrea about how Meryton handled that coverage. She initially held out on the grounds that I'd poached her talent, but she relented at my promise to leave Meryton flyers at the door.

I scan the message, ignoring Andrea's "subtle" inquiry after Jane and Charles.

With the (massive) exception of Andrea's honeypotting allusions, thinking about Jane and Charles makes me smile. Jane's been on cloud nine since last weekend. Granted, it's Jane, so his cloud nine looks like a cloud eleven, but the man's effervescence warms my heart. He and Charles have seen one another every day, meeting up after Jane's voice lessons and attending his gigs together. Charles even went to last night's rehearsal in Bushwick, which had me assigning major brownie points. The guy's staying in the Meatpacking District; Bushwick's a hike.

That hour-long trek made it all the more surprising to learn that Darcy was also in attendance. But then, according to Jane, Charles has yet to make an appearance either unescorted by the handsome grump or without some mention of said grump's recent departure. I've decided to chalk the near omnipresence up to an unhealthy level of attachment on Darcy's part or evidence that Charles's friendship is an act of charity.

I shift in my chair, pretending it's not a squirm. Dillhole or not, that look from Saturday has initiated a number of fantasies this week. Not that I'd admit it aloud, but *lordy*. In my mind, Darcy and I have corrupted as many surfaces in Meryton as there are spaces to get horizontal—or vertical, with reasonable support. He's always very apologetic about the "tempting" comment; the Darcy in my head is an excellent groveler.

My email dings with a new message, stirring me from the semi-libidinous reverie. It's Marley, Pemberley's manager, confirming today's final walk-through. They've arranged the seating to fit my sketches to give me a feel for how the room will look Saturday.

I can head over right after lunch with Jane. I grab my purse and stroll to Toby's office on my way out. "I'm off. If you need caffeine, speak now, or you're going to be translating Italian."

❧ · ❧

"Okay," says Jane. "We'll see you guys in a few."

I narrow my eyes at the plural nouns, even as the implication sends a tingle up my spine. Jane proposed we meet Charles for coffee before I go to Pemberley, and it sounds like Charles will have a certain untemptable friend along. I made a point of not asking after Darcy on principle; internal me may entertain forgiveness, but real me has a little more pride than that.

Jane studiously ignores my look as he returns his phone to his back pocket. "Bennet," he warns, his voice cool. "Give him a chance. I know he rubbed you the wrong way . . ."

I cross my arms.

He sighs. "*Fine.* He said a shitty thing and I can't make it better. But that was over a week ago and you're being petty."

I frown. "Petty" is Jane's word of choice when I'm behaving in a way he considers beneath me. That's the burden of having a best friend who is a morally superior creature; they always expect you to be better than you actually are. It would be encouraging if I didn't get called "petty" so often.

"I get to take offense. That was my best material."

"Hmm." Jane taps his chin. "Sounds more like your pride than your brain."

I refuse to acknowledge the truth in the observation.

"Charles mentioned Darcy was with him, not that Darcy planned to stick around. If he does, you'll have to cope. And it's not like he *meant* to insult you. You were the one listening in."

"How is that supposed to be better?"

"I don't know," he says evenly. "I didn't think it through. They're a few blocks away. Get the pouting out of your system, maybe look at the nice stationery in the window here, then meet me in front of the cat hospital." He points across the nearest intersection, where the feline-centric clinic on the corner displays cats available for adoption. "Sound like a plan?"

I keep my head high. "I'm not pouting."

As Jane walks ahead, I stay in front of the letterpress store, waiting to look at the display until Jane is a few shops down. As I admire the lovely, albeit obvious, autumn-themed arrangement of paper products, I consider my reluctance to give Ol' Sexy Sourpuss the benefit of the doubt. There's a chance Jane might be right about Darcy, and I'd like to think he is, because, again: good face. If he's half as skilled at apologizing in the real world as his imagined counterpart is, there may be hope for him yet.

I give my reflection a cursory look, pretending it's an appeal to my vanity and nothing to do with the shiver I just suppressed. *Well done on selection, eight a.m. me.* Figure-flattering is a requirement for all my clothing, and today's floral wrap dress, with its fitted waist, is no exception. Tasteful, with a touch of oomph.

I consider my neckline. *Oh, what the hell.* I give a quick tug to the body of the dress, bringing the collar down to a less office-friendly level. Tasteful, but the "oomph" borders on "ooh la la."

I start down the sidewalk, the brush of air tingling against the newly exposed half inch of skin. My watch buzzes with an incoming text.

> **C:** Hey, Lizard! You up for playing tour guide around the end of the month? I've booked a couple of magazine shoots, and Gales needs "real" pizza.

My heart leaps. It's my cousin in California. I scan for Jane. He'll be excited, too. As much as he loves living in NYC, he misses SoCal, and at this point, Chloe and her fiancé are as much emotional touchstones as they are friends. I tug my phone from my purse. Yay! I type, sending the message with confetti. What are your dates? Who are the shoots with? As a makeup artist, Chloe has worked on fashion shoots all over the country, the lucky brat.

There's a lull in the traffic, so I cut across the street instead of using the crosswalk farther up. Jane's in front of the cat hospital, leaning in to look at the kittens available for adoption.

Movement above him catches my attention—something being pulled down from the side of the same building. Or, not *pulled*, but—I slow my pace—*falling?*

My chest tightens. The roll-down security gate above the window has come loose from the building. The metal frame wobbles forward, the side nearest me falling first, the other pulling free from the brick to follow—

Jane's backing away from the window, his attention still on the cats.

He's right below the damn thing. Does he not see it?

The frame arcs toward him in slow motion.

"*Jane!*" I dodge a guy on a scooter to keep Jane in my line of sight. His head turns a little, but his eyes stay on the window. "*Jane!*"

The frame comes down with a crash. Someone screams, and a cloud of dust billows from the area of impact.

I run toward it.

CHAPTER
6

Jane is on his side, boxed in by the frame. He's propped up on one elbow, free hand patting at the back of his head.

"Jane!" I hop over the crumpled metal and kneel beside him. "Jane? It's me, love."

His eyes wheel, searching blankly. A cold panic ripples through me, but his eyes finally focus. "Bennet, what—who hit me?" He shifts to press himself up and gasps, eyelids fluttering.

"Stay put," I order. "Are you okay?"

"We're going to be late . . ." He removes his hand from his head to motion toward me, and blood drips from his fingers.

"Whoa!" The chill weight of horror settles on my shoulders. "You're bleeding."

I glance at the growing crowd. Onlookers lean over the frame, though for the moment the metal's serving as a makeshift barrier. A guy in a baseball cap lifts his phone overhead and snaps a selfie with the scene as his backdrop.

"Can someone call 911?" I beg.

The small crowd moves for pockets and purses as if a unit of a hive mind. A man in a suit says, "I've got it," and angles his head toward his phone. "Hello? I have an emergency."

"Can anyone help?" I plead. "A doctor or a nurse?"

A few people search among the group, eyeing one another expectantly, but no takers. My stomach pitches, and the fear in Jane's wide eyes emphasizes how out of my depth I am. I place a hand on his shoulder. Blood drips onto my wrist, and I wince. "I'm going to check out the back of your head," I tell him, my voice far more solid than I actually feel.

His lashes flutter, but he nods.

"Try not to move." More blood lands on my hand. I brace myself and scoot behind him. With his shaved head, the damage is immediately clear: brown skin, and the pink of torn scalp bordered by bright red blood. At its center, a sliver of sheer white—

Bone.

I gasp, then place my hands to either side of the gash, pressing my thumbs together to close the wound. Blood oozes from the seam.

"Is it bad?" Jane's voice is high.

"It'll be fine," I choke out. I change my position to keep the pressure applied with one hand. The scene around me tips, my vision swimming.

I just saw Jane's skull.

"Bennet?"

Hopelessness tugs at me. I grit my teeth. Jane needs me to stay calm. "It's all good, hon. We'll get you taken care of—"

Jane goes limp, and I gasp, struggling with the dead weight to ease him onto my knees. My heart clenches. Tears stream down either side of his face.

"Dizzy." His lower lip trembles. "It *hurts*, Ben."

The pain in his voice edges me toward tears. "I'm so sorry, love. Just stay still." I stroke his cheek, my other hand still maintaining the pressure high on the back of his head.

He takes in a shuddering breath. "I hate crying like this." His jaw is stiff, like he's more offended by the indignity of the tears than the horrible circumstances around why he's crying. "Lying down, the tears get in my ears. I *hate* my ears getting wet."

"I know." The rare gripe is strangely reassuring. "I don't understand how you shower."

Jane chuckles, and the fist around my heart releases some.

"We'll get you taken care of." I keep my hand on the side of his face and look for the guy with the phone, hoping 911 has given him an ETA.

"*Jane!*"

At the name, I scan for a familiar face. It takes me a second pass to notice Charles emerging at the front row of onlookers, Darcy beside him.

Charles pales, his eyes darting around wildly as he approaches. "Oh my God, Jane!"

Jane stiffens. "Charles?"

Charles kneels, clasping one of Jane's hands in both of his. Even with my upside-down view, the relief on Jane's face at Charles's arrival is clear.

"What happened?" Charles asks, not taking his eyes from Jane.

Darcy takes a knee beside me. "Has someone called 911?" He leans in to see the wound. The move puts him within motorboat distance of my cleavage, which really shouldn't be in my awareness right now, but damn it, adrenaline does strange things to a gal's body chemistry.

"EMS should be here any minute," hollers the guy in the suit. I nod in thanks and get back to Darcy.

"The gate thing came down, hit Jane," I explain.

Darcy sits up, face tight in consideration as I meet his dark eyes. "Are *you* okay?" He touches my elbow. The unexpected contact has me taking in a sharp breath that extends until I fill my lungs. My head swims, then clears.

"I was down the street when it happened. But if you could find something for the bleed—"

Darcy produces a white handkerchief from a pocket, or perhaps thin air, and offers it to me. "Will this do? It's clean."

"Um, thank you." I take the hanky and press it to Jane's wound, grateful I no longer have to look at the brutal tear.

"Anything else?" Darcy's voice is brusque. He sounds . . . impatient? His eyes dart to his left wrist—

Did he just check his watch?

I scowl. "I'm sorry, is my friend's *head trauma* keeping you from something?"

Darcy stares at me, brows low in familiar dour bafflement. "Well, actually—"

Just then a teenager walks through the group of people, head bobbing to whatever's playing on his oversized headphones. He steps over Jane's legs without even acknowledging the scene.

"How about crowd control?" I snap, pointing to the teen. "If it's not too much to ask."

Darcy watches me another beat, jaw tense, before he stands. "All right!" His voice is commanding enough that I sit straighter. "Back it up!" He raises his hands, then takes two steps backward, gesturing for the others to follow. I wait for static from the bystanders, but the circle widens as everyone copies Darcy's move. The handful of people who crossed in front of metal frame retreat to the other side of it.

Darcy looks to me. "Good?" he asks, and gestures to Jane. "Or would you like me to have a go at sewing him up? I'd hate for you to question my commitment."

I lift my chin, though I feel a little sheepish for having been short with him. "I think we'll leave that to the professionals, but thank you."

A siren wails in the distance and I sigh in relief. *Thank God.* My hand has started to cramp, and I switch my hold, applying pressure with my left hand instead. I roll out my right, then brush at an itch on my forehead.

"That's blood," Charles blurts. "On your hand." He jumps to his feet. "I can't—"

"Charles?" Darcy says his name like a question and a warning. When I look at Charles more closely, he's gone paler than before. He takes a wobbly step back.

"Charles?" asks Jane, reaching for him.

"Are you . . ." Before I can finish my question, Charles's eyes roll back and his body drops.

"Shit!" Darcy lurches forward. He's too far away. Charles hits the ground, his fall broken by Jane, who grunts as his left thigh catches Charles's head.

"Charles?" Jane asks. "Hello?" He strains to look down to the form across his lap. At least Charles landed with his face toward Jane's toes and not his crotch.

"He's out," I say.

Jane stays rigid for another moment, then his body relaxes. "Okay." He feels around to the back of Charles's head and smooths over his fair hair, his movements as tender and relaxed as Charles was with him that first morning. It's sweet, really, despite the circumstances.

A pair of EMTs carve their way through the thinning crowd. They stop short at the arrangement of bodies.

"He's wounded," Darcy says, pointing to Jane. He shakes his head at Charles. "The other one fainted at the blood."

One of the EMTs squats beside me. "Can you keep him in this position while we put on a stabilizing collar?" At my nod, he aligns the low gurney beside Jane. His partner stands over Charles, brows low, as though he's not sure how to go about removing the unconscious impediment.

"How's the bleeding?" asks the EMT.

"It's deep," I warn him, and mouth, "*Bone,*" not wanting to alarm Jane.

The EMT nods, then holds out the neck brace. He gingerly slides it around Jane's neck, the rubber of his gloves tugging against my skin as they pass over my thighs.

"Sorry," he mutters, making an effort to keep his face out of my décolletage, then snaps the collar into place. "You can release the pressure. We'll get back on it once we get him on the stretcher. As soon as—" He nods to where EMT Two works with Darcy to get Charles off Jane. Charles is alert enough to contribute, and is escorted past the downed frame and away from the crowd. A moment later, the second EMT joins us.

"Ready?" the EMT beside me asks Jane, who gives him a thumbs-up.

I lift my fingers, relieved the handkerchief adheres to the wound so I don't have to see it again. The other EMT moves to Jane's feet, and they transition him to the gurney.

I get to my feet slowly, catching sight of the dried blood high on my bare leg and the grim state of my hands. *Good lord*, no wonder Charles fainted. My palms are coated, and there are dark red lines where Jane's blood leaked between my fingers.

"Bennet?" Jane asks, his voice timid.

"Right here, hon." I move to the gurney, taking his hand. He gives me a tight smile. Tears leak from the corners of his eyes, and I wipe them away with the base of my palm.

The EMT who helped with Charles approaches us. "Are you . . . family?"

"Roommates."

"Company policy only allows family to ride along. We're taking him to Beth Israel."

"I'll be right behind you," I say. "Jane?"

Jane squeezes my hand. "X-rays and stitches and a check for a concussion." He sighs, like the procedure is an inconvenience now that the shock has worn off. I guess that's an advantage of growing up in a family of folks in emergency medicine: even head trauma loses its mystique. "Please check on Charles, though?"

Jane's loaded into the ambulance, and the doors close as he waves goodbye. A police officer I didn't see arrive raps twice on the back of the ambulance, and the vehicle takes off, sirens blaring.

The cop approaches me, asking for my information, and we sidestep another cop, who tapes off the scene. I briefly describe what I witnessed. As the officer jots it down on her notepad, I survey my clothing for splatter. The dark, patterned fabric conceals anything on my dress, but the blood on my hands has dried, and the tight feeling makes my stomach lurch. I turn up my palms. My hands are shaking.

"May I?"

I start at the voice and find the officer gone, replaced by Darcy, who holds out a—I cock my head—a *wet-nap?*

It takes me another second to realize what he's offering. I nod and watch in dull silence as he takes my right hand by the wrist. His touch is light but secure as he moves the towelette along my palm, wiping down each finger individually before turning my hand over to inspect the back. The experience is oddly pleasant.

"Thank you." My words are breathless. My hands are still shaking, my system coming down from the flood of adrenaline, but he doesn't mention it.

Slowly, the blood fades from my hand. *His* blood, Jane's . . .

"I saw his skull," I say, thinking aloud.

Darcy pauses midwipe. "Seriously?"

I meet his eyes—*goddamn*, those lashes. "Yeah."

He doesn't say anything for a moment. Then his nose wrinkles. "Ew."

I don't know if it's the unfiltered response or an extension of my still being rattled, but I snort out a chuckle that bubbles into legitimate, albeit faintly hysterical, laughter. Darcy's eyes soften.

"Yeah." My laughter tapers off. "'Ew' is right."

Smiling faintly, he starts work on my other hand. The wet-nap is spent, his action doing little more than smearing, but I'm not about to say anything as he continues attending to my fingers.

He grips my fingertips, the rust-colored wipe between us as he rubs at the creases of my knuckles. "You have long fingers."

I huff out another shaky laugh. "Runs in my family. My mom can palm a basketball."

He turns my hand palm-up as he continues to clean/smear. I must have been off about his impatience earlier, because he is taking his time. "And the calluses?"

"I climb."

"Rock climbing?" His surprise is clear in his voice.

Talking is easing the jitters, so I let myself prattle. "I'm from Colorado. I grew up doing it, and there's a gym by our place in Park Slope."

"Such varied interests you have." He releases my hand. "Bennet of the Rocks and the Four of Clubs."

The light comment catches me off guard, and I laugh, even while it's tempered by the memory of the overheard dismissal. Though Charles did say the card made "quite the impression"—

Wait . . . Warmth twines through my ribs. *I didn't tell* Darcy *I go by Bennet* . . .

They've been talking. About *me.*

"Thank you." I hold up my semi-clean hands and look past them to survey Darcy a little more carefully. He's wearing dark jeans and a slim-fitting plaid button-up in red and navy, sleeves rolled to expose his muscled forearms in that particularly appealing *yes, please* way. Something else about him seems more relaxed, too. His hair, maybe, the way it's tousled but not styled, with a dusting of grays at his temples. He hasn't shaved, either, and—I will myself not to lean in—*are those grays in his stubble?*

That would be . . . agreeable.

"You'll want to wash them," he says. I bring my attention back to my hands. "But at least now you can go into a Starbucks without someone calling the police."

I shrug. "It's New York. As long as you keep bodily fluids to your-self, no one really minds. Though . . ." I wiggle my fingers with the same flourish I'd use after a glove peel. Darcy cocks his head slightly as he takes in the movement. "There might be an exception if the bodily fluids belong to someone else."

He chuckles, his features lighting up. The sight makes my heart stutter. His dark eyes crinkle, and the sound of his almost-laugh, rich and light, registers deep in my belly. His smile highlights the fullness of his lower lip—*How did I miss that feature the other night?*—and lingers as his attention grazes my neckline. A heartbeat later, his eyes are back on mine. I thank ten-minutes-ago me for that quick tug of my dress: ooh la la, indeed.

"Should we see how Charles is holding up?" I ask.

Darcy's smile turns wry. "I got him settled while the EMTs were working with Jane. Don't give him a hard time?" he requests. "I'm sure he's mortified. He's always had an issue with blood."

"Oh." The care for his friend's feelings is touching, even if it stings he thinks I would jab Charles about fainting. "Sure."

We find Charles seated on a bench. He gives a weak smile as we approach. "Sorry. Blood." He looses a long breath that puffs out his cheeks. "I can't do it."

He rolls his shoulders, like he's trying to shed what he saw, and gives himself a little shake. "Jane's been taken to a hospital?" He directs the question to me.

"Beth Israel. Stitches or staples, maybe, but he's going to be fine."

He brightens. "And you, Bennet! Really impressive. You were right in there. Amazing. Wasn't it amazing, Darcy?"

Darcy opens his mouth to respond—

"Incredible," Charles continues. "Have you done anything like that before?"

"No," I admit, though I would have appreciated getting Darcy's thoughts, thank you, Chatty Charlie. "And I hope never to again."

"You were totally running things," he insists.

"Fake it 'til you make it."

Charles laughs, and I glance at Darcy. His half smile is almost as earth-shattering as the full one. My gaze drops to his lower lip.

"Can we do anything for you?" Charles asks.

"No, but thank you. Darcy already helped with my hands." I hold them up. "Made me look less murder-y."

Charles stares at my upraised palms, then quickly averts his eyes. I remember the traces of blood left in the creases and clasp my hands behind my back as a courtesy.

"Thanks again for the wipe-down," I tell Darcy.

"It was the least I could do," he sniffs. "After you shot down my offer to sew Jane up myself."

I stare at him. Was that—a *joke*?

Unease slips into Darcy's stiff expression, and I realize he *was* joking. A twinkle of goodwill warms my chest. *Humor!* How encouraging. "Sorry. Jane's just particular about who performs minor surgery on his head. He's a real stickler about medical licensing."

Darcy nods thoughtfully, though the corners of his mouth quirk.

"I'm gonna find a place for a proper scrubbing, then head to the hospital."

"Bennet." Charles stands, then sits quickly, pressing his temples.

"Easy there." Darcy places a hand on his friend's shoulder, giving him a few pats.

Charles takes in a long breath. "Bennet, I'd like to come, too. If you think Jane wouldn't mind."

I grin. "He'd like that."

"Flowers, maybe?"

I nod, charmed by his nervous intensity. "That would go over well." I turn to Darcy, wondering if he'll be coming, too, but he's frowning at his watch. The flicker of goodwill I was feeling for him gutters. *This again?*

"I have an appointment," he mutters. "Would you like me to call you a car?"

"Oh, hell." I frown, remembering my commitment at Pemberley. I'll have to cancel. "Don't worry about the car, thanks—the hospital is a quick subway ride from here."

Darcy nods before eyeing Charles. "You're sure you're steady?"

"If I get woozy, I think Bennet is up to the task," he says cheerily.

"Ms. Bennet is quite the caregiver." Darcy says it with the same surprise as when he confirmed I climb, and I wonder if I should be flattered or offended.

I settle for indifferent. "What can I say? I contain multitudes."

"So it seems." Darcy studies my face like he's searching for something. When his eyes land on my lips, his chest rises suddenly, heaving me back to the night at Meryton. My face goes flushed, the heat curling the edges of my indifference.

He sets his shoulders so firmly it looks as though he's literally been reined back. "Give my best to Jane," he rumbles, and turns to walk away.

I blink. *That's . . . it?* I look to Charles for an explanation, but he just stands and sighs.

"Don't mind him. We're still looking for the spell that will turn him into a *real* boy."

I nod, watching Darcy's retreating form. Real boy or no, it *is* an excellent view.

✦ · ✦

"You're sure you're okay?" Charles asks, standing at the end of Jane's hospital bed. Charles has been in and out more times than I can count, retrieving little things for Jane: takeout from a Thai place down the street, a stunning peacock-blue cashmere throw from who knows where, and an assortment of shirts to choose from when Jane goes home tomorrow (today's ended up in a hazmat bag). "You don't need anything else?" He puts his hands on his hips and surveys the small space as if looking for something else to contribute.

"You've done too much already." Jane's words are thick from painkillers. He had local anesthesia for the stitches and received a solid dose of something after that's left him endearingly loopy. "Thank you."

"Absolutely." Charles beams. "If you need anything, don't hesitate to call. You, too, Bennet. Are you sure I can't pick up something for you? Something to change into tomorrow?"

I smile back. It seems Jane's dad's chief-surgeon influence extends to the opposite side of the country. Dr. Okogu pulled those very long strings to get his son a private room for the evening, as well as permission for me to stay as company. "Thank you, Charles. I'll be okay."

"I'll be back by eight tomorrow," he says, reaffirming his promise to be here for Jane's release, provided we get the go-ahead from his doctor.

"Thank you again for that," I say, meaning it. Toby was sympathetic when I called to tell him I wouldn't be back this afternoon but made a point of confirming I'd be in first thing.

"Happy to help." Charles rests a hand on Jane's foot, rubbing it gently through the throw. He draped the blanket over Jane with such care earlier, I felt like a voyeur. "Good night." He pats Jane's foot one last time, then walks out the door.

Jane smiles at the empty doorway. "I *really* like him, Ben."

"I like him, too," I say. "He's a sweetheart."

"I wanna call him."

"He left six seconds ago." I laugh. "Careful. He may not even be out of earshot."

"So? It's nice knowing someone likes you. And I know he likes me. He brought me flowers." Jane points to the generous arrangement of white orchids Charles bought on our way in.

"They are lovely." I scoot my chair closer, resting my elbows beside him on the mattress.

"I probably wouldn't have bought *him* flowers." His brow furrows. "I'd have wanted to but been afraid I was coming on too strong. I would have asked *you* for advice and you'd have told me to hold off, too. We're too guarded, Ben. We let each other be too guarded."

I prop my head up on my hand, a coil of anxiety twisting in my sternum. "Is this the head trauma talking?"

"Or the drugs. We *are* too cautious, though. At least I am. If you hadn't said anything last weekend, I never even would have sung Nina. Maybe I wouldn't have gotten to know Charles at all."

I study him. His brows are still low, eyes sharp despite the fog of medication.

"Promise me you'll talk to Andrea about the design stuff. For Meryton." He holds up his hand, warding off the protest I almost formed. "You don't want me talking to Charles about it and I won't. But you should talk to Andrea. You've let what happened hold you back for too long. Like I have, because of Marcus."

I blink in surprise. Jane and I have an unspoken agreement to maintain a polite distance from one another's major traumas, and he's just referenced both of them in a single breath. We talked around my past after brunch with Andrea, but *Marcus*? We don't even say his name. It's why he gave me the bedroom at our apartment: it had been theirs, and Jane didn't want anything to do with a space they'd shared so intimately.

Jane lifts his chin and points to himself. "Right? Big stuff." He grips my hand. "You heard the doctor today. A few more inches in either direction, and that thing could have killed me, Ben. It's crazy I only got clipped." He sighs. "There's enough out there that can actually take you out. No point in hiding from the things that will only hurt your heart."

"*Dance like nobody's watching*," I say, trying to parse out how much of this he's going to remember in the morning. "*Live like a giant piece of metal could rust free of its bolts and crush your skull tomorrow. That's inspirational. It'd be a lot to cross-stitch, but I think it would look great next to the front door. We can commission Ming."

He smacks my arm. "Don't make fun. I'm being wise."

"I'm sorry."

"Does Ming even cross-stitch?"

"I'll ask." I squeeze his hand, and he chuckles.

I lay my head on my arms. He has a point, and I should focus on it. Instead, I find myself tracing along the fingers of my right hand, following the path Darcy made with the towelette, and thinking about the way he looked at me earlier. *What were you looking for, Will Darcy?*

"Hey." Jane nudges me. "Seriously. Promise you'll talk to Andrea about the design plans." His voice is heavy with sleep and pharmaceuticals.

"I will." I kiss his hand. He smiles, closing his eyes. *"Promise."*

CHAPTER

7

I adjust the microphone of my headset. "You're sure you're going to be okay?"

"Bennet, I'm fine," Jane says, his voice cracking over the receiver. He came home from the hospital yesterday, turning in early after a quiet afternoon of hanging around the apartment with Charles. He was still sleeping when I left for work this morning. While I set his alarm with plenty of time before the follow-up with his doctor, I still wanted to check in.

I settle against the break room counter. "I'm sorry I can't go with you. Toby's figured out that his fun little business venture is officially a bicoastal operation. He's kind of wigging."

This is mostly true, but I don't want to go into detail, lest Jane feel guilty for having the audacity to get bludgeoned. I came in yesterday to a deluge of emails and an overwhelmed boss, whom I directed to take lunch out of the office today so he could get a moment to breathe. I won't be able to get in a makeup meeting at Pemberley, which is a bummer, but they were understanding about my "family emergency." Between the notes I sent in and my commitment to getting there early Saturday, everything should be fine.

"Don't worry," Jane insists. "Charles will be here in a few minutes. He's offered to set up a meeting with his lawyer to see if there's any grounds for a lawsuit. Negligence, or something?"

"Smart." I smile. "And generous. Think he's gotten Florence Nightingale syndrome?"

"Ben!" he scolds.

"I'm kidding! Jeez, it's like you've had a recent head trauma or something."

I turn to open the cabinet above the espresso machine for coffee beans. Toby should return in the next few minutes, and I figure he'll appreciate a dose of caffeine.

The doorbell buzzes in the background of my connection with Jane, and I hear him take in a sharp breath. "That's Charles!" he says with a smile I can hear. "I'm off. See you at eight?"

"You're sure you're up for it?"

"It's only one song, and I can't bail on Darlene," he says, referring to the revue's producer, a fellow burlesquer. "It's her debut with this show. And, Ben?"

"Yeah?"

"*You made me, promises, promises,*" he croons. My shoulders drop. "You promised you'd talk to Andrea, miss. I'm holding you to it. Ciao!"

He hangs up before I can get out a proper complaint.

"Brat." I tug down the headset so it rests around my neck. I was hoping he hadn't hung on to that.

I don't know why I'm so apprehensive. I *know* I'm good. And I believe in my ideas. Plus . . . hell, I am paying for those student loans; might as well apply the interior design degree to something. And what's the worst Andrea could do? I ask to show her what I have and she says no? Or she checks them out and doesn't like them?

Or what if she looks at them and *does* want to use them? A thrill skitters between my shoulder blades at the thought. I push it away and pull a blank shot. But as the espresso machine hisses and steams, the possibility pops up again: a fresh start in design.

"Ah, Liz!" says Toby from behind me.

I raise the tiny espresso cup in my hand, my back still toward him. "Single or double?"

"I might have gotten coffee out." His voice is heavy with playful chagrin.

I wheel around, prepared to scold him for cheating on his Italian trophy wife, but he's not alone. A good-looking, sandy-haired guy stands beside him, assessing me with a mild smile.

I focus on Toby, stepping up the sass for his associate's benefit. "Ignorance is no excuse for outsourcing." The smile on his companion spreads. It's a good smile.

Toby laughs. "I'm sorry. Wickham here might be in need of a second round?"

Another grin from this Wickham fellow. "If it isn't any trouble."

"Not at all."

"Toby! You have a minute?" one of the interns calls from the hall.

"Sorry, I'll be back. Liz, thank you . . ." Toby directs Wickham my way, then darts out.

Wickham shrugs. As he approaches, I perform a quick scan like I might to a guest at Meryton. Gray chinos, cuffs just grazing his ankles;

nice loafers; and an oxford with an oversized gingham print, sleeves rolled up in a way I've only seen in the window of the J.Crew Men's Shop. He has one more button undone than would be natural, a pair of aviators dangling from the neckline. The overall effect is a little try-hard, but his inviting expression is making up for it.

He arches a brow. "Liz, I presume?"

I nod. "Apparently, you're Wickham. And a bad influence?"

"George Wickham, at your service." He holds a hand to his chest. "And the coffee was one hundred percent me. I took the red-eye in from LAX."

"Another Californian," I muse. "What's going on out there? You're the third Golden State guy I've encountered recently."

"Hm." He bends to rest an elbow on the counter, propping his chin on his knuckles. "Should I be worried about the other two?"

I laugh at the blatant flirtation. "Confident. But no. One is currently seeing my roommate and"—I tip my head, considering—"jury's still out on the other one. By all means, bring your A-game."

He grins, straightening to extend his hand for a shake. "Liz, it's a pleasure to meet you."

"Will you be in town long?"

"A few weeks, but hopefully longer. I have a deal in the works," he explains. "I grew up on the Upper West and went to NYU, then headed to the left coast. But I miss New York. There's nowhere else like it."

I smile in agreement, then place a hand on the coffee grinder. "Single or *doppio*?"

"I'm guessing that second option is double, and yes to that, please."

"*Doppio* it is." I measure out the grounds, using the scale Toby purchased for the precise eighteen grams. "So, will you be at this weekend's party?"

"Toby just told me about that. Am I right to assume you organized it?"

"One of my many duties."

"Then I'm sure it will be an unforgettable event."

I tamp the espresso into the filter. "You always this smooth?"

"Only when the company warrants."

"*Wow.*" He is quick, I'll give him that. "Save some material for Saturday. Do you have the details or should I get your email from Toby?"

"How about I give you my number and you can text me the information?"

"But then you would have my number."

"Yes, I would, wouldn't I?" He says it as though he didn't come to the conclusion himself. His eyes say otherwise.

I let out a sigh for effect, though I purse my lips in legitimate consideration. He's cute, even with the cheese-oozing. He's also receptive, which is a far cry from Mr. Tolerable, however pleasant Monday's wet-nap massage was. He's at least worthy of maintaining a text exchange; further assessment can be administered Saturday.

"Tell you what." I pull the espresso, raising my voice over the din. "Give me your email, and I'll get back to you."

Wickham smiles, and Toby pokes his head back into the break room. "Toby, your Liz is a firecracker. Where did you find her?"

"Craigslist?" Toby looks between us. "You need a sec, or—"

"We're good." I hand Wickham the double shot. The crema is a perfect shade of brown. "You have ten seconds before the flavor changes."

Wickham raises his eyebrows.

"She's right," says Toby, joining us. "She took a class."

Wickham tosses back the coffee, returning the cup to the saucer with a short clatter. "Liz, that was exceptional." He places the cup and saucer in my waiting palm, and his fingers graze mine during the handoff. He winks at me, then shifts to drape an arm over Toby's shoulders. "All right. Show me around your empire, bud."

◆ · ◆

The phone's ringing shatters the quiet of the lobby, but I let it go two rings before picking up, just to maintain my air of diligence. I don't have to look at the "Toby" icon on the cradle to know who's calling.

"Work It, this is Liz. How can I help you?"

"You know, Liz, I don't think I can wait until Saturday."

I turn to face my boss's office, where Wickham leans against the desk. He waves, Toby's phone sandwiched between his shoulder and ear. After their tour of the Work It "empire" wrapped, the guys posted up in Toby's office until Toby was summoned to handle a question with HR. Wickham's been boring a hole in the side of my head since. It's been fun to ignore him, though I'm almost offended he held out as long as he did.

"Is that so?" I ask.

"After hearing how you take a phone call? I'm powerless."

"I *did* watch a video."

"On phone etiquette?"

"I take my continuing education seriously."

"That settles it," he says with authority. "I have to ask you out for a drink tonight."

"Sure."

"Really?"

"I respect risk-takers." I face my computer screen again and make a few purposeful strikes of the keyboard, even though I'm only deleting spam from my inbox. "We can meet at Mother's Ruin, over on Spring," I say, because I may or may not have spent the head-boring minutes making a list of possible options should he have greater ambitions than casual flirting. I look at Wickham, who smiles faintly. "Six work?"

His smile spreads. "I look forward to it."

━━ · ━━

Wickham is already at the bar when I arrive. He raises his glass, a Manhattan, if I had to guess, beckoning me over.

"Hold up." He halts me with a high palm, then does a double take. "I'm sorry, I had a clever setup for conversation, but you've thrown me off with this—" He points to my dress.

I cast a glance at my reflection in the gold-framed mirror behind the bar. While the pale blue retro sundress was perfectly subdued with the cropped cardigan I had on earlier, I opted to go without the layer for drinks. Now the keyhole opening between the bust and the waistline is visible. Ditto the triangular patch of skin it exposes.

I press a hand to the knot at my bust. "This old thing?"

He lets out a low whistle of approval. "Damn. That's all I can say. Now!" He knits his fingers together and rests them on the bar top. "Back to my clever conversational setup. What was the most valuable lesson you got from that phone etiquette video?"

"Angling for my secrets?" I take the seat next to him, then reach below the bar to hang my purse as I give the bartender my order. Ruin is known for their frozen drinks, dispensed from a giant slushy machine. Today's offering is a mint-green gin concoction.

Wickham gestures to indicate the drink will go on his tab. I nod my thanks.

"Just one tip?" he asks.

"Smile during your greeting." I grin for emphasis. "The caller will hear the smile in your voice. Even if you're faking it."

He claps, laughing. "I'm going to steal that. So, Liz Bennet." He stirs his drink with his straw. "Short for Elizabeth, I presume?"

"One of my many names, yes. Thank you," I say, accepting my drink from the bartender. "Cheers." I raise my glass, and Wickham taps his to it.

He arches a brow as he takes a drink. "I'm sticking a pin in that 'names' business, because I have a feeling there's a story there. Where are you from, Ms. Many Names? You carry yourself like a native New Yorker, though something about that doesn't feel right. Maybe your willingness to fake a smile?"

This gets a real smile. "New Yorkers get a bad rap on the attitude thing. They prefer expedience. But you're right," I continue. "I'm from Colorado."

"What brought you here?"

A pang of anxiety lances through my chest. "I needed a change," I say, the reason accurate, if weak.

He nods. "Rocky Mountains to skyscrapers would be a contrast."

"It would." The thread of conversation snags on Jane's insistence about opening up, and I let it pull up a qualifier. *Be brave.* "But I was in LA at the time."

"Oh yeah? Nice. What were you there for?"

The anxiety winds through my rib cage, and I take a longer pull than necessary from my drink. I wince at the resulting brain freeze.

Being brave is hard. No wonder it took Jane a controlled substance and a knock on the noggin. "Work, mostly."

"Gracing another office with your excellent phone etiquette?"

Another out. This one grazes my pride, and I shake my head. "No. I was at an architecture and design firm. It's what I went to grad school for."

He leans away, looking me up and down as if to assess me in light of this new information. "You're an architect?"

"Interior design. I won an internship my last semester and it took me to LA."

"Nice. Are you just at Toby's while you look for a design job, then?"

"The internship ended *badly*." The words come out more easily than I'd have expected, if I'd ever expected myself to say them at all.

A sympathetic tug appears between Wickham's eyebrows, and the tension relaxes its grip on my shoulders. He aims a finger gun my way. "I have something for that. Shot?"

I feign horror. "On a *Wednesday*?"

"It's after five. And your face got so sad."

"A reposado, then. To *nurse*."

"I don't know what that is, but I'm sure the barman does."

As Wickham places the order, I question the wisdom of letting Jane's drug-addled moment of clarity inform my decision-making. What happened in LA was supposed to stay there; even thinking about it resurrects a lot of grief. But Wickham's assumption that I was an admin there felt like an erasure of a major part of my life, however painful that time ended up being.

At Work It, I've thrown myself into my commitment to competence. If I'm going to be an admin, I'm going to be indispensable. If the ongoing bafflement with the espresso machine is any indication, I'll maintain that label indefinitely. The same goes for kittening. If I'm going to do it, I'm going to be the best at it. While it's usually a stepping stone to performing, I'm happy participating in the show the way I do.

I'm proud of the work I do at Work It. I'm proud of what I've turned my gig at Meryton into. I'm also proud of what I accomplished before New York. Maybe—I stir my drink. Maybe I shouldn't let the bad tarnish the good.

The bartender pushes two snifters of clear liquid across the bar.

Wickham raises one. "Cheers."

"Don't shoot it," I warn. "It's not espresso. Sip it."

He does, and nods. "Ooh, I like it. What is this stuff?"

"A tequila. My cousin's fiancé is a chef. He introduced me to it when I was in LA."

Wickham takes another sip of the liquor. "About that time . . ." He shakes his head. "I'm sorry, I don't mean to pry."

"No, it's fine. It's just a shitty, embarrassing situation."

I take a bracing pull of the reposado, the smoky burn a pleasant contrast to the slushy's sweetness. "I went to the Art Institute in Denver. When I won the internship, it was a big deal. I was competing with students from programs across the country. It was me, from the blip of a school in Colorado, who won, which was huge for my program—"

And I failed them.

"How was it? In LA?" Wickham asks.

The question rouses a hint of the same rush I felt the first few weeks at the firm, the combination of excitement and possibility and pride that my work had proved me worthy of the experience. "It was like grad school, where everyone has a common passion, similar knowledge. Seeing what they were working on was *inspiring*. So much renovation to downtown. There's great design down there, and even being adjacent to the efforts to restore it was . . ." I shake my head, at a loss for words.

"Exciting?" Wickham supplies.

"Incredible. I was brought onto a team of the younger folks on staff. The lead was newish, too. Super encouraging. He was a real champion for me, and when he was given a restaurant project, I was his right hand. We worked round the clock, lots of nights.

"When it came time to present, Roger said it was a one-on-one meeting with the client." I swirl the straw in my drink, mixing the liquid in with slush in the middle of the glass. This is the part I don't even let myself think about. But I've gotten this far in the story, which is something, even if it feels like my chest is caving in.

"Have you ever fallen?" I ask. "From somewhere high enough to actually hurt?"

Wickham's brows crease as he cocks a smile. "Can't say I've had the misfortune."

"I have. I rock climb, and in high school, I was bouldering, which is without ropes. It's about traversing along the wall, not going up. But I went for a route higher up than I should have, and a hold gave."

Wickham cringes.

"The sandstone crumbled. It came loose from the wall and broke into pieces as I held it. I even have a scar." I turn up my left palm to show the faint white line bisecting it. "I'd clung to the rubble so hard the doctor had to dig it out with tweezers."

Wickham nods, but his brows are low enough that I know my aside isn't explaining itself.

"Feeling that rock give way . . ." I search for the words. "I knew I was screwed. And that's almost the worst part. The anticipation. When Roger said he had to present alone, the rock broke away all over again. It was the same sensation. Something that had been secure fell apart in my hand. Pain was coming, and I'd have to wait for it."

"What happened?"

"For one, he'd been telling our coworkers I'd tried to sleep with him—"

"What?" Wickham leans away, eyes wide. "Why would he do that?"

"Paper trail. He'd started circulating the rumor pretty early. Got it on record with HR. He timed it so that while I was having a sit-down about my 'impropriety' during those late nights at the office, he was presenting my work to the client as his," I force out. "He'd repackaged it to resemble an evolution of his design scheme."

"Damn."

"I came out of the meeting feeling like I'd been hit by a truck. Meanwhile, Roger was getting back slaps and handshakes in the conference room."

"And when you spoke up, it sounded like you were lashing out because of the HR thing." Wickham's voice is dull with shock.

"It took me a few days to piece it together." I huff out a mirthless laugh. "At least gravity had the decency to crack my rib quickly."

My side aches at the comparison. There's more overlap in that Venn diagram. The shame of overconfidence, of having reached too far, having placed myself higher than I belonged. Of trusting something, someone, I shouldn't have.

"I don't know if everyone believed him. There was already bad blood with some other designers because I'd been the favorite. Besides, he was the established designer and he presented the concept. In the end, no one backed me up, so I left. A family friend out here was going through his own shit and needed a roommate, so I moved. I'd never even been to New York before. At least I had some experience with a subway, after downtown LA," I add, but my smile feels heavy.

"Have you considered getting back into design since?"

"Yes and no." I run my thumb over the scar on my palm. I didn't climb for six weeks after my fall. Partly doctor's orders, waiting for my body to heal. Mostly, it was the hit my confidence had taken. Baby steps brought me back: indoor bouldering, some top-roping on routes I knew well, and after a few months I was back at the same wall, staying well below the damaged shelf.

The drawings I've done of Meryton shuffle through my mind like a deck of cards. *More baby steps?*

"I looked before I left LA. It turns out, a sexual harassment claim and a reputation for claiming the work of others doesn't make for good reference material. And now, three years on, I'd hardly be competitive. My portfolio's ancient, I have no recommendations and no internship experience I can actually discuss."

Wickham nods, looking thoughtful, and his shoulders drop. "Liz, I really am sorry to hear that. I—I had a similar experience. Something that should have been mine was ripped away, and . . ." He gives me a wan smile. "I guess I *have* fallen."

"Shitty thing to have in common." I grimace. "I don't usually talk about what happened. It's not like I have a chip on my shoulder about being an admin—"

"Especially with how good you are at it."

The compliment is a balm. "I'm torn between hating what happened then and not wanting it to define who I am now, or what choices I make. There might be something on the horizon, I . . ." I chew my bottom lip. "Thanks for listening. Sorry I prattled."

"My pleasure. You have an excellent prattling voice, too."

"How about you?" I pat his hand as casually as I can. "You said you have some deal in the works?"

He winks. "It's not locked down. I don't want to jinx it."

"You another tech wunderkind?"

He laughs, then talks about getting to know Toby back at UCLA. I am the opposite of surprised to learn that Toby was his tutor in one of their business classes, that my sweet-natured boss "had no game," and that Wickham's role after passing the class was as wingman when they went out.

He bumps my shoulder. "So. Toby mentioned you have an interesting weekend gig?"

"Oh?" The syllable comes out sharp. I never know how people will react to my involvement in the burlesque scene. I wonder what opinions Wickham might have—he's not giving off the Wall Street–asshole vibe, but I've been disappointed before.

He holds up his hands in surrender. "He wasn't being judgmental. I looked into Meryton. Pretty swank."

My hackles drop. "I love it. I'm the stage kitten, so I pick up what they take off."

"I confess I don't know a lot about burlesque." His smile is almost shy, a far cry from the cocksure swagger he had for so much of our exchange. "Would you mind if I come by some time?"

I would decidedly not mind this. "Tonight's a jazz show, but if it's burlesque that has you interested, my roommate's singing at a revue in Bushwick in an hour. It'll take about as much time to get there, but it's a solid lineup."

"Man, I wish I could. But it's still work hours on the West Coast, and I have calls." He holds up his glass. "This should make them pretty interesting, though." He clinks his glass with mine before we both take another drink.

I wiggle my eyebrows, ignoring the faint disappointment accompanying the burn in my chest. "Just remember to smile."

CHAPTER

❖ · 8 · ❖

"Is this heaven?" I ask.

"You're blocking the doorway," says Jane. He plucks my admission from my fingers and hands it to the guy at the door, who wears an MP armband and helmet.

"Don't care," I say, but let Jane nudge me past the threshold. I send my attention around the room, not wanting to miss a single detail. The venue where Jane's performing tonight has a USO theme, and whoever decorated it went all out. The little foyer is walled with framed photos of Bob Hope: dancing with Raquel Welch, flashing a peace sign with Ann-Margret, and mingling with countless soldiers over decades of service.

Jane keeps pushing me forward as I risk whiplash trying to take it all in, but I stop short to gawk at the bar. Above it protrudes the nose of a plane, complete with a bikini-clad blonde lounging against the words "California Girl."

"This is awesome," I marvel. "In the purest sense of the word. I am *awed* right now."

"Darlene's brother owns the bar," Jane explains, switching from pushing to tugging. "Their grandfather had a ton of memorabilia, and they've been all over the Eastern Seaboard for the rest. Tonight's show is the kickoff for the bar's opening weekend."

I nod, still agog. The show's title is *Red, White, and Boobs*. I was prepared for something patriotic, but this is next-level.

Jane gets me to the far end of the bar, where Ming waves to us from beside an oversized Uncle Sam *I Want YOU!* army recruitment poster. She's dressed in a navy blue onesie, a red kerchief in her hair à la Rosie the Riveter, though the way her jumpsuit is unbuttoned to expose the center of her coordinating polka-dotted bra is more in keeping with the "and Boobs" element of the evening.

"Would you get a load of this place?" She points up, one arm hugging Jane. "It has a freaking *plane*!"

I get a hug, too. When she releases me, I fold my hands in prayer. "Is there any way I can get a rush on the dress I brought you last week? That party for my day job is this weekend and I found incentive to step it up."

Ming's smile turns knowing, and she flicks the little tie at my bust. "Does this *incentive* have a name?"

"Our Kitten is on her *second* outing of the evening." Jane pats me on the shoulder. Between my texts on the subway ride and our conversation after we met up at the station, Jane is well informed of Wickham's many redeeming qualities. He couldn't believe how thoroughly

I'd spilled my guts to the guy. "He has my approval," Jane said. "Anyone who cracks you open on the first go has to be worthy."

I wiggle my eyebrows, and Ming cackles.

"I'm close to done, anyway," she says.

"Thank you! Seal the deal with a beverage?"

She gestures to the bar. "Obviously."

I raise my hand for the bartender's attention. Ming orders a beer and I get a cherry Coke, still feeling the effects from drinks with my "incentive."

Jane declines. "I'm gonna go warm up." He tips his hat, a new fedora he's wearing to cover his stitches. It's one of four he and Charles—which is to say, Charles—splurged on after this morning's checkup.

Ming nods toward Jane, who disappears through the curtains at stage right. "So. Thor's backing Andrea's bid for the building." She doesn't bother to phrase it as a question.

"Yup."

"Hm." Ming takes a pull from her beer. "The god of thunder was at your place when I checked on Jane earlier. Jane was totally gaga. Showing off his new hats, blasting Madonna. I haven't seen him like that since he was with Marcus." She smiles, but it doesn't meet her eyes.

"What's up?"

She screws up her face in thought. "Don't get me wrong, I love seeing Jane back at his full wattage. But I wonder if it's smart for him to be so obvious."

"He's being brave!"

"Like I said, I love it, but . . . I dunno." She rests an elbow against the bar. "Andrea's still talking like Jane's sealed the deal by hooking up with Charles. I swear, if she makes another 'sugar daddy' comment, I'm gonna scream."

"She's saying that to you, too?" I'd been hoping she'd at least keep that nonsense limited to me and Jane.

"So tacky of her, right? I thought the Brits were supposed to have better manners than us."

"Nah. When they're gross, it only *sounds* prettier."

"Anyway, I would hate for Charles to get the wrong idea. Like, that Jane's been aboard the sugar-daddy train this whole time, y'know?"

I nod.

"Ah!" Ming points past me. "Speak of the devil, here's Thor."

Charles is just inside the front door, cradling a bouquet of white roses. Spotting us, he smiles broadly and trots over. "Bennet, Ming, hey! Isn't this place great?" He cranes his neck, looking over the room. "Jane already backstage?"

I nod, and we settle into conversation. Charles was here for one of Jane's rehearsals, and he points out a few more intriguing details among the memorabilia.

"I met the owner, too. Super-nice guy," says Charles. "He's offered to walk me through some front-of-the-house stuff once the deal with Meryton goes through."

Ming raises her eyebrows. "Either you're feeling very optimistic, or Darlene's brother didn't explain the 'Loose Lips Sink Ships' poster by the bathroom."

Charles smiles. "I figured word was out by now. But I also do think we have a real chance of picking up the property." He crosses his fingers.

I cross mine, too. But as Charles shows Ming the bullet holes in the plane nose above us, my thoughts dim. He's all in, clearly, but on the off chance the deal falls apart, or the owner decides to pass things off to that nephew, I wonder what will happen. Andrea said the guy would likely stick with the burlesque concept, but what if he didn't?

The idea evokes an emptiness I haven't felt in a long time. I'd be able to find a kitten gig with another show, but the dynamic of our group would be hard to maintain. It's not as if we'd be able to up and move to another location; not *everyone* has a brother with a bar in Bushwick.

Our situation at Meryton is unique. Most burlesque shows are set up like tonight's, at a bar with a stage, where attendees pay a cover charge or buy tickets, and the producer gives a cut to the venue and the participants. The shows run once or twice a month at most, and performers have to hustle to get enough of these gigs to cover their costuming budget alone, to say nothing of housing and feeding themselves. The steadiness of Meryton is a gift to anyone who manages to land a position there, which is what makes keeping it going so critical.

As showtime nears, the room fills with familiar faces, crowding out the barren feeling enough that I smile; there's half a deck's worth of burlesquers in the audience. That's something I love about the scene, how supportive performers are of one another. There are occasionally squabbles about who gets to use a certain song, or someone will bite a piece of choreography from another dancer. There's certainly no shortage of drama in our personal lives, but at the end of the day, we show up for one another.

The band files onto the stage, the same quintet that works weekends at Meryton. The guys are dressed in khaki service chinos, though based on the distribution of pieces, it looks like they only had two full costumes and divided them among the crew. They take their places and coax out a few notes, starting into a warm-up tune. The energy in the room shifts, conversations going quiet, and my nerves quake with a vicarious thrill.

Johnny pokes his head out from between the curtains at stage right, tugging on an army-green baseball cap as he talks to Arthur.

"Should we grab seats?" Charles asks.

I pick up my drink, pausing when a woman joins Johnny, who retreats through the curtains. The woman looks side to side, blue-black victory rolls framing her pale face as she scans the room wide-eyed.

"There's Darlene!" Ming announces, and waves.

Darlene spots us and her jaw drops in a gasp of relief. The rest of her emerges from the curtains, dressed in the classic green khakis of a field nurse, the red-cross band on her arm embellished with sequins.

She hurries toward us. "You're about to save my *life*. Sola . . . ," she says, naming one of tonight's performers. "The zipper broke on the flight suit she's peeling out of and she's *stuck* in it. Jewbilee is doing the best she can, but—"

Ming tosses back the last of her beer, planting the empty glass on the bar. "I'm on it."

"Thank you." She turns to Charles. "Sorry. I don't really know you or how you can help."

"Moral support?" he supplies cheerily.

"I'll take it." She points at me. "Can you stretch for time?"

"What do you have in mind?"

"A sample peel? I'd ask tonight's kitten, but"—she mimes pulling something close—"her current position is load-bearing. Sola's costume is *tight*."

At the words "sample peel," my heart rate gallops, stomping out the remnants of emptiness from earlier. I try to sound blasé. "Can do."

"You're a lifesaver. Can I snag you a glove from one of the girls?"

"That would be great."

"Thank you, sweetie. I'll get you two bubbles as payment, but for now"—she tugs on Ming's arm—"we have a zipper to fix."

The women depart. My butterflies begin to stretch their wings, taking short, experimental flights around my midsection. I only get to do a sample peel at Meryton when we have a less experienced host filling in for Johnny, so this is a treat.

"What's this about a glove?" Charles asks.

"Some shows start with the kitten taking off something simple to get the audience feisty," I explain. "They don't always hoot 'n' holler until they've been properly encouraged." I cast an eye over the room again. With so many performers in the house, enthusiasm shouldn't be a problem, but the peel should give the folks backstage time to mend the zipper.

The house lights come down. The band transitions to a big-band rendition of Johnny's intro song, and the emcee strolls onto the stage. His usual tux has been replaced with a field jacket decorated with morale patches, like the one in the pictures of Bob Hope. He keeps his back to the audience as he wiggles his tush, lining up an imagined shot with a golf club.

"Fore!" He swings, and the follow-through turns his torso to the crowd. He grins, like he's just realized we're here. "Why, hello there, kiddies."

As Johnny sings, his standard tune tailored to emphasize the "bush" in Bushwick, Darlene slips from the curtains to the short steps beside the stage. I push off from the bar and join her.

"Will this do?" she whispers, handing me a red opera-length glove. "It's a left."

"Perfect." I wiggle my fingers into the glove, tugging the shaft over my bicep. "How goes the zipper?"

"Ming's a miracle worker. We'll probably only need a few minutes. Pop a pastie!" She blows me a kiss, then retreats backstage.

I'm straightening the seam along the inside of my arm when Johnny announces, "Beautiful people, please, put your hands together for our special guest"—a second spotlight turns on, wheeling around the stage before landing on me—"Miss Kitten Caboodle!"

The spotlight fries my butterflies midflight. I take the stage with a wave, the crowd's cheer flooding me with adrenaline. By the time I reach Johnny, I'm floating.

Johnny mouths me a "*Thank you*" before returning to the audience. "This delectable kitty cat will be providing a demonstration of what to expect tonight. So, pay close attention. This will all be on the final exam." Johnny backs toward the wings of the stage, then gives another swing with his golf club. "Take it away, Kitten!"

At that, the band begins to play a slow, sultry rendition of "Summertime." I adjust my expression to meet it, shifting from "cheeky assistant" to "siren" in the time it takes to form a pout. I extend the arm with the glove across my chest, gliding my hand from wrist to upper arm, showcasing the glove. Absently, I smooth my thumb over the bare skin between the glove and the wide shoulder strap of my dress, as though distracted by the contact.

It's the same tactic I employed when I knew Darcy was watching me at Meryton, enticing my audience to imagine their hands in place of mine. The thrill tonight, however, is totally different from the hot little buzz I experienced under Darcy's gaze. That was personal, almost intimate. Now I have an entire room in my thrall and I feel drunk off it.

Making contact with the tips of the glove, I grip the seam at the end of the middle finger, then tug. But the sample peel isn't only about getting the crowd to make some noise; it can also set the tone: a little cheek goes a long way. I pretend to struggle. Gritting my teeth, I yank at the fingers of the glove, grabbing at the ends of all four without letting the glove budge.

My character fights to rein in her frustration, shooting the crowd a tight smile as they chuckle at her plight. My body hums with adrenaline, my skin alive with the heat from the spotlight and the attention of the crowd, and I bring my hands in front of me, pressing my upper arms in to exaggerate my cleavage as I grapple. Laughter and wolf whistles stream from the crowd, punctuated by Ming's distinct cackle.

Ming! They must be done with the zipper. Time to wrap up.

I jerk the elbow of my pulling arm to suggest the glove has given way and roll my shoulders, transitioning back to sex kitten, eliciting more laughter.

I bite the tip of my gloved pinkie finger, tugging enough to get some slack. The move is repeated finger by finger until I'm at my thumb. I bring my hands to one side of my face and slowly pull my left hand free of the glove, making an unbroken traverse along the low neckline of my dress, fingers splayed to maintain tension in the glove.

I let my fingers slip free and catch hold of the edge. With a grip on either end, I shimmy it over my chest, adding a little jiggle below. More clapping.

Draping the glove over my shoulder, I brandish my now bare left arm with showgirl flair. I caress my arm from wrist to elbow, raising my hand toward my face, and freeze.

The audience stills, as though everyone in the room is holding their breath. A slow smile spreads across my face. Moments like this remind me I'm more than "Kitten Caboodle." I'm more than a tattered reputation at a design firm, a crushed dream, or the only person in an office who bothered to use Google Translate to work a fancy espresso maker.

I twinkle my newly exposed fingers with a grin, and the audience thunders with applause.

I'm Elizabeth Bennet. And I'm invincible.

CHAPTER

❖ 9 ❖

I exit the stage vibrating from the excitement. Darlene gestures toward me from the bar with a flute of bubbles. I walk toward her, still quaking, and smile at the shouts of support as I skirt the crowd.

"Well done!" Darlene passes me the glass.

My hand shakes so violently the liquid threatens to spill. I take a long pull from the rim. The sweet effervescence pairs wonderfully with my giddiness. Through the buzzing in my ears, I make out Johnny introducing Sola. The performer leaps through the curtains like a starburst in her rhinestone-studded flight suit, and Darlene regales me with the tale of the treacherous zipper.

My heart rate slowly gets back to normal, and I cheer along with Sola's peel. After the reveal, which leaves Sola in coordinating American flag pasties and G-string, Darlene excuses herself and sneaks backstage to prep for her own number.

I spot Ming and Charles on the other side of the room. They're in the center of a row, so I take a seat at an empty high-top along the far wall. I holler as Johnny introduces Jewbilee, whose routine is a tribute to the women's baseball league. Darlene's medic-themed peel follows, leaving the stage littered with yards of bandage wrapping for the kitten to sweep up. Then it's Jane's turn.

The song starts with the same big-band flair from Johnny's opener, and I don't recognize the tune until Jane croons, *"It had to be you."* His singing is more subdued than I'd have expected from the intro, and there's something about his delivery I can't pin down. I cross my arms, trying to place the vibe. It's more direct, almost focused. The energy builds as he infuses more feeling into each word, until each lyric is bursting with—

My heart squeezes. It's *joy*.

Jane can enchant a room, inspire passion and love notes and phone numbers from unsuspecting listeners. But I haven't heard him sing like *this* in years. It takes me back to the day I met him, at a barbecue at my cousin's in Silver Lake. Jane and Marcus were in for a visit, and Jane sang "Walking on Sunshine." His joy that day was infectious, but I haven't seen it since.

By the time Jane reaches the chorus, the whole room is swaying. It isn't the seductive spell of Nina, but it's magic all the same. An instrumental break follows, and Arthur beckons Jane to join him at the piano. Jane takes over playing for an extended solo that goes a long way toward justifying his tuition at Juilliard. My heart gives another squeeze. Watching him play is always a treat, but this is something else.

The rest of the band joins in, trumpet and drums and bass and sax meeting Jane's exuberance with each note. He returns to the mic; there's no question that every word that follows is meant for Charles.

My vision swims with tears. When did this happen? It's been less than two weeks. I look from Jane to Charles and back again. There's just enough light from the stage to illuminate Charles's smile, and Jane—

Jane drops to his knees. I gasp, thinking of Monday's accident, but he keeps singing, radiating bliss and pointing at Charles with every "*you.*" He belts out the last five words of the song, and Charles tosses the bouquet just as Jane's voice tapers. By some miracle, Jane catches the flowers in his free hand. The curtain drops, concealing the stage at the exact moment the music ends, and the audience erupts in cheers.

My seat gives me a clear shot to the stairs, and I charge backstage as the applause roars on. The guys in the band carry on almost as loudly as the crowd on the opposite side of the curtain, high-fiving and congratulating Jane on his performance. Jane is still on his knees, panting, and I rush to him for a hug.

"Jane, that was fantastic! How are you? Your head okay?" I ask. His heartbeat is racing.

"I don't know what happened," he says, gasping. "It's like . . . I *felt* the song."

"You're really taking that bravery thing seriously, aren't you?"

He fans himself, cradling the roses in the crook of one arm. For a moment, he admires the bouquet, smiling. But the smile fades. I meet his eyes, and he worries his bottom lip. "Seeing him out there, after Monday and the past few days, I *had* to show him how I feel, Ben." Jane's eyes are wide. "Do you think he got it? What I was trying to say?"

I laugh. "From where I was sitting? I'd say loud and clear."

◆ · ◆

Johnny announces intermission and the house lights come up, filtering through the curtain to wash the stage in a soft red glow. Jane and I move to the stairs to find most of the audience filing toward the bar. The flow of bodies has created a blockade on the far side of the room, stranding Ming and Charles, who wave to us excitedly.

"Should we cross the stage to get to them?" asks Jane. "Oh! I didn't know Darcy was coming with Charles."

"*What?*"

Jane points to the increasingly crowded bar, where Darcy stands beside Ginn and Tonic. Beside, to be sure; the Twins are huddled with their backs to Darcy, making his exclusion clear.

"Meet you over there?" Jane suggests, already starting across the stage. "I'll get Ming and Charles and we'll make our way to you guys."

I nod, still puzzling through Darcy's unexpected attendance as I head toward the semi-trio. While I can't fathom why he'd make the trip out here, I can't help but wonder when he arrived. *Did he see the peel?*

Tonic catches my eye and elbows Ginn. They wave, the movement as synchronized as when they're performing. Behind them, Darcy gives me the kind of strained nod generally reserved for hostage victims trying to signal distress without alerting their captor. He's back to the more formal look he wore at Meryton: a trim-cut suit, though no tie, his shirt open at the collar.

Ginn beams at me. "Kitten! That peel was hot." She has her arms outstretched like she wants to hug, then claps her hands to my upper arms. "Tag." She releases me. "You're it."

"What?"

She hitches her thumb over her shoulder. "Tall Guy is friends with Jane's boo, but he doesn't speak and it's creeping us out. He's all yours." She takes Tonic's hand, and the two stride away.

I turn to Darcy with an apologetic grimace.

"I take no offense," he says. "Small talk with new people has never been my strong suit."

"Ah," I say thoughtfully, though his admission makes me smile. I rest my elbow on the bar and lean in like I'm going to share a secret. To my surprise, Darcy lowers his face closer, and I pick up the faintest trace of his body heat.

"I can relate. I'm *not* a good dancer. It's part of why I kitten." I tip my head. "Though I've always figured it's my own fault—because I don't take the time to practice."

This gets me a smirk and a tease of the fullness a proper smile would give his lower lip. "Perhaps I'll fare better now that I have a more compelling partner."

I clap my hands. "That could almost be a compliment. You should fit those into conversation if you ever get stuck. People love compliments." He flashes a quick smile and my curiosity wins out. "When did you get here?" The question's a more subtle version of the *"Did you see me perform?"* I'm hoping to have answered.

"I missed some of the beginning. I—" He frowns. "I'm sorry, you've mentioned that before, that not being able to dance is part of why you kitten. Is the other part the . . ."

I get a little flutter that he's interested enough to ask after something so personal, but I leave him hanging on principle. He's *at* a burlesque show; he should be able to name the main activity.

After a few seconds, his mouth goes tight, and I offer, "Stripping?" He winces at the word but nods. "It's all an act."

I wait a beat, wondering if this is that same deadpan humor as Monday, but his brow stays furrowed. "Literally, yes, Darcy. This is a show. That you paid to attend," I remind him. "Where the performers make a production of removing clothing."

He looks around the room with narrowed eyes. "I don't trust it."

I laugh. "*Trust?* What does trust have to do with it?"

"There's just a veneer of artifice about the whole thing."

I arch a brow. "Have we just circled back to the idea of this being a show?"

"It feels . . . manipulative."

I watch him, my skin creeping with unease. In my years in the scene, I haven't heard anyone refer to what we do as *manipulative*. *Cheap?* Sure. And a whole table of women once accused me of debasing myself; curious, given that they'd chosen to spend their evening in an establishment specializing in said supposed debasement.

But *manipulative?*

I drum my fingers on the bar, then point at him. "What was the last play you saw?"

He clears his throat. "How is that—"

"What was the last play you saw?"

"*The Lion King.*"

"*The*—really?"

His brows twitch down. I regret not tempering my response but, *really?* "It's a stunning production," he says stiffly.

I nod in a way I hope is diplomatic. "Agreed. 'Circle of Life' gets me every time. But"—I raise a finger—"when you saw it, were you upset that there weren't actual lions onstage? That the play is all actors, *pretending* to be animals?"

"That would hardly—"

I gesture to the stage. "How is this different?"

"Watching a woman take off her clothes is a far cry from watching a man in face paint pretend to be grass."

I laugh. "Be careful saying something like that in this crowd. So many New York creatives in one room, there's bound to be a few who'd *kill* to play grass."

Another half smile.

"Is it the nudity, then?" I ask. "Is that what makes it manipulative?"

The half smile vanishes. A furrow develops between his brows. "It's so . . ."

"Intimate?" I offer, choosing a word he used that night at Meryton. I liked that bit . . . before all the talk of a certain lack of temptation.

"Something like that. Have you done it? The . . . stripping." He gets the word out so quickly this time, he practically trips over it.

"A few times. Student showcases after the intro course at the School of Burlesque."

"And you had no hesitations?"

"It's all about context," I say. "For me, onstage, the context was, 'This is where I take off my clothes for appreciative strangers.' At Meryton, it's, 'This is where I mince about in very little and hustle pasties.'"

"Ah. Does it bother people?"

The question is posed innocently enough, but a warning bell sounds in my head all the same. I know what he's getting at. This time, however, he's going to have to do the heavy lifting himself.

I cock my head, feigning confusion. "What people? My parents?"

"No, I—" Darcy's eyes widen. "Your *parents* have been to Meryton?"

"A few times. They love it. Well, their first time visiting, my dad was put out that his shrimp was overcooked. But he'll play poker with the guys, and I swear, Ming calls my mom more often than I do.

They're like this." I cross the middle and index fingers of my right hand. "They came out here for Christmas last year, and we all did dinner together at the club. Mom and I cooked," I add, smiling in earnest. "Andrea was such a fan of our mashed potatoes, Meryton uses our family recipe now."

"The potatoes were excellent," he says, more to himself than me. He shakes his head. "That's not what I was asking. I meant if your involvement in burlesque bothers the men you date. Presuming you date men, that is."

At last, we have reached the inevitable. Other iterations of the question flood my memory, sneers from guests at Meryton, all male, asking, "Does your *boyfriend* let you do this?" The idea that I need any man's permission to do whatever the hell I want with *my* goddamn body . . .

Even worse, it *has* been a problem. Sure, men get excited when they learn I'm involved in the scene, but the novelty wears off. Either I'm a hypocrite for refusing to bring my Kitten persona into the bedroom, or the guys see me in action and suddenly there's no difference between my kittening and literal solicitation. One such fellow took particular offense to my hip-checking a Russian blocking the curtain-call stampede. He interrupted the show to berate me and challenge the Russian to "take it outside" with him. It was mortifying.

I draw in a slow breath, willing myself to calm. Perhaps this is all some elaborate setup for Darcy's own forward-thinking views on female liberation.

"I date men. And it has bothered some. It turns out most like the idea but not the reality."

He purses his lips as though I've confirmed his suspicions.

The gesture gets my hackles up, but I press on. "However, I don't imagine it would be a problem to anyone worthwhile."

He frowns. "Is it inappropriate that a man prefer his partner not be partially naked in front of strangers?"

"He might have his *preferences*," I say tightly. "But it's not his decision. It's not his body."

"That isn't what—"

"Y'know," I interrupt, "I think I understand that 'trust' issue of yours. In your experience, a woman takes off her clothes in front of you and you've only ever seen the action as something she's doing for you. It's never crossed your mind that getting naked is fun or exciting for those women. It's only been a prelude to sex. In burlesque, stripping isn't about sex at all. It isn't about bringing *you* pleasure. You can't get your head around that, so you don't trust it."

Darcy opens his mouth to reply, and I step closer.

"Just because burlesque appeals to men doesn't make it an appeal *to* men," I say, my tone shaded dark by every aggravating past conversation I've had on the subject. "We all have our reasons for performing—"

"And what's your reason?" He asks it like he's been waiting for the opportunity.

I don't miss a beat. "Knowing I can."

He lets out a huff. "How is that a reason?"

"How is it not?" I counter. "When is a person more vulnerable than when she's naked? Then amplify that by however many people are in the audience. It's not something everyone can do. It's not something that everyone *wants* to do. But it matters to me. I see strength in it. And joy. I found it at a point when I needed those things."

"And then what?" he asks.

"What do you mean?"

"You know you can be naked in front of a crowd. So now what?" His dark eyes are intent.

I shake my head. "There doesn't have to be anything else."

"You're saying it's some kind of personal benchmark of bravery. So, what is there for you to be brave about?"

My lizard brain lashes against the inquiry. However, a part of me a few rungs higher on the evolutionary ladder concedes this is a very good question.

"You said you found it at a point when you needed it," he continues. "Did it fix whatever that was? Fulfill that need?"

This is an opening. More of that bravery of Jane's. I could explain to him what the scene means to me. How it gave me a reason to get out and explore the city, turned into the creative outlet I desperately needed, and made me feel whole again—

My stomach twists. *Whole. Invincible.* But what have I done with that strength? Because if I haven't used it to get back to design, then all this is little more than a rhinestone-studded crutch.

The realization stings like betrayal.

Darcy's dark eyes soften, like he's picked up on the fact that his question just undid two-plus years of emotional scaffolding. I could be flattered that he's tuned in to me enough to notice the shift, but I ride the unsettling vulnerability straight into anger.

"Why are you even here?" I growl.

He takes in a breath—

"Hey, you two!" Ming puts a hand on my shoulder. "Solid peel, girl. You missed a great opportunity, though." She hooks a finger into the keyhole at my bust and tugs. "I'd have threaded the glove through here, flossed a bit between the boobies."

I smack her hand away. *Damn.* That would have been inspired.

She grins at Darcy. "How about you, handsome? You enjoy Kitten's performance?"

I prepare to tell her he missed it, but Darcy clears his throat.

"I have reason to doubt it was meant as an appeal to my tastes," he says.

I glare at him, face heating. "You said you were late."

"I missed part of Johnny's opening. Not you."

"Aw, feel manipulated?" I ask in a mocking coo.

"I said I didn't trust it." His eyes fix on mine, dipping briefly to where the tie at my bust is still crooked from Ming's tug. My cheeks flare again. "Not that I didn't like it."

My breath stutters.

"If you'll excuse me." Darcy nods at me. "I need to get going. Enjoy the rest of the show. Bennet. Ms. DyNasty."

He walks away, and it is an act of sheer willpower not to stare after him. Maybe he did learn a little about conversational flattery.

"Did I detect some tension between the two of you?" Ming plucks at the tie again. "Of the *sexual* variety?"

"Tension, yes." I force my jaw to relax before I get a headache. "Sexual . . ."

"Also yes?"

The cash register dings. The bartender pulls out a series of bills, counting out change, then takes the money to a tall figure at the far end of the bar. I narrow my eyes. Darcy and his damn hundos.

He leaves a few bills on the bar and folds the rest into his money clip. As he tucks the cash into his jacket pocket, his eyes fall on me. Like he's expecting my attention.

I arch a brow, defiant. He smiles, slow and languid and knowing, and goddamn it all, I am helpless against the pull to watch what the smile does to his lower lip. The world tips slightly.

And then he's out the door.

I rub my temples. He shouldn't get to look like that and be a condescending poo.

And he certainly shouldn't be asking me the kind of questions I should be asking myself.

Ming studies me, clearly amused.

I drop my hands. "What?"

"Nothing," she says. "It's so cute to see you all hot and bothered."

"I'm *not*—"

She waves off my protest. "It's just lust. Now come on, let's socialize." She arches a brow. "Unless you're gonna trail the guy and ravage him in an alley."

I decide to ignore the sudden spike in my pulse. "Ming, *please*. I'm a lady."

CHAPTER

10

Toby shakes his head. "Liz, you have outdone yourself."

I grin, even though he isn't watching me. Twenty feet above us, Ginn and Tonic are radiant in all-white ensembles, contrasting brilliantly with the red silks dangling from Pemberley's ceiling. The costumes are more conservative than what they wear at the club, for obvious reasons, and while they won't be taking anything off tonight, performing a peel is hardly the most impressive feat in their collective wheelhouse.

"So . . ." Toby's head drops to the side as he follows a sudden movement from Ginn. "Where's this show you work weekends?"

I hold back a laugh at the idea of Toby at the club. His heart would *stop.* "Tribeca."

"Interesting," he says, voice distant.

I join him in appreciating the Twins' skills, their choreography all the more enchanting in the larger space. At Meryton, they are the clear focal point; there's nowhere else to look. But in a room easily five times the size, the fact that they have more than two hundred people admiring them from all corners of the space highlights just how arresting they can be.

Tonic begins a wrap maneuver I recognize, moving more slowly than she's done the times Jane and I have watched her and Ginn at their practice space. When she spots me, she freezes.

I sigh, then hold up my index finger and mouth, "*One time.*"

She beams and continues her ascent, twining the silk around her body more quickly.

I nudge Toby. "Brace yourself."

Tonic reaches the peak of her climb and leans back, holding the silk with one hand and arcing her other arm up and over her supine form. After a moment in the pose, she releases her grip, unraveling from the fabric with dizzying speed.

Toby lurches forward as if to catch her from his place twenty paces across the room, but I grab his elbow. "Easy."

He remains in a hunched position, hands outstretched. It's actually endearing; everyone else circled around the Twins' landing pad has the opposite reaction: gasping, followed by a quick retreat. A few collide with the railings around the edges of the platforms, narrowly avoiding a dip in the indoor lake. Tonic halts her fall inches above the startled onlookers. A beat of silence follows as she rotates above them in a casual recline. The guests recover with applause, and Toby lets loose a steadying breath. I pat his shoulder, then go to check on the evening's other, more subdued source of entertainment at the piano.

When I get to Jane, he's in the middle of a Gershwin piece, and I'm reminded of Wednesday's surprise performance. We haven't talked about the direction his song took that night, but then, I don't think we need to. If the multiple consecutive evenings he's spent out with Charles are any indication, Jane hasn't had to spell things out for him, either.

"How are you doing, darling?" I take a seat beside him.

"I love these corporate gigs. Show up, look pretty—"

"You always look pretty."

He sends me an air kiss. "I wouldn't want to do these exclusively, but it's nice to come up with a set list and go to town." His fingers dance along the piano keys with a playful flourish.

"Glad I could hook you up, then." I flick the brim of his fedora; the navy felt coordinates perfectly with his suit. "Plans for after?"

"A movie. Charles hasn't seen *My Beautiful Laundrette*!" he says, clearly scandalized.

"*Quelle horreur!*"

"You're more than welcome to join, but that dress says you have greater aspirations."

I sit taller, and the fashion tape anchoring the open back of my dress tugs against my shoulder blades. Tape aside, the dress fits like a glove. Through some tailoring sorcery, Ming darted and tucked the bust of the garnet sheath into cups and transformed the scoop neckline into a daring—but tasteful—sweetheart.

Alas, it seems I've wasted the dress's debut. The party has been going on for more than an hour and so far, Wickham's a no-show. We've texted a few times since our drinks at Ruin, but I haven't heard from him since yesterday's exchange about Toby's new hoverboard. Part of me wants to check with Toby to see if he's gotten any word, but I refuse—whether because of principle or pride, I'm not sure.

"Go put that thing to work." Jane bumps me with his hip, nudging me down the bench until I stand. "You're going to spend hours organizing Ming's costuming supplies to pay for it, anyway."

"The party's all coworkers and their plus-ones," I say, though he has a point. We are celebrating a merger, after all: surely someone here's worth a little *personal* merging. With that in mind, I return to the main gathering area around the lake, feeling out the vibe the way I would at the show. While it doesn't buzz like Meryton, the crowd has a good, light energy. My performers are happy, the guests are enjoying themselves, and my boss is in a state of near-drooling adulation. I am officially off duty.

I beeline for the nearest waiter, accepting a pair of bacon-wrapped dates with a smile. His not-so-subtle appraisal of me and my dress takes some of the sting out of Wickham's no-show. Chewing contentedly, I stroll to the railing bordering the lake with an eye on the drink server on the island across from me.

When I came to finalize the layout before the event, I had to sit down to absorb it all. It's been years since anything I had a hand in designing has been realized, and while I can hardly take responsibility for the grandeur of the space itself, seeing the little touches I suggested was oddly affecting. The tea lights dotting the surface of the lake had been idle doodling; I didn't realize I'd submitted them with the Work It plans. Marley, Pemberley's manager, confided that when the owner saw them in my sketches, he insisted on tracking down floating votives to make them a regular feature.

Pride blossoms in my chest as I dwell on the votives drifting below. The lotus styling is a nice contrast to the industrial vibe of the rest of the space. The exposed steel beams and iron railing around the lake needed softening, which is why I suggested the ivory bunting. I didn't anticipate it would serve as padding, too.

I lean a hip into the railing, drumming my fingernails against the metal. This place is being wasted as a venue for some generic event like this—even if said event has been meticulously coordinated. A proper show here would be incredible.

The bar for *Red, White, and Boobs* spurred a series of design concepts on the subway ride home that night. When Meryton's limited scale couldn't accommodate my idea for a custom chandelier for the Twins to work from, I upgraded to Pemberley. I already had the digital renderings of the current space, so it was easy enough to play with some ideas when I got home.

And on my ride into work the next morning. And during yesterday's lunch break.

Behind me, Jane starts playing "An American in Paris." The tune's urgency is a little out of place, but I close my eyes, letting my vision unfold in time with the rise and fall of the notes. Conceal the out-of-place barn wood at the back of the stage with a dark, solid drape. For the stage: plush red velvet curtains with gold tassels and coordinating bunting for depth. The footlights can stay, but with shells to tie in with the classic look of the curtains.

A collective gasp stirs me from my daydream. The vision peels away in time for me to watch Ginn, not to be outdone by Tonic, finish her own death spiral. She dangles in front of one of the managers from out of town—the Seattle branch, I think—and tousles his hair. He stares in naked adoration. *Lord.* And I thought Toby was on the verge of drooling.

I search again for a drink server. The one I spotted earlier has moved to another platform and—*oh, hello*—to get to him I'll have to pass a very well-filled-out suit on the catwalk. Its owner has his back to me, head angled toward the action on the silks. I move toward my initial target while preparing to steal a better glance at the second. Not that the rear view isn't appealing.

Appealing and . . . *familiar?*

I almost choke on my last bite of date. With a startled cough, I spin away, heart rate accelerating as I try to compose myself. This makes no sense. He wouldn't be here. Unless he's a plus-one? Or his tush has a doppelgänger . . .

One way to find out. I clear my throat, take in a breath, and turn to face Will Darcy . . .

. . . who is already looking my way.

Heat flares across my skin. I've interrupted enough oglers to know the signs of lingering appreciation, and Darcy's half-second delay before he makes eye contact tells me he's been admiring the view. He continues to study me with the same vague look the interns get when I change the Wi-Fi password: the situation is possible but incompatible with expectations.

I wait him out, glad I had a moment to process his presence before he discovered mine. Now that the surprise is ebbing and there's no risk of my choking on finger food, exasperation takes center stage. My date no-shows, yet here we have the guy whose follow-up to condemning my favorite pastime as "manipulative" was to set my world askew. *And* I've caught him checking out my butt. *What chaos god did I offend?*

I'll let the butt thing slide—the dress really is flattering, and I know my assets—but seeing him in the space I've devoted creative energy to feels like a violation. Part of why I ended up sketching on the ride home the other night was to distract myself from the push and pull of our argument. I'd wanted to write him off completely, but that goddamn smile before he walked out kept teaming up with the look at Meryton, and his comment about catching my peel: *"I said I didn't trust it. Not that I didn't like it."*

And *holy hell* can the man wear a suit.

His eyes go wide. It is tremendously satisfying. *"Bennet?"*

"Darcy," I say with all the coolness of my ten-second advantage.

The shock shifts to intrigue as he strolls my way, nodding politely to the people he has to move around. He maintains eye contact as he walks.

I roll my shoulders. He is *very* good with eye contact.

His attention drops down and up my figure, and I suppress a shiver.

He is also skilled at *not* making eye contact.

"Seeing Jane at the piano was surprising enough, then the aerialists, and now you." He smiles, resting a hand on the railing. "No one's going to start taking clothes off, are they?"

The candor threatens to throw me. "Nah. My boss is already enraptured." I indicate Toby, who is probably going to need a chiropractor after tonight. Has he even moved since I walked away? "He wouldn't know what to do with himself."

"You're with Work It?"

"I'm the executive assistant."

"That—you're *EBenAdmin*." He says my email handle with meaningful realization. "You have excellent correspondence skills."

"This is where I ask you how you know that."

"I was cc'd on some emails. You really came through on that liability insurance."

"Still not connecting the dots," I say, though I don't mind the tease. Is he being *coy*? The prospect tingles across my shoulders.

"As owner of the venue, it felt like I should be included in that kind of decision."

The tingle gives way to shock. "Come again?"

"Pemberley's been in my family for ages," he says with a shrug. "It's been several things over the years, but now we're hosting events. Which I suppose you know, seeing as you rented it."

I nod, still trying to wrap my brain around the new information. The beautiful space I've spent the past three days sketching belongs to *him*? I'm going to have to look up chaos gods when I get home, because this level of coincidence feels suspiciously divine.

"This means I was the meeting you had to get to the other day. With Jane," he says, as though coming to the conclusion as he speaks.

"That's why you were in such a rush." I grimace. "I hope you were coming in anyway."

"There's always something to do around here," he says with a half smile. "I appreciate that you cited it as a family emergency."

"It was."

He nods slowly, eyes roaming my face. "You put a lot of personality in those emails. Professional, but just enough cheek to keep them interesting. I looked forward to receiving them."

Flirting. This is definitely flirtation. But Darcy? *Mr. Tolerable* himself, flirting? He who doesn't "trust" my beloved avocation? It rouses a prickle of annoyance, though the sensation is outmatched by the sudden coil of pleasure twining in my belly.

Which is also annoying.

"Ah! Finn!" he calls to a server bearing a tray of champagne flutes.

The waiter, a young guy with a head of unruly copper curls, stops and smiles. "Will! Good to see you. Would you and the lady like a drink?"

"Bennet?"

"Sure."

Darcy takes a champagne flute from either side of the tray, mindful to keep the waiter's load balanced. He hands me a glass and I nod my thanks.

"Is this your last semester at NYU, or will you have another left?"

"One more," Finn says. "The workload's been brutal. But the internship is going well. I can't thank you enough for that."

"No trouble," says Darcy. He turns a little, making me more a part of the conversation. "I did my family the disservice of failing to go to law school myself. It would have been a crime to waste those connections. Besides"—he points to Finn—"you did the work."

Finn nods, going pink in the cheeks. "Thanks anyway," he insists, and raises his tray. "Sorry, I gotta keep moving these. Great seeing you. I'll tell Fitz you said hello." He sends me another little nod and moves on.

"Finn's interning at my uncle's law firm," Darcy explains. "I'm sure Fitz is running him ragged, but it's great experience." He lifts his glass. I tip mine against it and echo his offered, "Cheers." We watch one another as we drink.

"I take it you booked the night's entertainment?" he inquires.

I shrug, dwelling on the decency—hell, generosity—of his hooking up that waiter. "It would be a crime to waste the connections."

"I never would have thought about employing the space the way you are. You have a creative perspective."

"I have experience in design." The temptation to go into detail collides with my better judgment. I'm not about to admit to the hours I've spent fantasizing about remodeling this room, not when he's been so dismissive of what I'd like to see play out on its stage. "Between that and working at Meryton, I can't look at a crossbeam without consider-ing how Ginn and Tonic might use it to scare the hell out of people."

"That spiraling move is harrowing," he says, and while he's smil-ing faintly, I catch a flicker of disappointment in his dark eyes. "Made me glad I insisted on the landing pad."

I laugh; he *was* persistent. "If you're going to let aerialists perform here, you may want to invest in your own. Lugging that thing up from Brooklyn earned me a few enemies on the Two train."

"The mat's yours?"

"It's a bouldering mat. For climbing."

"That's right. One of those varied interests of yours."

He remembers. A pleasant sparking zips up my spine. I crane my neck and locate a corner of the black mat through the legs of the guests. "I don't know why I moved with it. I only ever climb in-doors now. But guests say it's not bad to sleep on. I can't guarantee it's totally up to the standard of some insurance policies, though. If you see the owner"—I hold a finger to my lips—"it's probably best to play dumb."

He fights a smile, which does as much for his features as actually smiling does. His eyes make another heart-stopping pass over me. "Jane's an excellent pianist." He turns, leaning against the railing. I shift, too, getting a view of Jane chatting with the head of Work It's HR. Jane carries on playing and laughs at something she says, not missing a note. "Juilliard, right?"

I nod, though the question threatens to rub me the wrong way. While I'm not surprised that it would have come up in conversation between Jane and Charles, I doubt my humble Jane would have shared it with Darcy. More likely, Charles felt compelled to announce his boyfriend's pedigree to build Jane up for Darcy's approval.

I wonder how much Darcy might know. "Jane comes from a long line of doctors, so there was some grumbling."

"Hmm."

I take another drink. "I guess you can relate?"

"A bit." He looks over my face, attention dropping to my lips before a blink has his eyes to mine.

"Your boss . . ." He turns his attention to Toby, about whose neck health I am genuinely concerned. "Does he know how you spend your weekends?"

My temper flares, the question sending me back to our tense exchange in Bushwick. "Are you asking if he knows his glorified receptionist moonlights as a glorified stripper, or if he'd care if he knew?"

"I meant if Meryton is something you're open with at Work It," he says coolly. "Though if you're concerned about your performance as an administrator, I suggest you add a signature to your emails. It would have saved us both some stress the other day."

"You certainly were eager to get here," I gripe, though his humor has taken the edge off my irritation. Plus, he's probably right about the email signature. "A few coworkers have come in," I say, getting back to the question. "It makes for an entertaining Monday when they see me at the front desk and their last memory is of me in my undies."

"I'm sure they're fine." He raises his glass for a drink. "It's a good memory."

The comment dances over my skin like a shower of sparks. This guy is a custom suit full of contradictions. Me in my undies is a good memory, while in the moment I was deemed merely "tolerable." He doesn't "trust" burlesque, but he liked my peel.

"Who are you right now?" The question falls out of me before I can stop it.

His mouth quirks. There's a smoldering in his eyes I can't ignore. It aligns so closely with a look I received from imagined Darcy in a particularly ambitious groveling session that my mouth goes a little dry. I take a restorative gulp of champagne.

"Why do you ask?"

"You're different here than you've been the other times we've met. You've *smiled*."

He chuckles, and I wonder what it would take to get a real laugh out of him. At this point, it would feel like an accomplishment. "Am I not supposed to?"

"Rumor has it you don't like crowds."

He winces. "That is an understatement."

"I'd hate to startle you," I stage-whisper, and Darcy shifts the tiniest bit closer. His proximity has me edging nearer. "There's over two hundred people down here. Excluding waitstaff. You sure you can cope?"

"Hmm." The thoughtful sound is so low, my toes curl. "Now that you mention it, I think I've hit my threshold. Would you be interested in a better view?" He points to the second level, which I haven't had the chance to explore. Centered on the upper floor is a large window, like an announcer's box at a stadium. "My office."

I toss back the last splash of my champagne, and there's a good chance I'm flinging away my better judgment in the same movement. This is definitely a questionable decision, but I can consider my motivation later. "Lead the way."

CHAPTER

· 11 ·

Upstairs, the door to Darcy's office is open, and he gestures for me to step in ahead of him. I'm immediately drawn to the framed black and white photograph of Pemberley's exterior dominating the opposite wall. The venue's name is spelled out in lights on a wide marquee, a feature that sadly no longer exists, but the distinct sunburst above the front doors is visible, and the tile on the front step is the same. The brick building's been maintained so well that aside from the missing signage, the photo could have been taken yesterday.

"Opening night," Darcy says from behind me. "Or close to it. Pemberley was originally a vaudeville club, but it never brought in the crowds like the Palace or places on Broadway."

"Really?" I say, still examining the photo. "You should put all that on the website. The photo, too. It's fantastic."

"That's—that's a very good call."

Footsteps sound against the hardwood floor, then soften to a whisper over carpeting. I turn to find him at a desk. He picks up a pen from the broad surface, then jots something down on a yellow legal pad; he knows a good idea when he hears it.

I look over the room. The space is tidy but lived-in, with a number of curios to plunder for secrets about their owner. The far wall is bisected by a deep-blue curtain—it must be the window I saw from downstairs—and below it is a table bearing a series of framed photos. *Jackpot.*

First is a photo of Darcy in a cap and gown beside a stern-looking, mustachioed older man I assume is his dad. Next is a shot of an elementary-age Darcy in a school uniform, standing, based on the sunburst above him, outside of Pemberley. His gap-toothed smile is brilliant. It makes my chest go a little gooey: he loved this place even then.

"Ah!" I pick up the next picture, featuring a familiar, perpetually grinning blond in what appears to be a small boat. Charles's navy tank has "Cal" across it in yellow letters, and I realize I've solved the mystery of Thor's calluses and physique: Jane's beau is a rower. This must be his college team. I look at the rower behind him—

Darcy. The photo's captured him midstroke, arm muscles bunched as he pulls the oars toward himself. Charles is in the same position, but the focus in Darcy's face is far more *effective.*

I'm about to ask if he still rows when another item on the table catches my eye. I wheel on Darcy, still by the desk.

"William Darcy!" I force a stern expression as I point to the catering tray, where two miniature beef Wellingtons languish alongside a few mini quiches and a trio of bacon-wrapped dates. "Are these from my party?"

"Would you believe me if I claimed I was performing quality control?" At my laugh, his lips pull in against a repentant smile. It's even more appealing than the rowing photo. "I have a weakness for finger foods. And those Wellingtons are outstanding. I think I've had five."

"There will be plenty," I assure him, and he starts to cross the room. "Besides, I told Jane and the Twins to bring Tupperware for leftovers."

"You take care of your own." He stops by the door. "I need to hit the light, otherwise people can see in from downstairs. Is that okay?"

I nod, and he flicks the switch. The only illumination in the room comes from the brass-shaded lamp at his desk, the warm glow making the room feel suddenly intimate. Some nocturnal instinct has me turn away, granting Darcy the view I caught him indulging in downstairs. The thought of his eyes on me again has me leaning against the table for support.

His body heat buffets my exposed back as he reaches to my right for the curtain pull. "As promised." The words brush the nape of my neck. *How close* is *he?*

I'm white-knuckling the edge of the table when the curtains part. My legs almost give out altogether. "Oh," I sigh.

The view is spectacular. From here, the tea lights twinkle like new stars, and the railing's gauzy bunting is almost ethereal. The sight of Ginn and Tonic on the silks adds to the unearthly vibe, the pair twirling like nymphs out of mythology. The possibilities for this space are truly endless. It's overwhelming.

After a few moments of silent reverence, I ask, "What happened after the vaudeville show didn't pan out?"

Darcy's next to me now; I didn't notice him move. "Restaurants, mostly, a dinner theater for a time in the seventies. But it's been vacant for about ten years now. An aunt wanted to give another restaurant a go but only got partway through remodeling—"

"That explains the barn wood!" I glare at the offending scab of pine. "Ugh. Everyone was doing barn wood then."

He glances toward the stage, brow furrowed. "What's wrong with barn wood?"

"Nothing," I say, deadpan, and grin. "When it's on a barn."

"Brutal," he says, but it comes out with a tinge of approval.

"You asked." I nod at the window. "So, this is it, then? No aspirations beyond an open venue?"

"It keeps the lights on."

"Huh." I let my gaze fall over the room below, glittering with potential. "Kind of a waste, isn't it?"

Darcy doesn't reply. I look over at him, and his eyes have gone distant, a slight frown on his face. He seems—hurt?

"It's safe, though. From a business standpoint." I have no idea what I'm saying. "That was rude of me." *Ugh. Why do I feel bad?*

He blinks as though coming back to himself. "Your word choice just struck a nerve. It's not the first time I've been told I'm failing to meet expectations."

"Law school again?"

"Among other things."

I cock my head. "If you didn't go into law, what do you do for work? Other than Pemberley, I mean."

"You—" His forehead creases. "You don't know?"

"I'm comfortable with 'Will Darcy: Man of Business,' but I'd imagine you have a more accurate job title."

Darcy huffs a small laugh. He still looks surprised. "I'm just used to people Googling me."

"Sorry to disappoint?"

"Not at all. It's refreshing. I'm a private wealth manager."

"And are private wealth managers typically Google-worthy?"

He smirks. "Hardly. Basically, I tell very rich people how and where to spend their money and occasionally help them work around estate taxes."

I wrinkle my nose. "That sounds morally questionable."

"It feels that way sometimes. But the estate taxes are usually avoided through establishing charitable foundations, so morally, it's more of a wash."

"Is it . . ." I think back to our last conversation. "Fulfilling?"

His mind must go to the same place, because his responding look is shrewd. "Is what you do?"

"I asked first."

"I'm pretty sure *I* asked first. But no." He says it plainly. "My work is not fulfilling. But I'm good at it. I majored in business, interned in college, established a client base. It isn't a dream job, but in some cases, I've been able to help other people achieve their dreams, so . . ."

"Another wash?"

"I guess." His dull tone suggests otherwise.

"Then what would be fulfilling?"

"That's the million-dollar question."

"Probably more, in your case."

He looks at me from the corner of his eye. "That's the tone I got from your emails, by the way."

"You said cheeky. That bordered on insolent."

Another huff. *Will I ever get a proper laugh out of this guy?*

"What would be fulfilling?" He asks it more to himself than me, eyes on the window. "I really would love to see something done with this place. Pemberley could be so much more. It *deserves* to be more. I just haven't found the inspiration."

I smile despite myself; I've been feeling the same way. I've played with several Meryton ideas here, and while it's all quality work, they lack something. Some element is missing. Even though I'm sketching it all out for my own benefit, it feels like I'm failing the building somehow by not presenting her best self.

Darcy clears his throat. "Bennet, when we spoke in Bushwick, I—"

"Showed your ass?"

"Did I?" His face scrunches, voice high with cartoonish skepticism. It's adorable.

"Yeah. Y'did."

He turns to rest his weight against the table. "I'm still getting used to the whole burlesque . . . scene. It's a lot to take in."

I screw up my face like he did. "Is it?"

"When Charles asked me to look over the properties he was considering, he only gave me hard numbers. Property value, revenue, and a description of the businesses operating in each. Meryton was listed as a 'cabaret.' So I was a little thrown when I arrived to find out that Charles had not only put in an offer without consulting me, but that the 'cabaret' was—"

"A threat to your virtue?"

He eyes me flatly, but the corners of that fine mouth of his twitch. "Not as described."

"Huh. Seems you should have done some Googling. That's some sloppy man-of-businessing."

"You—" He presses his lips together, the attempt to hide his smile betrayed by a delightful crinkling around his eyes. "What I'm taking forever to say is that you were right. About my trust issues. That's a

Darcy family standard. If we had a coat of arms, it would just be an old man, clutching money, giving side-eye. I don't want to be that way. It's partly why I've spent my adult life on the other side of the country."

He sighs. "But I've also had enough experiences to reinforce the family habit. So you'll have to forgive me for needing time to adjust to a community that takes something I understand as intimate and treats it as something recreational."

"So, you admit it," I muse. "You see clothing coming off and it gives you a certain expectation."

He frowns. "It's not as though I'm expecting—"

"That's not what I'm saying." I laugh. "You may have trust issues, but I think the bigger problem is a limited imagination."

Darcy crosses his arms, settling in. "Then please, Ms. Bennet, broaden my perspective."

The flirtatious edge to his request inspires a score of Ming-like replies, but I keep them to myself. I have a point to make.

I hop onto the table, mindful not to bump any photos, and settle beside the purloined canapés. "The first day of my Burlesque 101 class, we're introduced to tassel twirls. We practice, and we're having a great time with it. It's very satisfying."

"I'll take your word for it."

"Out of nowhere, one gal starts crying. But she's also smiling. She apologizes, but the tears keep flowing. And she explains, 'I have two kids. I nursed both of them, and I never thought my boobs would do anything cool again!'"

"Okay—"

I throw up my arms. "Her boobs were hers again! They were fun, not functional. She was reclaiming part of herself, and it made her so happy, she cried. We all cried. It was a moment."

I turn to face him, my knee bumping the tray between us. "I've been witness to so many of those moments in the scene that, frankly, it's offensive to have someone reduce it to something purely sexual."

Darcy nods slowly, like he's taking this all in.

"Maybe saying 'We all have our reasons' wasn't the right way to put it," I admit. "It's more that there's so much to get out of performing. Onstage, being cheered for, you're not thinking, 'These people are pumped about this glove coming off!' The rush comes from being celebrated, that you deserve to be celebrated. And if you get onstage and someone gives you a hard time? Sure, it sucks, but it proves you can survive a hit. And knowing you have that kind of strength in you can inform other parts of your life and make you brave enough to do other things that scare you—"

I swallow hard as the truth in my statement rings back to the inconvenient revelation from our last exchange. "If you let it."

Beside me, Darcy is silent. His lips part, and I wait for him to say something. He only watches me. His look isn't assessing, though there's something thoughtful about it. I watch back. *What is he seeing?*

"I apologize. I can see I wasn't respectful the other night. Thank you for being patient enough to explain."

"Thank you for listening." I smile as the shadow I've been refusing to acknowledge for the past few days suddenly clears. "You don't have to 'get' burlesque. But I don't want you thinking there's some grand conspiracy going on onstage. It's supposed to be fun. Fun for the performers and the audience. Whether it's titillation or shock or amusement varies, but the audience is supposed to be having a good time. So, if you're not experiencing that, I'm really sorry." I grin. "Because it's a blast."

"*That* definitely comes across. Though I don't know if that's made it more or less disorienting, given my limited perspective."

"Is there no *fun* in intimacy?"

"I didn't say that. Though I can't say I've ever experienced *shimmying* during an intimate moment."

"Hmm." I fight back a smile. "Then I'm sorry about that, too."

His smile takes that lower lip of his from appealing to irresistible. Just as I commit to searing the image into my brain, he laughs. The full-bodied sound ignites my entire nervous system. And I was right; it does feel like an accomplishment.

He's still laughing when a "Will?" comes from the doorway.

A middle-aged woman in cat's-eye glasses enters the office. It's Marley, the GM. She looks at us with a mix of relief and surprise.

"Marley." Darcy's voice is bright. He straightens from his perch on the table, and I hop down beside him. "I'm assuming you've met?" He places his hand on the small of my largely exposed back. His fingers tense against me, sending a current of pleasure up and down my spine. He leans to look at the point of contact. I hold my breath. *Bless you, Ming, and your many strands of sequins.*

Across from us, Marley grins. "Sorry to interrupt, but I need to steal Will. I didn't realize you were still around," she tells him. "The caterers are looking for extra burners."

Darcy grimaces and hisses a low, "Shit," between his teeth, which my heart rate finds particularly appealing. "I don't think they ended up getting ordered." His hand leaves me, and I force down the whine of disappointment that rises in my throat. "Let's—" He gestures to the door, then turns to me. "Sorry, Bennet. I'll need to figure this out and then—" He checks his watch. "I was supposed to leave half an hour ago."

"Oh?" The part about leaving sounded like an apology.

"Feel free to stay up here if you'd like." His gaze scorches over me again. "Will you be around midweek?"

"You know where to find me." My response is breathless. I remember we're not alone and turn to Marley. "Thanks again for everything. Good luck with the burners."

She smiles broadly, eyes darting to Darcy and back to me. "Anytime."

The two depart. I stay at the window, turning over the evening's unexpected . . . *everything*. Darcy owns this property. Darcy, who is, in fact, a fully realized human capable of remorse and introspection. Who makes a damn compelling flirt and is in search of inspiration for this beautiful space. My attention drifts to the rowing photo: the enticing cut of Darcy's muscles, the intensity in his expression, and that lower lip I'm finding ever more inviting.

A little shiver passes through me. *Goodness.* Any more inspiration on that front, and I may have a whole *other* infatuation to satisfy.

CHAPTER
❧ · 12 · ❧

I'm in the break room Monday morning, rinsing an espresso cup, when Toby steps in. Beside him, Wickham leans against the door frame. I arch a brow.

Honestly, I pretty well forgot about him until now. Yesterday passed in a flurry of design schemes, peppered with bouts of totally reasonable and not at all creepy Googling of Mr. William Darcy: Berkeley graduate, crew team captain, philanthropist, and curator of a number of excellent Spotify playlists now in my rotation.

"Liz, hey!" Toby's greeting is buoyed with relief and a hint of embarrassment. "Could you make us a couple lattes, please?"

"Can do," I say; he's never going to learn how to use the damn machine. Toby thanks me and continues down the hallway. Wickham turns to follow.

"Is whole milk good for you, Wickham?" I call. "Or would you prefer something with less substance?"

He blinks in surprise, then chuckles, strolling out.

Pulling each espresso only takes a few minutes. When I pour the hot milk into the second mug, I consider the rings of white disrupting the dark brown. I don't really care about the other night, but my pride bristles; I confided in the guy, and he didn't even have the decency to text me that he couldn't make it. I grab a stirrer and, with a sense of tremendous satisfaction, sketch "ASS" in the frothy milk.

Mugs in hand, I strut to the conference room where the guys have holed up, first distributing Toby's latte, then Wickham's. He smiles and winks, and I watch as he lifts the mug for a drink. The surprised laugh that follows has him spilling on the leg of his Nantucket Reds.

Works for me.

An hour later, he stops at my desk. The coffee spill has left a gratifying dark spot high on his left thigh.

"That was some stellar foam art, Ms. Bennet. Did you take a class for that, too, or did I stoke your creative passions?"

My smile is a baring of teeth. "I'd say you got off lightly. 'Hell hath no fury' and all that."

His face falls. "I'm sorry about Saturday. I—I have some history with the space where the party was. I didn't realize Pemberley was the venue until I was getting ready and . . ." He sighs. "I couldn't do it."

This is not impressive. "You had my contact info. You could have let me know."

"I know, and I'm sorry. I knew I'd be coming by today and would be able to explain face-to-face." He rocks forward, hands in his pockets. "*If* you'll let me take you to lunch?"

I purse my lips, expression purposefully bland. The "history" excuse doesn't hold water, and there's no reason to not text. If the plumber can text to tell me he has to cancel, there's no reason my plus-one can't. At the same time, he's apologizing in person, which, while late, and more in the spirit of "two birds, one stone" than I'd prefer, is worth more than a text.

"I have a nail appointment over lunch today," I lie. "We can do a drink after work—" Shoot, drinks would be an upgrade from the initial offer, and he hasn't earned that. I frown, as if something I'd forgotten popped up. "It would have to be in Brooklyn if you wanted tonight."

"Brooklyn works," he chirps. "You're in Park Slope?"

I nod. The N train might make this too easy. He should at least have to transfer. "Cobble Hill?"

"If all it takes to earn my way back into your good graces is the G train, you are indeed a benevolent goddess."

"Keep working on that goddess bit," I tell him, though my ego preens at the stroke. "I'm still on the vengeful side. A few sacrifices should edge me somewhere less volatile."

He holds a fist to his heart, bowing low. "I am ever your humble servant."

"Don't grovel. We'll meet at Clover Club at six thirty." I dismiss him with a regal wave.

"I look forward to it."

Head high, I gesture to the coffee stain on his leg. "And change your pants, acolyte."

◆ ― ◆

Wickham waves me over to the bar and I settle onto the vacant seat beside him. Clover Club's tufted leather stools are beasts, twice the size of a normal seat. Not an efficient use of space, but I like the way they keep the bar from getting too crowded.

"First," he begins. "Let's see the nails."

I extend my hand with a flourish, and he makes a show of inspecting the bright red polish. I got them done over lunch anyway.

"Excellent work. Your cuticles look exquisite." He gives my fingers a little squeeze. He changed his pants, the red chinos switched out for a teal pair. *Lord.* Does the guy not know about jeans?

I open the drink menu. "You've completed your first act of contrition, making the pilgrimage to the BK. I'll consider that a sacrifice of time. Are you prepared to sacrifice your financial stability?"

"If that's what it takes to regain your favor, Your Holiness."

"What did I say about groveling?"

The bartender takes my order and Wickham requests another Manhattan, finishing off the one he's been holding. Facing me, his lighthearted demeanor is gone. "What do you know about Pemberley?"

I watch him, unsure what to make of the sudden one-eighty. "More now than I did when I booked it. It turns out that the owner is buddies with my roommate's boyfriend. Will Darcy," I explain, enjoying the flutter I get at the name. "He inherited it and isn't sure what to do with it, so he's renting it out for events for now."

Wickham nods, expression dimming further.

I lose a little elevation. "What's this history of yours?"

The bartender hands us our drinks. I raise my glass for a toast, but Wickham's already taking a long pull from his Manhattan. He returns his drink to the bar with a loud clank of glass and shifting ice and asks, "How well do you know Will?"

"Not very." Though that's not quite true. I know he carries a hanky, what he studied in school, and that he went out of his way to hook that waiter up with an internship. If Charles is any indication, he cares a lot about the people he's close to, and while he can be snooty—and confounding—as hell, that eye contact of his is staggering.

I just can't figure the guy out. I'm still floored by Saturday's shift in personality, how friendly he was with the staff and the positive things he said about my input. But as tingle-inducing as all that is, it's the simple act of his apologizing I keep lingering on. He listened—really listened—when I explained what burlesque means to me.

Wickham nods, forehead creased. "That property, Pemberley? It's supposed to be mine."

Eh? "*Yours?*" I almost laugh. "How? He said it's been in his family for ages."

"When his father passed, I was supposed to receive it."

My eyebrows jump to my hairline.

"Will and I were close when we were younger. My dad worked for his father. And after my dad left, I was more or less absorbed into the Darcy clan."

I blink, thrown by the randomness of the connection. I really should have looked up those chaos gods. "How . . . generous?"

"Will never let me forget that I didn't really belong. His dad was the generous one. Even helped me with school." His dry chuckle is devoid of humor. "If Will ever knew, I'm sure he'd have been furious—the guy's tighter with his money than anyone I've ever known."

I nod, though this is contrary to my experience. I'd hardly say dropping forty bones on novelty playing cards and the most generous tip I've ever received is indicative of miserly living. Plus, he offered to call a car after Jane's accident. Not a cab or a Lyft, but a *car.*

"I'm sure he'd say I was taking advantage," Wickham continues, swirling his drink. His shoulders are slumped, his posture a portrait of disappointment. "He chose to go to school in California, and his dad's health took a turn for the worse. I was going to NYU, so it wasn't any trouble for me to check on him. At least at first. As his health declined, it took more and more of my time, and I eventually put school on hold.

"Will barely came around," he says, voice distant. "Even after I left NYU. It was my choice; the senior Darcy was adamant I not sacrifice my studies . . . What was it he'd say? Something like, 'Don't fret away your youth on an old bastard like me. Get out there and live!' But I couldn't abandon him. It wouldn't have been right."

I continue to nod, still trying to get my bearings.

"Pemberley was his favorite property. He knew Will lacked the imagination to do anything, too. I'd tell him about the ideas I had, and one day, he said, 'Screw it. Pemberley is yours.' Said he'd have the paperwork drawn up and it would go to me. I told him he was crazy, that it was too much, but Will was already getting everything else, and the senior Darcy was insistent.

"Then he passed . . ." He sighs, shaking his head. "Nothing. Will claimed no changes had been made to the will. I was devastated."

Wickham looks at me expectantly. I'm unsure what to say. It's all too dramatic, like I've been pulled into some epic feud. *Is this how I sounded when I talked about my internship?*

I straighten. "This is what you meant the last time we went out. This is your fall."

He gives me a wan smile, raising his palms my way. "No scars, but, yeah. Darcy tossed me a few grand to keep me from tarnishing his name. I should have used it to get a lawyer, but I was so broken down by losing that property, I had to get out of here. That's how I ended up in California. It's been the better part of a decade but"—another sigh—"it still kills."

"That's . . . really messed up?" It comes out as more of a question than a statement. Can all this be true? It certainly fits more comfortably with the pompous Darcy that first night at Meryton, rather than the amiable, human Pemberley Darcy. The disappointment is stunning.

My watch buzzes. "Excuse me," I say, though Wickham is already back to his drink, and I flick to the message at my wrist. It's Tonic, asking if I'm home. She left a lyra at our place and needs to pick it up. I get a twinge of guilt at the prospect of an easy exit and flit my eyes toward Wickham, who studies his now-empty glass.

I don't know what to do with this information about Darcy. If it's true, it's horrible. Even if Wickham's a flake, who would lie about something like this? Then again, who would deny someone their inheritance? Barring sociopathy in one party or another, neither makes sense.

"Shoot. A friend needs something from my apartment. I don't want to bail, though. Are you up for a walk?" I'm not sure what answer I'm hoping for but give him an apologetic smile.

"Another sacrifice for a vengeful goddess?" He raises his hand for the check. "My pleasure."

❖ · ❖

I sit on the rim of the bathtub, tapping my teeth together. Wickham's in my room. It's a more intimate setting than I would have preferred, but that's the downside of my arrangement with Jane: other than the kitchen, there's no neutral ground. At least I picked up my undies before leaving for work.

I don't know what I'm going to do with the guy. The business with Darcy isn't his fault, but Saturday established a higher flake factor than I'm willing to tolerate. Even the novelty of our exchanges has worn off. It's fun to banter with someone at the show, but going back and forth one-on-one like we do is exhausting.

I look at my watch. I've been in here a few minutes. Wickham may no longer be a romantic prospect, but there's no reason to imply gastrointestinal distress. When I come out, he's perched on the edge of my desk, eyes on his phone. I make a point of stepping on the squeaky floorboard past the threshold, and he flinches, almost dropping his phone at the sound.

I laugh. "Edgy much?"

"That floorboard is like a gunshot." He holds up his phone. "Family drama. Another deal I'm working on. My mom's new brother-in-law wants me to look over some of his holdings." He rolls his eyes, sliding the phone into a back pocket. "The guy's a total mess with his investments. I'm trying to talk him down from another disaster."

"So you're a *man of business*?" I ask, though the label doesn't feel nearly as cheeky as it did the other night.

"Exactly." He grins. "I should put that on a business card."

The front door rings and I excuse myself to buzz in the Twins. They arrive a minute later, Ginn tapping on her phone, Tonic greeting me with a smile.

"Thank you for hanging on to this," she says as I hand her the hoop. "With your and Jane's setup, you're the only people I can leave it with and not feel like I'm taking up valuable real estate."

"Hell-o," says Ginn, looking over my shoulder at Wickham. "And who are *you*?"

"Girls, this is George Wickham. Wickham, these are the Twins,

Ginn"—I indicate her—"and Tonic. The aerialists," I explain, having discussed details of the show with him on the walk home.

Ginn shoulders past Tonic to take Wickham's offered hand, and I choke back a laugh. *Easy, tiger.* "It's a pleasure to meet you."

His face splits into a wide grin. "The pleasure is all mine."

Tonic glances my way. I point discreetly between myself and Wickham, mouthing, "*Not together,*" though I appreciate that she checked.

Ginn has no such concerns, continuing to eye Wickham with zero regard for my potential property rights. "Are you familiar with what we do?"

"Ms. Bennet has given me some insight. However, if you're offering to demonstrate, I'd be glad to watch."

Ginn doesn't so much as look at Tonic. "We do love an audience."

"The practice space is only a few blocks away," Tonic adds, clearly perplexed.

Another broad smile from Wickham. He turns to me. "Liz?"

"I'm in for the evening," I say. "But you have a good time."

"You sure?" he asks, but he's looking at Ginn, who toys with the charm on the long necklace she wears. He follows the movement of her hand as it sways side to side, between the low—very low—V-neck of her shirt.

"Absolutely," I insist, relieved at the successful handoff. While Wickham seems brighter than he has been most of the evening, I'm still comfortable ceding any claim.

Wickham follows the Twins out. As I close the door, he flashes me a grin. "Hell of a photo, by the way." He winks, then trots to catch up with the girls.

Photo—oh!

I shut the door and dart back to my room. I look at the desk and—
oh, God—have to laugh. In the center of the workspace is the manila
folder with my Meryton designs, open to the five-by-seven print from
the card shoot.

"Nicely done, Bennet." I followed up my recent burst of inspiration
regarding Pemberley with updates to a Meryton idea. The card photo
was holding my place between the two sections. I pick up the picture,
recalling Ming's comment after the "thoroughly tolerable" burn: *"If
anyone can turn you down after the Four of Clubs, they're not worth
pursuing, anyway."* I put the photo back on the desk. "Well, Wickham,
you failed Ming's test."

Sitting, I flip to the Pemberley sketches. A pang of guilt lances
through me. It was supposed to go to Wickham.

I should have pressed for more details, asked him what his ideas
for the space had been, what vision he'd possessed that convinced the
senior Darcy to pass it to him. Does that even matter? In the end,
Darcy's father promised it to Wickham. Darcy disrespected that.

I know that kind of betrayal. I think back to when Wickham said
he could relate to my experience at the design firm in LA: *"Something
that should have been mine was ripped away."*

And it's Darcy's fault.

CHAPTER
13

JANE: Can you do me a HUGE favor
PLEASEOHPLEASEOHPLEASE?

ME: Don't be desperate.

JANE: Shush. Can you cover for the Jazz Night hostess?
I told Andrea I'd do it but Charles got Kinky Boots
tickets.

ME: You've seen Kinky Boots four times.

JANE: Not from the front row!

ME: Ugh.

JANE: Please? He goes back to LA tomorrow and it's
our last chance to hang out for a few weeks.

ME: FINE. But YOU have to bring me something to wear.

❖ · ❖

"Jane, you poo." I shiver, courtesy of the umpteenth draft I've caught this evening. The overzealous AC gusts by the hostess podium whenever someone opens or closes the front door. The dress Jane selected for me, the one from the Work It event, has my back exposed to the frigid current.

Icy blasts aside, I don't mind filling in. It's a hundred bucks cash for a few hours of work, and the entertainment is unbeatable. It's a blend of jazz, R & B, and a truly random assortment of contemporary hits. The modern songs are all performed with a soul-inspired twist, and I love hearing what each singer does with the material.

The show is in its last hour, and diners dance in the cramped space in front of the stage. It's the same band as the weekend shows, and Arthur shifts from one song to the next, seamlessly transitioning the end of Sam Cooke's "Cupid" into "I Put a Spell on You."

Ming is up.

I stray to the bar to watch her take the stage in a deep-blue evening gown. Like many performers, she can take on different roles at the club's shows: burlesque, host, or singer. She's no Jane, but the way she purrs, *"Because you're mine,"* transforms the lyrics into the most alluring threat.

Andrea is at the opposite end of the bar chatting with Michael. I still haven't asked her about the renovations. Jane nags me whenever he's home, though there's been less opportunity with his spending most evenings with Charles. Now I wonder if asking me to fill in for the hostess wasn't some ruse on his part. *Double poo.*

She catches my eye and raises a brow. I make a pitiful show of skulking back toward the hostess station, but Andrea shakes her head and pats the empty seat beside her. "Dinner service is over. Anyone else coming in can find the bar on their own. Care for a drink?"

"I'll take you up on that, thank you." I hop onto the offered stool.

Michael drapes himself over the bar, propping his chin in his hand. "What'll it be, kitty cat?"

"It *is* a weeknight. If I say 'velvet hammer,' does it give you any ideas?"

His eyes twinkle at the challenge. "Sweetie, I have a light rum that will do you right. Just a gentle tap on the noggin." He emphasizes "tap" with a mimed rap of his knuckles.

"I think you know I was offering you prosecco," Andrea mutters, but her mouth quirks as Michael gets to work.

"Better to ask forgiveness than permission?"

She cackles and takes a long drink off her martini. "You're a clever little thing, Kitten." She notes the back of my dress. "And gutsy. Good heavens, weren't you freezing at the podium? Standing there, you catch everything the AC can throw at you."

"You're telling me. And Jane brought the dress. His penance for roping me into covering for him."

"Ah, Michael said he was by earlier. That reminds me. Michael," she says as the bartender delivers my drink. "Fetch a Benjamin for Kitten, would you?"

I take a sip. The initial burn gives way to a sweet hint of coconut. "Michael, you're a genius." He shuts the cash register, handing me a stunning portrait of Mr. Franklin on linen. "Dangerous, but a genius." I tuck the bill under the band of my watch.

Andrea swirls her martini. "As relieved as I am anyone was available tonight, it would have been nice if it had been Jane. No offense, luv." She pats my hand. "Jane can also perform."

I take another sip. I didn't take offense in the first place, but the idea that I wouldn't be able to contribute more to the show rubs me the wrong way and nudges against a promise I made. I have more to offer.

"I . . ." My heart lodges in my throat. This may be my one opportunity to have a design realized. I know I have the strength to ask. I just need to use it.

My airway clears. "I want to talk to you about that."

Andrea's smile is knowing. "I wondered when you'd get around to this. You're the longest-running kitten we've had and the only one to ever content herself with the position." She flicks her attention toward the stage. "You want to get up with the big girls?"

"Not quite. What . . . what do you and Charles have planned for renovations?"

Her smile shifts to something more curious. "It will depend on the final number, whatever the purchase agreement is, though we have that pretty well hammered out. We've been looking at design firms. Astronomical, any of the ones worth a damn. A few haven't been interested in being involved with a venue with nudity, the *prigs*." She takes a drink. "Why do you ask?"

I shake my head; this would be better with a visual. "I don't have my file—"

Andrea eyes me over the rim of her glass. "Your *file*?"

"Of designs I've been working on. I have ideas I'd like you to consider for the renovation."

She crosses her arms, thin brows knitted together. "Do you have experience with interior design?"

"It's what I went to school for. I'm *good*," I say firmly. "I won an internship after I graduated, before I moved out here."

"Aren't you a receptionist by day?"

"Yeah," I admit. "Things got complicated with the internship. I—" I run out of steam. "Really complicated."

She snorts a laugh, revisiting her martini. "You find me one person without a complicated past and I'll show you someone who doesn't belong in New York." She tips her head. "I'd be delighted to take a look. No promises, mind you, but after the paperwork's been signed, you and I can have a sit-down with Charles, and we'll look at these designs of yours."

My jaw goes slack. *All I had to do was ask?*

Andrea laughs again. "You should see your face right now. You're looking half-soaked!"

I assume what she said is some Birmingham equivalent of "shocked dumb," because I'm at a loss for words. "Thank you?"

"I said I'd look and no promises. But if this is what suffices as good news for you, I'm happy to provide." She giggles. It's actually quite sinister, but for the moment, I can't think of anything I'd rather be hearing. "You're one of my girls, Kitten. It's the least I can do."

My heart thrashes in my rib cage, and when I raise my drink to take a sip, my hand is shaking. I asked. That was the first step. That's all it took, and I didn't have to go into any sordid details.

"Well, while I have you in such a light mood, perhaps you can tell me about this bloke the Twins are, I don't know . . . *seeing?*" Andrea asks. "Are they shagging him, you think? Both of them?"

I follow Andrea's gaze to a booth on the risers, where Wickham sits with the Twins. I was surprised to see *Wickham, 3* among the reservations when I came in earlier; I hadn't heard from him since Monday's drink. When their trio entered the restaurant, I almost laughed at the production. Wickham, in a black button-up shirt undone to the bottom of his sternum, looks like Jersey Zorro. Ginn and Tonic wear white . . . jumpsuits, maybe? Ginn's neckline competes with Wickham's. I can only imagine how much fashion tape is keeping her boobs in place.

"Who knows."

Andrea pats my hand again and rises from her stool, martini in tow. "Enjoy the rest of your evening. I have some numbers to look over. See you this weekend."

She makes her way toward her office back by the kitchen. When I finish my drink, I say good night to Michael, then swing by the trio on the risers. Wickham has his arms over the back of the banquette, Ginn tucked into one side of him, Tonic on the other. When I say good night, Tonic's brows go high, her mouth forming a hot-pink "O" of protest.

"So soon?" she asks.

"I have an early morning." It's technically true; nine would be early for anyone at this table. I'd be begging off regardless. While my interest in Wickham waned before their "arrangement" took off, I don't want to seem like a clinger.

Again, Tonic is the only one to respond with any degree of interest. "See you Saturday?" I nod. The farewell gesture gets a, "Later, Liz!" from Wickham, which, in turn, earns him a baffled frown from Ginn. Two-plus years working together, and it's possible she hasn't retained my real name.

I descend the short steps to the main dining area, pausing as I consider whether to change. My stuff is in the dressing room, but— my conversation with Andrea bubbles up again, and I smile. *I did it!* I asked her, and I'm getting a chance. Jane will be so proud of me. The thought of giving him a vicarious thrill makes me grin even more fiercely.

I give myself a shake and direct my attention to the couples dancing across from me. Some of the waitstaff dance among them, and Esteban sashays my way. I hold my hands up, warning him not to take on such a weak partner. He is undaunted, pulling me toward the floor.

"Look at you, Miss Smiley-Puss. Grinning all by your lonesome. Where are you running off to?" he asks, swaying his hips with finesse even Ming would envy.

"I have work in the morning."

"Psh. Day jobs. You need to go full vampire, like us." He channels a convincing Bela Lugosi, opening his arms to include the room. "Embrace the night!"

At my laugh, he drops one of my hands, holding the other high. He looks over my shoulder and grins. "I'm passing you off to someone *very* tasty," he whispers, maintaining the Romanian accent. "You can thank me later."

Esteban will flirt with peeling paint, so his assurances of tastiness mean nothing. He sets me twirling. I complete a full rotation before he releases me. A wobbly half turn later, I'm blindly accepting the hands of the supposedly tasty one. I'm struggling to stay upright when the hold at my waist pulls me in close. I gasp and brace my hands against broad shoulders, preparing to push away—

Only to find I've been spun right into the sturdy arms of Will Darcy.

For a moment, neither of us moves. We stand in a semi-embrace, his hands at my waist, my palms flattened high against his hard chest, and the music ends. As I grapple with whether I'm relieved or disappointed, the band starts another song, the piano dominating the first few bars. It takes me a moment to recognize the slowed-down version of Weezer's "Jacked Up."

Darcy glances at the hand resting above his heart. I watch in dull disbelief as he brings a hand up to cover it. His other hand edges to the center of my low back, palm and fingers pressing into bare skin. My pulse throbs. Tension melts from my shoulders as my awareness homes in on the soft heat of his hands. It's as though every nerve ending has relocated, shifted to ignite at the points of contact. I make a muddled vow to thank Jane for his impeccable choice in dresses.

We start to sway. He studies my face. Like always, I don't know what he's looking for, but as his dark eyes move over me, he can take as long as he'd like to find it. My eyes sting, informing me I'm staring, and I flutter my lids, not wanting to break the connection with a prolonged blink.

"You," I manage. "Why are . . ."

His Adam's apple bobs with a swallow. "Paperwork. For Charles."

I nod, though his response doesn't mean anything to me. Possibly because I'm transfixed by the way his mouth moves when he says "paperwork," the forward motion of his lips on the last syllable making me wonder what it would feel like if he said it against me, brushing his lips to the side of my neck. I inch closer, sliding my free hand to a more deliberate grip between his shoulder and neck. He closes his eyes, and when he opens them again, I swear his pupils have dilated.

I shake my head, woozy at the intensity. It's enough to rouse a prickle of irritation, the vague awareness that he's done something very, very wrong—

Darcy glides his thumb along my spine and the clarity is lost to a libidinous fog. His hand slides up between my shoulders, then down again. I arch into the caress without thinking, not that I'm able to do any thinking at the moment. My fingers curl reflexively, squeezing into the muscle of his shoulder beneath the soft chambray of his shirt.

"I . . ." *What was I going to say?*

Darcy lowers his head, his "Hmm?" tickling the side of my neck where his lips should be. He smells good. Clean, with a hint of some spice. I probably smell like rum. "What had you smiling earlier?" he asks.

A ripple passes through me. "An opportunity."

His "Hmm" is more thoughtful this time, but it makes me quiver just the same. "Whatever it is"—another languid swipe of his thumb—"I hope you find it fulfilling."

I'm about to thank him, but there's something else I should ask him about . . . *right?* I'm supposed to be mad at him, or, at least, not actively plotting to get him to put his mouth on my neck.

"I need to talk to you." I say it hoping to trigger whatever should follow. I sound dazed, even to myself, and I don't know why I was so sure a chat is in order when there are other things we could be doing instead. My fingers edge to his neck, tracing his hairline. The hand at my back presses more firmly. I let the gentle pressure guide me closer, and my next inhale has my chest brushing his.

His head dips lower. I hold my breath, angling my face toward him.

We definitely don't need to talk—

"What is he doing here?" He straightens, and the movement shifts a gust of air that matches the ice in his voice. His eyes are hard, fixed over my shoulder. *Oh, hell. Wickham.* My chest seizes. That shitshow is what was lodged in the depths of my brain. Damn sexy vibes had me sidelined.

Darcy's eyes meet mine again. His face softens some. "I'm sorry."

He skims his thumb along my spine, replacing my flash of indignation with ideas about where else his fingers might travel. "You want to talk, and I do, too, but Wickham . . ." The name settles like a stone in the pit of my stomach. "He's with your aerialists. Do you know him?" Darcy's tone thaws with another pass over my skin, his hand returning to the center of my back.

I don't turn to look at the party behind us; whether it's because I don't need to or because I don't want to create any separation between our bodies, I can't say. "He's friends with my boss." With some defiance, I add, "We've had drinks a few times."

Darcy takes in a breath. A thrill skitters through me. Is that— *jealousy?*

Do I care?

"You—" His lips press together, hand at my back tensing.

I do care. But I shouldn't. What Darcy did to Wickham was cruel. He disregarded his own father's final wishes to ruin the man, sent him fleeing across the country. Wickham may be a flake with exceptionally bad taste in going-out clothes, but no one deserves that. I know what that's like. It's taken me three years to get myself back on track, and my situation didn't have nearly as much baggage and history as what happened with these two. I keep that in the forefront of my mind, and push. "He has been unlucky to lose your friendship, it seems."

Darcy sneers. "He feed you the sob story? The poor urchin plays nursemaid to my father, then I come along and rip his dreams away?"

The callous comments twist my stomach into a tight knot. *Welcome back, Mr. Tolerable. It's been a while.* I drop the hand at his neck to his shoulder. "You've got the CliffsNotes version down."

His jaw sets. "Don't get in bed with him."

I pull back enough that his hand slides to my waist. "Ex*cuse* me?"

Darcy's eyes widen, the hand on mine pressing tight. "No! In business terms. Your boss, I hope, isn't bringing him on or investing with him, is he?"

I shake my head, still stinging at the earlier implication, though the mention of Toby makes me stay where I am. "Why?"

He sighs. "I wouldn't know where to start. Bennet—" My name comes out rough. "I need to speak to you as well. I—I can't right now." He sends another dark glance over my shoulder, then his attention returns to me. "Not now."

Disappointment and frustration grip my chest. Despite everything Wickham told me, I want to give in to the pull of this man. I want him to redeem himself. But there's no coming back from what he did.

"Why not?" I ask his lips.

"I'm sorry, I need to go." He releases me, taking a step back. But as my hand falls from his chest, he catches it, pressing my palm. "I'm sorry." His thumb glances over my pulse point. "I'm in California with Charles for the week, but I'll be back. And we'll talk. I promise."

He squeezes my hand again, and then he's gone, leaving a chill at every point where we shared contact.

CHAPTER
14

Ming pinches the extra material at my sides. "This good?"

I look in the full-length mirror. With the sides held by Ming, the dress hints at the potential I sensed at the vintage shop last week. The long-sleeved, shamrock-green mini was meant to fit and flare, which it'll do beautifully after Ming takes it in. Pearl buttons run down from the low V of the neckline to just below my belly button, revealing tiny peeks of skin between each fastener. The spaces are barely the width of a fingertip, but the neat dots of exposure push the dress to the spicy side of sweet.

I'm not exaggerating when I say, "Perfect."

"All right." Ming releases the right side and shifts to my left, plucking a straight pin from the (naturally) penis-shaped pincushion strapped to her wrist. "Prepare to be pinned."

"Ooh, Jane! Can you move the phone a little? I wanna see!" My cousin's voice comes out tinny from the phone's speaker.

Jane moves from his spot on the bed, where he's been lounging since commandeering my FaceTime session with Chloe to fill her in on the dream-turned-reality that is Charles Bingley. He points the back camera of my phone at the mirror, and Chloe squeals in delight.

"Ooh, looking good, Lizard. Ming, I know we haven't met yet, but let me just say, you are *skilled*."

"I know," says Ming, who starts pinning.

"So, Chloe, has Bennet told you *her* news?" Jane catches my eye in the mirror. I mouth for him to shut up, but he just grins. "She's getting back into the design game."

"*What?*" Chloe shrieks. "Jane, turn me around. Or switch cameras, whatever. I need to glare at Liz."

"Thanks so very much, Jane," I growl.

"Think of it as an insurance policy." He extends the PopSocket on my phone case, using it to nestle the phone in the space at the edge of my mirror. "The more people who know about your Meryton stuff, the more likely you are to actually go through with showing it off."

"I'm not going to flake," I say. "I want this."

"Lizard, I've been waiting three years for this! Tell me everything." On the screen, Chloe's at her vanity, working on a look for her upcoming shoots. Her bangs are pushed back in a headband, and since Jane stole my phone, she's made one eye up in a vibrant red ombre that covers the whole lid up to a thick, dark brow. "Meryton is where the burlesque show is, right?"

"Yes. But I haven't shown the powers that be anything yet," I clarify.

"Still, that's so great to hear," says Chloe. "I know what happened at the internship screwed with you. But I felt like you'd find your way back to it." She beams at me, and it's like a cross-country hug.

"Andrea said she and Charles would consider my work once the sale is final," I say. "There are no guarantees, but it feels really good to have even that sliver of a prospect out there."

"Speaking of *feeling good*." Ming prods me with the rounded end of a pin. "You going to tell everyone about the *other* highlight of that evening?"

I cut my eyes at her and she grins wickedly.

Chloe's brows peak. "Another highlight?"

"You made the most of the open back of that dress." Ming resumes her pinning. "Or, *he* did."

"Who is this now?" Jane asks.

Ming's dark eyes widen, her mouth going round in mock surprise. "Kitten, are you keeping secrets from our Sweet Jane?"

"I . . ." I clear my throat. The memory of Darcy's hands flares all over my back, but I chase it away, thinking of Wickham. "I don't know where I am with that."

"I can tell you where you *should* be with that. Somewhere horizontal and weight bearing. The two of you were radiating sex," Ming says.

"Weren't you downstairs?"

"I got a peek of the action. I thought he was going to stick his hand *into* the dress."

"That—" The idea of being close enough to Darcy for him to pull that off evicts any concern for poor, wronged Wickham.

We'd have to be pressed together fully, his hand sliding along my skin to edge beneath the dress, down to my waist . . .

I shiver.

"What did I just witness?" Jane asks in a high voice.

Chloe laughs. "I think I heard her ovulate."

"Shut up, all of you," I complain.

"Who is this even about? Wickham?" Jane ventures.

A cackle from Ming. "No offense to Kitten, but I think that guy is getting everything he 'needs' from the Twins." She tips her head, thoughtful. "Wasn't he the one you wanted a rush on that other dress for in the first place?"

I fiddle with one of the pearl buttons. "Yeah?"

"Interesting." She shifts to my opposite side, then points a pin at my reflection. "Aren't you supposed to be the 'stable' one in our sexy little family?"

"I never agreed to that. And yes, the dress was in case things got interesting with Wickham. He no-showed that night, I handed him off to the Twins, and now they're doing, I dunno, whatever it is they do with men."

"Ohmigod, the sexual intrigue of your world is too much for this old bride-to-be," Chloe submits. "I love it."

"It seems our beloved kitty cat," Ming continues with unnecessary gravitas, "has hooked her claws into a certain Mr. *Tolerable*."

"Darcy?" Jane sits upright on the edge of the bed, eyes narrowed but still smiling. "How dare you hold out on me!"

"*Fine.*" I sigh. "He came in—"

"That's right! Charles needed him to drop some paperwork off while he and I were out." He purses his lips. "I *meant* to ask if you played nicely."

Ming laughs, sordid as ever, but at Jane's mention of "paperwork" I'm back to imagining Darcy's lips forming the word against my neck . . . and everywhere else.

"Aah! She shivered again," Chloe hollers.

"Girl, I'm gonna have to sew cups into this thing if you're going to keep getting riled up," Ming warns. "You look like you're hiding pencil erasers up there."

I cross my arms over my chest, earning a poke from a straight pin. "We danced. It was . . ." I drop my arms to dislodge the pin. "Ming's right. It was very sexy and I liked what he did with his hands. But it's complicated—he and Wickham have a severely fucked-up history." I give the quick and dirty version of Wickham's claims about Pemberley and his relationship with Darcy's dad.

Ming grimaces. "That is some shady shit."

Jane shakes his head. "It doesn't make sense. Surely, they've both been deceived, in some way or another, gotten bad information from someone?" he says, as if the idea of such treachery is too foreign for his pure spirit to comprehend. I catch Ming's eye, and she smiles at our friend's unflappable good faith. "I'd hate to blame either of them if it's all some misunderstanding."

I laugh. "And now, Jane, please, tell me how we might forgive this mysterious third party with the 'bad information.' You'll have to clear them, too, or we'll be forced to think ill of somebody."

Jane ignores the snark. "But can you imagine how"—his brows lower as he searches for a word—"*disgraceful* it would be if Darcy truly treated someone who'd been so kind to his father in such a way? Someone he'd known all his life? No decent person would do that."

"Doesn't have to be decent to be worthy of lust." Ming places a reassuring hand on my shoulder. "You have my blessing to bone him anyway."

"Seconded," Chloe chimes.

"Thank you both," I say, deadpan. "I don't know. It's all jumbled.

And disappointing." I meet Jane's eyes in the mirror. "That night at Pemberley, he was charming and chatty and *flirty*—"

"Flirty?" Ming kneels to secure a pin at my waist. "He Who Could Not Be Tempted was *flirty*?"

I hold my hands up, mindful not to shift the dress.

"Do you think we could double-date?" Jane's question comes with an excited lilt.

"Don't you dare bring this up to Charles," I warn.

"I wonder if they've talked about it," he muses. "Darcy's with Charles in LA. Apparently he's considering a move back here, too."

Oh? According to Jane, Charles is looking into something permanent in Manhattan, a prospect that left Jane squirming in delight. But that Darcy might be sticking around, too . . .

"You going to be shivering again?" Ming points at my chest. "Warn me. You could put my eye out with those things."

I stick out my tongue.

"I could ask Charles about Wickham," Jane offers. "If you'd told me all this sooner I might have been able to find out before he left." A little light goes out of his eyes. "I suppose it wouldn't reflect well on Charles either," he says, voice low, "if he's friends with someone who could be so cruel."

I wince. I didn't consider that.

Jane's phone buzzes on the bed. His worry vanishes. "It's him," he announces, barely able to get the words out around his smile, and answers with a cool, "Hey, you." He waves goodbye to Chloe as he heads to his room.

I meet Ming's eyes in our reflection. She rolls hers. She hasn't brought up her "Jane needs to tone it down" theory since *Red, White, and Boobs*, but I have no doubt she's still thinking it.

"As exciting as your possible romantic developments are, I'm still swooning over the news that you're designing again," says Chloe. I look at the phone, and she's applying shadow to her other eye now. "I was preparing to have a come-to-Jesus over my visit."

"Why's that?"

She angles her head closer to the camera, filling the screen with her disapproving stare. "Liz, it's been three years of you working at that office and kittening. What exactly is the endgame?"

I glower at her. "Is my mom putting you up to this?"

"Genuine curiosity on my part."

"I don't know." I move to cross my arms but remember the pins and reconsider. "I could stick with Work It for . . . forever, I guess. And I like it. I'm good at it, and I'm useful. The pay is decent and I have insurance, plus it lets me do what I'd like with the show."

"And for the show, you're talking kittening, and now the design stuff?"

The *yes* is already on my tongue, but what comes out is, "Not quite."

Ming stops pinning. "Oh?"

"For the record, I am not about to abuse"—I point to my open bedroom door and Jane in his room beyond—"certain *connections*. But with a new owner, we could have more opportunities. I just keep thinking about the way you all had to scramble when the owner effed with scheduling last month."

"I remember Jane getting antsy about that. And there's something I don't get," says Chloe. "Why does the one location matter so much? Aren't there shows all over?"

"There are," says Ming. "And some other places pay a flat rate for performers, like Meryton, though no one else pays as well. For the majority of shows, what you make depends on audience turnout. I've hauled myself to Queens for a crowd smaller than the performance roster. I made less than my cab fare home."

"Ugh." Chloe's nose wrinkles. "That sucks."

"That's the hustle, baby. Unfortunately, that means spreading yourself all over the city." She gets back to the pins. "What do you have in mind, Kitten?"

"I don't know. But I feel like we're a wasted resource. Think about it: You're the most well-connected person in the scene. Everyone loves you—you could parlay that into some kind of managerial role, maybe? Or scouting new talent?"

Ming nods approvingly. "I do know the craft."

"It's worth thinking about. Something to give everyone more ownership. A way"—I think back to the office at Pemberley—"to take care of our own."

On the phone screen, Chloe nods, then frowns, turning slightly from the camera. "Gales?" she calls. The deep voice of her fiancé replies with something I can't make out before he fills the open doorway behind her.

Ming gasps as he approaches Chloe at the vanity. "Who is this thicc boi gracing the family exchange?"

Gales peers into the camera, confused, but Chloe pulls him in for a smooch on the cheek.

"Mine," she says. "And home early."

"That's our cue," I tell Ming. "Their schedules are brutal. They barely get to see one another."

"Aw, they're gonna do it," Ming coos. Gales's blue eyes threaten to bug out of his skull.

Chloe's laughter explodes from the phone. "Ming, I swear to God, when I get to New York, we're gonna be best friends."

"You'd be lucky to have me," Ming calls, and waves her goodbye.

"Hi and bye, Gales! We'll see you guys soon," I say, and tap the icon to end the chat.

We're quiet for a few minutes as Ming wraps up her pinning, the only sound the murmur of Jane's call in the other room punctuated by his bright laughter.

I think about that last turn in the conversation. The idea of taking care of my own, whatever that could mean, feels like an extension of designing for Meryton. When I first learned about the sale, sketching for the venue felt like a way to give back to the place. But it's not just the place, it's the people. *My* people. No matter the outcome of the sale, I want something stable for them.

Ming stands. "You're set. Change out of that and we'll make a decision about the cups after I take it in, n'kay, my little eraser smuggler?"

The allusion gets me thinking about Darcy's hands again. I didn't pay much attention to his fingers while we danced; I was too absorbed in how they felt. I imagine they're nimble and could make short work of these buttons . . .

Ming cackles. "Good *lord*, there you go again!"

CHAPTER

15

I pull myself up on the hold and the rope goes slack in front of me. I wait for Jane to pull my line taut, but it stays limp. The hand gripping the hot-pink skull-shaped hold starts to cramp, the muscles in my palm throbbing. "Take?" I call.

Nothing.

A higher foot placement lets me hook my elbow over the hold, and my fingers tingle with relief. I shake out my hand and peek over my shoulder to where Jane stands below me. His eyes are unfocused, hands slack on the rope that links us. I'm high enough on the wall to do some damage if he doesn't catch me.

"Jane, I can switch to an auto belay if you'd rather."

He blinks, shaking his head as he comes back to reality. "I'm sorry!" He feeds the line back quickly, taking up the slack so much my harness yanks at my thighs. I curl my arm more tightly around the hold to lessen the tug on my legs.

Jane sighs. "I'm sorry. It's—"

"I know," I assure him. "Just don't let me splat."

"I'm all yours."

I blow him a kiss and get back to the climb, jabbing my thumb into one of the skull's empty eye sockets to secure my grip. It's been weeks since I've come to the gym. The walls have been reset and my performance has been unimpressive. While I've gotten the rust off over the past hour, Pink Skull and his buddies are giving me more trouble than I'd like.

After a particularly graceless scramble, I get to the last hold and call to Jane again. "Take!"

"I've got you!" He tightens the rope. "You ready to come down?"

"Bring me home, baby."

"Go ahead."

I let go of the wall and descend, Jane smoothly feeding the line through his brake. When I reach the floor, I squat down for more slack, then straighten. "Off belay."

"You're off," he replies, and we release from the rope. "Sorry about earlier. That's such a no-no." He sighs. "I don't know why I'm letting this get to me. He's busy."

I nod, holding back what I know he's thinking: no one is too busy to send a text.

Saturday afternoon's call included a warning that Charles was going to be swamped for the coming days. Texts tapered off to nothing, with only a short check-in call on Sunday. Jane, being Jane, has taken it in stride, but after two days of silence I know it's weighing on him.

I try not to hold Charles's delinquency against him, but the man's inattention has derailed what started as a perfectly lovely week for Jane and me. After almost a month like two ships passing, we've finally had time to hang out together. Saturday's show was a blast, and I tagged along for Jane's after-hours performance with the band. We had brunch with Ming the next afternoon, where she theorized on the many ways that she suspected the Twins and Wickham enjoyed one of the bathrooms during Saturday's set break. Technically, it was only one theory with several interpretations on positioning, but she was thorough. And foul. Jane and I bought mimosas for the tables within earshot. At $3 a pop, we figured it was the least we could do for folks unprepared to wrap their weekend with the phrase "nightmarishly elastic" attributed to a human's pelvic region.

Evenings, I spent any free time working on my designs, with Jane giving input over episodes of *Drag Race*. But last night, when Charles missed their tentative phone date, Jane switched from Mama Ru to documentaries, getting in two episodes of *Blue Planet* before turning in. I'm trying not to read into it, but the slip into informational viewing sets off warning bells. Jane was deep-diving nature programming when I moved in. He was at the *River Monsters* stage of depression when I tasked him with showing me around Manhattan. I proposed climbing tonight to take his mind off things, but after his belay fail, I'm wishing I'd come up with a lower-risk activity.

Jane flexes his chalk-dusty fingers. The joints crackle and snap. "I think I'm done climbing. I'll still belay if you'd like."

I shake my head. "I'm pumpy." I turn over my forearms. They're swollen from the hour of climbing; my veins stick out like a mountain range on a topographical map. "I'm going to switch to bouldering till I burn out. Will you call out holds?"

Jane rolls his eyes. "You know you don't need me."

He's right. I rarely ask for input on routes. But I brought him to get him out of his head. I let my lip wobble.

He smiles. "Fine. You big baby."

We take off our harnesses and stash them in the cubbies in the benches flanking the bouldering area, then take a seat to wait for a space to free up. A buzzing rattles the bench. Jane's hand darts to his back pocket. I cross my fingers it's something from Charles, but my watch vibrates with an incoming message a second later. It's Andrea, to both me and Jane: an invitation to cover the door at Jazz Night. Jane's shoulders fall.

He slides his phone back into his pocket. "Mind if I take it?"

"She'd rather have you, anyway," I say, standing as a problem on the wall opens up. I grimace as I approach. *Yeesh.* The route starts with a brutal overhang. But the footholds are placed well; success will rest on whether my grip can last. I sit down at the base, flexing my fingers with an unsettling crack.

Behind me, Jane lets out a gasp.

"Have a little faith," I complain, and place my feet, reaching for the well-worn holds above eye level. Instinctively, I angle my body in and pull myself toward the wall—*sweetbabyjesus,* my forearms are on *fire!*

With a grunt, I get my body clear of the inversion. *Yes!* I secure my feet, pushing myself up higher—

"Sorry I was too chicken-shit to call," says Jane, his voice dull.

"What's that?" My hand trembles with the effort as I reach for the jug hold above me.

"The message I received from Charles," he says, barely audible.

"Wait, what?" Cold prickles up my spine. "*Charles?*"

"He says he's sorry." Jane's voice is choked. "And that it's over."

The two words jolt through me. "*What?*" My hands give out and

I drop from the wall, landing in a stumbling crouch. I shake it off and jog over the padded floor to Jane.

He holds up his phone, showing me the screen. "What do I do?"

"I—I don't know. What—" I take the offered phone and read the text in full: I'm sorry. It's over. Things are too complicated right now. Sorry I was too chicken-shit to call.

My heart gives a painful squeeze. Jane's breathing has gone shallow. He shakes his head, not blinking. "What . . . what did I do?" His voice is tortuously thin.

I hand back the phone. "Jane, no—"

He stands, looking side to side as if disoriented. "I'm going to go."

"I'm right with you." I move to grab our things.

"*No.*"

I pivot back so fast the grippy soles of my climbing shoes cling to the floor. I steady myself with a hand on the bench. "Jane?"

His lower lip trembles. He's blinking rapidly now. The silent struggle breaks my heart. "Thank you." He takes in a long breath. "But I need a minute. I'll be home later."

"You're sure—"

"*Please.*" The word rasps out of him. He presses his fingertips to his lips before holding his hand to his chest. "Please." His voice is steady, but his eyes plead with me.

I ache to give him a hug, to say something more—Jane's desperate expression warns me off. I don't like it, but I understand; with a hurt this fresh, I'd break down if anyone was remotely nice to me. After another moment, I gesture to the cubbies. "I'll grab your stuff. You . . . do what you need."

His lips pull in tight and he nods, then pads to the exit. I watch him slip on his street shoes, then he reaches for the fedora hanging from a peg by the door. It's one of the hats Charles bought for him after the accident.

Jane's hand hovers for a moment, then drops. Seconds pass, and his shoulders rise and fall with a long breath. He walks out. The hat stays.

➤ · ➤

At home, I put away our climbing gear and stash the abandoned fedora in my closet. I couldn't leave it behind. Jane looks great in it; Charles doesn't get to take that from him.

I lug my Meryton design folder to bed to look through while I prepare to wait up. Turning through the pages, the drawings barely register as I think about Jane. What was that text? *Sorry I was too chicken-shit to call?* Sure, Charles's very essence screamed "nonconfrontational," but dumping someone in a text? That's not cowardly. That's *cruel*—

Like what Darcy did to Wickham.

I drop my head against the pillows. To think, Jane fretted about Charles's being friends with someone who could treat a person so shamefully, and all the while Charles had it in himself to do the same.

My eyes drift over the designs on my lap. What might this mean for the Meryton sale? The thought twists my gut, sending me back to Andrea's tasteless comments at brunch last month. While I hate to think in those terms, a lot of people's livelihoods are potentially on the line with that deal. Not to mention what the sale has come to mean for me.

The prospect of sitting across from Charles, sharing my ideas with him, turns my stomach further. Would it be disloyal to Jane? If the sale goes through, will Jane stay at the club with Charles at the helm? We never see the current owner, so there's no reason to assume Charles would have any kind of presence, but still . . .

The door grinds with the turning of Jane's key, followed by the scrape over the doormat. The keys jangle as Jane hangs them on the hook in the hall, and his heavy footsteps make their way toward my room. I sit up against the headboard, closing the folder and putting it aside.

Jane trudges in, toeing off his shoes as he crosses the threshold into my room, not bothering to avoid the squeaky floorboard. I search his face to try to get a read on his feelings. All I see is the deliberate, flat look that greeted me the day I moved in three years ago. The familiar expression is worse than tears.

Without a word, he crosses to my bed and lies beside me, resting his head on my shoulder. I kiss the top of his head, a few inches away from the still-pink scar left by the accident, then rest my cheek against the spot.

I don't know how this happened, but I'll be damned if I don't get to the bottom of it.

CHAPTER
◆ 16 ◆

I keep track of Jane's viewing habits on our various streaming accounts from my work computer. In the days that follow Charles's text, he mainlines Werner Herzog's entire catalog before consuming the David Attenborough–narrated version of *Planet Earth*. I let that go without comment. When he starts re-viewing the same program with Sigourney Weaver's voice-over, however, I threaten to change all our passwords and recruit Ming to take him out for coffee.

Over the weekend, I learn more than I'd like about the use of bovine bile to control the spread of coral-eating starfish, but I'm cautiously optimistic. He performs at Meryton and, on Sunday, tears himself away from the Discovery Channel to help research a few ramen places for next week's visit from my cousin. By the time Monday rolls around, Jane's entertainment selections still favor the informative variety, but he's getting out of the apartment for more than just work, has come climbing with me twice, and ventures up to Manhattan to join Ming and me for lunch on Wednesday.

"I'll forget him," Jane announces, placing his napkin beside his plate. "Everything will go back to the way it was before."

I say nothing, but I'm helpless against the incredulous look that draws across my face.

"You doubt me," he says tightly. "Don't. I may think of him as the most pleasant man I've ever met, but that's all. I'm not going to be bitter about it. With a little time . . ."

His voice becomes strained, and he nudges at his side salad with his fork. Ming kicks me under the table. Jane clears his throat, sitting straighter in his chair. "At least I know it was an error of fancy on my side, and it has done no harm to anyone other than myself."

"Really?" I say. "Because the only thing that's keeping me from wanting to throttle him is the prospect that he's miserable, too." Ming raises her glass in solidarity.

Jane purses his lips. "It's not as though he *meant* to hurt me."

I scowl. Usually, Jane's insistence on universal goodwill is endearing. On this occasion, I cannot abide it. "He may not have *meant* to hurt you, but he still *did*. I'm holding it against him."

Jane's neutral expression wavers, and I hate myself for letting my pettiness show, even if it's in his defense.

I settle into my seat with an overwrought huff. "And I'm going to end up saying something shitty about him and then you'll be offended that I've spoken ill of someone you're determined not to hate because you're a goddamn angel and none of us deserve you, so you should probably tell me to shut up while you can."

Ming chuckles. Jane smiles, and it's the first real smile I've seen from him since last Tuesday.

"I love you," he reminds me. I blow him a kiss.

Jane is teaching a piano lesson in Chelsea after lunch, and we part ways outside the restaurant. Ming links arms with me as we watch Jane's retreating form. He's walking tall, but his stride has none of its usual pep. "You believe all that 'forget him' business?"

"I believe it's what he wants, but he's still watching the Discovery Channel. It isn't like what happened with Marcus," I assure her, and we turn to stroll toward the subway. "I'm not worried or anything. He's . . . disappointed?" It seems like the closest fit but doesn't quite cover the scene I've been coming home to. "Disappointed and hurt."

Ming shakes her head. "So shitty. And weird. Charles didn't seem the type to bail."

"I know, right?"

She slows to a halt, and we step aside to let other pedestrians pass. "You didn't tell Jane what I said about them, did you? That he needed to be careful about how excited he was?"

"God, no! That would hardly help."

"Good. I . . ." She grits her teeth. "I feel guilty suggesting that Jane might be even partially responsible for this, but if Charles got wind of the sugar-daddy bullshit—"

"Ugh. Maybe?" I try to remember the last time I heard Andrea spout off with that gross turn of phrase. Even if he did hear, it wouldn't be like Charles to take that sort of thing seriously. Then again, I didn't think he could be cruel or cowardly either.

"With Charles out of the picture," says Ming, walking again, "have you had any word from Mr. Tall, Dark, and Fuckable?"

"That's a good one. But no. At this point, I don't even know if I'm going to see the guy again."

"Boo," she jeers. "You should have at least gotten the chance to knock boots once, get him out of your system."

I don't reply. The boots-knocking is appealing, but Darcy has gained traction in my mind; I don't know that a quick roll could dislodge him. While New York isn't struggling for tall-dark-and-fuckables, since I've cleared my social calendar to be around for Jane, Will Darcy has gained legendary status in my subconscious. I've started more emails to his Pemberley account than I can number but never get past the subject line. Where do I start? *WTF is wrong with your best friend? Wickham, Pemberley, and unforgivable heartbreak? Re: Your mouth and the many words I'd like to feel it say against every square inch of me?*

"You still drawing, at least?" she presses. "If Chicken-Shit Charlie has ruined your chances with his buddy, he'd better not eff up the rest of your life."

"I'm still drawing." Jane's insisted that I not back out of working with Charles. I appreciate that he doesn't want me to miss out on the opportunity, but the prospect makes me feel like a jerk. I'm happy with my progress on Meryton, but whenever my thoughts stray to Darcy, my design work inevitably drifts to Pemberley. I even created a new file for the material. I've lost hours to sketching and have to shut the file in my desk to force myself to focus on Meryton. "I need to be careful, though. Last night, Jane was streaming *March of the Penguins*. I almost converted an entire concept to a solely black and white palette."

"Stark," she muses. "But glam. My red number would be fine as hell in that setup."

We arrive at the subway entrance at Bleecker. Ming squeezes my arm before releasing me. "Let me know if there's anything I can do for Jane. I'm good for lunch anytime."

"Sure. And thank you." I lean against the green railing around the subway entrance, then consider what gunk might be on it and straighten. "How might all this affect you?" I ask. "Meryton's sale, if things fall apart there."

Ming winces. "I'm scheduled with *Red, White, and Boobs* for the foreseeable future, but Darlene's so busy helping her brother with the bar, it's only one show every few weeks. Momma Fatima—do you know her? Drag queen out in Astoria? She's getting a show started. She's a great host, and there's potential there, but you know how it is." She shrugs. "Meryton is the most consistent gig in town."

I nod, frowning.

"You did get me started thinking about other applications for my skills, though, when we were talking to your cousin. I would be an amazing talent scout." She twirls the length of her ponytail around her index finger. "Worth exploring, anyway."

She's quiet for a moment, expression thoughtful. Then she tosses her hair over her shoulder. "Anyway. We'll see. But I should be done with the green dress in the next day or so."

"Let me know when you'd like to do the exchange and I'll have you eating like royalty."

"How's Friday? I can bring the dress by your office."

"Absolutely!" I say, excited by both the dress and having something to distract me from the all-consuming trifecta of Jane, Meryton, and Darcy. "Friday will be perfect. The rest of the staff is going to be out, for team-building, so it'll just be you and me. I'll make you a fancy coffee."

"Ooh la la!"

"Same menu as last time?" I ask.

"If it ain't broke . . ." She twinkles her fingers and descends to her train.

✦ · ✦

A few hours later, I'm at the intersection closest to my building, grandma cart loaded with my haul from Associated Supermarkets. A flash of red hair across the street catches my eye. Beside the door to the apartment lobby stand Ginn, Tonic, and Wickham. As I wait for the walk signal, I watch the trio, the girls' heads in close as Wickham says something.

Ginn spots me when I reach the curb. "Hey, Kitten!" she hollers. Tonic and Wickham start. Wickham recovers with a rakish grin. Tonic chews at her thumbnail.

"Hey." I push the cart their way. "What are you doing in this neck of the woods?"

"We wanted to see how Jane is." Ginn pushes her glossy lower lip forward in sympathy. Word got out about the breakup last weekend, when Esteban asked Jane if "Thor" was going to be in attendance. "Maybe take him out. I guess he's not in?"

The thoughtful gesture tugs at my chest a bit. "No, he had lessons all afternoon, but he should be back in the next twenty or so."

Ginn looks to Wickham, who shrugs, making his puffer vest crinkle. Tonic picks at her fingernails. No one says anything. And they're still in front of the door.

I raise an eyebrow. "Do you want to come up and wait?"

"Sure!" Ginn steps closer to the door.

Wickham and Tonic move my way. "Can I help with that?" Wickham reaches for my cart. I hand it over gratefully. Park Slope is aptly named, and the incline from the grocery store is killer on the days I'm prepping to cook for Ming.

"Thanks." I remove a bag to lighten the load, and Tonic takes it off my hands. I unlock the outside door, and we cram into the vestibule, through the interior door, and into the lobby. Wickham balks at the stairs, glancing at the cart.

"I'll get the wheel end if you don't mind walking backward," I offer. He gives me a thumbs-up, then guides the cart to the bottom stair. I get ahold of the base, and we start the trek, finding a groove after a few precarious steps.

Wickham nods at the cart. "This is a lot of food for two people."

"Closer to three. I have an exchange with Ming."

"An exchange?"

"For services rendered." I shift my grip, my recent return to climbing making my forearms complain under the weight of the cart. "The Twins do it, too. Ming's our go-to seamstress, and I pay her back by cleaning or doing meal prep. But when I cook for her, I get in portions for Jane and me, too."

"What's on the menu?"

"All stuff that can be frozen. Mostly mains and proteins. Getting Ming to eat her vegetables is an exercise in futility—she's like a four-year-old."

"Any way I can get in on this meal planning?" he asks, and wiggles his eyebrows.

I stop myself before I make a joke about whatever "services" he thinks he can provide in exchange. "So are things going well with that venture you mentioned? And the family thing?"

"I have a few irons in the fire."

I think of Darcy's warning, the question about my boss and Wickham. "You helping expand Toby's empire?"

"Toby has enough going on for now," he says, managing a shrug he probably regrets when it throws off his balance with the cart. "Work It is already coast-to-coast, though if I'd reached out sooner, I might have been able to offer Toby some guidance."

While I'm glad to hear he's not involving himself with anything Work It related, I bristle that Wickham thinks he could have swept in and done better than my boss did. Toby might be a goob, but he knows what he's doing.

Wickham hauls the cart onto the final landing. "I've had some inspiration lately. If I can get it together by the end of the month, I'll be money."

"Big month for a lot of people," I say, thinking of the Meryton sale and whatever it might mean for me. "Best of luck. And thanks for the assist."

Ginn and Tonic are at the door, Ginn leaning against the wall with her arms crossed, Tonic beside her, the grocery bag at her feet. She's picking at her nails again. I unlock the door and push it open, and Wickham reaches in over my head to hold it as I tug the cart in.

"Make yourselves at home." I tote the cart to the kitchen. "You want beer or wine?" I scan the counter, then remember the wine ended up in my room last night. I bailed on *March of the Penguins* about thirty minutes in and paired my time on the Meryton file with a tasty cabernet.

I turn and almost smack into Tonic, who holds out the bag she carried in. "Thanks." I place it on the counter. "That wine is in my room. Do you mind getting it while I start putting things away? It should be on the desk." Tonic nods, turning to go.

"I'll get it!" Wickham offers, appearing in the doorway with Ginn, and Tonic halts.

"On the desk," I repeat. He gives me a thumbs-up, disappearing down the hall.

Tonic watches him go, then leans in the doorway next to Ginn. "How *is* Jane?"

"Better," I say. "It's really sweet of you to offer to take him out."

Tonic sends a quick glance to Ginn, who doesn't return it, already walking toward Jane's room. Tonic's shoulders drop, and she chews at her index finger.

I wonder if Wickham has disturbed their dynamic. "You all right?"

Tonic flinches, then gives me an emphatic nod. "Yeah, totally. Just, um, thinking about Jane."

While I'm not sure I believe her, I nod and fetch a pair of wine-glasses from the cabinet. I point toward the sink. "The other two are on the drying rack," I say, then frown. "What is taking him so long on that wine? *Wickham*," I holler, and scoot past Tonic. "You get lost in here?"

"Sorry!" Wickham stands beside my desk, giving me a guilty smile. "I didn't get to take in the decor when I was in here last time. Your design skills are no joke."

I hug my arms, though I appreciate the praise.

Wickham leans in, checking out some family photos above my desk, but his eyes keep darting to the surface, then over to me. He laughs. "I'm sorry—" He holds up the five-by-seven of the pic from the Four of Clubs. It's officially become my bookmark for the Meryton file, which is open to the page I was looking over before I left for work this morning. "It's such an amazing shot."

I laugh, inured to any potential embarrassment at his seeing it.

"Thank you. It was a fluke, but I'm happy with it. Have you seen the one Ginn and Tonic took?"

"Ginn has a poster-sized version in her entryway."

"Just her?" I ask. "They don't live together?"

"Tonic lives with an aunt in the Seaport." He places the picture back on the stack of pages, tapping it absently before looking at me with a flat smile. "Has Darcy seen it?"

I grip my arms more tightly. "He bought a deck the first night he came in. Or, Charles did and had Darcy pay."

Wickham chuckles. There's an edge in it I don't like.

He settles against my desk. "Charles Bingley. I never understood his loyalty to Darcy. He worships Will. A total 'jump, how high' situation. It's almost embarrassing. Though it's probably why Will is so protective of him." His lips pull in sympathetically and his demeanor softens. "This stuff with your roommate is really screwed up. The Twins said Charles and Jane seemed legit."

I relax my arms a bit. "I thought so, too."

He scrubs his chin, leaning more of his weight against the desk. "Charles was always the friendlier of the two—more thoughtful. I wonder what changed. Maybe Will's influence." He rests his hands on the writing surface. "Though you were getting pretty friendly with ol' Darcy the other night."

The challenge in his tone makes my stomach curdle. "Excuse me?"

Wickham's smile evaporates, a muscle twitching in his jaw. He taps the desktop, fingers rapping tunelessly against the dark wood.

I blink. What the hell happened to the easygoing flake I had drinks with? "I know you two have a history—"

"Did Will say something about me?" The sharp question is more an accusation than an inquiry.

Or is it an admission? "Is there something to tell?"

Wickham's jaw goes tight. "He's not who you think he is," he says, as though I have even half a handle on what to expect from Will Darcy. "That man will do or say anything to protect what he values."

The comment lands hard, though I doubt my interpretation is what he wants me to get out of it. "Did you mean to imply that he values *me*, or is there something else you wanted to put across?"

He watches me for a moment, his gaze less severe, more assessing. "No." His voice is cool. "Though you've made a few things easier than they might have been before."

I throw up my hands. Does something happen when you spend your adulthood bouncing between the coasts? Because neither Darcy nor Wickham seems capable of a singular personality. "I don't know what you want me to say, Wickham. He said not to go into business with you. Unless you intend to poach me from Toby, I'd say the advice doesn't apply."

The cool mirth drops from him. He tips his head, eyes narrowing. I wait him out. I'm done with this. The Twins are acting weird, Wickham has turned into another person entirely, and I just want to turn on a movie and get started on Ming's meals. But the silence stretches on. What the hell does he want?

"Girls!" he calls. His smirk is back in place. "Let's head out."

Tonic appears in the doorway. "Weren't we waiting to see Jane?"

"Bennet said he's fine. Ginn," he says to the redhead, who has stepped in behind Tonic, "don't you two have a practice space reserved for six?"

Tonic's brow furrows, and Ginn drapes a hand over her partner's shoulder.

"That's right! Totally forgot about it. I got us in this morning.

Didn't I tell you?" Ginn looks at me. "Give Jane our best, though?" Her tone is too saccharine to be sincere.

I give her a tight smile. "Will do."

Ginn walks out and Wickham follows. Tonic lingers in the door-way. Her brow is still creased, and she holds her hands in to her chest, pressing back the cuticles of her right hand, one by one.

"Tonic?" I ask.

"I'm sorry," she blurts, taking a step back. "Tell Jane. I'm really, really sorry, Kitten."

I nod slowly. "Sure, I'll pass it along."

Her gaze is fixed on the floor between us. "I'll see you this weekend."

"I'll be there." I eye her. "Are you sure you're okay?"

"To-nic!" Ginn singsongs from the other side of the apartment. The front door scrapes over the mat. "Let's go!"

"I'll see you." Tonic darts down the hallway. I follow, catching sight of her in time to see her step out after Ginn. Wickham holds the door for the girls, then saunters to the opening with a tip of an imagi-nary cap my way.

"Ms. Bennet, thank you for your generous hospitality." The door shuts behind him.

I stare at where he was standing. What in the hell just happened?

CHAPTER
17

Friday afternoon, I relay Wickham's visit with the Twins to Ming.

She wrinkles her nose. "What's that all about?" she asks, and takes a sip of her latte.

We're in the break room at Work It, enjoying having the floor to ourselves while the rest of the staff is upstate. Toby's been traveling to check in with the new offices and asked me to organize a team-building day to make sure morale at HQ didn't fall off. It was sweet, like a new baby has arrived and Dad's taking the family dogs on special walkies so they don't feel neglected. I volunteered to stay behind and man the office in exchange for time off when my cousin visits.

"And for Tonic to be so skittish? I guess she's the more quiet of the two, though they're pretty evenly matched." Ming frowns. "This guy have a personality-zapping dick?"

I turn to catch my profile in the full-length mirror I brought in from the ladies' room. "I don't know what he *has*. However, I'd submit he *is* a dick of some kind."

Ming places her cup and saucer beside her on the counter. "Any aspirations for this dress, or are you going to put it out there and see what it reels in?"

"It's amazing, Ming. Truly." I sway side to side, letting it flare. The bodice fits like a second skin, highlighting the tiny gaps between the pearl buttons. It treads the line between sweet and saucy, leaning just enough in the direction of the latter I'll have to seriously consider where I show it off. I twirl a full 360 degrees, the draft created by my skirt giving me the shivers. The sensation continues after I stop, though. I check my profile again and see that the hem is caught on the right back fastener of my hold-ups, exposing my leg from just below my butt cheek.

I angle my backside toward Ming. "Any thoughts on how to avoid this?"

"Why would you want to? Look at that little tush. I wanna take a bite out of it." She gnashes her teeth, making grabby motions with her hands. "Also, I love that you're wearing a garter belt to your day job."

I peek at the clip keeping the thigh-high stocking in place. I don't generally wear them here, but it was cool enough to justify hosiery today. Plus, there's something fun about sneaking a feature of my Kitten persona into the office, even if I'm the only one who knows I've done it.

"What?" I bend over my leg, then straighten, trailing my palms from ankle to knee. I run a hand along my thigh, smoothing up my hamstring before dancing my fingertips over the top of the stocking. "These old things?" My sultry voice borders on cartoonish.

Ming snorts in a laugh, then releases a cackle that has her whole body shaking. "Hey, good-lookin'!"

I shimmy my hips, while Ming blots her eyes, still laughing. "Oh, no—not *you*." She nods to something—my chest seizes; *someone?*—behind me. "*Him*."

I cringe. *Welp, at least I could give the FedEx guy a thrill as well as my signature.*

I pivot the mirror to get a view of the door.

Oh. My. God. In the doorway stands none other than William Darcy.

I get a kick of that same high and low I've been feeling whenever I think of him: a swell of desire tinged with regret that I have to hate him for being friends with someone who hurt Jane, and for what he himself did to Wickham. His unexpected appearance sends the desire into overdrive.

The suit isn't helping. The not-quite-navy he's wearing is so impeccably cut, it's as though the jacket and trousers have been printed onto him. That upper-arm muscle I found so compelling in his rowing photo is obvious, like he's clenched tight—a possibility that does nothing to alleviate the revving in my nethers.

I take a breath and try to school my features into something resembling neutral. But based on Darcy's reflection, my face is not a priority; his focus is much lower. Warmth washes over me, and I free my hem with a quick tug. Darcy's eyes follow the movement as the skirt falls into place.

I spin to face him. "Darcy! What brings you here?"

"Sorry to interrupt, I—" He falters, blinking rapidly, before his eyes snap to mine. "I'm sorry. Where is everyone?"

I check my watch. "Doing trust falls in Rochester? The staff's at a team-building workshop. I stayed to man the fort."

He nods, then looks past me to Ming. She slithers from her perch on the counter and prowls toward him, her ruby smile nothing short of wicked. Darcy has the good sense to look worried.

"Kitten and I had some business to catch up on." She stops beside him. "Goods exchanged for services rendered."

Darcy's worry shifts to confusion. "Goods and services?"

"She's my go-to seamstress." I gesture at my dress. "I repay her by doing her meal prep."

Ming grins, tipping her head my way. "What do you think?" She crosses her arms over her chest, readjusting to tap her chin, as though she really is mulling over her handiwork. "I'm happy with the bodice." She points to my chest, demanding Darcy send his attention there. He offers no resistance, and I pray to the god of pencil erasers I can suppress any oncoming shiver, because Ming did not add cups. "I'm thinking I can do more to build in support up top, y'know?"

Darcy's forehead creases, eyes narrowed in study. "Suppor—"

" 'Cause she's not wearing a bra now, and I think—"

"*Ming!*" I warn.

Darcy's cheeks take on a hint of pink. "I'll defer to your professional opinion, Ms. DyNasty. I—" He pats at his breast pocket, then frowns. "I'm sorry. I knew I'd be in the area today so I planned to stop by with the refund on your deposit for the party, but I left Pemberley without the check."

Oh. So much for wanting to talk, too. Then again, with Ming practically circling him, this is hardly the time to bring up Charles and Jane. Or Wickham. Or to ask after his general dexterity with buttons. *Would you describe your fingers as* nimble, *Darcy?*

I wait for him to continue. He only stands there radiating discomfort. End of transmission. "Should I come pick it up instead?"

"I think that'd be best."

"No problem. I—"

"Or . . . no."

"You wanna give me a heads-up when you decide?"

He shakes his head. "This was my fault. I won't ask you to go across town for it. Would you be available to meet after work?"

"Sure." I extend the word on a laugh. "Are you okay, Darcy? You seem out of sorts."

"No, no, not at all," he says, the assurance rushed and not even slightly convincing. He proposes a bar around the corner, and we arrange to meet at five. "I'll even bring the check this time. Sorry for the inconvenience. And the interruption." He nods, the gesture oddly close to a bow, and heads out.

I watch his retreat, following his blurry outline on the opposite side of the frosted glass separating the break room from reception.

Ming stands beside me. "I think we're seeing some signs of temptation."

I nod, biting my lower lip. There's zero reason why he had to be the one to bring by the check. He could have sent Marley or a courier, or handled it digitally. And now we're having drinks . . .

Ming flicks the side of my boob hard enough that I yelp. I cradle the assaulted breast. "Dickhead!"

She cackles. "I'm definitely putting cups in that. Later, though. If you don't wear this out with him, you don't deserve it anyway."

When I get to the bar, I order a reposado, hoping that the burn will numb the guilt gnawing at my insides. Since Darcy left the office, I grappled with the decision to tell Jane about the rendezvous. Eventually, I elected not to. This is merely a business meeting taking place in a social setting. The check will be the priority.

And when that three-second transaction is complete, I'll grill him about Charles.

And Wickham.

Darcy appears just as the sting from the first sip of reposado subsides. "Good evening." His entire aspect is more at ease than it was at the office: broad smile, no tie, and when he hangs his jacket on the back of his chair, his sleeves are rolled up in that casual, appealing way. "How was the rest of your afternoon?"

"Fine," I say, watching him settle into his seat. The man seems perfectly content—a far cry from the anxiety ball he was at Work It. The bizarre contrast is enough to sideline my interrogation plan. "What was with you earlier? You seemed . . . off," I say, unsure how else to describe his behavior.

"A few things." The slow spread of his smile makes my thighs clench, and I submit an order to all erectile tissue to stand down. "I still can't believe I forgot the damn check. I guess I was distracted by the possibility of seeing you."

The admission is kindling to my libido, reigniting the blaze from a very sexy daydream I crafted after Ming left. A throwback to those imagined grovel sessions after I first met Darcy, updated to incorporate Toby's standing desk, adjusted to achieve the ideal height.

Rational thought cuts in like a bucket of cold water. Obviously, the "distraction" was because of Jane and Charles. I push the desk scenario aside.

"Then you had the issue with your dress and the—garter belt?" he asks.

I nod at the proper terminology while my neck warms at the reference.

"Yes." He smiles again. "That was . . . quite a sight to walk in on."

I arch a brow, unsure how to interpret this exceptional display of candor. However enjoyable my imagined desk-inclusive trysts, he's still Darcy. Prior to this afternoon, the last time I saw the man, he rushed out of Meryton after all but confirming the worst Wickham had said about him. That was more than two weeks ago, and he's made no effort to reach out since.

"You've seen me in less. *Way* less," I remind him, curling around the yellowing bruise on my ego.

"This was different. *Context*, as you put it. Seeing you like that in a break room on a Friday afternoon was . . . surprising."

I'm tempted to suggest we arrange to make seeing me in my garter belt on a Friday afternoon a little more commonplace, but instead I ask, "And is this unexpected peek of my gams so disorienting?"

"Knowing what you're wearing under that dress is disorienting." His voice is rough.

I forget to breathe. His eyes stay on mine, and I go on autopilot, covering with an old standby. "All in a day's work."

The intensity leaves his eyes, taking the heat and my confidence with it. It's like the dimming I saw when I evaded his design question at Pemberley, but worse. Lights out.

He nods toward my glass. "I'm going to get a drink," he says, voice flat. "You want anything else or are you okay?"

A dull heaviness settles in my chest, but I keep my face neutral. "I'm set, thanks."

He stands, then pats at the pockets of his trousers, first producing his phone, which he places on the table, then a folded check. He pushes it my way. "Lest I forget. *Again.*"

I stare after him as he strolls to the bar. *What the hell was that?* This guy turns on and off like there's a switch somewhere. I make a comment even remotely like something from the show, and it's lights out.

Darcy leans into the bar as he waits for the bartender, his closed-off expression lingering in profile. He looks my way, and I let him catch me watching. It goes against every lesson Ming ever gave on teasing, but I force myself to hold his gaze well beyond what would be considered cool or seductive. He smiles, glancing away again. Lights on.

My heart thunders. A one-and-done with him isn't going to be nearly enough to shake whatever's going on here. There's evidence enough of mutual attraction; even the time we got into it at *Red, White, and Boobs* was kind of hot. But every experience comes with an equal and opposite counter—Newton's Law of Flirtation and Repellence.

I want the lights-on Darcy, not the dour, dull grump-fest he switches into. Not the Darcy who's friends with someone who hurt Jane, and certainly not the man who ruined a childhood friend.

I pluck the folded check from the tabletop and tuck it into my purse, still trying to parse all this. The phone on the table buzzes and my hand goes to it instinctively. I turn it over, realizing it's Darcy's when I see Charles Bingley as the sender of the incoming message. I start to put it down—

CB: I'm getting weak. I need you to keep me from caving.

My stomach twists into a tight knot. *Jane.* It has to be about Jane. The phone buzzes again: I miss him.

The knot loosens. If Charles misses Jane so badly, maybe Darcy can talk some sense into him and tell him he's made a mista—

CB: I know what you said, but it felt real!

The relief drains out of me like there's a hole in my chest. I put the cell back on the table, facedown, pushing it toward Darcy's side. My blood rings in my ears. *What you said?* What could Darcy have—

Darcy places a coaster and a pint of beer on the table. He takes his seat with a strained smile, avoiding my gaze as he settles, readjusts, and shifts again. *Is he . . . fidgeting?* It's enough to rouse me from the turmoil brought on by the text. He meets my eyes, then raises his beer. "Cheers?" His voice is unsteady.

I clink my class to his without thinking. "Cheers." I take a too-large swallow of the reposado, and my eyes water.

Darcy's features relax, his shoulders losing some tension. He rests his elbows on the table, hand fixed at the base of the pint glass. "Clearly, I could have had someone else bring the check, or handled it online. But I wanted to see you."

I nod, my head still reeling at Charles's message. *What could he have said?*

"I know things are complicated right now. I wasn't expecting this. To feel . . ."

Feel. He said *feel.* Warmth blooms in my chest, flooding me, only to drain out of the hole bored by the words on his phone. The truth fills and hardens in the space: Darcy got Charles to leave Jane.

His brows go high with concern. "Are you okay?"

In my peripheral vision, I catch his hand reaching across the table, halting shy of mine. New disappointment piles onto the weight in my chest, threatening to crush me—I don't want him to stop. I *want* his hand on me.

He takes in a short breath. "You must allow me to say how much I admire you."

Admire?

I open my mouth to respond. His eyes dart to my lips, dropping lower long enough for my cheeks to burn. Despite everything, a smile tugs at the corner of my mouth, and he lights up again. That brightness pulls me toward him. But Jane—what did he do to make that happen? The question keeps me planted.

My head teems with too many thoughts, so I produce his words, instead: "'Thoroughly tolerable, but not enough to tempt *me*.'"

His brows come down. "What?"

The defensiveness in the clipped syllable breaks through the conflicting hot and cold overwhelming my senses, releasing the anger the slight can still manufacture. "I heard you. The first night you were at the show with Charles. You said—"

"I know what I said. I'm . . ." He leans back and expels a bitter laugh. "Wow. You held on to that."

My anger swells, crowding out all other emotions. "I appreciate you're not denying it. Real gentlemanly."

"How did you hear that? Were you in the room? No," he holds up his hand, the one that was close to mine, using it to fan away his questions. "That doesn't matter."

He peers at me in what I would otherwise guess was pure curiosity. "What is it, Bennet, that offended you? Or, what clearly continues to offend you? The fact your 'Kitten' routine didn't immediately win me over?" My jaw goes tight.

His eyes soften. "I appreciate what you do at the show. I know that it matters to you, but that night, you kittening, that wasn't real. That wasn't something to invest in. Not emotionally."

"What?" I ask, though I don't want to give him credit for trying to explain.

"Bennet, you looked incredible. And you were having fun, and that's great. I get that there's an art to it and it means something to you. But that doesn't change the fact that you were putting on an act. A moment ago, you slipped into an act. And that's not what I want from you."

The explanation threatens to dull my anger. I get what he's saying. That's what made flirting with him different. I initiated things playfully because of where we were. It limited the risk on my end, and if he didn't reciprocate, I could tell myself it was all part of the show. And maybe it was at the time—but now?

"The fact remains that in your club, a woman in her underwear"— he gestures to me before dropping his hand back where it was before, painfully close—"is simply a woman in a costume. Putting on a show. No matter how badly I want her."

No matter how badly I want her.

The words snag on my awareness like a ragged fingernail on tights. I stare at him. Color blooms in his cheeks, though his expression is plain. He didn't misspeak.

"Bennet?" He says my name softly, like a question.

I stretch my fingers forward, grazing his—

The phone beside us buzzes and I recoil. "You should get that," I choke out. "Charles is in a state."

Darcy's eyes drop to the phone. When he looks back, his face is hard. "You—"

"*'I'm getting weak,'*" I quote. "*'I need you to keep me from caving. I miss him . . .'*" I purse my lips. "*'I know what you said . . .'*"

Lights. Out. The shift is staggering. It makes the grim conclusion all the easier to accept.

"You're why Charles chucked Jane," I snap.

"Yes."

My chest squeezes at the cool admission, forcing a short breath. No hesitation, no regret. The confirmation stings like a slap in the face. "Why?" The word sounds so meek. "Why would you do that?" I point to the phone. "Charles obviously has feelings for him. Jane adored him. They were happy."

He hesitates, searching my face. Something like worry crosses his. "I thought it was a performance."

"A *performance?*"

"I assumed Andrea put him up to it," he says, back on the defensive. "She didn't exactly hide her comments about Jane's 'sugar daddy.'"

Oh, God. I didn't even think about Darcy's getting wind of that. "You took that *seriously?*"

"I know perfectly well how tactless that woman can be, Bennet. But you can't pretend she didn't think Jane and Charles's being together would work to her advantage."

I hate that I can't argue the point. I could kick myself for not telling Andrea to lay off that talk. "None of us even knew she was trying to buy Meryton until that first evening you came in," I say, though the excuse sounds feeble even to me. "And Jane had no idea about Charles's involvement until *after* he and Charles had already spent the night together."

"And what did Andrea say about that?" he asks, like I'm on my way to proving his point.

Again, I have no defense. "Jane adored Charles." My jaw is almost too tight to get the words out.

"That's another thing. Jane was just so . . ." He shakes his head. "*Affectionate*. It didn't seem possible that he could have felt so strongly so quickly."

Ming's warning pulses through my brain in time with my racing heartbeat. I insisted Jane's enthusiasm wouldn't be a problem, but Ming was right. It's gutting.

"*So?* I could say the same for Charles. Are you telling me *he* got to be head over heels for Jane, but Jane couldn't show the same?"

Darcy opens his mouth, but he doesn't reply.

"You didn't even consider that, did you?" I ask, incredulous.

Darcy seems shaken, too. His eyes are distant, brows high. "I was protecting him." His voice is hollow.

The excuse conjures Wickham's warning about Darcy's loyalty. My shallow, conceited ass interpreted it as a compliment, Wickham's being jealous. Did he suspect this? Was he trying to warn me?

"Protect him from what, Darcy? How can you possibly link this to the club? Hadn't you already shortlisted it for him?"

"Yes. But I—"

"Hadn't bothered confirming what the business inside actually was?" I toss my hands up. "Pretty major oversight for someone who's so goddamn protective."

Darcy's eyes are still unfocused, but they dart side to side, as though he's cataloging every missed step in his shitty excuse for rationalization.

"Honestly, even in whatever worst-case scenario you've imagined, how would Charles's being with Jane have impacted anything?"

"I would not abide my friend being used, no matter the outcome." Darcy curls his hands into fists, then relaxes them again. His voice is quieter when he adds, "Charles's money was only a secondary concern. My true fear was for his heart."

Neither of us says anything for a moment after that. Not that it matters. We're talking around the real problem, the ugly assumptions behind Darcy's fears for Charles's well-being. Those assumptions wouldn't just be about Jane, after all. They'd be about me, too. It almost hurts to ask, "Why would you suspect Jane of something like that? Because he's broke? Because he wants to sing? Because he's pursuing some dream? This is New York. Everybody here has a dream."

"What's yours, Bennet?"

I lean away from the table. "What?"

Darcy's face is hard again. Not his standard, starchy stiffness, but purposefully steeled. Shielded. "You mentioned experience in design. With so few programs in Colorado, it wasn't hard to determine where you went. And the school doesn't update its website much."

I feel the color drain from my face. The school's overwrought article about my internship win was searchable when I last checked, but that was years ago.

Darcy's expression is shrewd. "That firm was looking forward to bringing you on, too. Then, nothing. No trace of Elizabeth Bennet, aspiring designer."

"You *Googled* me?" I say with all the incredulity I can muster. The act itself isn't an issue, but the direction it's taken this already knotted conversation is threatening to derail me completely. What *is* on the firm's site about me? What does he know?

"Since I'm so *goddamn protective*, shouldn't I also consider what you might be trying to get out of my friend? I mean, interior designer is a pretty solid step up from stage kitten."

And there it is.

I push away from the table so hard my chair scrapes against the floor. People at neighboring tables stare, but I don't care.

Darcy rises, too. The lights are back on. "Bennet, I'm sorry. I—"

"Fuck you," I growl, my voice thick. "How dare you judge *me*?" The hurt fuels the anger already simmering in my core. I shove it back at him. "And you can keep kittening out of your mouth. I love that gig. It means something to me, and you *know* it." My voice wavers. I've made it clear that discovering burlesque was a turning point for me, and he's acting like it's a strike against my character?

"Who in the hell do you think you are?" I stand taller. "What dream do you have, Darcy? To hang out, doing fuck-all with that building you took from Wickham?"

At Wickham's name, Darcy's eyes narrow.

"Maybe you have Charles now, but how is he going to feel when he finds out you were so blinded by your goddamn paranoia that you steered him away from someone who loves him?"

A new agony takes root in the center of my chest. "This is where all that trust bullshit comes into play, isn't it? You think Jane's acting, so you can't trust him with Charles. And you think I'm acting, so you can't trust me. But you"—I point at him with a smile so fake it hurts—"you can't help wanting me anyway. And it's gutting you. Is that it?"

Darcy stares at me like I've pulled a gun on him.

"Quality commitment to that intimacy you care so much about. *Wow.*" I consider the mental gymnastics of trying to sort out the

Wickham situation, the time I devoted trying to get Darcy to see value in something I care about. And *this* is the person he is. I'm thinking aloud when I say, "What a *waste*."

He flinches. It's almost too small a gesture to note, but I'm so homed in on him I can't miss it. "What?" His voice is dark.

The reaction pulls me from my stupor. The word tumbled out of me, but his visceral reaction has jogged my memory. That night at the Work It event.

I take a step forward, chin high. "Charles's friendship. Pemberley. It's all wasted on you."

His jaw goes tight. "Say it again."

With pleasure. I move another step closer. Close enough to feel the anger rolling off of him. Close enough to touch him. My eyes drop to his lips. Close enough to . . . "It's. A. *Waste*."

His lips go tight. I watch them draw together, tension quaking in his jaw, and my ego swells at the successful hit. But at the same time, I ache to smooth the strain away. I want to touch him, pull him to me, run my tongue along the seam of his mouth and feel it soften and give against mine. It's dizzying.

The charge between us crackles. It pulls us toward one another, but everything said and done repels us with almost equal force. I meet his eyes again, and his look burns. He feels it, too.

"So this is your opinion of me?" he says, the words coated with bitterness.

We are so, *so* close. His focus lands on my lips. My face is on fire.

"Forgive me, then," he says, eyes still low on my face. "For wasting so much of your time."

He swipes his phone from the table, pausing only to yank his jacket from the back of his chair. Then he shoulders through the crowd I didn't realize has packed the bar. The eyes of other patrons weigh on me as I watch him go, the back of his head visible over a flock of women at the door before it disappears for good. I grip the table.

It's over.

CHAPTER

✦ 18 ✦

I settle against the wall in the stairwell, just below the top step. Ming's doing her red number, the same arrangement she wore the first time Charles and Darcy came by. God willing, she won't kill anyone with that damn shimmy belt.

Barely half my attention is on the performance. I've been distracted all day. I haven't told Jane what happened yesterday. What's the point? If Darcy was able to persuade Charles that Jane wasn't interested, how invested could Charles have been?

As much as I know I should be fixating on Darcy's interference, I keep going back to our final moments together. The heat and intensity of those last few seconds still make me light-headed.

No matter how badly I want her.

I shake it off, taking a second to scan the room. It's a full house. The crowd has a good energy, though I pray the two rowdy bachelorette parties are prepared to call it after this, because holy hell are they shattered.

Even the bar—

My blood flashes cold, then hot.

Darcy?

He's leaning to talk to Michael, who hands him a drink in a rocks glass. Darcy tosses back most of the contents in one go. For a moment, he looks into the glass, his shoulders going slack, then raises it to his lips to finish it off as he turns to face the dining room. Our eyes meet and I stare at him, mouth agape. What in the actual fuck is he doing here?

He freezes, the glass still at his lips, and it sends a hot wave of annoyance across my shoulders. You *don't get to be surprised. You came to* my *place of work.*

Slowly, he lowers the glass, placing it on the bar without taking his eyes off me, and starts my way.

I shake my head, ignoring the thundering in my rib cage and the sudden rush of blood to southern territories. Damn stupid hormones. I'm already fueled by burning hatred—no need for burning loins. Darcy stops at the edge of the dining room. He looks at the stage, like he's trying to determine if he can walk over without interrupting Ming. *Don't you dare—*

Beside me, a light flares. A guy in his midforties wearing a suit and tie makes his way up the stairs. His eyes are on his phone, the glowing screen illuminating his face as he rubs incriminatingly under his nose. He doesn't notice me until he's two steps below me.

I hold up a hand and confirm Ming's progress. She's at the bra reveal, and it'd be better if this guy wasn't milling through the crowd when she gets down to her tassels. I conjure an apologetic smile. "One sec. Ming's wrapping up and then you can take your seat."

Mr. Nose Candy gauges my authority with a quick, bleary-eyed scan but doesn't come any closer. Instead, he rests his back against the wall, tucking his phone into his pocket to watch Ming through the fine bars of the guardrail. I smile my thanks, then nod at Ginn and Tonic, who file up the stairs below him. I raise a finger to indicate the wait time, and they give me a thumbs-up, the casual gesture at odds with their dramatic ensembles.

Ming lets out a whoop and the red sequined bra goes flying, arcing toward the band. As I monitor the trajectory, my thoughts drift to Darcy. I cross my arms as tightly as the boning in my corset can allow and fight the urge to look at him, though his location is branded into my awareness. Yesterday's parting shots should have been more than sufficient. This bridge has been burned from both ends. What could he want?

When I flit my eyes in his direction, he's looking at something in his hand. I watch him for a second, observing the furrow to his brow, the high planes of his cheekbones—*damn it*! I veer back to Ming, who spins her tassels with glee. Why does he have to be so appealing? Why can't his outsides match his insides?

The guy on the stair says something I can't quite make out, and I lean closer.

"What was that?" I ask, eyes still on Ming.

"I said it should be you up there. You have the better body." His voice is slick with amusement; he seems to think this is very clever. *Gross.*

I don't even look at him. "Alas, this is as much of me as you'll be seeing this evening."

"You sure about that?"

Oh, for Christ's sake. I peer at the guy, who's still wiping his nose.

His forehead glistens with sweat. "In your case? It's a *promise*." I shift one step higher on the stairs to give myself some space, then return my resentment to Darcy. I glance his way again, prepared to glare if his attention is directed at me, but when I find him, he's looking past me. His eyebrows are low, and he's craning his neck as if to see—

Hot fingertips slide up the outside of my thigh.

I start and cut my eyes at the fellow below me on the stair. He watches me, smile defiant as he moves his fingers higher on my leg.

"I like your tights." His voice is thick and throaty. "Such an interesting texture."

My rage at the uninvited contact is a hot, liquid thing. Adrenaline surges through me, fight and flight battling for supremacy, and my body seizes. The guy oozes entitlement, watching me as his hand slides to the back of my thigh.

Bile rises in my throat. He angles his hand inward, higher . . .

I lean down with a saccharine smile. The guy is sweating bullets, his pupils blasted, and there's a tiny fragment of white powder in his right nostril. His smugness increases with my proximity: satisfaction at successful seduction via grope.

I bat my lashes. "I can make it look like an accident."

It takes a moment for my words to register, honey sweet and low as they are. His eyes dart to mine, hand halting at the point where my thigh meets my ass. My smile drips with venom as I look pointedly past him, down the steep stairwell to the dim landing below. My groper follows my gaze. Ginn and Tonic have stepped aside, gesturing down the void with showgirl flair; I forgot they were here.

The man wheels back to me, eyes wide. I'm shaking, my bright façade gone. "This may be a foreign concept for you, but in this room, you don't touch without permission. So get your fucking hand *off my leg.*" I bite out the last three words.

He looks to where his fingers rest against my thigh and jerks his hand back, like he's come in contact with an open flame. His Adam's apple bobs.

I'm spared further interaction as Ming descends the stairs in a flurry of feathers. I head to the stage, maneuvering through the crowd without sparing a look behind me. Rage gives way to a sick pitch in my stomach. The ghost of the creep's hand clings to my hamstring, the invasion like a fresh wound. Tears sting my eyes. *Bastard. Goddamn bastard.*

I retrieve Ming's costume on autopilot, Johnny's commentary muted by the blood rushing in my ears. I'm off the stage before I remember to loosen the silks for the Twins' aerial set and double back, fumbling with the fabric with unsteady hands while trying to keep Ming's gown from sliding from the crook of my elbow. When I finish, I hightail it to the stairs, registering that the asshole is gone while narrowly missing Ginn on the top step. I blurt an apology. Tonic calls after me in a too-soft voice, but I don't look back.

In the dressing room, Ming sits in the corner, cooling off with one of the oversized feathered fans from the number she'll do later. Jane's doing vocal exercises in the supply closet. I fight a sob of relief. He'd be able to tell something is wrong and I can't talk about this now.

I make short work of hanging Ming's costume. The shimmy belt rattles in my quaking hands as I drape it over the hanger beside the bra and gloves.

"Thank you, Kitten," Ming calls from her corner. I risk a glance. Her eyes are closed, fan resting on her chest.

Jane's singing stops. The doorknob to the supply closet rattles, and I bolt for the hall, praying that one of the bathrooms is open. A minute to myself. Just a minute . . .

At the landing, there's no line, though both rooms are occupied. I consider the coat check, but one of the restroom doors swings open. I keep my eyes averted when a woman steps out, holding the door open for me. Thanking her, I dart in, locking the door behind me.

I grip the rim of the sink. My next breath is a ragged gasp. I'm shaking. I still feel him on me.

I straighten and clench my hands into fists, pulling them into my chest. It was nothing. He barely touched me. It could have been so much worse. And I froze. I didn't even defend myself. I was a bystander to my own groping. How? How did I just stand there and take it?

Only until I didn't. I focus on that: my threat, not the delay. But what if he'd done more?

I cover my mouth to stifle a sob, and the tacky feeling of my lipstick has me yanking my hand away. Crimson smears run along my palm. The tears I've been fighting spill over, and anxiety tightens across my skin. No, no, no, I can't fall apart. I have to clean up after the Twins. There's still the back half of the show . . .

I fumble for some toilet paper, wiping away the rest of the wrecked lipstick before blotting at the tears tracking down my cheeks. Great. Just perfect. It's a small mercy when I check the mirror and my eye makeup is still intact. *God bless waterproof mascara.*

Here. This happened here, at Meryton. *My* Meryton. It's profane.

I conjure the final look on his face, try to savor the fear in his eyes, but all I can come up with is the smug smile.

What if he comes looking for me?

The thought cuts off my breathing in a whimper. A new bolt of adrenaline shoots through me. *No, there's no way* . . . I try to rationalize. Jane and Ming are just a shout away and there's a club full of people upstairs.

I grip the doorknob, turning it slowly. The button of the lock clicks out against my palm. I brave a step out and am greeted by a tiaraed bride-to-be who moves forward in relief. She lurches past, barely letting me step aside before she shuts the door behind her.

I massage my temples. Two years. Two years and no one's been grabby before . . .

"Bennet?"

My stomach falls. *Darcy.* I completely forgot about William *goddamn* Darcy.

I remember the look he had earlier, spotting the guy about to feel me up. Brilliant. He probably caught the whole thing. Shame floods my cheeks, and I grit my teeth. Tonight just keeps getting better.

I leash the ugly feelings and look to where I heard his voice. He stands on the far side of the room, near the coat check. I toss up a hand. "Congratulations, Darcy. You're now the *second*-to-last person I could possibly want to see right now."

"He's gone," he says tightly. "I told Michael. He got the bouncer and sent the guy packing."

"You—what?" I search his face, confident I'll see judgment, some self-righteous attitude. All I find is open concern.

"I hope I didn't overstep," he continues, moving toward me. "I should have asked you first. It just seemed—"

"No!" The swell of appreciation mingles with the adrenaline coursing through my system, making a heady cocktail of hormones. *Why is he here? Why would he do that for me after yesterday?* "Thank you."

A trio of girls from one of the bachelorette parties makes its giggling way down the stairs. I tip my head toward the coat check. Darcy follows me into the tiny space, letting the curtain fall back over the opening. I hit the dimmer switch, bringing the light up just enough that we're not in total darkness, but not so much that he can get too clear a look at my face. We're standing on opposite sides of the almost-room, but it only separates us by a few feet.

He looks around. "This was where you were when you overheard me talking to Charles."

I slump against the wall. I don't want to talk about that, to be reminded of yesterday on top of the degrading moment he just witnessed. But he's watching me too carefully, so I ask, "Why are you here?"

His eyebrows are low, as though I've interrupted some inner monologue. "I need to give you something. But . . ." He studies my face, his jaw tight. "Later. First, are you okay?"

I answer honestly. "No." The broken word sets my cheeks ablaze, and I have to look away. My nameless assailant's face flashes in my memory, and fresh tears sting my eyes.

"Would—" Darcy stands straighter, feet planted like he's squaring off. "Would you like to hit me?"

A strangled half laugh escapes me. I blink back the tears. "*What?*"

His shoulders fall. "Given what happened, I thought you might need a release."

"And you figured *hitting you* would do that for me?"

"I assumed it might hold some appeal after yesterday."

The man can be astute, I'll give him that. "A generous offer, Darcy, but I'll pass."

He nods, rubbing the back of his neck. Did he really think I'd take him up on the offer to *hit* him? All because some creep—I flinch at the specter of that unwanted touch.

Darcy tenses, scanning me for some sign of damage. His genuine concern tangles with my roiling emotions, and I blurt the first thing that comes to mind:

"Kiss me?"

He nods, but then my words register with both of us. Darcy manages a baffled, "W-what?" as my brain screams, *What the fuck did I just say?*

I gasp and fling a hand over my mouth. "I'm sorry!" I curl my hand into my chest, fingers cold against the rising heat. *OHMIGOD!* "That was totally inappropriate. I—I don't know. It's probably because you said 'release'?" I fumble for an explanation. "I want to feel something I've asked for, something good. I just don't want to feel *him*."

Darcy still hasn't blinked.

"I'm sorry," I repeat. "Forget it."

He comes to, eyelids fluttering. A cautious smile plucks at one side of his mouth. "So, kissing me would be . . . good?"

I did say that. *This night just got so much worse. What the hell. What in the actual—*

"Okay," he says.

I wonder if I can commit seppuku with one of the wooden hangers behind Darcy's head. "Don't. I'm . . . I don't know what I'm saying. It's stupid. I—"

"Bennet." Darcy half-smiles, looking almost—*self-conscious?* It's enough to give me pause. Is he even capable of that? "I don't want to make light of the situation," he says. "But you can't think I wouldn't be interested."

Yesterday's brutal comments echo in my mind. He should hate me. I wanted him to. "After everything—"

"It's hardly a sacrifice to kiss a beautiful woman."

My mouth is already open to protest, but his comment has me snapping my jaw shut so hard my teeth click. *Beautiful?*

Before I can dissect his response, he steps forward, holding his hands out, palms up, like a surgeon who's scrubbed in. "Do I have permission?"

The word choice confirms he was able to make out what I hissed at that asshole, and it's almost enough to mortify me anew. But he says it so carefully, I know he's not giving me a hard time; he's asking for my consent. Asking. Not taking. The emotions tumble in me: anger and humiliation and want. The appeal of having an outlet, of feeling *him*, is too strong to deny.

I nod slowly. "Yes. Please." *Oh, God, Bennet. Please? Really?*

Darcy closes the space between us, placing a hand at my waist. The heat of his palm sears through the layers of silk and boning, and I silently celebrate my skimpy costume.

His hold tightens.

I stop shaking. And breathing.

My hands rise to his chest, resting lightly on either side of the line of buttons on his shirt. He brings his fingertips to my chin, tipping my face up to his. He's focused solely on my mouth, his look so intense, I have to close my eyes. *How is this happening? How is this what I need right now? How—*

His lips press to mine.

He's gentle, lips moving tentatively as though feeling me out, trying to gauge my commitment to this remedy. But, *oh*—his lips are soft, and his tongue, teasing along my upper lip, is cool from what he was drinking before he found me. I savor the unexpected sensation, but the whole thing, the extremes of the past five minutes, is too much to process.

So I stop trying. And I kiss him back.

Darcy shifts a hand to cup my cheek, fusing me to him with the arm at my waist. His tongue sweeps along my lower lip, then presses in to tangle with mine. My knees threaten to buckle. *This is a distraction. It's still Darcy. He's why Jane is hurting. He's a proud, rude shit. You're using him. You're using him.*

Then I find myself sliding my hands up to knead the thick muscle between his neck and shoulder, drawing a sharp intake of breath from him. The sound cuts off the monologue in my head, and my number one priority is getting him to do it again.

My hands scorch down his chest. I make a tactile record of him through his shirt, registering the firmness of his pectorals and the muscle along his rib cage, then lower, tracing the ridges of his abdominal muscles. The path leads down to the defined outlines of his hipbones, and I track them to the waist of his trousers, where I let my fingertips rest on his belt. He, in turn, has moved one hand so low that it's technically pressing against the top of my ass, and the other cradles my head, cushioning me as he backs me against the wall.

The hand at the top of my rear eases down, following the outside of my hip to the top of my thigh. I melt into the contact, and it's a testament to my loyalty to Jane that I keep myself from wrapping my leg around him. I nip at his bottom lip, and he gasps again. *Good* God, *that sound—*

I resolve to apologize to Jane.

I arch, lifting my knee slightly, and in a display of impeccable instincts, he pulls my leg up against the outside of his. Then he's everywhere, kneading my hamstring and backside. He smooths me over, as if working to erase the contact from before, to overpower the unwanted imprint. It works. Each movement is long and slow and deliberate, until there's no trace of the intruder, only him. Only Darcy.

When I wrap my arms around his neck, he tugs my leg higher, hand moving farther inward on the underside of my thigh, grazing the edge of my panties. I angle toward his hand—

And let out a yelp of pain.

We break the kiss at the same time. Darcy shifts his hold, lowering my leg the millimeters necessary to dislodge the corset boning jutting into the top of my quad.

He lifts his face from mine. "Are you—"

I shake my head. My heart hammers against my sternum, and I'm grateful for the wall because I don't think I could stand on my own. "Corset," I pant. "Not ideal for . . . this."

"Ah," he breathes, and smiles faintly. He kisses my temple, then my cheekbone, and angles down to the corner of my mouth, lingering there.

I try to slow my breathing, exquisitely aware of the brush of my lips against his at every tiny movement. It would be so easy to get back to it, to turn my head or dart out the tip of my tongue, to taste him again—

"Thank you for your service," I manage, the words cool, though they come out on a shaky breath.

He chuckles, nuzzling lazily against my cheek. "Anytime." He presses a kiss below my ear, and I'm glad the position of his face prevents him from seeing the ecstasy crossing mine. He smiles against me. "This was a much better idea than what I offered."

I giggle, and he gives me a little squeeze.

"Did it help?" His question dances across my skin.

"A bit." I smile. "Thanks for not making me feel like a creep for asking."

He straightens enough that I have to look up at him. One hand cups my face. "Bennet, kissing you isn't a sacrifice. Touching you . . ." He rubs his thumb along my cheekbone and I close my eyes, almost purring at the contact.

He lets out a low sigh. "I'm just sorry it wasn't under better circumstances."

I flutter my eyes open, checking to see if there's any hint of what I'm gleaning from his comment in his expression. I'm met with the same intensity from earlier. My knees go wobbly again.

"I should let you get back to work," he says distantly, but makes no effort to extract himself. His thumb follows the line of my cheekbone, his other hand still massaging my thigh, maintaining a circular path that traverses from hip to knee. Less dangerous territory than where we were, but the ache he roused between my legs is relentless.

Slowly, I unravel myself from him, easing my hands from his neck to his chest. I relax my leg enough that it begins to slide from his hand, but he doesn't let it drop. Instead, he guides me back to standing by gliding his hand along my thigh until his palm casually cups my rear, which is a very neat trick. When he steps back, the cool of the room fills in the space between us. I roll my shoulders at the sudden chill.

He's still close, watching me with a faint smile. My eyes keep dropping to his mouth, his kiss-bruised lips. I bite my lower lip to keep in a laugh; it's a really, *really* good thing I got rid of my lipstick earlier.

Ice weaves through my rib cage. *Jane!* Oh, God, I just threw myself at the architect of Jane's misery. "This doesn't change—"

"I know." His face goes stony and he takes another step back. He pulls an envelope from his back pocket and holds it out to me. "I hope this helps."

I press away from the wall to accept the envelope. "You holding someone for ransom?"

"Just . . . read it? Please." He's written my name on it. His penmanship is excellent.

"Sure."

"Bennet." He has one hand on the curtain of the coat closet and starts to draw it back. "I'm going to fix this," he says firmly. "Everything with Jane and Charles. I'm sorry. I'm going to take care of it." His gaze drifts over my face, darting lower just long enough to test my resolve. His eyes meet mine again, and he smiles. "I'd really like a chance for better circumstances."

He passes through the curtain. I wait a beat, wondering— hoping?—he'll come back, then sag into the wall again. The lack of oxygen and rerouted blood flow and the sheer unbelievability of what just happened set the room spinning around me. That was the hottest thing I've ever experienced. Holy . . .

I shake my head, trying to rattle my brain back online, while the tightness low in my belly makes a compelling case for throwing myself out of the room and up the stairs after him. I force myself to wait in the alcove for another minute before exiting. Disappointment blooms when I see that neither guest waiting for the restrooms is Darcy loitering for a second round of ravishment.

The envelope is heavy in my hands. *Better circumstances . . .*

I'm still in a daze as I stagger toward the dressing room. My lips are tender, buzzing from the friction, and my blood thrills through my veins. I run my index finger along the bottom of my corset, finding the errant bit of metal responsible for cutting the interlude short. I don't know whether to curse the thing or thank it. If it hadn't poked me, how much farther would his hand have gone?

Andrea intercepts me in the hall. She swirls her martini. "You missed the Twins' silk. Ginn had to wrap it after the set."

I stop short. *Shit*—I forgot about their performance. Or, really, the world, for a few minutes. "I'm so sorry, Andrea. I—"

"It's sound, luv." Her voice is gentle. "They explained what happened on the stairs, said you might be needing a moment." She purses her red lips. "That handsy bastard. The nerve of some people! We got rid of him, just so you know. The staff's been informed, and Martin will keep an eye out at the door. He's not welcome here again." She pats me on the shoulder. "We always have your back, you girls. And those stairs are treacherous." Her tone is leading. "Good thing we have liability insurance."

I smile, blinking back sudden tears. Whether the house would back me up didn't even cross my mind; I guess I took it for granted that they would.

Andrea must see how close I am to crying, because her head cocks sympathetically. She lets out a gentle, "Oh, kitty cat."

A moment later, a shrewd smile spreads across her painted face. She takes my chin in her hand, turning my head side to side. Her laugh is a brilliant cackle.

"Snog rash. You little minx." She releases me, then pats my cheek. "Good for you."

◆ · ◆

At home, I sit in bed. Distantly, I'm aware of having brought my Meryton file with me, but when I look at the drawings, they hardly register. Almost nothing about my evening does.

Darcy's letter sits in the middle of the open folder. The envelope bears the distinct upside-down logo of the Standard Hotel, and the paper inside is coordinating stationery. I hesitate, looking at the folded pages. *A chance for better circumstances.*

Unfolding the paper, I find four solid pages, written in a neat, though cramped, hand, and a pair of business cards. One is for his uncle, Fitzwilliam Darcy, Esq., partner at *Darcy, Darcy, and de Bourgh.* On the back is a note: *Should you require further testimony on the subject of George Wickham, feel free to contact Fitz.* Interesting.

Card two is for Marley at Pemberley, with the accompanying explanation that she's a family friend who can discuss what happened in the weeks following the passing of Darcy Senior. I eye the letter. What have I gotten myself into?

Bennet,

   Allow me to assure you, this isn't a retread of last night. You owe me nothing, and that includes your time. But I humbly ask that you read this, if only to have a fuller picture of the circumstances surrounding the grievances you listed: my separating Charles from your dear Jane and shameful treatment of George Wickham.

   What I observed in Charles was unlike anything I've seen in him before. Never has he been so freely affectionate with a partner, nor so light and at ease. But instead of respecting the source of that affection, I only considered how it might be used to hurt my friend, and I took that consideration too far.

   Charles's confidence has never been steady. I confess to using that knowledge to undermine his hope that Jane returned his affections. Jane's own enthusiasm, as well as Andrea's repeated allusions to how Charles's involvement in the club would be "beneficial" to Jane and applauding Jane for landing a "sugar daddy," convinced me I was acting in my friend's best interest.

I won't condemn my instincts, but I can regret acting on them without doing my due diligence. You were right; I never once allowed that Jane's attachment to Charles might have been as legitimate as Charles's obvious affection for Jane. For that, I am profoundly sorry. I should have discussed their relationship with you before jumping to any conclusion. However, I feared confirming the worst—that you, too, were in on some ruse—more than I wished to exonerate your friend. This was sheer cowardice on my part. Cowardice, and a predisposition toward distrust I hope to, if not validate, at least explain to your satisfaction in the course of this letter.

For now, as it was my action and inaction that caused this separation between our friends, I will take it upon myself to mend the rift.

Regarding Wickham . . . that is its own painful series of complications.

As boys we were close, but we drifted apart in high school. I became more involved in crew and preparing for college, while he committed his time to . . . other pursuits. The resale of classmates' Ritalin was rumored to be his endeavor, and accusations about similar schemes circulated during his time at NYU. Ultimately, he took a leave of absence that coincided with my father's final months and began visiting him frequently.

Despite the circumstances of Wickham's availability, I was glad to have a familiar face checking in on my father. Wickham accompanied him to specialists and kept me updated on Dad's condition. When I'd comment on his visible deterioration, Wickham would assure me that I'd simply caught Dad on a "bad" day or that recent, alarming bloodwork had been compromised by a medication. Trusting my old friend, I believed my father's health stable.

After a few months of this, my uncle, Fitz, flew to LA to confront me over neglecting Dad. He explained that Wickham had made it clear I couldn't be bothered to visit. Wickham had convinced family and friends I'd simply abandoned my only living parent. As it was, doctors believed Dad had weeks—days, possibly—left, though even those grim estimates proved optimistic. Dad died that night, sometime while my plane was taxiing into JFK. I didn't get to say goodbye.

Then came Wickham's claim of the inheritance. Fitz was executor of the estate and had received no notes on the subject, nor had any changes to Dad's will been made to back Wickham's assertions. We did, however, discover a sum of money missing from my father's personal accounts. There was no guarantee that the blame could be placed on Wickham, but there were no other suspects. When pressed, he claimed his innocence and would not relent on the issue of Pemberley. In the end, my father's lawyers and I chose to extend him a few thousand dollars, though now I believe he uses the generosity as further evidence of my plot against him. Personally, I have not spoken with him since my father's passing.

For all my insistence upon it, trust is, in the end, a choice. I have ample evidence to support my stance with Wickham—electing to trust the man again would be sheer folly. But in matters of the heart, as with Jane and Charles, I cannot seek evidence of absolute truth. Your steadfast belief in Jane's affection is where I must satisfy my need for fact, and I trust you. I choose to trust you.

At the beginning of this letter I claimed that you had only two grievances, but I know I'm guilty of more. As for the comments you overheard the night we met, I know I said I didn't have to explain myself, but I want to.

I won't mince words: it offends me that you are so committed to your first impression of me, while my impression of you has not stopped evolving. Seeing you care for Jane that day on the sidewalk secured my interest more than any playing card could, however alluring its image (and make no mistake, it is; I have looked at that card more times than would be considered gentlemanly).

Further, the wit you expressed that night at the show was practiced: skillful, but not genuine. The way you've conducted yourself in our meetings that followed has shown me just how quick and clever you are. Our correspondence as you secured Pemberley for Work It's function revealed the scope of your professionalism and tenacity; you are owed a far better title than "glorified receptionist."

Similarly, I deeply regret suggesting that your kittening was a detriment. The comment was unkind, informed by old prejudices and mobilized in anger. Between your cheeky emails, your care for Jane, and, whether I "trusted" it or not, your playful, stunningly sexy persona at Meryton, you had me well and fully enchanted before that night at Pemberley. The push and pull of my attraction to you and my concerns over manipulation were unsettling, though to hear you phrase it yesterday, that I wanted to have you anyway, revealed the depth of my delusion. You are, delightfully, the sum of your parts, Ms. Bennet/Kitten/EBenAdmin.

I will be on the West Coast for the remainder of the month, but business has me back in New York in two weeks. If you would care to further discuss anything mentioned here, it would be my pleasure to meet and do so. Better still, if the contents of this letter have softened your opinion of me, I would be honored by your company over dinner. I leave it entirely to you. If this has left you unmoved, know I will see that as a sign that you prefer I stay away and I will respect that desire.

Yours,
William Darcy

I'm stunned.

I read the letter a second time and still come away feeling like I've been hit by a truck. Both times, reading that he "undermined" Charles's faith in Jane sets my teeth on edge, and the confirmation of what he alluded to last night—that he thought I may have been in on the imagined scheme, too—lands like a slap. But after reading the rest of the letter, I can't be mad at him. Yes, he directed Charles away from Jane, but he was confident he was doing so in his friend's best interest, and as much as I hate to admit it, I see how he came to that conclusion.

I scrub my hands over my face. Damn it all. I haven't let myself consider Darcy's explanation last night, his insistence that Jane's behavior was a performance, but Ming was right. Jane's exuberance, Andrea's tactlessness, Charles's uncertainty, and Darcy's experience with Wickham's duplicity collided with the worst possible outcome.

That he was afraid I might have been involved in some Charles-swindling plot isn't exactly sunny. *But*—I flip to page 3 and his admission that any suspicion was no match for his attraction to me. Given the origin of his cautious tendencies, that's actually a solid compliment.

He's apologized for the things I took offense to personally, and well, I might add.

And he's looked at my card. A *lot*.

Wickham, on the other hand . . . I feel like a dupe. The guy's only gotten shadier each time I've seen him; he was downright hostile when he came by with the Twins. Given what I now know of both men, that Wickham could take advantage of an infirm senior Darcy is more believable than any malice Wickham ever claimed on Darcy's part. The sheer depth of Wickham's betrayal of his childhood friend, someone who had trusted him with the care of his own father, makes me nauseous. That Wickham would go so far as to cause Darcy to lose out on whatever last, precious time he could have spent with his dad? It's irredeemable.

I look at the pair of business cards beside me on the bed. Irredeemable, and easily corroborated. But I don't want to think about Wickham. That's its own mess, and I'll have to decide what to tell the Twins about his past.

I scan the last paragraph of the letter a third time, giggling aloud at the overwrought invitation to dinner as I recall just how thoroughly I "softened" to him in the coat check.

I trace the five letters above his signature.

I've been wrong about so much.

And I couldn't be happier about it.

CHAPTER
19

"Lizard!" My cousin spins on her bar stool, hopping down to meet me with arms open wide. I rush into the hug, sending her staggering back a few steps, her slightly lower center of gravity keeping us upright.

"Sorry!" I loosen my grip. She's still laughing, though the body slam was overkill. "I'm so happy to see you. Both of you," I say as her fiancé approaches and hugs me, too. There's no risk of knocking him down; the guy's a beast.

"Have a seat." Gales nods to the bar. "I'm gonna grab another beer. You want anything to drink?"

"Sure, thank you." I point to the champagne flute next to Chloe as I shrug out of my jacket. "I'll have what she's having."

I sit, taking in what I can see of the main floor of the hotel. White subway tile, gold accents, and lots of reclaimed wood. If there aren't knockoff Eames chairs somewhere on this floor, I'll eat my hat. Chloe props her elbows on the table, hands in clenched fists below her chin, near shaking with her own excitement.

"How's your room?" I ask.

"Tiny! Gales can barely turn around in it. But it's great. All we need."

Chloe casts a glance to Gales, who's off chatting with the bartender. She practically glows. These two are a living vision board, proof that anyone in my age range is capable of functional adulthood. Chloe already had a side hustle as a makeup artist before she finished her undergraduate degree. After that, she got formal training and expanded her freelancing to the thriving business it is today. Meanwhile, Gales went to culinary school and has been working at a restaurant that rocked the Sunset Strip last year when it received a Michelin star. The hours are hard on them, but when they're together, it's something you can get lost in.

As always, my cousin looks amazing. Her makeup is flawless, as well it should be, and her white-blond hair's been styled in a severe undercut, parted to one side to show the buzz beneath.

People never believe we're related. She's her dad's side of the family, a sun-worshipping Elliot of light hair and tan-ready skin, while my coloring favors *my* dad: dark, wavy hair, and a complexion the sun only greets to singe. But if any casual observer can look beyond that, they'll see our moms' influence, the sisters' faces shaping our own.

Most people just can't get past the hair.

I blink away sudden tears, surprised at the intensity of my reaction to them. Chloe eyes me, her tan face creased with worry. "Lizzy, are you—"

"I'm really glad to see you," I say. "Things have been . . . complicated recently."

"Any of those complications have to do with why Jane has been so off? Yesterday, he texted me some factoid about pandas. It makes a gal worry."

Gales returns in time to catch the end of her comment and hands me my glass. We toast, and he looks my way as we drink, brows low over his bright blue eyes.

"Philip asked us to feel things out while we're here," he says, mentioning Jane's older brother, Gales's college roommate. They're how Jane and I were introduced. "This isn't like with Marcus, is it?"

"No. It's not great." I'm fighting a smile. "But I think it's on its way to being remedied."

"Explain," my cousin demands.

I frown. "You were so much better with vagueness before him." Directness is Gales's only approach to communication. He grins, bringing an arm around the back of Chloe's bar stool. She leans into him, unruffled by my complaint.

I summarize the past few weeks, including Andrea's unsavory commentary, which Jane glossed over in his Charles-centric gush-fest with Chloe. When I get to Darcy's involvement in the breakup, Chloe's hackles rise.

"Ugh. Dickhead," Chloe complains.

"He said he was going to make it right," I say, defensive. "For me."

Chloe's hostility tapers to intrigue. "Wait, Darcy's the handsy dress guy, right?"

"Yes."

"So, we like this?" she asks.

"It is . . ."

"Complicated?" Gales offers.

"Understatement. With him, it's been intense since day one. The pull is relentless."

Gales elbows Chloe. She rolls her eyes but leans against him.

"Yes," she says. "I know something about that feeling." Gales sits a little taller, if that's even possible.

"The two of you," I grumble. "Anyway, everything is on hold until Darcy gets things straightened out with Charles and Jane."

"Oof." Chloe winces. "The anticipation has to be killing you."

"It's excruciating."

"I hate to interrupt," says Gales, "but I'm pretty sure the two of you are getting into a subject you'd enjoy more without my participation."

I hold a hand to my chest. "You don't want to hear about the hottie I made out with in the coat check?"

"I'm sure he's dreamy." Gales finishes the last of his beer. "However, there's a Japanese knife shop in Tribeca I'd like to check out." He rubs his palms together in excitement. "They have a sharpening demo in about thirty, so I'm going to take off. Unless you want to go, too?" He eyes us skeptically.

Chloe pats his forearm. "I think you'll get more out of it without us, babe."

"Fair enough. It's only an hour long, so gimme a ring if you get into something." He rises from the stool, leaning in to give Chloe a kiss on the temple. He brings two fingers to his brow, then tosses me a casual salute. "Lizard."

Chloe's eyes follow Gales to the lobby, then she meets my gaze. "You good with your drink? We can go to the lounge area, if you want. Better chairs."

I follow her around the corner to a space with couches and the requisite faux Eames. Chloe takes a seat, placing her drink on the marble table between our chairs. "So, back to you and this Darcy. Does he have any redeeming characteristics beyond *intensity*?"

I slump forward, resting my elbows on my knees. "He really, really does. And I really, really decided not to let myself acknowledge them because I am a petty poo."

"Ah, pettiness." Chloe pats my hand. "It's a family trait, I'm afraid."

"The first night he came in, he was . . . unresponsive to my wiles. And I overheard him tell Charles I wasn't 'tempting' enough for him."

Chloe scowls. I can practically see her own vanity ruffling. "Yet there was happy time in coat check?"

"Oh, yeah." I fill her in and explain the letter.

"Now what?" she asks. "He's at least partially responsible for Jane's heartache, and I'm assuming you had other reasons for not acknowledging his finer points, outside of the 'tempting' thing. What's making this guy so compelling?" She takes a sip from her drink.

"It's . . . different with him. None of the lines from the show work. I can't fall back on the one-liners or playing the game. There *is* no game. Which is hot. And challenging. Which is also hot."

"Is there banter?"

"Yes. But again, it's only effective when it's natural. Like, when I'm legitimately entertained that he's stolen finger food from my party."

"So, he's into you. *You,* you."

"Yes, *me,* me." *Delightfully the sum of my parts.* "It's freaking me out."

Chloe snorts out a laugh. "I'm not going to warn you about the sheer depth of the smit you're in, because I think you know, but freaking out like this? It's a good sign. What's he like?"

"He's generous. Ambitious, but thoughtful about it. Like he wants to do something that matters. He lets me handle my own shit," I say, thinking of Jane's accident and the groper on the stairs, "then comes in with a solid assist. He said some things about burlesque that were a little too close to crappy comments guys have made about it in the past. Now I know it was part of him trying to come to terms with it all. I'm not used to that, to people reconsidering their first impressions of the scene."

Chloe nods.

"I was also receiving some solid misinformation from another guy he has bad blood with." The allusion to Wickham makes my skin crawl. I called Marley yesterday, claiming Darcy had recommended her as a character reference for Mr. George Wickham, which isn't too much of a stretch. She went *off,* revealing an endearing protectiveness for Darcy and no shortage of colorful descriptors for the "feckless con" who betrayed him. Her input made a text to the Twins all the more imperative, though I only heard back from Ginn, who sent a thumbs-up and reminded me they weren't on the schedule at Meryton this weekend.

I shake my head. "Anyway, it was easier to believe what *he* had to say about Darcy because it jibed with my first impression."

"Nothing like a little confirmation bias to skew your perspective."

I groan. "You sound like Gales."

"It's sexually transmitted. Anyway, I have no doubt that you and this Darcy will find a room with a proper door and hash it out," she says with an air of finality. "How is the show? I looked up their website. It needs some work."

"I'm hoping Charles will get on that once the building changes hands. Probably when they remodel."

Chloe sips from her champagne flute. When I get to "remodel," she lowers the glass. "You still working toward that?"

"Yes," I say, though I'm telling my armrest, not her. "It was a good distraction while Jane was streaming episodes of *Dog Whisperer.*"

Chloe waits me out, sipping contentedly at her drink.

"Hold on." I reach for my bag, pulling out my Meryton folder. Among the pages is the print for my playing card. I hand it to her as I flip through the drawings, trying to find the best place to start. "Here's this, by the way."

"What—ohmigod! You're a *naughty* kitten! Holy hell, woman. That's awesome. What's it from?"

I explain the cards and pasties and how I get a commission, mostly to brace myself for sharing the folder. I don't doubt she recognizes it as stalling, though I appreciate that she lets me get away with it.

"Has your fellow seen this?" She hands back the photo.

Part of me feels like I should correct her for the "your fellow" line, but I enjoy hearing it too much. "Yes. Though not this large. He bought a deck of cards the first time he came to the show."

"We're coming to Saturday's show then, obviously."

"There's a two-top with your names on it."

"Bueno. Now, gimme that." She reaches for the folder. "I want to bear witness to your triumphant return to the world of interior design."

"Easy with the hyperbole," I say, passing the file. "Nothing's been decided yet."

"Whatever." Chloe smiles faintly as she opens the file, revealing a recent doodling of the club. "This . . ." Her voice trails off in consideration. Her smile broadens. "This is your Meryton?"

"Yeah."

She props her elbow on the arm of her chair, chin in hand as she pores over the file. My butterflies, usually nocturnal, flutter anxiously as I watch her turn page after page.

"Lizard . . ." Chloe studies a rendering inspired by a

black-and-gold wallpaper pattern featuring items from the Met's grand entry hall. Feathery wings freeze in anticipation, dispersing as a huge smile spreads across her face. "This is *gorgeous*."

She opens a page I've folded over on itself, studying it for a moment before turning the paper my way; it's an older sketch of Pemberley. Must have gotten in with the Meryton stuff by mistake. "What's this?"

"Pemberley. It's a space Darcy owns."

"Here?"

At my nod, she leans back, eyebrows high. "So Jane's with the guy who is buying the club, and you're having coat-check make-outs with a guy who already owns New York real estate?"

"Darcy inherited the venue. It's a family thing."

"Is that a *water* feature?"

"Yup. I have a whole other file on Pemberley. The space is *beyond* stunning. Actually, since Darcy gave me his letter, I've devoted more time to Pemberley than Meryton.

"Anyway." I clap my hands together like a schoolmarm commanding attention. "I've dominated the conversation long enough. How are things with you? How's work?"

Chloe lights up. She built her business entirely on her own, and it means everything to her. "Grueling. And great. I have two shoots lined up this week and will be completely at your mercy as to how to get to either of them. One's in Midtown, the other's a loft in Tribeca, I think? Or FiDi? That giant white mall thing totally disoriented me last time, so whatever you can do to get me situated will be appreciated."

"Can do."

We finish our drinks and return our glassware to the bar, then head out through the lobby. The hotel is a bit west of my normal stomping grounds, but we make a right outside the double doors with

Gales's knife shop as our destination. On the way, I find the building where Chloe's first gig is taking place, and we stake out a few to-go restaurants nearby, which she says is critical.

"I never trust anyone to provide good food." She points at a craft services tent near a street that's been blocked off for filming. It's a constant in New York; I'm so used to seeing the shooting schedules taped on lampposts that I barely notice them anymore. We meet up with Gales, who is the proud owner of two new knives, and Chloe and I do our best to greet "Storm Cloud" and "Sky Piercer" with suitable reverence. Then we're off to the subway, buying MetroCards and planning our route to Greenpoint, where Gales is to be reunited with his favorite pizza at Paulie Gee's.

An hour later, we're enjoying the hot-honey-and-sausage-laden Hellboy when my watch buzzes with a text. Normally, I'd let it go, but the one that follows, and the one after, get my attention.

J: !!?!?!?

CHARLES IS AT THE BAR

BENNET!

"Oh, *whoa*." I don't realize I've said it out loud until Chloe and Gales look up from their pizza. "Sorry. Things just got interesting." I get my phone and pull up Jane's number. "Excuse me."

Jane answers on the first ring. "*Bennet,*" he whispers. "*I'm hiding in the stairwell. What do I do?*"

On the other side of the table, Chloe and Gales blink at the over-heard intensity.

"Well, for one," I say, "shame on him for dropping in unan-nounced at your work."

"Do you really think I'm thinking about *manners* right now?" Jane's whisper-shriek is incredulous and so very un-Jane.

"Sorry! No, just . . . hear him out."

"What?"

"I'll explain later, or maybe Charles will. He's been a wreck, so . . . let him talk?"

A pause. Jane sniffs. "He's been a wreck?"

I smile. "You've both gotten a raw deal, and I'll go into it when I get home. Just be honest with him, Jane."

He's quiet for a long moment. Then, quietly, "I've missed him so much, Ben."

My heart turns to mush. "I think we both know what you need to do."

"Yeah," he says, already lost to whatever he's scheming. "N'kay. Bye, Ben."

"Bye, babe. Be brave." I slip my phone back into my purse. Darcy must have cleared things up with Charles. Giddiness washes over me, and I let out a giggle. He did it.

Gales and Chloe watch me with mild interest. "I take it we won't be seeing Jane later?" Gales offers.

I grin. "I have a feeling he won't be resurfacing for a *while*."

CHAPTER

20

"Let's go inside." Chloe reaches for the door.

I swat her hand. "No."

"You're the one's who's been raving about this place. I wanna see it."

Chloe's shoot wrapped before lunch because the actress she was working with ended up getting whisked away to rehab. I've taken the day off to kick around the city with her, and after we met up with Jane and Charles, who briefly emerged from their cocoon of bliss for lunch, she requested a peek at Pemberley.

"You're seeing plenty." I point to the sunrise motif above the double doors. "The lighter bits in between the brass? I'll bet it's mother-of-pearl. Probably original, too . . ."

"Huh." She sounds less than impressed. "I thought that was half a clock."

"You pain me."

Chloe makes for the door again.

"No! What—"

"Don't be a weenie. It's probably locked." She tugs and the door opens toward her. Her jaw drops in exaggerated surprise. "Or maybe not!"

"Chloe—"

She opens the door wider. "What is your deal? Mr. Happy Hands is on the other side of the country and you've been here before. If we're busted, say you left a jacket or something."

"*Chloe.*"

"*Lizard.*" She mimics the warning in my tone. "You only made lunch suggestions that would get us to this part of town, anyway. Let's make the most of your little ruse, eh?"

I glare at her. I thought I'd been clever about lunch.

And I do want to go inside. Desperately. Since showing Chloe my work, I've spent all my downtime on a Pemberley design. The drawing I started to defuse my frustration with Darcy at *Red, White, and Boobs* has been the jumping-off point to more concepts than I can count, but the version inspired by the sunburst has quickly become my favorite. It's evolving well enough, but something about it hasn't quite gelled. Trespassing aside, a fresh view of the space *would* be helpful.

When I don't say anything else, Chloe wiggles her eyebrows and darts into the building. The door slowly whispers toward shut.

I lunge for the handle. "*Brat.*"

❦

Chloe is halfway up the catwalk by the time I get to her.

"Oh, Lizzy," she says admiringly, "it's beautiful. And you're right. The barn wood has to go."

I turn in a slow circle, trying to take it all in. Most of the lights on the main floor are off, but sunlight streams in from the windows upstairs to illuminate the catwalk. Without the attendees from the Work It event, Pemberley is the torturous blank slate it was the first time I saw it. The sheer potential is almost overwhelming.

Chloe bumps my shoulder, returning me to the present. "Is this going to be like your first trip to LA when I took you to Union Station and you cried?"

"Oh, hush." I nudge her back. Though her allusion to the train station tickles my brain. That missing element . . .

"*Tile!*" I scurry to the railing around the lake and peer into the dark water. "Tiling the lake . . ." The vision unfurls, washing over the scene in front of me. "Not white, like subway tile, that's everywhere now. But . . . taking a color from the mother-of-pearl?" I riffle through other memories from that day with Chloe, our walking tour of the Historic Core of downtown LA. The Bradbury Building, the Million Dollar Theater, and the grand dame herself—

I gasp. "The Eastern Columbia Building!"

Chloe frowns. "What's—oh, yeah! In LA. The turquoise one with the clock tower." She looks into the lake. "Ooh, that blue would be perfect."

I nod, bouncing on the balls of my feet. The pop of color would liven up the room without distracting from the architecture or taking the focus from the stage. I already colored in gold accents, and warmer lighting would balance the cool of the imagined tile. Chloe's bemused smile tells me just how bonkers excited I must look, but I don't care. "This has been plaguing me for weeks. It's all clicked." I shake my head, still not quite believing it. "It's *perfect*."

"That's awesome," she says. "Especially because I think we're about to get kicked out." Chloe waves, and I realize her attention is behind and above me. "Hi there!"

"Bennet?"

The low voice sends a shiver down my spine, and my pulse kicks up another notch. No. Effing. Way.

I wheel to find Darcy peering at us from the second floor. For a moment, we gawk in silence. If anything, he looks as stunned as I feel—though I hope my version looks even half as appealing as his. He's dressed in a white T-shirt and jeans, and holy bespectacled hotness, he's wearing glasses. With the sunlight coming in behind him, he's an urban Adonis.

And he's *here*.

Useless, I toss him a wave. "Hiya."

"What, ah—" He takes off his glasses, hurriedly hooking them on the neck of his shirt. It takes him three tries. "Are you here for something?"

Oh, God. Chloe and I just barged in here like we owned the place. "No—"

"She wanted to show me the building," Chloe says. "I'm Chloe, by the way. Are you *Darcy*?" She says his name with incriminating enthusiasm.

. . . and now he knows I've been talking about him. "I thought you were gone until next week," I say, hoping to sideline his own realization. "I was going to reach out—"

"I flew back with Charles." He slides his hands into his pockets, rocking back on his heels. "You may have noticed he couldn't stay away."

Charles. Charles, who just sat across from me for forty-five minutes of sushi and idle chitchat, knew Darcy was here and didn't say anything. That little . . . "Yeah, I *did* notice. He didn't say anything about you."

"I asked him not to," he says quickly. "I didn't want to impose."

My forehead wrinkles. The idea of his being an imposition on anything other than my recent dry spell is too foreign a concept until I recall that all our reunions have taken place in my head.

"No!" *Too loud; jeez, Bennet, keep it together.* I take in a breath, willing myself to slow down. "Not at all. Thanks for the consideration, but . . . no. You're no imposition."

"You wanna come down here?" Chloe calls, her hands cupped around her mouth. "Or would you rather keep hollering from different floors?"

Darcy huffs out an anxious laugh, which—anxious? He does that? "I'll be right there." He turns and disappears from view.

"Holy shit," I hiss, trying to keep my voice down. "He's *here.*"

"And he's nummy. Well done, Lizard." Chloe scans my face. "Your lipstick is good, nothing's smudged." She points to the front of my dress. "Good call on the wrap, but let's—" She pinches the fabric below my bust and gives a quick downward tug; I'm too stunned to protest. "Just right. The girls look great—hey!"

Darcy strides our way.

"Sorry for the breaking and entering." Chloe extends a hand. "Chloe, again. I'm Liz's cousin. Just visiting."

Darcy shakes her hand with a smile. "You sleeping on the infamous bouldering mat?"

I blink, thrown by the unexpected callback to a month-old conversation. A snort escapes me at the visual of Gales trying to make himself comfortable on the mat, let alone share it with Chloe.

"*No,*" I say. "They're in a place in SoHo. She's a makeup artist here for some photo shoots. But her fiancé is a chef, so any time she's not working has revolved around eating . . ." I look at Chloe, who shrugs.

"Eating," she agrees.

"Where have you hit so far?" Darcy asks.

It takes me a moment to process the question. He's *here*, with all his biceps-baring appeal. I didn't even think about what his arms would look like. I want to touch them. "Paulie Gee's, Curry-Ya, Mission Chinese—"

"There's a Mission here?" he asks.

"Two. One in Chinatown, the other's in Bushwick."

"Huh. I've been to the original in San Francisco. Great food."

Step it up, Bennet. You're treading dangerously close to small talk. "We're going to Ippudo tonight." The angle in my voice is mortifying. "If you'd like to join us?" I add, less leading.

He tips his head, watching me as though he's trying to gauge whether I'm serious. I hold my breath. A slow smile brightens his eyes, and my toes curl so hard, I hear the joints pop inside my pumps. "I have client calls on and off until eight." He grits his teeth. "*And* an overseas call at ten. But I can meet up in between?"

"Drinks?" My voice gets back to that mortifying lilt.

"Absolutely." The word "absolutely" now ranks with "paperwork" as one I'd very much like to feel him say against me. I fumble for my phone for something to do that isn't launching myself onto his face to determine which word would be the most pleasing. "I'll give you my number."

I pull up his contact info with his Pemberley email address. I really was going to give myself until next week to get in touch. But he's here *now*. He recites his number and I punch it into the phone.

"I look forward to it, then."

Chloe lets out a little, "Oop," plucking her phone from her purse. "Pardon me." She steps away to take the call, though the glimpse I get of her lock screen tells me it's an act. "Hey, H," she adds, tossing in the nickname of a friend back home. *Thorough.*

Her kitten heels click along the catwalk, fading as she reaches the carpet in the lobby. Then it's just Darcy and me.

"Your tours of Manhattan usually include empty buildings?" he asks, voice low.

"I love the space." It comes out with more emotion than I'm prepared for.

His eyes dance over me. "I'm glad."

I'm completely useless again. I want his face on my face. And everywhere else. Ugh, we are wearing far too many clothes right now.

"Thank you for the letter. And everything with Jane and Charles. It . . . meant a lot. To them," I swallow hard. "To me."

He meets my gaze. "I had incentive."

Adrenaline skips through me. "More than the intrinsic value of reuniting your best friend with someone who adores him and whom he adores in return?"

His laugh is just as satisfying as it was the first time I heard it. "I'd consider taking offense to that, Ms. Bennet, but I'd rather assure you that yes, I had far more incentive. Just don't get smug about it."

I bat my lashes, aiming for coy. For once, I hope I'm not pulling it off. "Too late."

◆ · ◆

I am a wreck all afternoon. I pester Chloe with repeat analyses of my interaction with Darcy, which she counters by reminding me she was there, assuring me he's clearly "feeling it," and demanding I stop obsessing, because I sound like a loon.

I keep my phone in my lap through dinner and holler, "Wilfie and Nell!" when he sends a text suggesting the bar for drinks.

"It's good," offers a man sitting across from me at the large community table. "There's a hell of a men's day spa a few doors down." He nods to Gales, who doesn't seem sure what to do with the information.

I am then insufferably antsy, according to my good cousin, who demands we make the fifteen-minute walk to the bar to burn off some of my restless energy. She then does me the cruel disservice of letting herself get distracted by a stationery store on Christopher Street, which would be fine, if not for my sense of urgency. We arrive with Chloe's stockpile of greeting cards to find Darcy has secured a pair of two-tops by one of the windows flanking the bar's entrance. He's dressed as he was earlier, though there's no sign of his glasses. Pity.

He stands to greet us. We move toward each other, stopping just shy of—what? Are we hugging? Shaking hands?

"Hey." The hand he offers slips around my waist. I come in close, giving him a squeeze that is over too quickly. But his lips graze my cheek, and I get a hint of that same clean, slightly spiced scent I noticed the night we danced.

We sit, and he extends a hello to Chloe before I introduce Gales. As hands are shaken, I shift my leg closer to Darcy's.

"How was the ramen?" He places his hand on my knee. *Very yes.*

"Solid. Have you been?" Gales asks, the talk of food a reliable icebreaker with him.

"No. I've heard good things, though. Supposed to be the real deal, a guy downstairs making the noodles by hand and everything."

A server comes by for our drink orders, and when she leaves for the bar, Darcy looks over all three of us. "Before I forget, do you all have plans for Tuesday?"

"Not yet. It's our last night in town, so we're game for anything," says Chloe.

"Great. I got us seating at the chef's table at Brooklyn Fare."

The name doesn't mean anything to me, but I think Gales stops breathing.

"How did you swing that?" he asks, voice high with awe. "That is amazing. I am *amazed* right now. How—"

"No trouble at all," Darcy insists, and, in the same breath, continues with, "That's not true. It required some minor bribery on my part. But a family friend was ultimately persuaded to go elsewhere for dinner Tuesday."

"I hope the rest of their party doesn't mind," Chloe says.

"That's where the bribery came into play."

A smile tugs at my mouth as I watch the back-and-forth among the trio. So much for Darcy's not being good with new people.

"Have you eaten there?" Gales asks.

"Years ago. Not long after they got their first star," says Darcy. "Tiny place, still next to the grocery store in Brooklyn."

"Now they're up to—" Gales's thick eyebrows come down in thought. "Three stars?"

"Sounds fancy," says Chloe.

"It's on me. This was my doing. I insist," Darcy adds, cutting off Gales's protest.

Chloe sits back as the server returns with our drinks. "Sounds like we're in for a treat! Thank you."

Gales raises his beer. "To minor bribery."

"To minor bribery," we chorus, and clink glasses. As we drink, I watch Darcy over the rim of my wineglass. Catching me, he arches a brow and places his beer back on the table.

"Bare?" he whispers.

It takes the warm pass of his hand over my knee for his question to click. "Yeah. No stockings today." His hand moves in circles over my skin.

"So, Darcy," says Gales. "Liz mentioned you're in wealth management?"

"Will Darcy: Man of Business," I say.

Darcy chuckles. "Something like that. It's how I ended up at Meryton. A friend was looking to invest in property, and the club was the most promising of the options he found. Done right, Meryton could be extremely profitable. The current owner . . ." He lets out a huff of a laugh, then takes a drink of his beer. "He's wasting an opportunity."

"Speaking of Meryton," Chloe starts, "Gales and I are going to Lizzy's show tomorrow and she's being super coy about it. What's this place like, Darcy?"

"Chloe," I warn.

"The least we can do is go in prepared," she says.

Darcy shifts his grip a few inches higher on my leg, making me more receptive to this little game of my cousin's. "You're already more prepared than I was. The information I'd been given on the property described it as a cabaret. I did not expect clothing to come off."

"Or a kitten?" Chloe offers.

I narrow my eyes.

He rubs his hand up and down my leg, and—oh, Diane von Furstenberg, hallowed be thy name—the movement is enough to part my wrap dress, and his hand is high on bare thigh. "No," he says. "Nor a kitten."

I am suddenly much more forgiving of my cousin.

"The food is good. Not great, which is too bad—there's a lot of potential there," he says, directing the comment at Gales.

"Is this something your friend who's buying it plans to do?" he asks. "Change the kitchen?"

"It would be in his best interest," Darcy admits. "Even if the venue's focus isn't on the plates. I've come to appreciate those other elements."

The admission gets my pulse thrilling. I prop my chin in my hand. "Is that so?"

Darcy's hand moves over my leg slowly, fingertips lighting along the inside of my knee. "It is."

"That's something you've never mentioned, Liz," Gales says, interrupting perfectly good eye coitus. But Darcy continues stroking my leg, so I decide to let the big man live. "Maybe you've explained it to Chloe, but how'd you end up being part of the show?"

"I went in to watch Jane sing. I didn't know what to expect, either. All I knew about burlesque was that it was fancy stripping. And then Ming—you'll see her tomorrow—she went onstage and she was the most joyful, beautiful thing I'd ever seen."

The tip of my nose tingles, warning me of impending tears. "There she was, almost completely naked in front of a room full of people, and she had them all in the palm of her hand. I wanted to have that power, too. It was the first thing I'd wanted in months. And that made me realize how much I was letting myself be held back by what happened in LA, that I was living in this beautiful city and not getting to know any of it. It opened my eyes to what I was missing. I needed that push. After . . . after the internship blew up."

"You know about that?" Chloe asks Darcy.

"No, not specifically."

Chloe waits for my nod before continuing. "Her boss stole her ideas and passed them off as his own, and had been peddling BS about her being 'inappropriate' so she couldn't speak up," she says bitterly. "The fucker. I still—" She holds up a hand, matte red lips pressing into a hard line. "It's been three years, and you handled it the way you felt was right at the time, but *shit*. Your work was *so good*."

"It was."

"Which is why it's so great that you're drawing again," she says.

Gales's thick brows go high as he drinks. "Chloe mentioned that! Good for you. Your stuff was always amazing. Has she shown you?" he asks Darcy.

I answer for him. "I've been Googled."

"But has he seen your Meryton ideas?" Chloe asks, despite knowing the answer.

Darcy smiles. "Do you have a proposal for Charles?"

"Andrea said she'd talk to him once the sale was finalized. They'll take a look then," I explain.

"He'd be lucky to have you," says Darcy. "The few pieces in that article on your school's website were outstanding."

I grin. The fellow currently stroking my kneecap has casually referred to my work as "outstanding." A gal could get used to this.

Chloe cocks a brow in Darcy's direction. "If you could take a break from whatever's going on under the table, maybe Bennet could share some ideas for that forsaken barn wood."

Darcy's hand stiffens, and I cross my arms. "Why are you like this?"

Chloe wiggles her eyebrows and hitches a thumb toward Gales. "Do you see both of *his* hands?" Gales raises his left hand, but his right, which is closer to Chloe, remains out of sight.

A second later, Chloe jumps with a little "Yip!" and curls over her side toward Gales. "Ohmigod, stop!" she begs, laughing. She bumps the table from below, sending her drink sloshing. "There's a beverage here, man!"

"She has a spot on the back of her knee." Gales takes a long pull from his beer, other hand still tormenting his fiancée. "Liz, do you have it, too? Ticklish as hell. She can't function."

Chloe shrieks with laughter, eyes welling. A couple at the table next to us look over, clearly puzzled.

Darcy dances his fingers along my knee. "Interesting. Though . . ." He checks his watch. "I'm sorry, but I have to go. I have a call with a client in thirty."

"I'll walk you out." I cast a glance at Chloe, loading it with a subtle but direct *Don't even think about joining us.*

She takes the hint. "Want to share one more?" she asks Gales, dabbing at her eyes with a cocktail napkin.

"Sure." He extends his hand to Darcy. "Thank you for whatever you've done for Tuesday. If you offered up your firstborn, know I'm supremely grateful."

"My pleasure. The two of you will be at which show tomorrow? Charles and I were going to stop in during the ten o'clock."

"We'll be there. Ooh! Join us!" Chloe suggests.

"Perfect. See you two then," he says, and we head outside.

❧ · ❧

"This was fun." Darcy nods toward the bar. We've crossed to the opposite side of the street, where there's less foot traffic. "Chloe and Gales are great."

"Yeah, Mr. Not Good with New People. You seemed pretty comfortable with a couple you only just met."

"Easy. They were vetted by someone I trust."

The word "trust" makes my chest go warm, but I need to confirm we're seeing eye to eye on that subject. "Darcy, you've said that you appreciate what I do at the club, but I need you to know I'm not going to change that part of my life, even if you're not totally on board with it. That's mine. I'm going to have that flirty act in my undies a few nights a week. But with you"—I hook my fingers into his belt loops—"there's no act. Undies and flirting, yes. But no act."

"I'm very glad to hear that." He steps closer to take the lapels of my moto jacket in his fingers, gently gripping the ends as he studies me. "Would you like me to say something meaningful, or do you want me to admit how many times I looked at the Four of Clubs while I was gone?"

"About that—just how 'ungentlemanly' did you get with that thing?"

"I didn't have any other pictures of you. And I wanted to see your face."

"And the other ninety-eight percent of me?"

"It's what I had." His tone is all innocence, but his grin is wicked. He releases my jacket, hands settling on my waist. "I'm glad you stopped in earlier. I'm almost confident I had it in me to wait for you to reach out next week, but I'm glad I didn't have to find out."

"And if I hadn't?" I tug on the belt loops, edging us closer.

"I would have honored what I wrote. You wouldn't have seen me again. Though it was encouraging to hear you'd spoken to Marley. And, naturally, Charles passed along Jane's suspicions that I wasn't completely in the doghouse."

"Yes, well, I'm going to be having a word with Mr. Bingley," I grumble.

"You should. It was very sneaky of him."

"Hmm." I find the hem of his T-shirt, edging my fingers to the firm warmth of his abdomen. He hisses in a breath, hands going tight against me, and I no longer care about Charles and his sneaky, sneaky dealings. I'm too busy taking in Darcy's face. Those peaked eyebrows, his dark eyes, fixed so intently on me. The focus is intimidating, as though there's no input coming from anywhere but me.

And he *does* have gray in his stubble. Even in the limited light coming from the closed FedEx beside us, I can see the pale flecks in his five o'clock shadow. *Swoon.*

"I owe you an apology," I say. His brows draw together but relax as I skim my fingertips along the skin above his pant waist. I trace to the solid columns of muscle on either side of his spine, then back to his hips. Some heat returns to his eyes. "Last week. When I said everything was wasted on you. I said it to hurt you, and I'm sorry."

"It was an effective word choice." He half-smiles. "Thank you. I appreciate the apology." He brushes his thumb across my lower lip, the touch a painful tease. "Do I have per—"

I close the gap between us before he finishes the question.

There's no easing into this kiss, no feeling one another out. We dive right in, any self-control collapsing around the need for contact. His hands slide high on my rib cage, clutching at me. The desperation in his grip sets me spinning, libidinous thoughts shifting in time with my accelerating heartbeat. My kingdom for a room with a door, or even a curtain again—

His tongue strokes mine, and even my most negligible condition falls away. *Anything. Everything. Public indecency. Bring. It. ON.*

I arch toward one of his hands until he's cupping my breast, and he groans into my mouth. He kneads me through my dress and bra, thumb tracing the low neckline, brushing over the sensitive flesh spilling over the top of my bra.

Oh, am I glad for the partial darkness. And whatever foresight had me wearing my jacket out here. The leather has to be hiding these lovely goings-on—*right?*

He edges into the cup, and lower still, nudging against my erect nipple. I gasp.

He breaks the kiss, panting. "I have to go."

I mean to say, "No," but what comes up is a dreamy, disappointed, "Nuh."

He nuzzles below my ear, withdrawing his hand from my bra. I whine in protest. "You're going to have to act as my restraint right now." His words caress my neck. "Because mine is about tapped. If there weren't other people's money tied up in tonight's call, I'd be begging you to come back to my room."

To quote Ming: the basement is flooded.

My eyes shutter. "Tomorrow?" I press my body to his. Hard heat pulses against my thigh. *Oh, my—*

"God, yes." His head drops to my shoulder. "*Please.*" He says the word against my neck. It turns out "paperwork" and "absolutely" aren't the only contenders for pleasure; as long as it's his lips, I am on fire.

He kisses my neck. And again. And again, until he's traveled to my lips. I remember his comment about restraint, and this time I'm the one to pull away just to see if I can.

"Until then. Good night, Mr. Darcy," I murmur.

His lids are heavy, a faint smile displaying his lower lip in a way that leaves me no choice: I pop onto my toes to nip at it. He lets out a low sound that I could really get used to.

"Clear your Sunday, Ms. Bennet." He strokes my cheek. "You are going to take a lot of time."

CHAPTER

❖ 21 ❖

Ming joins me at the makeup station, peering into my open bag. "Are you changing?"

"Yup." I wiggle out of my girdle and toss it onto the vanity.

She laughs her throaty cackle. "Your Darcy's coming in at ten, isn't he?" His name stirs the anxious new breed of butterflies twitching in my midsection. *Darcy hornimus*, if I had to classify them.

I pluck a pair of rose-gold rhinestone pasties from my bag. The disks are designed like little starbursts, with the center providing coverage and smaller rhinestoned points branching out. I hold them in front of my boobs, tweaking the pasties so they catch the light. "Maybe."

Ming shakes her head, reaching for my roll of fashion tape. She cuts a piece off, then takes the pasties. "Girl, you have it bad."

I withdraw a sheer bra from my bag. The tag still dangles from one of the straps. "You have no idea."

Ming's jaw drops at the sight of my costume-to-be. "Shut. Up."

My stomach flips at her reaction. I wanted to step things up tonight, but if the getup is enough to scandalize Ming, I may need to reconsider. "Too much?"

"I didn't know you had it in you." She sniffs, wiping an imagined tear from her eye. "My little Kitten, slutting it up proper. It makes a pervert proud."

The finished look pushes away any apprehension about the switch. The pasties sparkle through the fine pink mesh of the bra cups, almost as indecent as I'd be without them. The panties are an opaque satin, while the garter belt is the same semi-transparent mesh as the bra. My nude stockings glint with scattered rhinestone detailing. I grin at my reflection in the mirror over Ming's makeup station. "For a worthy audience."

"Jesus Christ Superstar." Jane leans in the doorway. "I had no idea this was in the works." He gestures for me to spin. "Show off the rear view."

I dip my chin and turn in a slow circle, shaking my booty for emphasis.

"You are not coming home tonight, are you?" he asks.

"Not alone."

Chloe stops short in the doorway, freezing with an arm out to give Jane a hug. She helped with makeup before the eight o'clock, and I asked her to update my look for costume two. She falls against Jane. "You look more naked than if you actually were. What is this?"

"A little something special."

She finally exchanges hugs with Jane, who ducks into the supply closet to warm up his voice. "*Mr.* Special is upstairs with Charles and Gales," she tells me, and tips her head, still taking in the little there is of my outfit. "He's going to die. You're going to kill that poor man and there's nothing he can do about it."

Ming drapes herself over the back of her chair. "But what a way to go."

Chloe beckons me to a seat beside Ming. "I'm switching you to something softer. Still a red lip." She unzips her makeup kit. "I have a smooch-proof stain the two of you will appreciate."

Ming watches Chloe work. Despite Chloe's declaration of impending best friendship a few weeks ago, Ming had her reservations about letting a stranger handle her false eyelashes earlier. After Chloe showed her a new way to apply them, tipping the outside corners down for a dreamy, coquettish look, Ming's studied every brushstroke and pencil line like a dutiful student.

After a few moments of thoughtful silence, Ming leans back in her seat. "JOHNNY!" Chloe and I flinch at the sudden sound.

"WHAT?" Johnny replies from the hall, equally loud.

"Have Kitten do a sample peel for the ten o'clock!" Ming wiggles her eyebrows at me. "Get your evening started a little early," she says in a normal voice.

Peel? My Darcy-induced nerves start to quake in earnest, joining the kaleidoscope of preshow butterflies in their regular test flight.

"A peel?" Chloe asks.

"EH?" says Johnny.

"Kitten!" Ming barks. "Have her PEEL!"

"KITTEN?" A folding chair scrapes against the concrete floor in the other room, and Johnny's footsteps sound down the short hallway. "Kitten, do you want to do this or is Ming volunteering you—holy shit." Johnny finishes his statement as he steps into the room, getting an eyeful of my costume. He nearly drops his playing cards. "Oh, yeah. You're doing a peel. Lordy, Kitten. Warn a guy before he walks in on this." He cocks his head. "Or don't." He salutes me with the cards, then heads back to his game. I arch a brow at Ming.

She shrugs. "You can name your firstborn after me."

My preshow and pre-Darcy jitters careen wildly, colliding to create a feathery gob of anxiety and hormones. "Let's not get ahead of ourselves," I tell Ming, and go to the wardrobe rack and the little black dress I've left here for peels.

My hand hovers over the hanger. This feels like a test of my principles. I changed into my second outfit as a preview for later. But to peel in front of Darcy, knowing he's in the audience . . .

Just because burlesque appeals to men doesn't make it an appeal to men.

That very much remains the case. However, as I remove the dress from the hanger, I can't ignore the thrill at the thought of his watching. I finger the bright pink tassel looped onto the zipper pull. If he weren't here, I wouldn't even hesitate—I'd do it because *I* want to. And I did warn him I wouldn't be cutting this from my life.

I think back to Darcy's parting words last night, the heated moments leading up to it, our time in the coat check, the dance we shared . . .

A little invincibility might be just the thing.

❦

Twenty minutes later, I stand at the top of the stairs, a goddamn bundle of nerves. Naturally, Johnny has chosen tonight to try out a new bit and has been harassing a bachelorette for pictures of her intended since he wrapped his intro. I don't know how much longer I can stand the tension; if Johnny doesn't shut up and let me take off this dress, I'm going to yank him from the stage with his mike cord.

It's also getting hard to keep from watching a certain quartet. Andrea seated them in the same space Darcy and Charles had that first night, combining it with a neighboring table to make a four-top. Darcy watches me with open curiosity, his expression pleasantly intrigued, like he's trying to work something out and is enjoying the challenge. Every now and then his eyes shift low, and I imagine he's fantasizing about what I'm wearing under my comparably conservative dress.

"Ladies, gentlemen, sexy people across the spectrum," Johnny calls. I snap to attention. "Allow me to introduce you to Meryton's esteemed stage kitten, Miss . . ."—he draws out the title—"Kitten . . ."— the spotlight swerves toward me—"Caboodle!"

The cluster of wings in my chest vibrates so rapidly, it feels like it's going to tear itself apart. I stroll through the crowd, which offers polite applause, and ascend the stage to stand beside Johnny.

"For those who might not be familiar with how these shows work, Kitten is going to give you a chance to practice sharing your appreciation. What do you think, kitty cat—a glove peel?"

I raise my bare hands and screw my lips to the side in an exaggerated show of contemplation. Then I grin. I spin to present my back to the crowd, swaying just enough to send the tassel swinging side to side.

"Now, what do we have here?" Johnny edges to the side of the stage. The band takes their cue, kicking into Henry Mancini's "Baby Elephant Walk."

Working in time with the music, I reach my hand to the middle of my back and grasp the tassel, guiding it down the zipper track with practiced slowness. I shift my shoulders to further open the gap, the cool of the room and the heat of the spotlight dancing across the widening sliver of exposed skin. I face the diners again.

With a roll of my shoulder, the dress tumbles to my bicep, catching in the crook of my elbow. I wink, pressing delicately at the neckline of my dress to keep it in place. The applause is lively, but I'm looking for more. A roll of my other shoulder and the opposite side of my dress slides down, but with my off-center hold at the top of the dress, it falls farther, revealing the left cup of my bra and the glinting pastie below.

Gasps and whistles burst from the audience. Chloe bellows, "*Lizard!*" like a rowdy frat boy, and any residual self-doubt evaporates in a feathery cloud. I can't make out Darcy over the stage lights, but knowing he's watching makes my pulse thrill. It's not just us, and this is hardly intimate, but this peel has turned into the jumping-off point for the rest of our evening.

Returning to the production, I draw my lips into an exaggerated O of surprise, then smile again. I arch an eyebrow and lift one finger from the top of my dress. Then another.

The room is still. At the next beat of the song, I pull my hand away completely and let the top of the dress fall, the straps tumbling past my hands until—

The dress catches at my hips. I stare wide-eyed at the point where the dress sits, the front draped over the skirt like an apron. The waist of my garter belt is visible, as well as the bare skin above my undies, framed by the arch formed by the stays of the belt. I pout and shimmy, but the dress doesn't budge.

I hold up a finger in faux realization and turn my back to the crowd again. Hooking my thumbs into the fabric at my hips, I edge the dress down, leaning over as I guide it past the rise of my satin-clad backside. Once it's cleared my rear, the dress falls freely to the floor, mercifully not snagging on any of the rhinestones in my tights. I straighten, slowly running my hands up the sides and backs of my thighs.

When I reach my full height, I extend my hand demurely. Johnny moves forward to take my fingertips, and I step out of my dress with dainty, ladylike steps. I face the audience again, surveying the length of myself and brushing away some invisible dust. Satisfied, I raise my arms in a classic showgirl pose, beaming wide. The crowd goes wild. My heart thrashes, and I let out a giddy laugh.

"Ladies and gentlemen," Johnny hollers, "Kitten Caboodle!"

I'm about to descend the stage when I remember my kitten duties. I step one foot into the puddle of my dress, then kick up my heel, fingers crossed that I have my timing right. The move lifts the dress enough that I catch it, then smoothly drape it over my arm. As I pass my table of supporters, Chloe throws her hands up in delight, and Gales and Charles keep up their applause, with Gales adding a wolf whistle. Darcy still hasn't moved. He's looking at me like he did the night we met, as though the final notes of "Feeling Good" linger in the air, and I'm due for a pouncing.

"Help me out, Darcy." I bump his shoulder with my hip, savoring the heat of his body so low on mine. "Was that 'cheeky' or 'insolent'?"

He opens his mouth to reply but ends up taking in a breath, a smile sneaking across his face. "That was all you."

"I have to warn you." Darcy plucks a key card from his money clip. "The room is . . . excessive."

I grin. If *he's* saying it's excessive, then it really must be something. "I'll try not to hold that against you."

"You're too kind." He presses the key to the panel above the doorknob, and the lock disengages with a robotic grinding.

The sound grates against the final, frayed thread of restraint I've been clinging to since the show wrapped. I could distract myself from the evening's trajectory while I had costume fragments to pick up and pasties to shill. But from the moment I stepped onto the main floor in my street clothes, it's been a countdown to this. Darcy called a car, we dropped off Chloe and Gales at an after-hours restaurant, and the next stop was the Standard. No discussion. No hesitation. I don't think I've taken a full breath since seeing the hotel's sign.

My breathing inches toward normal as I step into the room. The suite is paneled wall-to-wall in wood, with all the upholstery in shades of deep red. There's a dining table off to one side, flanked by a three-quarter banquette and a pair of chairs with red leather seats. Farther into the room is a platform with wedge-shaped cushions I assume are supposed to comprise a lounge space.

The only break in the color scheme is the floor-to-ceiling window that spans the exterior wall of the room. I walk toward it, drawn by the sweeping view of the Hudson. As I round the corner of the hallway, I can see into the sleeping area, and—

"Is the bed *round*?" I deposit my bag on the table and move toward the red disk. But before I get there, I note another oddity, a giant teacup bathtub between the foot of the bed and the window. "How many times have you used that?"

"In all the trips here?" He stands beside the dining table, his hands in his pockets. The hanging lamp over the table is the room's only source of light, and it bathes him in a soft glow. "Zero."

"Ugh. You have no appreciation for luxury." I pivot back to the view.

He chuckles. "I appreciate they didn't slack on the *shower*." His reflection in the glass grows larger as he comes closer. He sheds his jacket along the way, tossing it onto the couch thing. "But if you'd prefer the tub, I'm game."

My eyes follow the progress of a ferry crossing the water below, but my remaining senses are homed in on Darcy's approach. He's close enough that the warmth of his body seeps into my back. I rest against his chest. I track a flat barge as it makes the slow trek toward New Jersey and focus on the steady rhythm of Darcy's heartbeat against me.

"You asked about the song," I say. The work of Henry Mancini was the only subject of conversation on our drive over. "But you didn't say what you thought of the peel."

"Hmm." The low sound rumbles against all points of contact. His deep inhale pushes me toward the glass; I drift back again as he breathes out. "I wanted to pull you off that stage and take you to the coat check."

I shiver. "Then you should know"—I turn to him, my back almost against the glass, and raise my chin, exposing the zipper pulled high on the rounded collar of my jacket—"I leave work at work."

No hesitation. He takes hold of the zipper and draws it down slowly, shifting to stand so close that his hand barely wedges into the space between us. I rest my hands at his waist. The jacket parts, and his hands come to my collar. He kisses my temple, then leans closer, his breath tickling the shell of my ear. "Do I have permission?"

When I nod, his stubble scrapes against me. "Do I?"

"Hm." He peels the jacket from my shoulders, smoothing the leather to rest at the bend of my elbows. I start to straighten my arms—

He pulls me roughly to him by my jacket, and I gasp. My arms are pinned to my sides, and my pulse leaps at the sudden restraint, lacing my desire with a rush of adrenaline I can taste. Darcy nudges my head aside with his own, pressing a kiss below my ear. "No."

A fresh jolt of surprise lances through me, sending all erectile tissue to delightful attention. He just said no.

He kisses lower, moving along my neck in a blazing path of lips and teeth and tongue. My breath catches, and he lifts his head, bringing his lips to mine. The relief is exquisite and immediate and not nearly enough; it's like trying to release a dam through a keyhole. My arms ache to hold him to me, to reciprocate, but his grip and the leather keep my arms bound, useless at my sides. The loss of control is unfamiliar and exhilarating, making every muscle below my belly button clench.

But I still have control of my body. I arch into him, searing myself against him from sternum to pelvis, savoring the solid resistance of his torso and abdomen. I angle myself further, grinding against his hip—

Darcy groans. *That is not his hip.*

He relaxes his grip, easing the jacket from my arms, and breaks the kiss to toss it onto the rim of the tub behind him. He takes stock of my dress, the deep V of the neckline and the buttons running from just above the center of my bra to an inch below my navel. He's seen it before.

He meets my eyes. "Do I still have permission?" I nod.

I stand as still as my thundering heartbeat will allow as he undoes the top button, his knuckles grazing the insides of my breasts. Not being allowed to touch him has gone from challenging to cruel, but the standard has been set.

"Do I have permission?" I rasp.

He runs a finger up and down my sternum, plucking at the center of my bra. I forget to breathe. He shakes his head slowly. "No." His voice is distant. He drags his finger down farther and releases another button. *So nimble.* "Not"—another button undone—"yet."

He drops to his knees. I blink in surprise, and his eyes meet mine. His pupils are so dilated, I can't tell where they end and his irises begin. Returning to the task at hand, he undoes the fasteners below my rib cage. He parts the material, kissing the skin between my bra and the top of the garter belt as his fingers continue their downward path. I dig my nails into my palms.

My buttons undone, his hands smooth down the sides of my skirt. He passes the short hemline, moving to my unsteady knees before reaching to my hamstrings, then up again. Cool hands meet the bare skin above my stockings, then cup my backside. He glances over the sensitive area between the back of my thigh and the bottom of my ass, and I have to rest against the window for balance.

Darcy traces along the elastic bordering the legs of my undies, halting at the straps of my garter belt. "Are you still wearing what you had on at the show?" His voice is rough. I grin.

Darcy groans, wincing as though pained, and presses his forehead low against my abdomen. He releases his hold and stands, moving his hand under the fabric at my shoulder, guiding it back and away from my body to reveal the cup of my bra. The rhinestone pastie glitters. "Oh, Bennet," he breathes.

I watch him study me. It isn't the bleary ogling of a guy freely enjoying eye candy or a lecherous glance at forbidden fruit. He saw me in this—less than this—just over an hour ago, yet his gaze is nothing short of reverent. It's as though I'm the lucky one to be looked at like this, rather than his being lucky for getting to view.

He blinks, eyes darting to the other side of my dress, as though he's just realized that breasts come in pairs. He pushes the dress aside and off my shoulder. I pull my arms free of the long sleeves, leaning away from the glass to let the dress fall to my waist. Darcy's hands glide down my sides, trailing along the elastic at the top of my garter belt, then push the dress down to fall from me completely.

Now I *am* dressed exactly as I was at the show. But I'm not performing a role, not riffling through preplanned responses. It's just me, being undressed by a man I want desperately. It's not unlike the high I get from being on the stage, but there's more to it. It's intimate. It's *real*.

"Do I have permission?" It gives me a new thrill to have to ask, now that he's established the risk I'll be turned down. When he nods,

I nearly swoon with relief. I get to work, shaky hands fumbling with the buttons of his shirt. When I finish, his hands quake against me, too.

We kiss, and his shoulders shift as he helps me remove the pristine button-up, lips parting from mine when I pull too hard to free his shoulder from his collar. The loss of contact makes me blink, and I'm suddenly aware that this is the first opportunity I've had to see him shirtless.

I rest against the glass to better appreciate the view. With the light coming in from the city, he's another incarnation of yesterday's urban Adonis. He is every bit as solid as his topography felt, his trim torso defined but not bulky, with a fine dusting of chest hair. His rib cage expands and contracts rapidly, intercostals shifting with each quick breath.

I press my hands to his sides, feeling the muscles ripple and the rumble of his responding groan. His skin is soft as I glide my palms around to the broad spread of his lats. "You still row?" I ask, breathless.

He leans in, forearms braced on either side of my head, caging me against the glass. His forehead presses to mine. "Five mornings a week."

"You're fantastically proportioned. Climbers are all lats." I bring my hands to his chest, pressing into his pectorals. I watch the flesh give. "They don't have *this*."

His laugh gusts against me, only to be sucked back in through his teeth when I trail my nails down his stomach. My fingertips light at his waistband, and his head drops to my shoulder. Sweat has beaded on his forehead.

"Do I have permission?" My mouth is dry. He nods against my

shoulder, his hair tickling along my jaw. I undo the tab, the button beyond, and finally take hold of the zipper below.

I feel every notch in the zipper track as it descends, letting the heel of my hand brush against his hard length. His breath hitches, the same sound that challenged my fortitude in the coat check. I reach into his open fly, molding my fingers to the impressive thickness enclosed in what I hope are boxer briefs.

"Please?" I ask, voice thick.

He picks me up. I wrap myself around him, relishing the heat of his firm abdomen between my legs. He turns to the bed and drops to his knees on the mattress, laying me against the comforter still bound to him. We kiss, the warmth and weight of him making me shake with the need for release. His hand grips my thigh, running along the suspender strap attaching my stocking, and the clip releases.

I break the kiss. "You just did that."

He shifts to his side, running his hand over the front of my thigh, stopping at the fastener there. Taking hold of the tiny ribbon between the rubber grip and the stocking, he tugs. The catch releases. He gives me a smug smile I'd have half a mind to wipe off his face if it didn't light up every nerve in my body. "I did my research."

Rising to his knees, he maintains a gentle hold on my thigh, keeping it elevated. He smooths his palms down the length of my leg to roll the fishnet stocking from me. He twirls it on the tip of his finger, looking a little too pleased with himself.

I narrow my eyes. "Beginner's luck."

He grins, letting the stocking fling from his finger, and slides his other hand up the length of my leg. He pauses to kiss the inside of my knee, then higher on my thigh, before lowering my leg to the bed.

I rest on my elbows and lift my other leg for him to take care of the second stocking. He makes short work of both fasteners, rolling the stocking down my leg just as before. The moment it's off my toes, he tosses it behind him and leans over me.

"I looked up how to take off the belt, too." His hand slides to my back, feeling for the catches there, and his lips meet mine again. We kiss with an urgency that builds with each hook and eye he releases. The garter belt goes slack.

He moves to his side and crooks a thumb beneath my bra strap. Eyes on mine, he guides the strap down my arm until the cup starts to follow, then watches its progress. The gauzy material slowly peels down, clear of the pastie, until the flesh of my breast is exposed. Light fingertips trace along the sensitive underside before palming me entirely. My body is molten.

He thumbs the pastie. "Will it hurt to take this off?"

"A little," I answer, voice husky.

"I'll be careful."

The three words are so reassuring my breath falters. I bite in my lips and nod.

The discomfort is minor as he tentatively edges around the starburst, prying it up with care. I look down, belatedly relieved the double-stick has remained adhered to the pastie and not my nipple, though the distinct wrinkling of tape is clear on my areola.

"You okay?" Darcy says it with a tenderness matched by the gentle caress of his thumb over the erect pink tissue. I nod, his touch ridding me of speech, and he smiles, cockiness and insecurity dancing in his dark eyes. "This helping?"

"Yes."

"Then this would probably be better." He lowers his mouth to my breast. The wet warmth is fresh torture, his long, gentle pulls inflaming the ache between my legs. I clutch at his neck, wanting to keep him put but desperate for him everywhere at the same time, not wanting to deny any part of my body his adoration. He kisses along my chest to the other breast, pulling down the bra cup quickly. The edge of my pastie catches on the material, tugging sharply enough that I yelp, then—*oh*—moan.

Darcy's brows go high, and I open my mouth to assure him I'm fine, but nothing comes out. The foreign mix of pain and pleasure mingles with my desire, and I swallow hard, weighing my response. "That was . . . good."

Understanding lights in his eyes. Watching me, he moves to the pastie, kissing and nibbling his way, drawing his teeth along the underside of my breast until I gasp. He maneuvers up, then eases his teeth to get a grip on one of the points of the starburst.

I take in a long breath, steadying myself. Then another. "Do it," I command, though it comes out a rasp.

He jerks his head and the pastie wrenches free with a sharp, clarifying pain that has me arching my back. I let out a gasping cry. My pulse throbs in my raw nipple, the beat there almost as insistent as the one between my legs, and Darcy's mouth closes on me, his tongue laving my aching bud. I lose my words on another rasp of pleasure as Darcy grips my hips, tongue and lips soothing the buzz of pain from my breast. One of his hands slides between my shoulders, unhooking my bra, and I pull my arms free of the straps.

His fingers press at the inside of my thigh. The responding surge of desire is so extreme, I flinch. He lifts his head from my chest, fingers pulling away, but I catch his hand. "No, it's not—" I can't complete a sentence. "Yes. Please. *More*."

He searches me for any hesitation as his hand drifts along the inside of my thigh to the corner of my panties with painful slowness. The heel of his palm presses against my sex, and I cry out his name. I angle myself against him, feeling him hard against my thigh. "Please," I pant. "I want you."

His eyes lock on mine. He's breathing hard, too. "Say it again." An echo of our fight last week, the counterpoint to every ugly thing I've ever said or thought about him.

"I want you." I guide his hand from my inner thigh to press against the seamless waist of my panties. "I want you, Darcy." My voice breaks.

He hooks his fingers into my panties, then pulls them down. He straightens, observing my form now clad only in the lights coming in from the window behind him. For a long moment he takes me in, his only movement the rise and fall of his chest. I quake in anticipation of his touch.

"Condom?" I rasp.

He retrieves the jacket he placed on the couch and produces a foil square from one of the pockets. Then he pulls down his boxer briefs, springing from the confines of the dark material. My fingers curl, wanting to touch his length, to feel him warm in my palm, and I shift against the velveteen slipcover. He takes in another long breath; at no point have his eyes left my body, and with each small movement from me, his body grows tighter, more ready.

Kneeling at the end of the bed, he takes hold of my calves and pulls me down to meet him, and my legs splay, revealing what's left of me he hasn't seen. He draws a hand over me slowly. "Jesus, Bennet." His eyes glaze. "You feel so good."

I writhe as he makes another pass across me, aware of the easy glide of his hand over the slick folds. I watch through hooded eyes as he coats his shaft in my wetness.

He leans over me, a hand resting beside my head as he positions himself at my entrance. "Ready?"

I arch my hips in assent, greeting his tip with my warmth. "Please."

He slides into me smoothly, farther and farther in until he's sheathed to the hilt. He begins to thrust. I raise my hips to meet him, shuddering at each partial withdrawal, clenching at every plunge. He holds me, our bodies pressed together from shoulder to pelvis, physically locked. The pressure in me builds.

We grind against one another, the press of his hand above my ass maintaining pressure exactly where I need it until I'm digging my nails into his back. My breath is a startled snarl.

A twist of his hips, and I'm biting at the muscle between his shoulder and neck. I'd be embarrassed by how quickly he's brought me to the breaking point, but I can't hold back. I don't want to with him. Not ever. He maintains his pace as my climax shatters me, the relief excruciating.

Goosebumps appear on the skin before me, and his body tenses. "Bennet," he cries, and I pull his face to mine. I kiss him, stroking my tongue along his as he releases, thrusting and shuddering, then slowing. He breaks the kiss to rest his forehead on mine. There's sweat on both our brows now, and we're panting.

"Holy shit, Bennet." His skin is blotchy and red, his hair tousled from my grip. It's the most disheveled he's ever looked *and* the most appealing, surpassing even the image of him in glasses.

I giggle, and his body rumbles with a low laugh. With me still reeling from the climax and him still *in* me, the movement rocks me with an aftershock. My hips buck and I gasp.

His eyes go wide, and he carefully withdraws. My giggles start up again, and Darcy collapses, one side of his body partially on top of me, an arm and a leg draped over my body. He smiles and I grin right back. That was worth the wait.

His eyes dart past me. "You wanna give that tub a go?"

◆ · ◆

"That first night I saw you," Darcy begins.

I turn my head to face him. I lie on my belly, resting my head on my arms. Darcy lounges beside me. He's propped on one elbow, running his free hand over my exposed backside. He begins at my shoulder, then sweeps down my back, rising up the incline of my ass, down to graze the top of my hamstring before reversing the route.

He smiles and shakes his head. "You scared the hell outta me."

I'm tempted to feign innocence, but the admission makes me smile. He watches his hand journey up and down my back. "I didn't know what to think. If you looking at me was part of the show, if that meant I was going to be singled out for something later."

I cast a meaningful glance at our current positions. "Are you thinking you weren't?"

"That's one hell of a long game, Ms. Bennet." His hand changes direction, cupping along my rear and moving side to side. "That first night, I was determined not to enjoy myself. Charles had made an offer on the property without seeing it, clearly had no idea what it entailed . . . I was fuming at him. And then you showed up and ruined my brooding with your 'One way to find out.'"

I laugh. "I was only trying to loosen you up. You were so starchy." I bite my lower lip. "And I didn't plan to listen in on your conversation that night," I add. "Ming and I were getting pasties, and I heard you guys out on the landing."

"Just think if you hadn't."

I give a dry chuckle. "It would have spared several people a lot of heartache—"

"I meant that we'd probably have been getting naked together a lot sooner."

"Ooh," I coo. "That, too."

His hand stills. "I'm sorry for what I said then. I was trying to get Charles to lay off, because I knew he'd keep pestering me all night if I didn't talk to you again. And I had my suspicions about the club, everyone being in on some scheme to ensnare Charles, or get to him through me—"

"You don't give much credit to your winning first impression," I say with a smirk.

"*That* was insolent. And deserved. I couldn't look at the cards until we'd moved on to the next bar. I wouldn't even let Charles open his. It took me two more drinks, but I found the Four of Clubs and that was it. I turned around and went back for you, but you were gone."

"You—you were with Charles when he came to see Jane!"

"You'd vanished into the night," he laments, and I laugh. "Then there you were, holding Jane's head together. I can't even talk about that glove peel. And the Work It party—"

"*Me?* You were the one being so damn charming and attentive. It almost interfered with my wounded pride."

"And I was wondering what you had on under the dress. I wanted to believe nothing." He looks off into the middle distance. "No bra, no panties . . ."

I laugh, but the idea gets me squirming. "How far did you get with those musings?"

"Nothing realistic. Just you. And me, confirming there was nothing on underneath."

"That's—"

"Then ravaging you on my desk."

I choke on my laugh. "Goodness, you're expedient."

"I already had you down to one item of clothing. At least I waited 'til we got to the office. It could have been the buffet table."

"Maybe another time."

"Oh?" Darcy nudges my shoulder and rolls me onto my back, exposing me to him. The insistent move makes me moan, but his eyes go soft. "Oh, no . . ."

His tone has me following his attention to my right breast. The nipple is marred with blotches of red; the rough removal of the pastie earlier must have ruptured some capillaries. His brow furrows in concern and he cups my breast. "Are you okay? I'm sorry—"

"I told you to do it," I remind him, and his face softens. "That was . . . new. For me." A flush rises in my cheeks and flares across my chest at the admission. Darcy watches the progression of pink with rapt interest. "I've never wanted that before. Roughness. I guess I trust you."

"Oh?"

I raise an eyebrow at the surprise in his voice, though I'm still trying to breathe normally. "What?"

"I trust you, too." He leaves my breast to rub along my side, his eyes doing that searching thing he's so prone to.

"What are you looking for?" My voice is a whisper.

He shakes his head, eyes still moving over my face. "I don't know. But every time, it's just been you. You're always *you*, whether you're selling pasties or tearing into me in a bar." He trails his fingers to my hip. "It's like I said after your peel tonight. It's all *you*." He slides his hand between my thighs. "Multitudes."

"Me?" I mean to sound thoughtful, but it turns into a moan as he makes a leisurely pass against my center. My hips buck.

His chest rises in that slow, smoldering way I've been thinking about since the night we met. The intake of breath that's supposed to precede a pounce. "God*damn*, Bennet."

The words scrape along my body, plucking a plea from amid the baiting little comments already on standby: "Please?"

Darcy's eyes meet mine, and at long last, the man pounces.

CHAPTER

❖ · 23 · ❖

"Morning." Darcy gives me a sleepy smile. He lies on his stomach, arms curled around his pillow like he spent what little time we slept hugging it. The bedsheet is tantalizingly low on his back, exposing the top of his rear.

I've been awake for a few minutes, languidly perusing the form I've gotten to know so well. It's been a lovely way to ease into consciousness; there's a particularly endearing freckle just above his left butt cheek I keep returning to. I'm considering naming it.

"I might have to duck out before housekeeping shows." I point at the window. Darcy peers over his shoulder, still hugging the pillow. The large pane of glass bears the incriminating stamp of my backside: two oblong prints for my shoulders and either side of my spine and a second pair of smaller spots where my butt was. There are multiple handprints, too; Darcy switched his grip while I was *otherwise* secured to the window.

Round two was . . . *ambitious*.

"I might need a picture of that."

I hold up my phone. "Way ahead of you."

He chuckles, scooting up to kiss my shoulder. Sadly, the sheet travels with him. "How are you?"

I prop myself up against the tufted velvet headboard, leaving the phone on the pillow beside me. "A little saddle-sore, but I'll manage." He grins, and I tap his nose. "Don't get cocky," I warn, but really, he can be as smug as he'd like.

He pushes away his pillow and scoots closer, kissing the notch in my collarbone before resting his head on my bare shoulder. I run my fingers through his thick hair. Definitely grays in there. *Yum.* He drapes an arm across me, snuffling a little like a dog might while getting comfortable. We're *cuddling.* It's so . . . quaint, considering everything else we've done in this room.

His hold shifts, the hand at my ribs edging inward, following the swell of my right breast, and he lets out a sympathetic noise as he cups around the nipple. The bruising has darkened to an ugly purple; I noticed it in the bathroom earlier.

I giggle. "Mr. Darcy, you've purpled my nurple."

He half-smiles. "I don't think I'm going to be able to forgive myself for this," he says, grazing the tender area with his fingertips.

My breath comes in tighter at his touch, my nipple pebbling. "You're well on your way to earning *my* forgiveness, if that helps."

"Hmm." His hand closes around me, and he kneads gently. The cool touch is soothing, but I pray that's not his sole incentive. My hips shift in time with his ministrations, and he lifts his head to watch me, settling on his side. He leaves my breast and traces the line of my body to the sheet draped over my hip. He pulls it away, tossing the cover to the foot of the bed, revealing our nakedness to the daylight.

"Jesus, Bennet," he breathes, taking me in with the same mix of reverence and desire as last night. I shiver. I feel exposed—too exposed, to the point of vulnerability. Again, a thrill rushes through me, not concern.

The sunlight makes shadows in the valleys and planes of his muscles; I want to run my fingers along every rise and fall, create an interactive map of his topography. Venturing lower, I find the morning has taken hold of a certain endowment. I decide I would like to take hold of said endowment myself.

My phone rings.

"No one who knows me would call before noon," I say, my focus low.

He's laughing as I push him onto his back, but the sound cuts short when I sit astride his hips and take hold of his hot length. Darcy sucks in a gasp, eyes shuttering before he palms my breasts. I release him, shifting until he's nestled against me, and scan for the condoms.

My phone starts up again.

Nope. *No chance.* I rock my hips, grinding over Darcy's erection. He leaves my breasts to grip my ass, holding me to him. A low sound escapes him. I increase my pace, and a prickle of sweat begins high between my shoulder blades, tension coiling in my belly. Holy goddamn hell, we're going to get me off like *this*. I'm close, so—

My phone starts ringing again, and I whine in frustration.

He pinches my tender nipple. "Finish, Bennet."

The authority in his voice shoves me over the edge. I come, gasping and calling out his name for the umpteenth time in I don't know how few hours. He keeps me firmly against him, maintaining that critical contact as the climax takes its time to crash and ebb. I collapse onto his chest, liquid.

Darcy rotates our bodies so he's on top of me, positioning himself against my still-quivering opening. "The hell did I do with those condoms?" he growls.

"By . . . window?" I pant.

Another phone begins to vibrate somewhere in the room. My phone joins in.

Darcy and I stare at one another. "Who's—"

"I don't know, but I hate them," I growl, fumbling for the phone. *Jane?* "Oh, for shit's—" I take the call. "*What?*"

"Why haven't you picked up?" Jane demands.

"I just did," I snap. "What—"

"Charles's deal fell through."

My chest goes tight. "What?"

Darcy must overhear Jane because his brow furrows. He climbs off me and strolls in all his naked loveliness to retrieve his phone from his jacket. When he looks at the screen, his shoulders fall. "Shit."

"He's talking to his lawyer now." Jane's words are fast and uneven. "We're out next month."

"*What?*"

"Andrea's beside herself. Has she tried calling you?"

"Maybe. My phone's on *Do Not Disturb* until nine on weekends. How's Charles handling it?" I turn to Darcy as he joins me on the bed. "Meryton's changing hands in a month."

"I don't understand how this happened. And Charles isn't picking up."

"He's talking to his lawyer." I go back to Jane, who's repeating my name. "Just catching Darcy up. I'm putting you on speaker."

"Charles is disappointed, but there's bigger shit at work here. Bennet." His tone grows insistent as his voice erupts from the speaker. "How much do you know about Wickham?"

Darcy lets out a sharp, "Fuck!" that has me cocking my head. He scrubs his palm down his face.

"Wickham?" I repeat—the name-drop is totally random to me.

"Because that's who Meryton went to!" says Jane. "*He's* the god-damn *nephew*."

The news cuts across my gut like a blade. "*What? How did we not know that?*"

"There's so much more to this, Ben. He has Ginn."

"*What?*"

"He has Ginn under contract."

The air rushes out of my lungs. Wickham's stolen the venue. Now Ginn, too? I'm about to ask *how* but instead say, "Tonic?"

"Nope. Just Ginn."

"They're inseparable!"

"Not anymore."

They let *him* come between them? "How binding is this contract?"

"I don't know, but, Bennet, that's not the worst of it. Did—" He takes in a long breath. "Did you show Wickham your Meryton designs?"

A chill slithers up my spine. Darcy's hand goes to my knee. "No. Wh-why?" The word leaves me slowly, churning awkwardly on my tongue. The cold spreads, the ghost of old trauma curling around my rib cage. "*Jane.*" I struggle for calm. "Why are you asking?"

Darcy's grip on my knee tightens. Jane sighs, and I know what's coming, even though I don't know how it's possible. I look at my palm, the fine white scar from the sandstone, and the familiar sensation of falling washes over me. It's happened again.

"Some wires got crossed in the email chain and Charles was forwarded pages of Wickham's proposal." Jane's voice is heavy with apology. "His concept? The big idea he used to get his uncle to hand it all off to him? It's one of *yours*."

My mouth opens but I don't know how to form the words. I catch bits and pieces as Jane describes elements from an older series of my drawings, one I abandoned to better realize at Pemberley. But his words are drowned out by the screaming in my head. *It's happened again. It's fucking happened again.*

I'm shaking. Every muscle in my body is rigid as I struggle against the onslaught of old hurts and the pain of this fresh betrayal. I trusted Wickham. I told him what happened in LA, and he used it as a blueprint to undermine the deal. To undermine *me*.

No, not just me. This time, I'm not falling alone. He's stolen more than ideas. He's stolen my second home. By coming between Ginn and Tonic, he's tearing apart my second family. He's potentially screwing over the people and place I value over almost anything, and he's using my work to make it happen.

"*NO.*" It comes out of me so sharply, Darcy flinches. "He doesn't get to do this. This isn't happening again. Meryton is *ours*."

"Could he be at Ginn's, you think?" I shove myself from the bed, scanning the room for the dress Darcy peeled from me. Was that really only a few hours ago? How can last night even exist on the same plane as the past five minutes?

I spot a hint of green by the window and beeline for it. "Do you know her address? Does Ming?" I pluck the dress from the floor, unearthing with it the wreckage of condom wrappers. "I swear to God, if he thinks—"

I turn to find Darcy in front of me. His dark eyes fix me to the spot, his concern so plain, my words catch, only to release as a strangled sob.

It's happened again. Logic threatens to derail my anger. My eyes well. What am I doing? Charging after the guy? Then what? Jane said the deal is done. Wickham has Meryton.

When my hold gave way in LA, it took days for me to hit the ground. The descent was gradual, the rumors and lies taking their time as I realized the floor was coming up to greet me. This is more like my actual fall: quick and unforgiving. Even the ache in my ribs feels the same. It revives the crushing ugliness that chased me from the other side of the country. Every brutal memory, every dirty look aimed at me in the days before I left. That I was nothing. The feelings pile on.

I let the dress slip from my fingers. It's over.

Darcy gestures for the phone. I raise it, Jane's worried voice carrying on in the space between us. "Jane?" His eyes stay on mine. "Hi, yeah. She'll call you back later. When Charles finishes with his lawyer, tell him to call me?"

Tears press against the backs of my eyes, and my mouth feels thick with the impending breakdown. Darcy places a hand on my cheek. I lean into it, covering his hand with mine, but I can't speak.

Darcy says it for me. "Wickham." The two syllables drip with venom, reminding me of their shared past.

"Did you know he was involved?" I ask.

"Not until the night at Meryton, when we danced." He takes the phone from my hand and tosses it onto the couch. "That's when I linked him to the owner. He's an uncle through marriage, so I wasn't sure about the connection until I checked. It's why I left so suddenly."

His mom's new brother-in-law. This was his "family thing."

"Why didn't you mention it?"

He thumbs my cheek. "I didn't think I needed to. Even when I confirmed the relation, it all but guaranteed the deal was Charles's. Wickham's completely unreliable. There was no way he could convince anyone to pass something of worth on to him. Not without—"

"My design." The words claw through me. I close my eyes, resting my bare back to the glass. "How could I have been so stupid?"

"Bennet—"

"He knew what happened in LA, Darcy." I push off the window. "I told him everything, and he fucking used it against me. Against all of us!"

I make it the handful of steps to the un-couch and collapse, folding over my knees. My whole body aches. I didn't realize how much I was banking on my foothold at Meryton as my way back into the field. This was my chance. And it's gone.

As the idea settles, my thoughts continue to bounce, lighting on one grim prospect before drifting to another. Where will the changing of hands leave the regular performers? Will anyone from the old guard be invited to stay on? Would anyone even want to? This was Jane's most stable gig, but with his connection to Charles, will he be cast out? What about Ming? Tonic?

Will I ever see Meryton again? The thought sucks the breath from me.

"Bennet?" Darcy's voice is tight with concern. He sits beside me, draping a plush black robe over my shoulders.

I shake my head, pulling the robe around me. It's a whole other level of gut punch. If I weren't already in a ball, the idea that I'll never see Meryton again would have me curling over my pitching stomach. But I can't go back in there, not with Wickham at the helm, seeing my work being realized under his name. I know we have a month, but there's no way he won't be around before then, gloating . . .

Darcy rubs my back, his hand brushing circles between my shoulder blades. For half a moment, some base impulse has me blaming him for not warning me when he could have. But the misdirected anger dies before I can fully realize the target. He warned me, in a way, and I let myself be suckered, however briefly. I left Wickham alone with something valuable.

I was so sure he was looking at my photos. I grit my teeth. Fucking vanity. *Way to go, Bennet.*

The guilt mingles with the anger and disappointment, churning like acid in my empty stomach. My ideas did this. Whatever the outcome for the others, it's my work that made it possible. *My* work is being used to hurt the people closest to me.

That's the thought I cling to, and it's enough to keep me from a total emotional free fall. I'm not falling alone.

"I can't run away this time, Darcy." My voice is thick with the threat of tears. "Too many other people were wrapped up in that deal."

"What do you want to do?"

"I—I don't know," I admit. "I'm somewhere between sobbing and screaming. But I want my people. I want to get everyone we can together and . . ." Again, I hit a wall. "Commiserate?"

I stand, pushing my arms through the sleeves of the robe as I consider the room. "Could everyone hang out up here?" Darcy looks pointedly past me to the window, and I remember the sex stamp. "Or somewhere we haven't sexually ransacked?"

He chuckles and stands. At some point, he put on a dark pair of boxer briefs. The cuts of muscle disappearing into his waistband provide a moment's reprieve from the misery of the last few minutes. "The hotel's restaurant has a private room. They're doing brunch, so I doubt the space is being used. I'll look into it."

"Then I'll rally the troops." The prospect is enough to inspire a tentative sprout of optimism, but I can't muster a smile. Darcy pulls me into a hug. The solid feeling of him is unexpectedly reassuring. I lean into it, greedy for the support.

He kisses the top of my head. "We'll figure this out."

I nod, because I want him to be right.

I just wish I believed him.

CHAPTER

24

Jane leans into me, the side of his head warm against mine as we huddle in the booth in the Standard's Wine Room. Darcy was right about the space's availability and was able to secure it for us until tonight's dinner service. I still don't know what we're going to do once everyone arrives, but just having Jane close has been enough to make me feel almost human.

"He got the plans the day he came by with the girls," he says with the empathy of a heart familiar with betrayal.

"It's obvious now. They were all acting *so* weird—" I grit my teeth, stung anew at the Twins' involvement, and grip the bag on my lap a little more tightly.

Something inside crinkles, so I relax my hold. When Jane spilled through the yellow revolving door and into the lobby, he was carrying two bags. One held a few days of work clothing for me, as he'd rightly anticipated I planned to extend my sleepover with Darcy. The green messenger bag currently in my lap came at the advisement of Charles's lawyer, who suggested we go through my work for evidence of earlier stages of the design Wickham stole. I've been clinging to it since Jane explained what was inside, but I haven't brought myself to look in.

"I'm sorry if anything got wrinkled," Jane says, indicating the bag. "I was a little flustered and swept everything off the top of your desk into the thing. I think your pen cup ended up in it."

I laugh. It feels good. "Thank you, boo."

"You okay? I mean, all things considered."

"It will be good to get everyone here, I think. Have us all on the same page. Charles," I say, and sit up as he joins the table, scooting into the booth to sit on Jane's other side. "I'm so sorry about your deal."

"It's pretty awful." He sighs, shoulders falling, looking for all the world like a reprimanded golden retriever. One glance at Jane has him perking up some. "But I've already gotten more than I could have dreamed from the arrangement."

Jane purses his lips against his smile, but his eyes go bright. "*You.*"

Darcy makes his way toward us, sliding his phone into his back pocket as he walks. I stand and join him at the end of the room's long dining table.

"Fitz isn't the strongest on intellectual property," he says, "but he's gotten hold of the partner who is. She agrees with Charles's lawyer about going over your work."

I grip the strap of the bag, my nails digging into the cotton weave.

Darcy's eyes go soft. "It's your call, Bennet. I don't want to stress you any further, but they want us to act quickly. I'm happy to go, so you can stay with everyone here. If you'd rather send copies, we can do that. Or you and I can take them up there together."

"No. You can take them," I say, though I still don't let go of the bag. "But I can't. I can't look at them right now. It's raw, is all."

Darcy reaches out, but instead of taking the bag, he rests his hands on my upper arms, gently guiding me closer. "It's up to you."

"If you go, will you stay with them? With the designs, I mean. I know I'm being paranoid, but I don't want my stuff with people I don't know. I trust you."

I said it last night, but something about repeating the words now makes the room go still. Because I mean it. I trust him. Not because I'm trying to be brave, but because he deserves it. Darcy's made missteps and gone above and beyond to remedy them—he's proven himself.

His throat constricts in a swallow. "Of course."

"You don't have to do all this," I say belatedly. "I appreciate it, but don't feel obl—"

"Bennet." His face is tight, not in the lights-out way, but paired with the set of his shoulders, he's clearly holding himself in check. It's actually pretty hot. "You know my history with Wickham. On one level, this is just another underhanded move from him, but he's brought you into this, and he's screwed up an opportunity for Charles. I've half a mind to hunt him down so you could strangle him with your garter belt."

This gets a rusty laugh. "A little kinky, no?"

Some of the tension leaves him. "I'm in this, too, Bennet. Right now, I can offer the legal angle. IP is tricky, but I'm going to do everything I can. You just give yourself a break." When I frown, he rubs my cheek. "This isn't your fault."

The sentiment is so ludicrous I could laugh, but the gentle way he says it has me drawing in a breath instead. My chest expands beyond the crushing tightness it's been bound in since Jane's call. The relief is dizzying. Darcy's face is already angled toward mine, and I tug him in for a kiss that makes me deeply appreciative of the complimentary toothbrushes in the suite's bathroom.

When we come up for air, he looks a little shell-shocked. "What was that for?"

"Saying what I needed to hear." I give him another quick peck. "Even if I don't believe it."

"Well, I do." He squeezes my shoulders, then lets me go. I hand him the bag, and he takes it, pulling the strap over his head to wear it cross-body, like I did.

"Call me if you need anything. I'll be in touch," he adds, patting the bag. It makes a crunching sound, like crumpling paper, and he winces.

"You might want to look through that on your way," I say. "I think there was an X-Acto knife in with my pens."

"Will do." He gives me a final kiss on the cheek. I watch him stroll down the room, and he opens the door, stepping back to let Ming enter before stepping out.

Her leopard-print caftan billows as she struts my way, a pitcher of mimosas aloft in one clawed hand, like she's presenting a prized kill. "I figured we could use a little something." She deposits her bounty on the table, then yanks me to her for a fierce hug. "What a morning, eh?"

"Understatement," I manage to say, the air in my lungs forced out by the crush of her boobs. "Have you heard from the band?"

She releases me to smother Jane and then Charles, who have joined us and squeak out salutations of their own. "They're playing a booze cruise on the Hudson. Johnny, too. I'm going to give them a shout later." She bumps me with her hip. "How'd your night go, by the way? Mr. Tall Dark and Fuckable got you walking funny?"

Normally, I'd groan, but Ming's steadfast commitment to filth is actually refreshing. Charles doubles over in laughter, and Jane lets out an exasperated, *"Ming!"*

"A lady never tells," I say.

She cackles. "If I see one, I'll keep that in mind."

The door clatters open: Andrea. "What bullshit," she announces, voice booming as she strides the length of the room. She has also grabbed a pitcher of mimosas, though I doubt she intends to share. "It's bad enough to have been swindled, but betrayed by Ginn? Criminal! To say nothing of what that scoundrel did to you." She rests a hanky-laden hand on my shoulder. "Oh, darling, I should have asked you to show me your work, gotten it on record . . ."

Fresh guilt piles on. If I'd been braver sooner, maybe if I'd spoken to Andrea earlier or had my work with me the night I finally did . . . Would that have changed anything?

Tonic slips in through the still-open door. The room goes silent, and I have to remind myself to breathe. Her gaze immediately drops to the floor.

"I sent her a text, too," Ming says quietly. "She's lost . . . a lot, I think."

Tonic bites the nail of her right thumb. The gesture takes me back to that day at my apartment, and the tightness in my chest eases some. I walk toward her, and it's as though my approach has untethered her from the spot at the door, as she half-runs to meet me. "I'm so sorry, Kitten!" she chokes out. "He said you'd shown him the designs and he wanted another look. I didn't know he'd taken them until this morning!"

I nod. With her in front of me, her face tearstained and puffy, I'm not angry, and I'm willing to take her at her word that she didn't mean any harm. After all, I was taken in by Wickham, too.

"It's . . . not cool. But thank you for the apology. Have you heard from Ginn?" I ask, not sure if I should. "What happened?"

Tonic's shoulders slump, her eyes welling. "She wasn't at our practice space this morning. When I texted, she wrote back, *Sorry. Under contract with W. Solo act. Huge opportunity! Couldn't say no!*" Her hand strays to her left side as she recites the message. I wince: her tattoo, the one that coordinates with Ginn's.

"Would you like a hug," I offer, "or will that make you cry?"

"I could go for a hug," she says in a small voice.

I wrap my arms around her and give her a squeeze. The girl is solid wiry muscle and trembles like a whippet as quiet sobs overtake her. A moment later, Jane joins the hug from behind Tonic, and a pair of softballs jam between my shoulder blades as another pair of arms envelops me; Ming. Andrea reaches over Jane to pat Tonic's shoulder.

Here are my people. The thought almost makes me smile, but it falters immediately. I try to remember what Darcy said about not blaming myself, but I can't help it. Wickham had his own connection to the club, but I'm the one who let him embed himself in the group. I drew the plans that stole the deal. I'm why we're here, trying to keep this found family from fracturing.

The thought becomes less grim as I dwell on it. I *am* why we're all here. I got us gathered in one place. The group hug slowly disbands. A tear slips down my cheek, and as I take in the faces around me, I'm not the only one whose eyes are wet.

This is worth fighting for.

→ · ←

"So." The word comes out wobbly. I clear my throat. "The deal fell through."

Even though everyone has had a few hours to process the information, the words suck the life out of the group. Shoulders droop, brows crease, and the only sounds for a few seconds are a sniffle from Tonic and the low hum of the room's wine fridges.

"Andrea," I ask, "do you have any idea what to expect from the next few weeks?"

She sighs. "You have a month before he closes for renovations. Bookings and schedules are good through then, assuming any of you can stomach the idea. Tonic, luv . . ." Andrea looks to Tonic, who chews on her thumbnail, not meeting anyone's eyes. "I don't know what you can expect. It's a hideous situation for you."

Tonic nods, eyes still downcast. Ming throws an arm over her shoulder, tugging her close.

"I'm already out." Andrea takes a dramatic pull from her mimosa. "That Wickham bastard is coming in this week to get a feel for how things are run. He said I was welcome to help transition, but I told him to stuff it. It's humiliating enough to be shoved aside after so many years there. I'm not going to stand by and watch him steal it."

"Likes he's stolen everything else," Ming mutters.

The heavy silence falls over us again.

"Oh, good! You are in here. Gales!"

I turn at the unexpected voice to find Chloe at the open door. She charges toward our booth, and I rise to meet her. Gales follows her in, carrying mimosa pitcher number three, and closes the door behind him.

"Ohmigod." She wraps me in a hug. "Are you okay?" She holds me at arm's length, eyes narrowed. "Are we plotting revenge? We're here to plot revenge, right?"

Gales adds his pitcher to the table, then hugs me, too. "You hanging in there, Lizard?"

"It's been a weird morning," I say, though their sudden appearance is adding to the surreality. "What are you two doing here?"

"You're family!" Chloe slides into the booth beside Ming, and everyone shifts to make room for the new arrivals. "And Jane's one of my favorite people. Plus, Ming let me set her lashes last night. That's a sacred act of bonding."

Ming drops her head to Chloe's shoulder. "We're basically married."

"Hey," Gales protests, but he's smiling, and sits beside his erstwhile fiancée.

Ming waggles her eyebrows. "I'd be happy to share."

I grab a chair from the long dining table behind me, pulling it to the head of the table we're gathered around. "But how did you know to come here?"

"That was me," Charles says, hand half-raised. "I sent him a text. We had coffee with Darcy yesterday afternoon."

Gales sighs, sinking against the dark leather, and Chloe puts a hand over one of his. "We had a theoretical stake in the plan, too."

I cock my head. "How's that?"

Chloe taps her teeth together, like she's priming her jaw for a confession. "We're considering a move. That's why we're out here this week. My gigs were a trial run for something long-term."

"What?" A tentative spark of happiness warms in my chest. "You're coming here?"

"Nothing's been decided," Chloe says quickly. "I'm not sure how much time I'd want to commit to the job here, how much I'd still freelance. But . . . yeah." She fights a smile. "It's huge."

"So, I've been looking into kitchens," says Gales. "Mostly sous positions. But at coffee yesterday, Charles and I got to talking. Charles needed a chef, and I had some thoughts for a menu." He half-smiles. "It went well."

I arch a brow at Charles.

"Darcy's doing, mostly. I think he made a point of steering the conversation. But Gales had a bunch of ideas," he says, tipping his head toward his would-be employee. "I spoke to his chef in LA and he agreed: this guy is going places."

Their consistent use of the past tense snuffs out my little glow of happiness. I cross my arms over my chest. "So on top of everything else, Gales has been screwed out of his first kitchen."

Chloe shakes her head. "Lizard, honey, nothing was official."

"It was just an offer," Gales adds.

"But does this mean you're less likely to take your job here, Chloe?" I ask.

"If Meryton had worked out—" She looks at Gales, then shrugs. "That would have sealed the deal. But it's still on the table."

I rake my fingers through my hair. The room bottoms out around me, and the nauseating falling sensation rocks my sense of equilibrium. The phantom pain in my ribs flares, and my left hand feels hot—

"No!" The word bursts out of me, bouncing off the wine-bottle-lined walls, and eight pairs of wide eyes are on me. "Fuck Wickham. We're not letting him win. Meryton was going to be your investment, Charles. Your first kitchen." I point to Gales, and looking between Jane and Ming, I say, "Your most reliable gig. Tonic's been screwed out of a partnership. Andrea, Meryton was practically your life's work."

Ming steeples her fingers, angling them to point at me. "Chloe mentioned revenge. Is that where your head is?"

I don't know where my head is, but I know what I feel, and I know what I don't want. "Meryton was home, but only because we were in it. Without us, all Wickham has is a building and a drawing."

"Both of which are fairly important," says Chloe.

"But we have *us*. Performers. A chef. Someone with almost twenty years' experience running a club. We have a solid financial backer." I don't know where the idea comes from, but when it settles in my mind, it's obvious: "We'll find another property for the show and move it there."

Across from me, several mouths open, budding protests clear on their respective faces, but I press on.

"Charles," I say before anyone can interrupt me with "logic," "you looked into other places in the area, right?"

He blinks, uncertain. "Yeah. But I know most have been sold by now. Even if any are still available, you're talking about adding the entire purchasing process on top of any remodeling. That's time Wickham doesn't have to spend."

"But it's possible?" I ask, unwilling to be derailed.

"Nowhere else had that Meryton magic." He smiles. "But most of that was you all, anyway."

"And you'd still want to invest in something?"

"Absolutely."

I look at Andrea. "You still game?"

"And undermine that Wickham shit? With pleasure. But Charles is right, Kitten," she says, voice heavy. "This would be a huge undertaking, and incredibly time-consuming."

"Let's not worry about time. Let's focus on what we can control."

"Time still matters, though, Ben," says Jane. "Most of us don't have day jobs. If this is going to take a few months, that's time without a chunk of income for most of us."

"Which would have been the case during Meryton's remodel, too," I say, hoping to combat the group's stubborn practicality with some of my own. "Could we produce the show somewhere else for a while?"

"If you're willing to trek to Astoria, the club Momma works out of has nights free," Ming offers. "And I know Darlene would give us a night or two out in Bushwick, but I'd hate to ask. She's doing her own thing out there, and I don't want to cut into that, y'know?"

I nod. "Understood."

Chloe tugs at the neck of her shirt, a nervous habit she's had since we were kids, and I brace myself. "I don't want to be a spoilsport, Lizard. If all this works out, great. Perfect, really. It would be a huge opportunity for a lot of people . . ."

Gales places one of his big hands over hers and nods. "But as it stands, it's uneven ground for us to pin our futures on."

"I get it." It stings, but I do. "But outside of all that, say Charles and Andrea luck onto a property and we could get this off the ground in a reasonable amount of time. Or," I add, desperate, "Darcy and his uncle find out some legal way to get Meryton back to us. He's with lawyers right now, looking through my work to see if there's a way to link my stuff to what Wickham stole. If that pans out, there's a chance Wickham won't be able to keep the club. That's two scenarios where we're still together."

I'm losing them, though I don't think I ever had them in the first place. And I don't blame them. I've been here before. Again, the feeling of falling threatens to knock me from my seat.

Jane's gaze is too pitying for me to hold. "Meryton was a reliable gig, but gigs come and go, Ben—"

"What if it was more than a gig?" I ask without thinking, but there's something to it. The conversation I had with Ming and Chloe, Ming's thoughts on scouting . . . "What if it was something you had a stake in? Not the property, but the concept." A new hope ignites in my chest, burning brighter than before. It's like Friday's moment of inspiration with Chloe at Pemberley: this is *it*. "What if we all did?"

Tonic looks up from her thumb-chewing. "All of us?"

Andrea eyes me, tapping the base of her champagne flute. "What's going on in that clever head of yours, kitty cat?"

"Whatever will get you all to consider this?" I admit, and she snorts back a laugh. "Like Chloe said, it could be a huge opportunity, but only if we make it one. So think about it. What would we want the show to look like? And I mean in every capacity. Do we want an overall theme for the venue—"

"Ugh," says Ming. "No. I love what Darlene's doing, but I'd hate to have that kind of a restriction. Theme nights? Sure. And holiday shows—"

I clap. "Yes! This is what I'm talking about. We were completely at the mercy of the last owner. And not to say that Charles would treat us poorly"—I look to Charles, and he holds up his hands, like he's showing he's unarmed—"but we can make this work for all of us. Let's get into the bones of this thing."

The faces across from me brim with hope too tempered with reason to act on.

"I know it's a long shot. And maybe it's stupid to get fired up like this. Maybe—" I snap my mouth shut to trap in what I was about to say. *Maybe it is just me.*

"Ben?" Jane takes my hand. "What is it?"

I keep my focus on Jane's elegant fingers. "Jane and Chloe and Gales know, but I gave up a huge opportunity a few years back because of something like this." I let out a dry laugh. "Exactly like this, actually. Someone stole my ideas. I told Wickham about it, and that's probably how he got this whole shady, shitty enterprise rolling. But when it happened, I ran away. And I don't regret it. I can't."

I meet Jane's worried gaze and smile. "The move brought me to you." I squeeze his fingers. "It introduced me to burlesque and Meryton and so many things and people I can't imagine living without anymore. I only regret leaving LA for the reasons I did and for hiding from that shame so long, I didn't realize it didn't have a hold over me anymore."

As I say it, I realize it's true. What happened then wasn't my fault, but how I reacted was my choice. The same goes for today, and I'm going to choose better. I squeeze Jane's hand again. He's smiling at me, eyes shiny. "I'm not letting this happen again. Not to us."

"Besides," says Ming, "we have three pitchers of mimosas and a swanky private room." She raises her nearly empty glass. "What the hell else are we going to do?"

I release Jane's hand to clap mine together. "Then let's get to work."

❧ · ❧

We lose the room at four, a little earlier than anticipated, but we've been plenty productive. Charles has already lined up viewings at three properties, and Ming and Jane have come up with a dozen potential performers, as well as a solid list of themes and events specific to certain numbers the prospective acts perform. We've filled pages of hotel stationery with ideas, and I tote them to the suite upstairs, where I spend another hour trying to turn them into something cohesive.

I'm still sprawled on the couch thing when the suite's lock grinds to announce Darcy's return. He doesn't have the bag, and while it makes my stomach twist just a little, I knew that would be the case. He called before he left to ask if the lawyers could hang on to my work a little longer.

"Hey there." He toes off his shoes before stepping over the big wedge-shaped cushion forming the back of the couch. His socks are patterned with little sriracha bottles.

"Any thoughts from Fitz's people?" I ask.

He settles beside me, stretching his long legs out against mine. "We should know in a day or two. His firm is good, but if anything comes of this, it's going to take a lot of time."

I groan. "That's the theme for today."

"I'd say your brain trust is the exception to that. When I checked in with Charles, he about talked my ear off. Are you all really going to stick this out?"

My heart gives a little kick. "More than that. We've started a business plan." The words come out high, like I don't quite believe them, despite the evidence on my lap.

"A business plan? Now you're speaking my language."

"Everyone has a role, or some involvement outside of performing..." I don't even try to temper my enthusiasm. "If this works, it's going to be a boon for the whole crew."

"Would you be comfortable sharing it with me?" he asks, plucking his glasses from the neck of his shirt.

"With Will Darcy: Man of Business? I'd be honored." I look at the top page, even though I don't need to. "Andrea for operations. She's available and interested and has been doing this for the better part of two decades. She and Charles already had that sorted, so no surprises there."

He nods. "Easy enough."

"Ming for talent acquisition. Scouting, anyway, on a commission basis. We actually kicked that thought around a while back. And Ming *and* Jane for program development. Still trying to figure out what kind of pay scale to use there, if it's something to lump together with gigs or if there's a salary consideration."

"It's a good thought. What else?"

"We got hold of Esteban and he's getting in touch with the wait and kitchen staffs. Michael for the bar. The band and Johnny are in, too." I drum my fingers against my knee. The next item came to mind while the others were still here, but I didn't write it down.

"Tonic is going to need some help, I think. She didn't say anything directly, and I don't want her to feel like a charity case." I worry my bottom lip. "Depending on the insurance Charles gets, I think that renting her space a few times a week to teach aerial lessons would be a kindness."

"You two clear things up as far as Wickham?"

"Yeah. She was blindsided, too."

"Unless there's a significant difference in cost as far as insurance, you might let her do it free of charge. Those lessons wouldn't interfere with programming, would they?"

I lean my shoulder into his, and he wraps an arm around me. "You are an outstanding sounding board."

"It's why they pay me the big bucks."

"As far as a chef . . . Chloe and Gales are undecided. But best-case scenario, Gales would be in the kitchen. Rumor has it, I have you to thank for that?"

"I merely invited him to coffee with Charles and me. And then nudged the conversation in a very specific direction."

I heave an overwrought sigh. "Already keeping secrets from me."

"If you're asking me to apologize for prioritizing sex with you over recounting how I spent my afternoon, I can." He nuzzles under my ear. "But I wouldn't mean it."

I shiver as goose bumps erupt along my arm. "Valid point." He kisses my neck, and I clear my throat before continuing. "Chloe's only request was that she gets to do portfolio shoots in any finished space."

"You all are really thinking ahead. Bennet, this is impressive. Compare where you are now to where you were this morning."

"It feels good. It might just be the contrast with how shitty everything felt *then*, but this . . ." I face him, resting my arm on the cushion. "I know everyone's in this together, but it feels like mine, a little. And I like that."

"Must be nice," he says, and I raise a brow. That sounded like regret. "Still . . ." He flips through the pages, shifting closer to look them over. His nearness is enough to redirect my attention. "I can't help noticing you haven't listed anything for yourself here."

"I'll be maintaining my kittening duties. And Charles admitted that Ming terrifies him, and that he doesn't want to risk favoring acts Jane proposes, so I'll have final say on new performers. But I already have a full-time job. Work It is entering a new phase, and I'm not going to bail on them, even in our dream scenario. As for long-term . . ."

I didn't express this to anyone else, either, and it feels like a confession. "I want the flexibility to pursue more design work. If we get this off the ground, I don't want it to be a one-and-done for me."

He doesn't say anything for a few seconds, his attention still on the pages in my lap. I wonder if he even heard me, but he blinks, lashes fluttering. His eyes take their sweet time traveling up my torso, and when his gaze meets mine, it's nothing short of lascivious. "I'm very glad to hear that." His voice is a rumble.

The heat coming from him is sudden, but I am more than happy to accommodate the shift. I pick up the pages from my lap, depositing them on the other side of the cushion.

"Speaking as a designer . . ." I point to the window across from us. The evidence of last night's romp had been wiped clean by the time I got back to the room, and the window is an almost unbroken pane of sunset orange. "The view could use a little . . . *je ne sais quoi*, no?"

"Hmm." He sounds convincingly thoughtful as his fingers close on my knee. "I'd hate for your designerly sensibilities to be offended."

I'm still laughing when he springs on me, rolling me to my back.

Darcy smooths his hand under my dress, up my thigh, over my hip—then cocks his head, shifting his hand back down again. "You're not wearing underwear."

"'No bra, no panties,'" I quote. His eyes dart to my neckline, and I finger the bare space between the buttons at my chest. "It's your fantasy. Not your office, but I thought we could improvise."

He reaches to remove his glasses, and I catch his hand.

"No," I say. "Keep 'em on."

CHAPTER

❖ · 25 · ❖

Tuesday evening, after dinner with Chloe and Gales, I stand on the catwalk at Pemberley, head pitched back as I take in the empty room. Even in the partial darkness, the space is a dreamscape.

The house lights come up gradually as Darcy hits the switches upstairs, bringing the room to life one feature at a time. I see each element as rendered in my sketches, like an animation cel has been placed over reality. The lake: tiled. Barn wood: gone, possibly burned in some ceremonial cleansing. The existing chrome balanced with gold accents.

Soon, I promise myself. Once we get everything situated with Meryton, I'll talk to Darcy about this. Maybe sneak in one night and rip down the barn wood myself.

The last two days have passed in a blur. Charles and Andrea have already looked at two potential properties and have another viewing lined up for tomorrow. There's still a chance, however slim, that something could come from the IP angle, that Fitz and his team could uncover a means to get Meryton back to Charles and Andrea. I haven't even raised the subject with Darcy since Sunday. But then, with our respective work schedules limiting our time together, we've been prioritizing *non*verbal exchanges.

I hear Darcy's footsteps behind me. "Did you get what you needed?" I ask, and turn to face him. My stomach flips over. He's carrying the green messenger bag Jane put my design work in Sunday.

Darcy stops short at my reaction, his eyes soft with apology as he gestures to the nearest island. I sigh but step onto it, taking a seat in a round booth. He slides in beside me and places the bag on the table, pulling out a manila folder. Brightly colored tabs protrude from the top and sides, as though the contents have been sorted and labeled. "Sunday, you said it was too raw to look through these. But would it be okay now?"

In answer, I open the file. But my bravado ends there. The first page is a version of the design scheme Wickham stole, as rendered at Pemberley. My chest constricts, and two days of positive momentum can't restrain the reprimand that bounces in my skull: *so, so stupid.*

Darcy puts his hand on my back, and I lean into his touch. "This is the one he has, but at Meryton?"

"Yes. I don't know how I didn't miss those drawings. Maybe because I'd already moved the idea to Pemberley?" With a pang, I realize it's the one I started the night I met Darcy, with the dark matte arc behind the stage.

"One of several set here." He puts the page aside to reveal another Pemberley sketch, then another. My stomach riots. Jane said he'd swept everything from my desk into that bag, but in the general chaos of the day, I failed to consider what that *everything* might entail. Of course the Pemberley work would be there: I spent Saturday morning finalizing the plan inspired by the Eastern Columbia Building. And now Darcy's seen the depth of my obsession with his family's property. *Goody.*

I avoid eye contact, feeling uncomfortably exposed as the plans are arranged on the table. There are four concepts, most iterations of ideas started at Meryton, though the one with the Eastern's color scheme is its own. Seeing them laid out gives me a bittersweet swell of pride, despite my embarrassment. This is the best work I've done.

"Tell me about this one." Darcy picks up the page of turquoise and blues. My heart leaps.

I can't help smiling. "Do you know the Eastern Columbia Building?"

"In . . . downtown LA. Huh." He looks over the page again, dropping his arm from me to pull the supporting illustrations toward him. "A college friend of mine has a place in there. What made you think of it for Pemberley?"

"Chloe jogged my memory the other day. I visited her in LA when I was an undergrad. She took me on a tour of the Historic Core and saved the Eastern for last. It was . . ." Sudden emotion swells in my throat. "Like the first time I saw Ming perform. *Inspiring.* It's why I went to design school. That's what made the internship so important," I say, running my fingers over the sketch. "It felt like it was meant to be, going back to within walking distance of the building that got me hooked on design in the first place. When everything fell apart, it felt a lot less like fate and more like cruel irony." I let out a mirthless laugh. "Kind of like now."

Darcy doesn't say anything.

I close my eyes and force out the truth I've been trying to avoid since I saw that bag in Darcy's hands. "We're not getting Meryton back, are we? Your uncle . . ."

"It's not hopeless, Bennet," he says, too softly for the words to feel believable. "If you're willing to wait, they can pursue this. And you could get a ruling in your favor. But"—he pauses—"there's no guarantee."

My eyes burn, and I wrinkle my nose, hoping to keep the tears at bay. I didn't realize I was hanging on to that sliver of hope. Letting go, it's like picking sandstone from my palm all over again.

"Which is why we're here now." Darcy rests a hand on the Eastern design. "I've been fielding proposals for Pemberley for months. This is better than anything I've seen from any design firm. This . . ." His eyes drift over the page. "This is genius."

This blows Friday's casual "outstanding" out of the water. "Thank you."

"With your permission, I'd like to apply this design to Pemberley."

"You'd like—"

"And, if you're interested"—he pauses, eyes watchful on me—"move the Meryton productions here. Permanently."

I gawk at him, speechless.

He lets me stare for a few seconds. When it's clear that I'm incapable of vocalizing, he raises an eyebrow. "Please?"

I'm already shaking my head. "Darcy, you can't—"

"I've run the numbers. Charles and Andrea have the liquid capital for the renovations. You and yours have the plan."

Me and mine. "Seriously?" My voice is high with disbelief. Or is it shock? *My* concept at Pemberley. A new home for the show.

"I don't want you to feel pressured." There's an undercurrent of concern to his voice. "In this scenario, we actually have time. There's no buying process. Still, you say the word, and I have a short list of contractors to review your plans."

I'm back to dumb amazement. "This is huge, Darcy. *Huge*," I say emphatically. "And don't be offering because . . ." I try to produce something a little more subtle than "because we keep leaving sex stamps on the window of your hotel room," but nothing comes to mind.

He looks amused at my plight.

I nudge him with my knee. "You *know*."

Darcy turns his attention to the table, leaning to peer under it, then braces his foot against the pedestal leg. A quick push creates another foot of space between himself and the tabletop. He reaches for me. "C'mere."

I roll my eyes but slide onto his lap. The snug fit of my dress only allows me to straddle one of his thighs. "You're kind of proving my point."

He chuckles. "I can't promise that the two are mutually exclusive. And if the idea makes you uncomfortable, we can slow down. I'd rather not slow on *either* front"—he squeezes my hips for emphasis—"but this is your call."

I appreciate his assurances, and good *God* is this prospect exciting. But I keep a leash on my enthusiasm. "It feels . . . *impulsive*."

"I'd like to refer to Friday evening as a testament to my restraint."

"When you specifically asked that *I* act as your restraint?"

"Details." He tucks a lock of hair behind my ear. "I've had your work in mind for weeks now, Bennet, since I saw that article on your school's site. If Meryton hadn't fallen through, I'd have asked for your input on Pemberley anyway." His lips quirk into a half smile. "Assuming we'd been restored to civil terms."

"Only civil?" I ask, for no other reason than to voice something that isn't the giddy acceptance of his offer currently dancing on my tongue.

"I'm glad you told me to look through the bag before I got to the firm. First, because that five-by-seven almost killed me. Finn, too. I picked him up on the way to Fitz, and he was with me when I found it. I've never seen anyone blush that hard." His head falls to the seat back. He peers at me through hooded eyes. "Was that your *bookmark?*"

"*It's what I had,*" I say, affecting the same innocent tone he took when I gave him a hard time about looking at my card.

"Then there was your vision of Pemberley. Like something out of a dream. It was hard to focus on anything at Fitz's. I was crawling out of my skin, wanting to get back to the hotel to beg your permission to use it. And I was going to." He smooths his hands down my arms. "But I didn't want to get in your way if that design scheme ended up being what you wanted for your new Meryton. Then you had your plan. And it hit me, looking at what you'd put together, that this was the perfect opportunity for all of us. But I didn't want to cut in on something if Charles wanted to strike out on his own."

"What changed? Why are you asking me now?"

"I couldn't stop thinking about it." He frowns thoughtfully. "My work life revolves around spending other people's money, Bennet. I want to build something of my own. The fact that it involved something so exceptional for this building?" His hands find the exposed skin of my back and my breathing goes tight. "You said it yourself.

Pemberley means a lot to me. I wouldn't trust it to just anyone. I've been waiting the better part of my life for inspiration. You're it."

The word "inspiration" weaves through my rib cage; it's going on the list with "paperwork" and "absolutely." I slide my hand along the stubble of his jaw, trying to ground myself. "And if we *fail*? This is your money, Darcy."

"Every investment has risks. If we remodel and the concept flops . . ." He tips his head side to side, as though weighing the potential outcome. "Not ideal, but hardly ruinous. Pemberley would return to being a rental venue, and a particularly stunning one at that. You would still get to see your plan realized, and—"

"Will still have failed, once again putting my friends' careers in jeopardy, and—oh, yeah—losing you and Charles and Andrea a *bunch* of money—"

"Which could happen in any scenario: here, anywhere else Charles found, the original Meryton. Where's the optimism you had five minutes ago?"

I purse my lips. "What about Pemberley's current bookings?"

He tucks his chin, considering. "We have a smattering the next few months. The majority are far enough out that their relocating shouldn't be an issue."

He's *really* thought about this. "We're going to have to look at that before we go any farther."

His hands scoot to just above my rear. "I have everything in my office."

But he doesn't move. I don't either. A smile makes its way across his face.

"What?" I ask.

"You said *we*."

"If we're doing this, then *we* are doing this," I say. His smile widens and I press a finger to the tip of his nose. "I said *if*. I want everything in writing."

"As a *man of business*, I wouldn't have it any other way."

I bite my lower lip. He didn't even balk at the suggestion. He's committed.

My brain reels. What else should I be asking right now? I only sat in on a few negotiations at my internship; even then, most of the financial details had already been finalized by the time we got to the table. I screw my face up in thought, but I can't hold back my grin any longer. "You want us here."

"I do."

"You want to use my design."

"And I want to pay you for your work. I've seen quotes from several firms. I can guarantee a competitive rate."

I press my fingertips to his lips to shush him. "One step at a time." Having my design realized at Pemberley is already a dream coming true, and the chance to share this with my nearest and dearest has me light-headed. Talking about money would probably make me pass out.

"It was your work, Bennet." He hooks his fingers into the front of my dress, right where, if I were wearing one, the straps of a bra would connect to cups. He uses the hold to pull me close and kisses my neck, letting his lips linger. "You *inspired* me."

My breath shudders as his tongue flits against my jawline. "I have to run it by everyone. Package deal." I'm rambling, trying to get out the last of my transactional concerns before I'm completely swept away by the giddiness tugging at me and the very real inclination to explore the weight-bearing properties of the table behind me.

"Funny you should mention that," he says into the skin below my ear. "Because I suspect we're about to be interrupted."

As if on cue, Darcy's phone vibrates on the bench seat. I glare down at it—

CB: Please don't forget that we're up here and can see everything u2r doing.

"What?" I look up, scanning the floor above. My attention settles on movement in the darkened window of Darcy's office. A light turns on—

I gasp. Andrea, Tonic, Ming, Esteban, and Michael. Even Chloe and Gales—how did they beat us here? Everyone is up there, faces and hands pressed to the glass like they're scouring a zoo exhibit for an evasive resident.

And there's Jane, alternately looking between me and his phone, and Charles, who waves both arms. Is he—I squint—holding bottles of champagne?

My watch buzzes with a text. I read it aloud for Darcy, though it's hard to make out the letters through my sudden tears. *"Can we please come down? Charles is fit to burst and we're all dying. Why were we asked to bring bubbles?* Yes!" I half-blurt, half-sob. I wave with both hands, beckoning them to the ground floor. A second later, everyone's vanished from the window, leaving handprints and lipstick smudges on the glass, then they're crowding the railing to the right of the office.

"Lizard," hollers Chloe. "Why are we here?"

Darcy looks at me. He cups the sides of my face, thumbing away my tears. "It's your call."

"I'm in," I pronounce, and kiss him, heedless of our audience. His arms wrap around me, his fingers twining in my hair as his tongue dances across my upper lip. My heart feels like it's going to explode.

"Kitten!" Ming shouts. "We popping corks or do we have to wait for Darcy to pop his?"

I break the kiss and sit up, wiping away the now-flowing tears. "Get down here!" I wrap my arms around Darcy's neck and press my forehead to his. "We're home."

CHAPTER

✦ · 26 · ✦

Across from me, Diva de los Muertos runs her fingers over one of the rhinestones glued to her temple, prying off the gem and placing it in a pile with the others she's removed. Her face is painted like a sugar skull, the rhinestones detailing flowers she drew for her performance.

Beneath the table, Darcy's fingers drum an anxious beat on my knee, but I'm not concerned: Diva's a go. Since last month's meeting of the minds we've signed a good half-dozen performers to Pemberley and not a single one has even asked for time to think it over. The consistent, well-paying gig is an easy sell, and once we explain the scandal surrounding the show's inception, the offer is just too juicy to pass up.

Ming gives a thumbs-up from her spot at a makeup table behind Diva. She's thrown herself into scouting, attending shows most nights and taking gigs featuring promising new faces, like Diva. The only downside has been these late-night treks to see the potential hires for myself. I'd thought we could have them come to Pemberley, but Ming put the kibosh on that, saying, "Audience chemistry is a critical part of any burlesque performance." A valid point, and she didn't even punctuate it with anything vulgar.

Diva pries off one more rhinestone, turning it over between her fingertips. "I'm in."

Darcy's hand finally stills, and I bump my knee against his. He's been a solid wingman on these recruiting trips, though before tonight I've only brought him along to negotiate with musical acts Jane has scouted. He's come a long way since the night we met, but for him, sitting across from a woman clad only in pasties and a G-string— when that woman isn't me, anyway—still feels like an intrusion.

But Diva's bone-and-flower motif wasn't limited to her face. Her peel gradually revealed a painted skeleton, the white body paint illuminated by a blacklight onstage. The contrast against her dark skin was so dramatic, she looked like an improbably buxom wraith. Even this close, she appears to be wearing a skeleton costume. The illusion is probably why Darcy is more at ease.

"Ming's given me a heads-up on the drama," says Diva. "I promise to keep it on the DL, so no worries." She mimes zipping her mouth shut. The skeletal grin painted over her lips makes the gesture alarmingly realistic.

"Thank you," I say. "It'll all get out eventually, but the discretion is appreciated."

She scoops the pile of discarded rhinestones from the table to her palm. "I have a few shows booked further out than your opening night, so shoot me a schedule and I'll see if there are any conflicts. If you guys can promise a regular gig, you've got me."

She stands, gesturing to her body paint. "If you'll excuse me, I have a date with a hose. Shut up, Ming," she adds, not even looking at the other dancer, whose low chuckle is already rumbling with filth.

With Diva sorted, we turn our attention to Momma, the show's producer and emcee. Ming insisted we arrive on time to catch Momma's opening number, and I'm glad she did. The towering drag queen burst onto the stage with a full-bodied performance of "When You're Good to Mama" that had me itching to hand her a contract, and her version of "Fever," punctuated with deadpan asides about the questionable couples referenced in the song, got more laughs than most of Johnny's standards. Her commentary on Pocahontas and Captain Smith had Darcy wiping away tears.

"Anything on your mind, or did you just ask me to sit down so I wouldn't think you were poaching my talent?" Momma's tone is innocent, but her overlined smile is knowing. Her show has been a launching pad for several new acts, like Diva, but has also become a go-to for established performers who want to try out a new routine. Ming's number tonight was a stunning, subdued peel with fans of trailing blue silk set to "You Look so Fine." It was riveting, totally unlike anything I've ever seen from her, though she insists she still has a few kinks to sort out.

"Did Ming tell you we were coming by?" I ignore Ming's feigned gasp of indignation.

Momma inspects her nails, the red acrylics filed to points. "I don't break out 'Fever' for most Wednesday-night crowds."

"We're looking for someone to fill in for Johnny when he's on tour in March," I say.

"Go on." Her voice is a purr.

"We're thinking we'd start you off with a few spots as a featured singer. If you like the feel of the space, you'd sub for Johnny when he has other commitments. His annual Foul-Entine's Day thing's already scheduled for a Saturday, and there will probably be others once a month or so."

"Is that all?"

"Ming's assembling a Thursday-night set. More of a variety show than classical burlesque," says Darcy. "It will need a host."

"We don't need an answer right away." I draw a business card from my purse, grabbing a pen from the table to write the date of opening night on the back. "If you can make it, we'll save you a table."

Momma spears the card between her talons, turning it over to look at the date. "I can make myself available." She tucks the card into the vast stuffing of her bosom. "Now for the after-show rounds. Momma needs a drink." She sashays through the fringed curtain separating the dressing room from the front of the house.

"She's the first soft 'yes' we've gotten," Darcy muses, eyes on the still-swaying curtain. "Everyone else has been enthusiastic."

Ming drapes her garment bag over the table. "She *did* say she needed a drink . . ."

"That's my cue, right? I'm the closer?" Darcy looks to me for confirmation. At my laugh, he rises. "You need anything?"

"Other than a stimulant?" Ming slides into Darcy's vacant seat. She puts her feet on my lap. "I saw you yawning during my set. It makes a gal doubt her sex appeal."

I wrinkle my nose in apology, stifling another yawn. Between Work It, renovations, scouting missions, and my private nocturnal activities with Darcy, I'm spread thin.

Work It is still taking up the better part of forty hours a week, though Toby's been understanding with the odd times I've had to duck out for contractor meetings. He blames himself for not warning me off of Wickham, and he was mortified to learn about the idea theft, though not entirely surprised. It turns out they weren't as close as Wickham's visits led me to believe, and Toby was secretly relieved when Wickham's interest in me was redirected.

"No, thanks," I tell Darcy, who's already at the curtain. "Go land us a drag queen!"

"I'm out, too," says Ming, shifting her feet off me. She plants a noisy kiss on the top of my head. "Might hit TD 'n' F up for a shot, though. Part of my finder's fee."

"He still doesn't know what it means when you call him that." I fold my arms on the table and rest my head.

"He doesn't know he's *Tall, Dark, and Fuckable*?" She nudges me. "What kind of girlfriend *are* you?"

I shut my eyes. "A tactful one?"

"Overrated. Later, lover."

The metallic shifting of rings on the curtain rod announces Ming's departure, and I let myself enjoy the quiet for a few minutes, the dull murmur of the crowd at the front of the house providing a white noise that threatens to put me to sleep. A vibration on my wrist brings me back from the brink.

C: WE GOT IT! I'm a Brooklynite, baby!

I smile and reply with a confetti emoji. The last-minute apartment posting is why Chloe had to bow out of tonight's scouting mission. She and Gales got here two weeks ago, and while the rate on the Airbnb they booked isn't totally gouging them, Chloe and Gales are ready for a home of their own.

I'm about to rest my head again when Momma's pink bouffant pokes through the curtain.

"The deejay isn't back here, is he?" Her voice is low with annoyance, far from the playful lilt of her stage persona.

"Sorry. Just me."

She lets out a huff, then raises a champagne flute. "Your fella's a generous one. Got me a glass of the house's finest."

I arch a brow.

Momma purses her lips, like I've called her out for waxing her nose hairs. "*So* I signed on to sing at Pemberley a couple of times." She points a claw at me. "You'd better wow me at that opening." She backs away from the curtain, then leans in again. "And if the deejay shows up, tell him I'm gonna skin him."

I sit up, stretching. "Y'know, Momma, that's *exactly* the kind of energy we're looking for. This bodes well." She disappears from view with a mischievous cackle that could rival Ming's.

Another yawn overtakes me and I stand, fishing my phone from my purse to check my email. The contractor sent photos of the day's work at Pemberley. I pace the room and scroll through the shots, noting where he made the changes we discussed to the floor tile in the entryway. Chrome veins extend from the base of the doors, radiating over the floor like the rays of the sunburst over Pemberley's entrance. It's even better than I imagined.

I blink back sudden tears. They sneak up on me every now and then. I got to lay the final few tiles in the lake: four tiny red pieces, cut and assembled into the shape of a cat—or rather, as Darcy pointed out, a *kitten*—nestled in the sea of turquoise. That got me. And Jane won't lay off me for what happened when he performed the inaugural sound check. Seeing my favorite person performing on the stage that had only been a dream a few weeks before had me on the verge of tears anyway, but then the brat sang "Rainbow Connection." I lost it. Charles is still texting me pictures of Kermit.

I put away my phone and stroll to the far side of the room, letting my attention drift over the flyers and announcements that extend from floor to ceiling. I did my best to ignore them while we met with Diva and Momma, but now I scan for advertisements regarding a talent search for Meryton.

Ming's made sure that news of what she's dubbed "the Meryton Massacre" has spread across the scene. Performers and producers have been warned off the SoCal snake in chinos, and anyone worth their eyelash glue is so disgusted by Ginn's betrayal that she's having a hard time booking gigs. Rumor has it they've still managed to pull in a few acts, mostly new, hungry performers who don't mind the taint of Wickham's underhanded dealings and Ginn's treachery, but I haven't encountered a single established burlesquer supportive of their venture.

As I study the thumbtacked and taped pages, the most recent addition seems to be the bold-lettered announcement for the debut of *Red, White, and Boobs*, which is out of date by three months. I tug it free, revealing a sign for *Johnny Ryall's XXXMas Sextacular*—from four years ago?

Jeez. I reach to snag that page, too, but something shiny catches my eye. A . . . *doorknob?* As the thought registers, the door swings toward me in a flurry of rustling paper. I stagger back with a yelp, narrowly missing death by a thousand paper cuts. As the door starts to close, two men file inside.

The door shuts with a violent clang that has the pair swiveling toward me. One is the show's errant deejay.

The other is Wickham. Every muscle in my body goes tight.

The deejay approaches me, wide-eyed. "Shit! Were you right there? I'm sorry!" His head bobs side to side as he surveys me for damage. "It didn't clock you, did it?"

"No, I'm fine," I say flatly. I'm watching Wickham, who is studiously avoiding my gaze. This was inevitable. The burlesque scene isn't that big; we were bound to run into one another at some point. Granted, I didn't anticipate the meeting's taking place after a near-clobbering with a stage door. At least, not with *me* on the receiving end.

Over the past month, I've entertained numerous revenge scenarios. My favorite had him crawling down the catwalk at Pemberley on his knees, his stupid chinos covered in coffee stains, as he begged my forgiveness. In this fantasy, it's Pemberley's opening night. I'm onstage in a fabulous showgirl headdress, chin high and looking regal as hell as I coolly deliver my verdict: "No." He weeps and wets his pants. It's on the cover of the *New York Post* the next day.

The deejay turns to Wickham. "I'll get back to you on that proposal, man. I haven't been hurting for gigs, and—" He checks his phone for the time. "Oh, shit! I should be onstage. Momma's gonna kill me. I'll be in touch." He calls the last bit over his shoulder as he pushes through the curtain to the front of the house.

Wickham watches him go, then turns to me. His discomfort has morphed to a sly smile. "Bennet." He says my name with a practiced mix of surprise and bemusement.

Dickhead. "I don't have anything to say to you." My voice is dangerously calm.

He has the audacity to look hurt. "Bennet—"

"That's *Liz* to you," I snap. "You knew what happened in California. You knew, and you—" I cut myself off, wishing I didn't say anything at all. If nothing else, he wants a reaction. The least I can do is deny him that. "You're not worth this."

"That's too bad," he says, the mask of hurt replaced with a condescending smirk. "Because we're looking for a kitten."

I stare back, more offended than stung. At my silence, he lets out a little laugh. He thinks he's won, and why shouldn't he? I gave him the blueprint for my undoing, and he knows what's supposed to happen after: my retreat.

I wait for the old ugly voices to chime in. For the sneers of my cohorts to resurface, some echo of those events to pull me down. I wait for the falling sensation that accompanied those memories. But it doesn't happen. That nightmare's run its course. If Wickham thinks he's going to take its place, I've found a stage door his face can meet.

"I have my sights set on something bigger."

"You find another show?" he asks, curious.

"You never did have much of an imagination, Wickham." Darcy emerges from behind the curtain. The sight of him is enough to get my insides coiling, but Wickham's reaction provides a very different kind of pleasure.

His nostrils flare, his posture going stiff, his eyes widening as the dots connect. He swallows hard. "Pem-*Pemberley*?" He seems to choke on the name.

I just grin.

"You really think you can get in on this?" he spits. His eyes dart frantically from Darcy to me. "You think there's room for *two*?"

"I guess we'll find out," I say as Darcy comes to stand beside me. "In any case, we're set to open in two months. And from what I hear, you haven't even gotten started on remodeling at Meryton, no?"

Wickham's jaw goes slack.

"How's the talent search going, Wickham?" I screw up my face in a mockery of sympathy. "Having a hard time finding folks to join you? Like, maybe word's gotten out that you're a conniving asshole and they might want to think twice before signing with you?"

Wickham frowns, brows drawn as though something he's been trying to piece together has fallen into place—and he doesn't like where it's landed.

"How about staffing?" I step closer. Wickham steps back. "You weren't able to put up money to retain the Meryton crew during renos. And, again, there's the small detail of your lack of integrity, so any good-faith offer on your part might not be enough to make them stick around."

"We have the talent. We have the staff. We have twice the occupancy . . ." Darcy looks at me expectantly.

I smile, reveling in anticipation of the coup de grâce. "And we have *my* concept. You snagged the wrong sketch, man. What we've done to Pemberley? With the lake? And those ceilings!" I press my hand to my heart. "Ginn can tell you. Aerial performances there are *epic*."

Wickham's face purples.

"So did I find another show?" My voice goes dark. "*No.* I *made* one."

A pop of static comes from beyond the curtain, followed by the intro to "All That Jazz." The playful tune adds to the surreality of the moment. *My* moment. The rush is better than performing, surpassing invincibility. I am vibrating with triumph.

Wickham still hasn't moved. I don't even think he's breathing.

"That's the spirit, Wick," says Darcy. "Bennet, do you need anything else or do you want to press on?"

I'd love to keep staring down Wickham, to watch him have to slink away or wait to see if any of that groveling I've imagined ends up

318 · Vanessa King

taking place. But this closing beat is too good to pass up. I take Darcy's hand and he beams at me, eyes alight with heat and something like pride.

"Looks like you're getting a 'fall' after all, Wickham," I say, enjoying the way he flinches as I lead Darcy past him. "Might want to brace yourself. I have a feeling the landing is gonna be rough."

I yank at the doorknob, pulling open the camouflaged door. Wickham's almost-silent "Shit" of defeat barely registers over the rustle of paper, but it is the sweetest sound I could have ever hoped for.

Darcy and I are deposited into an alley and a group of smokers. We weave through them and I pick up the pace, the mix of victory and giddiness propelling me like a shot of adrenaline straight to the heart. We get around the corner before I slow, then pull Darcy up the steps of a darkened barbershop. I move to the stair above him, bringing us to eye level. One look at his grin, and I'm undone. I press my lips to his.

It's fast and firm and hungry, and he kisses back with the same intensity, taking the last step and backing me against the storefront. His hands slide to my waist, then under the skirt of my dress to grip my thighs. A second later I have my legs wrapped around him. He's already hard, the front of his trousers and the wisp of material covering me a negligible barrier against the insistent press of his length. He surges against me, and I moan—

A flash of red and blue lights makes me flinch, and we separate with a shared gasp. Darcy hunches over me protectively, but beyond his shoulder I see the cop car moving up the street and away from us. The siren starts to blare and the cruiser speeds off.

I let out a wobbly laugh. "That may have counted as public indecency." I loosen my grip on Darcy's shoulders enough to look at his face. Even in the near dark, he looks shell-shocked. A giggle escapes me. The sound borders on manic. "*Wickham*. I hate that guy."

Darcy presses his forehead to mine, still breathing heavily. "If this is how you handle hate, I'd be more than happy to review your enemies list with you."

"I keep that list at home."

He lets out a low sound I've learned is a promise. His fingers press into my hamstring and I suck in a whimper. "Then I'm calling us a car."

Opening Night

I cannot fix on the <u>penis</u>, *or the* <u>member</u>, *or the* <u>man-meat</u>, *or the* <del>bratwurst</del>, *which laid the* <u>erection</u>. *It is too long a* <u>phallus</u>. *I was in the* <u>junk</u> *before I knew that I had* <u>dong</u>

I glance over the Mad Libs sheet at Ming, who trembles with suppressed laughter. "You found a thesaurus, I'll give you that."

"It doesn't even make sense," says Momma, reading over my shoulder. "The last one is supposed to be a verb."

"Poetic license." Ming chuckles and resumes her eyelash application.

Chloe sits on the edge of Ming's makeup station, nodding as Ming presses her fingertips to the far edge of either eyelid, angling the lashes down. "*Voilà!* The student's become the master."

Ming flutters her lids, making the tinsel highlights in her false lashes glimmer. "God, I'm gorgeous." She blows herself a kiss.

I roll my eyes, but I'm actually grateful for Ming's unwavering Ming-ness; the consistency is making the evening a little less surreal. We're less than an hour to showtime, and I'm pretty sure my entire midsection is comprised of quaking wings. The bulk of the crowd is friends and family, so we could bomb and still get a warm reception, but every moment I'm not actively engaged in show prep, my brain reminds me just how much has led up to tonight, how many people are bound to its success, and I have to remind myself to breathe.

Beside me, the dumbwaiter's squeaking pulley announces the imminent arrival of the preshow bubbly. The delivery settles with a rattle of glassware, and I raise the hatch for the bucket and flutes.

"I love that thing." Momma grabs a handful of stems to distribute around the dressing room. She was with Ming last week when Ming dropped by the club to set up her makeup station, and she volunteered to work tonight's grand opening. After that, we floated the option to all our new regulars. Everyone available accepted. The dressing room is packed, but so far, the excitement is making up for any accidental elbowing, and there's been zero squabbling. I have to hand it to Ming: she might have the sense of humor of a fourteen-year-old boy, but the woman is a master of group dynamics.

The room's design was inspired by the velvet-and-tassels look I wrote off as too fussy for upstairs. Half a dozen vanities line the walls, each centered in front of a pleated curtain of pale pink velvet. I initially planned to cover the walls in the fabric, but Ming said the sketches looked "labial," and, frankly, there was no unseeing that.

Each vanity is framed by bare bulbs, creating a halo of light around every station, and there's a coordinating pink ottoman in the center of the room. The thing's going to be covered in body glitter by the end of the night, but that feels fitting.

I flick the light switch by the door of the vocalist warm-up space. A moment later, the light above the door blinks in response: Jane letting me know he'll be a moment. The little room is fully insulated. Nary a sound escapes to or from the dressing room; impressive, but I miss hearing Jane's vocal exercises.

My watch buzzes with a text. D: Office?

I grin. Darcy and I haven't seen one another since this morning, and I hoped to check in before showtime. I scribble back: 10 min?

When I look up, Chloe meets my eyes in Ming's vanity mirror. "What's that smile about, Lizard? Darcy need you to buff his desk?"

The room erupts in a chorus of faux-scandalized "*Ooooh!*"s.

"I told you about that in confidence." I point at Ming, who bats her enhanced lashes innocently. "I blame you for this. She was perfectly well behaved before you."

"Ten points if he figures out how to get that costume off of you."

I shake my head but admire my reflection in her vanity mirror all the same. The playsuit makes me look like a superhero by way of a classic Playboy bunny, sans tail and ears. The plum satin is inset with velvet panels of the same color and is the most luxurious thing I've ever worn. The perilously deep V at the neckline required a whole other level of fashion tape, but that's only a safeguard against all the bending over I'll have to do during the show; the fit is perfection.

Diva trails Momma, pouring prosecco into the glasses, and I hand out the rest of the stems. Andrea presses through the curtain at the door, scowling at the tablet she holds.

"God, spare me the self-importance of an Academy Award

nominee's personal assistant." Andrea holds the tablet to her chest, taking a restorative gulp of her martini. "I was just on the phone for ten minutes with some brat who wouldn't divulge whom, exactly, she was making a reservation for. Like I'm going to call the damn *Post*? Chloe, dear, do any of your clients use 'Janet Doe' for reservations? I need to know if it's anyone worth putting up with."

Chloe narrows her eyes in thought. "Yes." She nods. "And *yes*. *Very* worth it. But her assistant is the worst."

"Noted and noted." Andrea hands off her martini glass to Diva, who freezes, rhinestone-studded brows drawn in confusion. Andrea taps furiously onto the tablet, then retrieves her glass. Diva shrugs and presses on.

"And, Tonic," Andrea continues, "can you tell your boyfriend he can't have the front island at stage right every goddamn weekend you're booked? He looks like a baby mob accountant."

Tonic covers her face with her hands and the room titters with giggles. Toby and Tonic was a pairing I couldn't have anticipated. Unbeknownst to me, Toby snagged one of the business cards for Tonic's aerial lessons at the Work It event, then spent the better part of a month trying to get up the nerve to make an appointment. Now I'm scheduling their weekend getaways and gleaning more than I'd like from calls to the office with contractors about where Toby's installing aerial hardware in his new penthouse.

As far as I'm concerned, Toby can carve his initials into that front table. A few posts from his social media accounts, and Pemberley's due to become *the* place for every techie and creative who can deign to be seen outside of Brooklyn on weekends.

I arch a brow. "Change your mind about separating business and pleasure, Andrea?"

"Never," she says. "But he can at least explore the room. How are things down here?"

"Great," I say, and thank Diva as she fills my glass. Jane emerges from his warm-up space in time to be handed the final flute, and suddenly all eyes are on me. Tonic turns down the music, and my butterflies still for a moment.

"How 'bout a toast from our fearless leader?" Jane suggests.

"No speeches," I warn. "I'll start crying and it will be 'Rainbow Connection' all over again." I cast my attention around the room. "Thank you for being part of this. It's literally a dream come true, and it wouldn't have been possible without you. I adore you all, even if you're kind of nasty." This gets everyone chuckling, and I raise my glass before the tickling behind my eyes results in anything detrimental to my eyeliner. "Pop a pastie!"

"Pop a pastie!" they chorus, and we all drink.

"Alrighty." I turn to Jane. "I'm going upstairs, but I'll be back in time—"

"Oh, we're not done with you yet." Jane pulls me to his side, free arm linking with mine, and I realize that no one else has gone back to their preshow routine.

"It turns out that Ming doesn't cross-stitch," Jane continues. A memory flickers at the edge of my awareness. *Cross-stitch?*

"*But*," says Ming, "Tonic does."

Tonic steps forward holding a leopard-print gift bag. It's long, probably meant for a bottle of wine. "It wasn't any trouble," she says, handing me the bag. "The challenge was finding a frame the right size."

I nod, still clueless, and push past the pink tissue paper to pull out something in a gold-colored frame. Behind the glass is a cross-stitch with letters in the same blue-green we used to tile upstairs, the words surrounded with tiny flowers of blue-green and gold.

"*Dance like nobody's watching.*" The words are a tight fit around the sudden lump in my throat. "*Live like a giant piece of metal could crush your skull tomorrow.*"

"Did I get it right?" Jane asks. "I was pretty muddled, but I wrote down what I could remember the next day. It felt worthy of preservation."

"I—" I'm at a loss. "Thank you."

"Thank *you*, Kitten," says Tonic. "For this opportunity. Especially after . . . everything."

"Your costume is my thank-you," says Ming. "But thank you, also."

"You've done something special here, Kitten," Andrea says, martini aloft. "I'm honored to be part of it."

"Well done, Lizard," Chloe offers, and the newer performers chime in with thanks of their own.

Jane wraps me in a hug, kissing my cheek. "This is what being brave gets you."

"I . . ." I look over each of them in turn. My cousin, who believed in me enough to move her entire life out here. Ming, in her unrelenting, filthy glory. Andrea, who, for all her faults, has pulled every string, thread, and line of spider silk in her arsenal to make tonight a success. Tonic, coming into her own. Momma, Diva, and our other new performers, brought into our weird, sexy family.

And Jane. *My* Jane. The reason I found them all in the first place.

A new feeling starts to take shape amid the quaking nerves and the excitement overwhelming the rest of my awareness. It's familiar, and positive, and I know that if I give it an inch, it will absolutely destroy my makeup.

I laugh. "I just pick up panties."

Jane squeezes my arm. "You hush." He raises his glass. "To Kitten!"

"To Kitten!" the others call, and toss back their glasses. A moment later, Blondie is blasting from the speakers, and everyone returns to their final preparations. I leave the framed cross-stitch at my makeup station, arranging it beside the postcard of the Eastern Columbia Building Darcy mailed me while he was in LA last month.

"Okay," I announce to the room. "*Now* I'm going upstairs."

"Be back in time for me to do your lips," Chloe calls, and I give her a thumbs-up.

On my way out, I place my hand on the green, egg-shaped light fixture beside the curtained exit. Andrea rescued it from Meryton after our emergency meeting that grim day, and the light was the final element to the room. The contact helps banish the jitters about as much as it ever did, which is to say, hardly, but I'm happy to have part of our old home with us.

Moving through the curtain, I pause in front of the open door of the band's dressing room. The guys sit at their poker table, suit jackets hanging on the wardrobe rack at the back of the room. I spot Johnny's gold sharkskin among the black. It's the least offensive of his lineup. While that's not saying much, it is my favorite.

"Thirty minutes to showtime, fellas," I say.

"Thanks, Kitten!" Johnny looks up from his hand, eyes darting to the others at the table. He nods toward Dion, whose back is to me, and arches a brow.

I can see Dion's cards. Unless Johnny is holding a particularly great hand, he's SOL against Dion's four of a kind. I grimace, and Johnny's shoulders sag.

He waves me off. "Pop a pastie, kiddo."

I continue down the hall to a short set of stairs and one of the exit points to the main floor. I wait, hand on the knob, and listen to the murmur of the gathering crowd on the other side. The faint twitch of nerves flutters in my stomach. This is it.

I take in a long breath, trying to steady myself. I don't know what to expect from my first look at the crowd. The excited buzz from the dressing room has given way to that other, unnamed sensation. Whatever it is, it's good; a little unwieldy, but good. When I open the door, sound swells into my ears: laughter, chatter, and the clinking of barware. I round the corner into the bar, and my breath catches.

The bar is almost full, guests enjoying drinks and conversation as they wait to be seated. The seats on the islands are filling up with our VIPs, and the tables between the islands and the bar are mostly seated as well. Across from me, Marley beckons to a group I recognize as friends of Chloe's in from California, escorting them to the catwalk. Andrea's resumed her post at the hostess station, fielding a phone call. She throws her head back, clearly exasperated, and plucks her martini from the podium.

Looking around, there's no question we've maintained the Russian contingency, and I spot a penis-tipped tiara among a group of women with sashes that read, "Karli's Gettin' Hitched!" No sign of any fratty Wall Streeters, though. I suspect their attendance had more to do with Meryton's proximity to the Financial District than any particular fondness for the club, but it works for me: Wickham can have all the coked-up broker bros he wants—assuming Meryton ever opens.

The thought passes over me like a cold shadow. Our renovation crew had friends on the Meryton job and kept us abreast of the setbacks that befell the other operation. It seems a few purloined sketches of a design scheme do not a cohesive concept make, and when pressed for clarity on "his" vision, Wickham struggled to expand beyond what he'd snatched from me. This cost him two reputable contractors, and when he finally found someone willing to work with the incomplete concept, Wickham couldn't pony up for the deposit.

The bold-lettered sign that went up a few days after Meryton's last show read, "REMODELING: Under New Management!" It was replaced a month later with "Schedule Your New Year's Eve Event!" Last week, a handwritten note was taped over the vinyl sign: "Grand Opening: TBD."

When Tonic sent me the picture, my stomach bottomed out. Wickham's spiraling descent toward failure should be satisfying; instead, it's just sad. We may have transplanted the heart of the place, but it hurts to see Meryton being treated so shamefully.

"Hey, kitty cat," calls Michael. "Feeling proud?"

I smile back, glad for the distraction, and sidle up to the bar. It didn't need much updating, though the tile on the floor is a larger version of what we used in the lake, and the liquor cases lining the wall behind Michael were illuminated to highlight the sunburst motif framing them. "More like having an out-of-body experience. How's it going?"

"Beautiful chaos." He resumes pouring a row of shots. "You girls get your bubbles?"

"Sure did. Thank you kindly."

He smiles, then looks over my shoulder. "Esteban!" He points to the tray of shot glasses. "For island two."

Esteban pulls the tray across the bar. "Why don't the Russkies do bottle service? Always *vashe zdorovie* one round at a time." He sends an air kiss my way. "Kitten, your parents are adorable, telling the Ivans all about their talented baby."

I groan. "They haven't been too mortifying, have they?" I step on the bottom rung of a bar stool to get a better view of the frontmost islands, where friends and family have been seated. My mom is on the catwalk chatting with a broad-shouldered man in a suit. She points toward the stage, and I smile. When my parents got in yesterday, I gave them a tour. Mom wasn't able to fathom the barn wood, either.

"It's cute," says Esteban, offering me his hand as I step down from the stool. "They've been talking nonstop, pointing out details in the room. Your dad had them hunting for the tile kitten. It was precious." He hefts the tray of shot glasses. "Careful. You may have some former KGB over for the holidays."

He departs with the shots, and I finally make my way to the stairs up to the second floor. At the first landing, I find Charles pacing the short platform. I have to look away before I laugh outright. The guy is truly sunshine incarnate; even his anxious stride is optimistic.

"Bennet!" He holds up his hands with a wince. "Sorry. You're Kitten right now. And what even is this outfit?"

I shimmy my shoulders. "It's called a playsuit."

"Ming?"

"Naturally. And how do you feel, sir?" I look over his jacket for any boxlike protrusions. "Nervous?"

Charles grins and reaches into his breast pocket, producing a shining platinum band dotted with tiny diamonds. I helped him pick out the engagement ring last month, but seeing it now, I press a hand to my chest in an earnest swoon. "High quality, with sparkle to spare. Just like our Jane."

"I'm glad you're here. I need a second opinion. I'm waiting until after the show. *Maybe.* I don't want to distract him asking before he goes on, but I'm afraid that if I wait, I'll throw myself onstage halfway through 'It Had to Be You' and propose then and there." He wrinkles his nose. "What do you think?"

"Waiting makes sense to me," I say. "It's a little close to showtime now anyway. But if he's singing and the spirit moves you, I say charge up there and bend that knee."

"Darcy said the same thing! And with Jane's family and everyone here, it's too perfect." He sighs. "I love him so much."

"Yeah, you do."

He gives himself a little shake. "Thanks, Ben—*Kitten*. Pop a pastie!"

I watch him trot down the stairs, then finish my trek to the second floor. We opted against seating the upper level tonight, and I weave around the empty tables and chairs to the open office door.

When I look in, Darcy is at the window, observing the gathering crowd. My heart gives a familiar squeeze. He'd do this during renovations: quietly survey the day's progress. It's similar to how I catch him looking at me at times, no longer searching, but with something like wonder. I feel a different kind of pull toward him in these moments— he's admiring something I contributed to. I had the vision, and he had the means to make it real. Together, we've created something.

Walking in, I place my steps to the side of the rug, letting my heels click on the floorboards to announce my arrival. He looks my way and I stop short, momentarily breathless at the intensity in his gaze. It's that wonder again. There's no getting used to it.

"Wow," he says.

I continue toward him, executing a turn to reveal how little there is to the back of my costume.

"I repeat: wow."

"Thank you." I reach into his open jacket to place my hands on his waist. The contact is more grounding than the green egg could ever hope to be. "Ming yelled at me because she had to let out the bodice twice. Seems our climbing has made me Hulk out."

"Your trapezii *are* looking prominent these days." He runs his hands over the sloping muscle on either side of my neck. I clench my fingers at the shiver that follows. "It looks good on you." He cocks his head, eyes at my neckline. "Fashion tape?"

"Always."

"A careful removal then?"

The allusion sends a warm tingle over me. "You really haven't forgiven yourself for the nurpling, have you?"

"It is my greatest shame," he says, deadpan, then gives me a squeeze. "How was the interview?"

I grit my teeth, revisited by a hint of the nerves I had earlier. The last round of permits filed with the city caught the eye of a clerk with a particular fondness for Pemberley and a friend at an architecture magazine. A few days later I was offered an interview about the remodel. As luck would have it, there was a design conference going on in Newark this week, where a contributing writer and onetime mentor to me would be presenting. I'd been in touch with my old professor during renovations but hadn't seen her since before I went to LA. Touring Pemberley with her this afternoon was an absolution I didn't know I still needed.

"Exciting. Unreal. It helped that it was conducted by a friendly face."

"I look forward to reading it. Your *parents*"—he grins around the word—"are *very* excited."

I snort out a laugh. "My *parents* are well on their way to adopting the errant adult children of oligarchs." I release him to look down at the frontmost island, where Esteban is distributing vodka shots to my parents' table. One island over, a table of Russians raise their glasses, several making a gesturing motion to their new friends. At the neighboring island on the opposite side of the catwalk, members of the construction crew sit at one table, Chloe's friends at another. Both groups raise their glasses as well. My parents hesitate, but Gales's folks go for it, and my mom's sister laughs, she and my uncle joining in. To my surprise, it's suddenly bottoms up all around.

Jane's parents and brother join my family's island, Charles in tow, which inspires further enthusiasm from the Russians. Esteban retreats, presumably for more vodka. Chloe and Gales step aside on the catwalk to let him pass, then are rushed by the crew in from California, exchanging hugs.

That feeling from downstairs washes over me again. The people I care most about are in this building, a space that's the actualization of three years of work and a dream I'd all but given up on. It's where so many of those people have the opportunity to see their own dreams play out, onstage and off, or simply find the stability to continue pursuing their passion.

This isn't Meryton. And it never will be. It's so much more than that.

I blink back the tears, throat going tight. "Thank you for believing in me."

"Thank you for trusting me with your vision." His smile is soft. "I have something for you." He takes my hand and leads me to the desk. On the much-celebrated surface is a box about the size of the one Andrea's tablet came in, only black velvet instead of white cardboard.

Darcy beckons me toward it. "Go ahead."

I run my fingers over the soft exterior, unsure what to expect as I lift the lid—

"Oh!" My hand flies to my chest. It's a gold, bib-style necklace designed like the Pemberley sunburst. Where the original piece is inlaid with mother-of-pearl, the necklace is open, save for the centermost point, which is solid. "It looks like something out of a Klimt painting."

"Ming helped with the measurements; she suggested I have an extra link put in to accommodate any increase in muscle mass."

"It's beautiful, Darcy." I lift it from the box. It's light, despite its size.

"May I?" Darcy takes the necklace and I turn my back to him, letting him fit it around my neck. Links connecting the rays of the sunburst shift to conform to my collarbones, the squared end of the center resting just above my cleavage. Even from my upside-down view, it's stunning.

"I thought it would coordinate well with what you wear here." He kisses the back of my neck, brushing his lips along my hairline. "And what you don't."

"Thank you." I turn and bring my arms around his neck. "It's perfect."

Darcy's watching me with that soft smile again. He places his hands at my waist. "Did I ever tell you about the cheeky admin who had me intrigued after a few email exchanges?"

"Cheeky admin . . ." I mean to sound thoughtful, but Darcy leans closer and the proximity leaves me legitimately muddled. "Wasn't she more of a 'glorified receptionist'?"

"Hardly." He nuzzles the side of my neck, tweaking my earlobe with his teeth. "I was devastated when she had to cancel a meeting we'd scheduled. I even showed up at the party she coordinated," he murmurs. "Hoping I'd get to meet her."

I laugh and trace the skin above his collar. "You weren't afraid of coming off like a weirdo?"

"I played it pretty cool," he says, brushing his lips against my neck. He smiles against me as my laughter tapers. "And the stage kitten. She bewitched me."

Instinct compels me to say something clever. This time I wait. I'm getting good at waiting. Having a comeback at the ready can be satisfying, but sometimes the payoff is better when I let silence do the heavy lifting.

Darcy meets my eyes. "And the brilliant designer who realized the potential of a place I've cherished since childhood. They ended up being one person. One wonderful, beautiful, clever, terrifying force of nature. They were all you."

He strokes the side of my face. I close my eyes, leaning into the touch. His fingers trace my jawline. "And I get to love you." He says it like he's awed at his good fortune. And I think I recognize it because I feel the same way about him.

In the months we've spent together, across the many (many) surfaces of Pemberley, we haven't said this to one another yet. It's not as though the sentiment's been missing; I feel it from him every day, in that staggering look of wonder, the sleepy smile I get each morning, and every moment we share in between. And yet, now that I have heard him say it, I don't know how I've gone so long without it.

I flutter my eyes open. "I love you, too, Darcy." My words are thick with the threat of tears. "All of you."

Wonder and lust battle it out behind his eyes. "Your cousin is going to kill me if you cry."

I laugh. "She really will." I let go of him to fan my face. "Can you say something sexy? Quick: propose a new desk fantasy."

He chuckles. "I actually think we're doing fine in that department." He flicks his attention up and down my form, dark eyes promising trouble. "But if you think I'm not planning how to peel you out of that thing, you don't know me at all."

The words send a current through my nervous system. "Ah! That did it. Equal parts horny and emotional."

He groans. "Now *I'm* distracted. I'm imagining you in only that necklace." Darcy brings his face closer to mine. "You're going to have to act as my restraint again."

"I think we've established that I am *not* the woman for that job." I pull him to me for a kiss. It's slow and sweet, but I consider the desk's proximity anyway. His thumb kneads my jaw, the hand at my waist sliding up to press between my shoulder blades, and my fingers curl reflexively. *Holy hell, this man . . .*

As we kiss, I'm buoyed by a rush of adrenaline and confidence. It's like the high I get onstage, the intensity topping even the moment I watched Wickham realize his scheme was over. Pemberley actualized. Stability for my favorite people. The fact that there's no way Charles is going to make it through the show without proposing to Jane.

And I know what to call that feeling I haven't been able to place tonight. It's obvious now, but Darcy's the one to give it a name. It's *love*. Love for this place, these people, this work, this man, *this desk* . . .

I slowly run the tip of my tongue along his upper lip. I smile. It stretches across my face until I can no longer kiss him properly, and he smiles, too, then laughs.

"What?" he asks, the question brushing my lips.

"You love me."

"I do."

My wrist buzzes with a text, and I remember that we have a very big evening ahead of us. I pull him in for another kiss, heart bursting. "See you after the show."

He grins. "Pop a pastie."

ACKNOWLEDGMENTS

To my parents, Jim and Lisa. Dad, whose sheer adoration instilled in me the kind of confidence usually found in serial killers, which manifested in me the audacity to think I could write something. Mumsie, you raised me with a love for the written word that has been responsible for some of my favorite things in life. You are my first and most steadfast cheerleader on this writing journey. Thank you.

To my mother-in-law, Cheryl, the best human I know, whose 2010 Christmas gift, a Gotham Writers Workshop Intro to Novel Writing course, literally changed my life. Thank you.

Thank you to World Famous *BOB*, whose confidence class was the first step in my discovering this sexy, sequined world, and Jo Weldon, headmistress of the New York School of Burlesque, who recommended I drop into Duane Park and ask about kittening. Amber Ray, Gal Friday, Peekaboo Pointe, and Medianoche: you may have zero memory of Toodles, but I'll never forget you. And a tip of the hat to Murray Hill—I think my dad still has a shirt with your face on it.

To the Second Drafters: thank you for nudging me along those first few years with kind words for my dialogue and stubborn demands for "plot." A special nod to Bill, my New York dad, who, in his own words, is "probably the person furthest from this book's intended demographic" but did enjoy it. And the Seattle revision crew, which never did get a proper name. Thanks for the feedback and the hangouts. My *Popstar* ticket stub is on my desk.

Erin, you beautiful tropical fish, who, as I gripe-messaged about not knowing what to work on, casually mentioned you were modernizing an older story and took zero offense when I text-screamed, "I HAVE TO GO I'VE HAD AN INSPIRATION," and departed our chat to start outlining this novel. Thank you for taking a seat next to me at SCBWI—even if my hair had you thinking I was someone way cooler.

This book would not have happened without my fabulous critters at Critique Circle. Thank you for picking at my repeated words and letting me know when I'd written something entertaining but clearly for myself, and for telling me that if I did, in fact, plan to have an audience at some point, I should maybe drop the whole scene if I'd like to keep their attention. Harsh, but valid. So, D. K. Deters, Jason Caldwell, Jill Storm, Lydia Eato Harris, Sania Plum, and Stacie H: thank you, thank you, thank you.

Lots of love and appreciation to the friends who have been subjected to countless drafts, random chapters, and abandoned stories for . . . ever? J Dawg, Megan, and Athia (my Phoenix mom), thank you. And, Polly, ohmigoodness. You're simply the best. Thank you for being part of our chosen family.

To my agent, Tara—you are a dream come true and worth every minute of those four months I waited for you to open to queries. Thank you to Margo, who scooped this up mere days into NYC's 2020 shutdown, and Tricja, with her keen eye for those entertaining but perhaps unnecessary moments I hadn't quite excised, who carried this book through to completion. Aja, my eagle-eyed copy editor, thanks for catching my bad math and keeping Ms. Bennet from blushing too often. No one should have to highlight the word "back" so many times in one paragraph.

And Derek. My boo. Thank you for the time and the space I needed to make this happen. I love you. Let's snuggle.

DISCUSSION QUESTIONS

1. In *A Certain Appeal*, Bennet and Darcy have an intense first meeting. What did they think of each other? What were your first impressions of these two characters?

2. The novel is set in the glamorous and lively New York City burlesque world. Did you know anything about burlesque before reading? How did your perceptions change?

3. What relationship do the various characters have to burlesque? How do they use it to enhance their self-confidence?

4. In *A Certain Appeal*, the author, Vanessa King, transplants the characters of Jane Austen's *Pride and Prejudice* to the modern day. How does that classic help ground the story? In what ways does it feel different from the original?

5. Aside from the two main leads, the book is full of many lovable

secondary characters. Who were some of your favorites? How did they bring the burlesque world to life?

6. Discuss the experience that leads Bennet to New York City and her administrative job. How does Bennet grow in her design journey throughout the book?

7. How do Bennet's connections to certain buildings line up with specific life choices and important stages of her life? How do these places impact her creative visions?

8. Before he gets to know Bennet more, Darcy has a skeptical view of burlesque. How do his reservations affect their relationship, and why does that change?

9. What do you think is in store for Bennet, Darcy, and the other characters?

ABOUT THE AUTHOR

© *Emerald Boes Photography*

VANESSA KING spent two years in the New York City burlesque scene and has the glitter in her pumps to prove it. *A Certain Appeal* is her debut novel and love letter to the dynamic, sexy world of twirling tassels and eyelash glue. When not writing, King enjoys reading, wielding a glue gun, and the contrast of red nails against a chrome barbell. She lives in Colorado with her husband and daughter.

VISIT VANESSA KING ONLINE

VanessaLKing.com
🐦 VuhVuhDanessa
📷 VanessaLeighKing